MISSING

Other Books by Amy Kulp

Stand-Alone Novels:
- Innocent

Poster series:
1. **Missing**
2. Wanted*

*Read the first chapter in the back

MISSING

Amy Kulp

First paperback edition November 2022.

ISBN 9798985930917 (paperback)

Published by Amy Kulp

Partially edited by Christa Gumbravich

For business inquiries, contact amy.kulp1@gmail.com
For more information, visit the author's webpage at
http://amykulp.weebly.com

To my mom, family, and friends for all of their continued love and support.

Shoutout to my two dogs - Maisey and Scooter. They always let me bounce my ideas off of them.

Chapter 1-

I stopped breathing when I saw the new kid walk into my class. I noticed everyone else stopped what they were doing and stared too. An elbow attached to my boyfriend jarred into my side purposely. As he smirked at me, I realized that I was caught red-handed. I was staring. My cheeks blushed a deep red while my neck ducked down like a turtle. Hearing Chad chuckle at my reaction, I ducked my head lower from the embarrassment.

I finally looked back up when the new kid passed my desk and sat in the back corner. I sniffed as he walked by and realized that he also smelt good. It smelt like he just got out of the shower and put deodorant on. I sniffed again and realized that he wasn't wearing that disgusting cologne that Chad wears. I couldn't even sniff in Chad's direction; it was so strong. My nose always burned whenever I nuzzled it into Chad's neck. Maybe I was just allergic to what Chad wore. A coughing attack usually ruined the romantic mood he tried to set for us.

I had to admit that the new kid was amazingly hot. He did not have bulky muscles, but he was tall, which made up for the fact. His eyes were a deep brown that shone in the sunlight. His lips were plump and moisturized; any girl would've died for them.

Most girls from my school probably wouldn't go for him though. He was the type of guy who didn't wear snapbacks, muscle shirts, or anything that the typical boy here wears. He had a button-down shirt and he buttoned them up to his neck. I admit that I always fell for guys who wore those shirts. He had skinny jeans on and contrary to the typical boy in this school, you couldn't see his underwear. That was only speculation though. I was too embarrassed to look.

I let myself pack up slowly as Chad attempted to hold a conversation with me about his football career. He thought it would be a real hit and he's been offered a couple of full scholarships.

I only smiled.

I supported his career options 100% but he didn't support mine. Instead of doing cheerleading as he wanted, I played soccer. He doesn't understand that my dream is to go to the Olympics for soccer. Not be on the sideline cheering for him.

The reason Chad wants me to do cheerleading is because of the status quo. The footballers are supposed to date cheerleaders. He took a major risk even talking to me. Thankfully, everyone knew not to mess with me because my father was very capable of killing each of them.

Seriously, every time I have a boyfriend he shows them his gun and knife collection. He then explains what knife or gun he would use for how bad he broke my heart.

Usually, the boy would have police sent to my house but my dad has all of his needed permits.

Chad was the first to stay even though my dad doesn't approve of him. My mom just liked him because he was eye candy. If she had to like him for his personality, she probably wouldn't be seen around me if he was at the house.

I understand though.

Chad is extremely… demanding. He gets what he wants when he wants it. The only thing he hasn't been able to take from me is my V-card and I don't want to lose that yet. Especially not to Chad.

It's just a high school fling.

If you get married to your high school crush, I will gladly sign your divorce papers. I admit sometimes I do believe that Chad and I should be married but other times I'm always on the verge of breaking up with him. I usually think through my anger and realize that I need to let people's flaws go.

Chad grabbed my hand randomly and pulled me down the hall to my next class. I was surprised by his actions since he never held my hand in school and sometimes he wouldn't dare to be caught with me. This was especially true if I was wearing sweatpants or something he deemed embarrassing. He smiled at me and kissed me on the lips before shoving me into the classroom.

Still in shock, I sat down at a random desk and thought about what was going on. Maybe he was jealous of another cute couple. He was a very jealous person and he would go a long way to stalk people and prove that we were a better couple than them.

I always feel bad about it though.

"Can I sit here?" Knocking myself out of my daydream, I looked up and nodded as the new student sat down next to me. "I'm Miguel."

"Miguel?" I questioned. I threw the idea around in my head for a couple of minutes and then nodded my head. "Suits you." He smiled a bit at the comment and then pulled out his schedule. "Need help?" I quickly asked.

He showed me his schedule and I read over it a couple of times. I was surprised to see we had the majority of classes together. Out of nine classes, we had six together and three near each other. I could basically walk to all of his classes, to my locker, and then back to mine and still be on time.

"We're in basically the same classes," I reported. He seemed a little surprised but I saw a smirk playing on his lips. "So I guess I could just show you to most of them. Hold on, let me write down the ones we don't have in the same period." I quickly doodled his schedule down on a piece of paper and smiled. "I'll just meet you at the door of each classroom I don't have with you and I'll show you to your others."

"That'd be great," he replied with a smile.

"You know, it's a bit weird," I whispered. "Usually nobody has the same schedule."

                                        AMY KULP

That's when he turned forward and decided to pay attention to class. He had a smile on his lips the whole class period like he knew an inside secret that I wasn't in on. Like it was about me.

"Okay class, you may talk for the last five minutes," the teacher announced.

I instantly turned toward Miguel. "I don't think I mentioned my name before," I said. "I'm Emily."

"Hi, Emily." He smiled at me and I smiled back but I felt a blush creep on my face. He chuckled a bit once he noticed but that only made me blush even more. "You know, you're cute when you blush."

"You know, I have a boyfriend."

"You know, I already know that."

"How?"

"He was acting very jealous when I was going to go up and talk to you during the last period." I felt my lips press together hard and I faced the front of the classroom, interrupting anything he was about to say to me.

I was still going to show him to our next class but almost everybody knows that Chad is very jealous. If he saw me talking to any other boy that he didn't approve of, he would automatically assume I was cheating and then continue to lecture me for hours upon hours. He was like my dad.

When the bell decided to finally ring and wake me from my thoughts, I had already gathered my books and had started out the door. If the new boy wanted to follow me around to our next class, he would just have to catch up to the normal speed of an anxious senior.

"Hey there!" I heard Chad yell. I turned around and continued walking backward as he jogged up to hug me. "Where are you heading off to?"

"You already know my schedule but I'm showing Miguel to all of our classes," I repeated. "He has a lot of classes with me."

"Whose Miguel?" He squeezed my shoulders tighter and I felt his muscles begin to tighten.

"He's the new guy. Don't worry he's chill," I replied. Once those words left my mouth, I instantly cringed at my slang. Chill?

"I don't know about him. He doesn't look right."

"What do you mean? He looks perfectly fine."

"I don't know, he just seems too…" I knew where this was going and I knew Chad was going to say something stereotypical about Miguel.

That was the bad thing about being with Chad. He was stuck in a poor mindset. I disapproved of it completely but Chad was brought up in a first-class very snobby and prude white family. They hated anyone different than them and were huge racists. Nobody would ever call them out on it though. I still have yet to meet them because Chad knows that my mom is Latina.

It just aggravates me when people judge others by their skin color, eye color, sex, deformity, mental progression, or looks. People should be judged by their personalities because nothing else matters.

Having a nice personality and being attractive is a nice combination though.

I will admit that I do tend to judge people before I meet them. Even if they look like a snob to me, I will still give them a fair chance at being nice to me, and half of the time, they exceed my expectations.

"Emily, are you ever going to wait for me?"

I felt everyone turn to stare at me and Chad together. Once Miguel reached us, Chad clamped his hand on my shoulder tightly but Miguel didn't seem to notice it. He walked right beside me with a sly smile on his face.

When we reached the doorway to the classroom, Chad spun me around and kissed me hard on the lips. I backed away from him and squirmed out of his grip and went inside the classroom. I hated shoving my relationship into other people's faces.

I know I'm going to hear a lot about it later though because Chad was going to lecture me about how I'm his girlfriend and not Miguel's. I would just roll my eyes and get a makeup kiss that I never really wanted. It was like a routine with Chad and me.

And I was sick of it.

Chapter 2--

I began to tie my hair up in a ponytail when I heard the locker room doors creak open. I froze in place and peered around the mirror that I was looking in. I was double-checking that it was just one of the girls coming in for a break from practice. Sometimes people snuck in here after school to try and find valuables that may have been left behind. I have never caught anyone doing this and even if I did, I wouldn't do anything. I waited a few more seconds before trying to fumble with my hair again.

After five more minutes of struggling to put my hair up, I shrugged and let it fall down my back. It's not like I was trying to impress anyone as I was working out anyway. My hair would usually stick to my forehead and back of my neck anyway. By the time I was done working out, the hair tie wasn't tight against my crown anymore either. When I decided my hair was good, I went to my bag to grab my phone before going into the weight room.

There was no one here but that was usual for now. The sports that had practice today were either finishing up or they were just starting. Most people feel like they're unwelcome when they're not playing a sport that season, but everyone could use it at any time. Normally you had to have one other person in the weight room, but I knew what I was doing. I've been here so many times that I knew what my routine was and today it just happened to be weight day. Of course, I knew you were supposed to switch between leg day and arm day, but I just did them both on the same day. Every other day it would then be cardio. Maybe it's not healthy for me to do it, but I hate doing legs and arms separately. I like the burn my body feels when I do it all in one day and the day I do cardio, the burning in my lungs makes it all feel better.

I put my earbuds in as the air conditioning kicked on and smiled as an upbeat song sang through my ears. I knew that it was normal to listen to rock and heavy metal when you were working out, but I preferred classic pop and bubblegum pop. I often got mocked by Chad for listening to half of the artists I like, but I can't change who I am. Who cares that I like boybands? Why can't I like any band or artist without being mocked? I turned the volume up on my phone and listened for a second before looking around the gym.

What did I want to start on? After I'm done with the treadmill, do I want to do legs or arms? I walked over to the treadmill and thought about it for a moment. I walked at a slower pace than my usual walk and thought. I was very unstable on the treadmill because my balance and coordination are off, but once I got the hang of it I was usually okay with it. Even though the treadmill is cardio, I always used it to warm up. Maybe that was just me, but I always sweated the most when I walked on the treadmill. Weights didn't make me sweat, it just made me ache and I loved that feeling.

After a quick ten-minute walk, I turned the machine off and slowly got off it. I turned my music up and walked over to the weights. I wasn't a fan of them, but I guess I should start with the harder stuff. The only reason these were so tough for me was that I had terrible posture. I was always being corrected when coaches were around and if I was close with people, they corrected me too. However, that quickly stopped once Chad claimed me as his.

Not even my girls would dare touch me when he or his buds are around.

I wiped my hands on my pants for a moment before gripping the weights. Another reason I hated weights was that I was so afraid I would drop them on myself. I sweat too much for it to be normal and my hands will sweat for no reason. It could be the middle of the winter and they will be sweating. Chad finds it disgusting which is why he's not fond of holding my hand.

After a quick work out with the free weights, I decided to do legs and finish early today. I wasn't feeling it today and although I knew I would hate myself later for it, I knew that it would probably be the best thing for me. I had a lot of homework to do tonight anyway. So I quickly changed my song to one that fitted my mood and rushed through leg weights with that song.

As soon as I got up, my legs wiggled like they were jello. I stood still for a moment until I regained my composure and went for my gym bag. I grabbed my water bottle from it and then headed back towards the locker room. I had my school stuff in here and even though I was tempted to get a shower, I didn't. It was a beautiful day out and even though I drove here today, I was going to run home. I quit early so I will give myself this last pep talk.

I opened up my gym locker and placed my bag inside. I had to stack it up and slam the locker shut or it would all come piling out. That will be a problem for me tomorrow. I knew I had to take some of my work out clothes home because most of them weren't mine. My mom hasn't worked out in a while, but most of them were hers. She usually just lounges in them now and even though I wish I could say I could do that, my weight would gain back instantly.

My music continued to blast as I started making my way outside. I passed my car and smiled as I began to jog. It hurt because my backpack kept hitting me in the back, but I only had one book in here and it felt light today.

Being a former fat kid gave me so many self-esteem problems. Chad only started liking me when I started losing weight. I know it's messed up to even let him into my life after that, but I didn't have any friends. I thought that this was my chance to finally have someone. Although I was right, I sometimes wish I hadn't let Chad talk to me. Even though we're the school's power couple, we fought more than we did anything else. He was so controlling and although I usually let him get his way, I fought beforehand. I knew as soon as I got home that my phone would be blown up with notifications from him. He would start sweetly and slowly it would turn into a more controlling situation.

I was looking forward to seeing them as I turned into my driveway. I huffed and puffed for a little bit before opening the door to my house. The wifi sucked around here so when I didn't hear the notifications immediately, I didn't worry about it. Instead, I just threw my backpack on the couch and ran upstairs to take a shower.

I put my showering playlist on from my phone and sang along as I put shampoo in my hair. I got out five minutes later and turned the music off. I looked at my phone and saw that I had only two notifications.

From an unknown number.

I listened to the voicemail that was placed, but it was just a bunch of mumble-jumble. So I looked at the text that was sent to me.

Unknown   hey I think I grabbed ur history book on accident

My eyebrows instantly shot up with confusion. I know that I packed my history book in my backpack before I left for the work out. I tugged the towel around my body a little tighter and opened the bathroom door. I went downstairs as fast as I could and grabbed my bookbag. My parents weren't home this early, but I was

                                    AMY KULP

still always nervous that they would surprise me by being home one day.

As soon as I closed the door to my room, I unzipped the backpack and noticed that my history book was indeed missing. I didn't know what to think because I know that I put it in before I left. I had to study for the test that was tomorrow. How was I supposed to study now? I didn't want to fail because I had to keep my grades up for soccer season. History was the hardest class for me because I found it so boring.

I looked back at my phone and was curious as to who had it. I was in the middle of two people in that class so it had to be between the two. I knew it couldn't possibly be Miguel though because he didn't have my number. So that only left Bri. I looked back at the number though and was confused even more. I have her number plugged into my phone. Even though we weren't the best of friends, she's on my soccer team and I made sure I had all of the girls' numbers in case we had to cancel a practice or if we wanted to schedule an extra one.

I shook my head and didn't reply to the text. I'm just hoping whoever it was that texted me had my book. I was going to stress though because if I couldn't study, I didn't know how I was going to pass tomorrow's test. The hardest thing about it is our teacher teaches like he's teaching college kids. He doesn't care if you understand it or not, he says the information that he thinks is important and then gives us questions that we would be able to answer that was in the textbook.

I guess I would wing it…

✳✳

"Chad, stop," I said between kisses. He pressed his lips harder on mine as more students came down the hall. I attempted to get away from the harsh kisses, but I was already pressed against the locker. I could see some students give us dirty glares as they caught us making out around their lockers. I was very uncomfortable with it, but Chad loved to show off the relationship when he was jealous. Although I wasn't sure who he was jealous of since he knew that no one else would go to me without his consent. As soon as Chad attempted to add tongue into the mix, I used most of my strength to give me some space. "Stop." He smiled at me like he thought I was joking and wrapped his arms around my waist so that his hands were caressing my butt.

"How am I supposed to control myself when you look so amazing?" His hands squeezed and I let out a little peep. I have to admit even though most of the attention he was giving me was unwanted, I had a weakness when he complimented me and touched my lower back. I smiled up at him and since he was taller, I stood on my tiptoes to peck him on the lips. He smiled through it and he bent his head down to get more. I smiled up at him and gave him a little smirk before lowering myself to my actual height. "Is that all I get?"

                                    AMY KULP

I smiled and wrapped my arms around his neck. I must admit that I was a sucker for him. Even if he was controlling sometimes, he was my best friend. I parted my lips to kiss him again, but before we could we were both interrupted.

"Hey, Emily." We both looked over to where Miguel was standing and I let go of Chad. Chad was reluctant to let go of me completely so instead, he wrapped his arm around my side. Miguel looked at Chad for a minute before shaking his head and producing my history book from his bag. "I'm sorry, I didn't realize that I took this until it was too late." My eyes instantly got wide as I looked at it. I grabbed it from him and was a bit confused. "Once again I'm sorry." He smiled a bit nervously and before I got anything out of my mouth, he started to leave.

"Thanks," I whispered once he was gone. I continued to look at the book in my hand and then looked toward Chad. He didn't have any emotion on his face so I knew he was thinking about something. "What?"

"Why did he have your book?" I bent down a bit to get to my lower locker and placed it in the bottom of it. Once I got back up, I could tell that Chad was shamelessly staring at my butt, but I didn't mind.

"I don't know."

"I thought you were studying last night."

"I couldn't. I didn't have my book."

"You took it home with you last night," Chad said matter-of-factly. I looked over at him and raised an eyebrow. "You were stressing about the test and I watched you put it in your bag." I nodded my head and thought so too. Of course, we were both wrong because it wasn't in there. "Were you two studying together last night?"

"What? No," I said a little too quickly. Chad raised an eyebrow at me and I felt myself blush. I sound so guilty, but truth is, Chad wanted to hang out last night, but he didn't bother texting me because he knew I was busy studying.

"Em, I watched you put it in your bag and all of a sudden, he has it?" Chad stepped a little away from me and I knew what it sounded like. I stepped closer to him and wrapped my arms around his waist. I pulled him closer to me and I knew he wouldn't resist. Chad is a physical guy and he likes every ounce of attention I give him because we haven't exactly done anything yet. I'm a prude and Chad is okay with that, but sometimes I feel like he wishes I wasn't.

"Chad, I don't even know how he got it." He wrapped his arms around me too and although I knew he didn't believe me, I didn't know what else to tell him. This was the truth. "When I got home, I got a voicemail and a text from an unknown number saying they had it. I'm assuming it was his number now. But I swear, I didn't even meet him last night."

"How did he have your number?" I shrugged my shoulders and let go of him. Chad let go too and I was stunned for a moment. Did he think I would cheat on him with someone I didn't even know? "Did you give it to him?" I nodded my head and leaned into him. This time it was Chad's turn to be surprised.

Honestly, I'm not one for personal contact if it isn't hugging and Chad knows this. When I'm uncertain about something, I always act like this. It was weird to even think about how he could've gotten my number because not many people have it.

Chad.

My mom.

My dad.

My soccer team.

No one else.

"Let me walk you to your next class," Chad said. I nodded my head and he grabbed my hand. I quickly wrapped my hand in his because this was a rare opportunity. Neither of us talked while we were walking to my class. I pecked his lips goodbye and as the warning bell sounded, I knew that he was risking getting detention to make sure that I was okay.

I smiled.

Chapter3---

I closed my eyes and tapped my pencil against my lips for a moment to think. Time was running out while I was taking this test and the teacher didn't care; it was due by the end of class. I looked at the clock and noticed that I really only had ten minutes left. When I looked back down at my test, I had half a page left to go. Since the last one was a writing assignment, I knew that I had to get the rest of the multiple-choice done or I would be screwed. Counting off how much time I had left though distracted me and I couldn't concentrate hard enough to figure out the multiple-choice. I instinctively raised my hand and the teacher cleared his throat.

"No, you cannot have more time."

My arm fell back down and I pouted amongst myself. Knowing that the writing assignment was worth most of the grade though, I skipped the multiple-choice and read what I had to do. It was an easy assignment and I was quickly done within five minutes. However, this only left me three minutes to do ten more problems of multiple-choice. I held my breath as I struggled to keep myself from crying. I guessed on most of the front page already and I didn't want to fail.

I really loved soccer.

Next to me, I could feel Bri and Miguel's stares as I struggled. I was sure that I was the only one left that was doing my test and I could feel the impatience in the room growing. Or maybe that was just me being insecure about myself again.

"Em," Miguel whispered. He nudged his arm into my side and slid his paper a little closer to me. At first, my eyes darted away from the page because I don't cheat. However, I did check a few of my already answered answers and memorized some. I felt so guilty, but I ended up cheating off of him. I'm sure my face was pale by the end of the class and as the bell rang, I knew that I had to do the last two by myself.

"Miss Emily," the teacher said impatiently. He tapped his foot and I wrote down two random answers. I looked up at him with a pained expression and he smiled politely at me. He grabbed it gently from me and I got up from my desk.

Outside was Chad and he was waiting for me anxiously. I instantly wrapped my arms around his waist and hugged him. Chad instantly hugged back and knowing that this wasn't usually how I greeted him, he knew that something was wrong. He rubbed my back until I was ready to let go and even then I didn't want to face the world.

"We have lunch next, do you want to skip?" he asked. I shook my head and he chuckled a bit. "I didn't mean school, do you want to hang out in the band room or something?" I nodded my head and even though I didn't belong in the fine arts, I knew Chad found it to be a safe place to go.

We carefully walked through the halls and I pressed my body harder into Chad's. As we went walking through the halls I could feel little tears gathering in the corner of my eyes. Although they were trying to escape, I wasn't going to let them and instead blinked them back. It was very uncharacteristic of me to cry or cheat. I already broke one of those actions, so I wasn't going to let myself cry at school.

"Stay here, okay? I want to see if the band room is open." I nodded my head and Chad left my side for a moment.

Although Chad was the star quarterback of our school, he really loved the fine arts. He didn't play an instrument, but he loved to sing. I was constantly going to his concerts they had at school and I loved watching him when he starred in the school musical. Despite him being a hot shot on the stage and the field, being a jock and into the fine arts wasn't popular. There was a big wave of people who were divided among the fine arts or sports. Just like people were divided about whether a soccer player and a quarterback should be dating.

It was supposed to be Chad and Bri.

Not Chad and Emily.

I did love Bri though. She was such a sweet girl with an amazing smile. She had a few people who didn't like her, but that was because they were jealous of her. Specifically, they were jealous of her boyfriend. Her

                                    AMY KULP

boyfriend was the pitcher of the baseball team and possibly the most attractive guy in our school. He loved screwing around with her and they were constantly on and off. She didn't deserve half of the things he was doing to her, but she accepted it. After all, she didn't want to lose her best friend. But Bri was a cheerleader and a soccer player. She wasn't the head captain, but that was only because she wasn't a football cheerleader—she was a basketball cheerleader. I guarantee if she stuck it out for both of the seasons, she would be captain. The coach doesn't let anyone be captain unless they're on both of the seasons. However, soccer and football season are at the same time and a lot of the schedules were conflicted. Since she wanted to do both, she didn't see a problem with just doing basketball cheerleading. I have to admit I was jealous though. She was an amazing soccer player. I wish I could be in her shoes, but at the same time, I don't. We were both co-captains of the soccer team.

Although I'm not the best soccer player, I am fairly decent. I'm not quite sure how I became the captain, but I just know that the coach didn't like it when the girls voted for me. She wanted Bri to be the only captain since she was the best one for the team. I always wanted to know why I was the captain, but then I realized that I'm better at helping other girls. Don't get me wrong, sometimes I get in moods where I don't like anyone, but I always try to give pointers. Plus I've been on the team longer than Bri has. It has always been a mystery to me why they chose both of us, but I'm sure by the end of the season I'll get a straight answer.

"Sorry I took so long," Chad said. He shrugged his head and huffed for a moment. "The flutists are currently practicing for the winter concert so I'd rather not rush them. I think the stage is open though." I nodded my head and Chad wrapped his arm back around my waist. We quietly walked along and when Chad looked through the doors, he didn't even hesitate to bring me in.

I really wish Chad would've looked though. There were a couple of kids practicing their songs on the piano and when they noticed us, they stopped practicing for a moment.

"Did you come to practice?" Holli asked. She smiled up at him and although I was standing right there, she refused to make eye contact with me. Chad nodded his head and he tightened his grip around my waist. I'm not sure if he was trying to hint to her that I was here or whether he was being protective, but Holli didn't give up. "You're bound to get the Christmas solo, are you sure you don't want to practice?"

I saw it in Chad's eyes. I saw the longing in them. He wanted to practice, but he continued to nod his head no. He smiled politely at her, but he turned his back on her as soon as he could. In a moment or two, they were back to singing and I could tell he wanted to start too.

"You could go practice with them if you want."

"No, I want to be with you," he whispered. I nodded my head and he brought me off the stage and into the audience. We sat in the first couple of chairs and I could feel a couple of the kids' eyes on us. "Don't worry about them, okay?"

I nodded my head. I was never really worried about any of them. Even if Holli was really pretty, I didn't worry about her interfering. Holli didn't have a constant boyfriend, but she was constantly hooking up with people. She was beautiful look-wise, but evil-hearted when it came to personality. She was also one of the flyers for the cheerleading squad and she always participated in the musicals. She usually doesn't get leads, but I'm sure she will soon. She was a really good singer.

It was no secret that she wanted to get with Chad and it was no secret that Chad didn't want to get with her. Even if he is a meathead, Chad would never be mean to anyone. He loved other people and although he seemed like a dick to most people, I've never actually seen him be flat-out mean to anyone.

Except for Miguel.

"So what's been bothering you?" Chad asked me. I shrugged my shoulders for a moment and listened to the music that was flowing from the piano. I closed my eyes for a moment to listen and without realizing it, I guess I must've fallen asleep.

Chad wasn't happy with me when I woke up.

Chad wouldn't let me explain when I woke up.

Chad broke up with me when I woke up.

All because of Miguel.

Chapter 4-----

I put my bag in my locker for a moment and breathed in a shaky sigh. Once I was done with my work out I would force myself to talk to Chad. He has been avoiding me all day and although I couldn't really blame him, I knew that it would be hard for me to admit the truth. I'm not sure if he told anyone about our breakup or not, but if they had, I know that girls would be pining over him already. Knowing Chad, he would be going after them as well. He didn't need much time to recover from a broken heart. Even though our relationship wasn't the best, I knew that if our breakup was official, it would be hard for me to get over it so quickly.

I plugged my headphones into my ears and looked for a song to use for my work out. As soon as I found a slow song to represent my sadness, I shook my head and kept the song playing. It wasn't really a work out song, but it would get me going. I went over to where the sinks were and silently sang to myself as I quickly dribbled water onto my face. Afterward, I quickly patted myself dry and threw my hair up into a higher ponytail. It was hard to get the hair off of my neck since it was so long, but it was still manageable. However, if I didn't cut my hair soon, it would always touch my neck no matter how high I had it.

I gave myself one last look-over before nodding my head and making my way toward the work out room. Once again, there wasn't anyone in the room so I just shook my head. I thought that the football players would be here already. It didn't matter to me whether they were here or not though because I knew my routine. Besides, the boys always added a little pressure when I worked out. I knew that they stared every time I squatted or bent over and despite how uncomfortable it made me to know this, I continued to do my normal routine. If Chad were to see them checking me out, he would straighten them right out and make sure they would never look at me that way again. Now I'm sure he wouldn't care that much.

Just thinking about it made me a little bit nauseous. As if someone could see me and I was having a conversation with them, I shrugged my shoulders. I have to admit, I stared at the guys when they were working out too. Not in a sexual way, but I just loved looking at people's posture. Some people found it easier to do sumo squats while some people like narrow squats. Some people don't use weights while they squat, some do. It depends on preference and what the goal is.

For me, once soccer ends, I won't be doing as much running. I'll just be trying to build some muscle and flexibility in my body. I probably won't come to our weight room after school every day either. It would most likely be every other day. Especially as the year goes on and the assignments get harder to complete.

After ten minutes on the treadmill, I slowed it to a walk and looked around the room for a bit. Since there was no one else in the room, I knew I probably shouldn't do as much with the weights. I didn't want to get hurt and not be able to breathe if they dropped on my chest.

Calculating the current weight, I dropped one of the weights off of each side and threw a little one on the sides. I shook my head for a moment and recalculated the numbers again. I sighed slightly and took off another big weight. I didn't want to hurt myself while no one was around.

As I slowly got underneath the bar, I felt my arm tear my earphone out of my ear. I sighed for a moment, but couldn't do anything to fix it. I already had the bar in my hands. I began doing some reps and my breathing began to form a sort of pant to them.

"Do you want a spotter?"

Instantly my balance caught me off guard and my arm gave out as I had jumped in surprise. I felt the bar fall onto my chest and slowly roll towards my throat. The person behind me grabbed at the bar, but even though they had just offered to be my spotter, they couldn't take it off of me. My vision instantly went blurry, but we were both still struggling to get it off of me. I choked in the air that I couldn't breathe and finally, I began seeing black splotches.

I gave up trying to get it off of me.

                                   AMY KULP

Chapter 5 -----

As soon as I became somewhat conscious, I kept my eyes closed and listened to my surroundings. I felt the pain coming from my chest and even though I wanted to remain quiet, I couldn't keep my intake of breath quiet. I immediately opened my eyes and tried to bring my arms up to my side, but I felt a force pin them back down. When I adjusted my eyes so that I was able to see better, I saw a somewhat familiar face in front of me. I didn't say anything as I looked around the room and saw all of the football boys surrounding me. Nobody was lifting and everybody was paying attention to us.

"Remain still, the nurse is on her way," the coach said. I looked at him and barely nodded my head. I forced myself to go back into a planked position and watched the ceiling above me. "You know the rules, Emily. Why were you here alone?"

"Leave her alone, coach," one of the boys said. "She's had a rough night as it is." I attempted to look for the culprit who was talking, but I knew that I didn't have much visibility for my eyes. What I saw was whatever was directly above me.

"We have rules for a reason," he said. He looked back down at me and gripped my wrist. "Are you okay?"

he asked. I didn't say anything and felt myself begin to wonder if I truly was. I was having trouble breathing, but I knew that was noticeable. My chest was going in and out too fast and I knew that there had to be some sort of bruise that was forming. That weight was too heavy for me to lift off of me once I was out of breath and Miguel had no chance of getting it off of me. No offense to him, but it was clear that he was weak since he didn't have any muscles. It was made even clearer to me when he couldn't take the weights off of me.

"Where's Miguel?" I asked. I couldn't see anyone's face, but from the surrounding areas, even the small scuffing of people's shoes was stopped. There were only the machines working and the small buzz of the overhead lights. I attempted to look at the coach, but he didn't answer. I wanted an answer, but before I could even ask again, the nurse was back and persisted with me with one-hundred questions a minute.

"The ambulance will be here any minute, we called as soon as I was notified," she rambled. "I'm just here until they come. Are you hurting anywhere?"

"Of course she is. A weight was lying on her chest and she was passed out. Who knows how long she was there for?" I immediately knew it was Chad who was talking. From the sound of his voice, I also knew that he was very close to me. I reached silently for his hand and even though we may have been broken up, he grabbed at it in desperation. "Emily are you okay?" I didn't reply and even though I could have made the situation easier, I decided I was in too much pain.

It hurts to talk.

It hurts to breathe.

"They're here!" one of the boys yelled. I nodded my head and even though they began loading me up in the ambulance, I held onto Chad's hand the entire time. I felt a slight tug at our hands and I knew that they were going to put some resistance up for Chad coming along.

"Only family members." Even though I wanted to put up a fight, I didn't. I immediately let go of Chad's fingers and saw his gaze as they began to close the doors shut.

"I'll meet you there, okay?"

I just nodded my head and closed my eyes.

****

I have been lying in this bed for about an hour without doing anything. The doctors have already done their tests and even though my family had come, I asked them to wait in the hallway. I knew that this had hurt some of them to hear, but I just wanted to be alone. Even when Chad came into my room, I asked him to leave before he even got a word out. It would be surprising to me if he were waiting in the room though. I imagine that he had just gone home instead of waiting. I don't know why I wanted to be alone though. Normally I would crave for Chad or my mom, but with what had happened in the weight room, I had a couple of questions to ask myself before I could answer anyone else's.

Where was Miguel once I woke up? None of the football players seemed to even think that Miguel was in there. The coach made it very clear to me that no one had been in there when they got in the room. I was perfectly fine lifting that weight amount, but when it slipped from my grasp, Miguel should've helped me get it off. Even if he wasn't strong enough to lift it off, he could've just slid it to one part of the ground. This brings me to my second question:

Did Miguel leave me there to die? I can't exactly answer this one and I don't think anyone can except for Miguel. To be honest, if I asked him about it, he wouldn't tell me the truth. Nobody with common sense would. Maybe he went to get someone and it took him forever to find someone.

Did Chad forgive me? It seemed as if he had forgiven me by the way he was clutching onto my hand. He wanted to protect me and even though it was in front of his boys and they would make fun of him for it, he skipped out on practice to come and find me. I wasn't sure if he just wanted to make sure I was okay or if he thought that I had done that on purpose. Either way, I really did just want to explain to him that I have never cheated on him and I never will. He never let me explain that to him and even if he wants to stay broken up afterward, at least he'll know the truth.

I clicked a button I was given by the nurses and waited patiently for one to show up at the door. When one did, she came in swiftly and smiled sweetly at me.

"Can you get Chad?" I asked. She nodded her head and I listened as her shoes clicked against the ground. It was such a soothing sound. Within seconds, the clicking sounds were getting louder and I knew that she was on her A-game.

He came in quietly and he refused to look me in the eye as he sat down next to me. I stayed silent for a moment too and watched as the nurse left the room. I waited a couple of seconds and opened my mouth to talk.

Chad remained quiet as I told him the truth. He had a blank face so I wasn't able to tell if he was believing me or not. Either way, I explained what the text had meant and even though he hated people who cheat on tests, I knew that he hated people who cheat on other people more. As I came to the end, I just looked at Chad and his face remained blank.

He simply just nodded his head. I'm not exactly sure what that meant, but I wasn't able to ask him about it. The doctor came in with my results and even though my family wasn't around, he still told me about them. The only thing that kept running through my mind was what Chad had asked the doctor.

"Would she still be able to play soccer with damaged lungs?"

The doctor seemed very uneasy about answering this question. Initially, he was going to shrug his shoulders, but he thought better of it. Don't asthmatic people do sports all of the time? Is being asthmatic and having a collapsed lung even the same thing? I knew they weren't, but soccer was my life. I mean I would rather heal if I needed to because I don't want to risk the chance of anything happening to me, but I still really loved soccer.

I must've spaced out from when Chad and the doctor were talking because the next thing I knew was that he was leaving to talk to my family. I looked over at Chad, but he seemed heartbroken as he looked at me with pity. He shook his head and even though I still wasn't sure of our relationship status, he bent over and hugged me. As soon as he did, I wheezed out some breath and Chad recoiled. He looked like he was afraid to touch me, but I quickly shook that realization off of him when I sat up and forced a hug upon him.

"So," I whispered as I ended our hug. I looked him in the eyes and I'm sure he knew what I wanted to clear up in the air. He scratched his neck for a moment and I could see the uneasy tension in the air. He looked rather guilty about something and since he wouldn't meet my eyes, I could only think of the worst things he could've done. I sat up on my bed and faced straight ahead of me as I thought. I wouldn't ask because I didn't want to be petty, but I was definitely going to be hurt and passive-aggressive about it. "Oh."

He wasn't replying and although I really wanted him to, I wasn't going to force it upon him. He came to visit me in the hospital after all. He skipped his football practice for me too. Even if we weren't going to be a

                    AMY KULP

couple, we would probably still be friends.
Right?

Chapter 6 -------

As soon as I was told that I could go home from the hospital, I was ecstatic. I didn't realize that I would be just as bored at home as I was in the hospital. The only difference is that I am much more comfortable in the house. It's hard getting around though and my family isn't there all day to babysit me. My intentions were to get any homework that Chad has been dropping off at my house done, but I do not have the self-discipline for that. I constantly need to be watched over and reminded that I should be focusing on my schoolwork. I do not know how people can just stay focused on studying. In school, you're forced to be there and pay attention because you can have your phone taken away from you. I could sleep at home, but at school, you would get in trouble for that. Who's going to punish me for napping on the couch? I won't. If anything, I would reward myself with more naps.

I have been sleeping a lot and just wishing that someone would text me. I haven't gotten any texts from anyone - not even Chad. He drops my homework off on my porch and when my parents come home they find it. It's irritating to me that he won't even talk to me about what is going on with us. It seems that he doesn't want to be with me over a text message about cheating on the test. It wasn't my fault that he had confused cheating with cheating on him. I won't forget his face though when I had told him that though. He seemed guilty.

Did he cheat on me? I don't have anyone who would tell me if he was. The football players and theater kids are loyal to him. The soccer players are loyal to me, but I'm not all buddy-buddy with them. I opened my phone up and scrolled through my previous messages for a bit. I stared at Miguel's last message he sent me and bit my lip. I don't know who he is loyal to or if he has even found his niche at the school, but I had a lot to blame him for. I wasn't able to attend soccer practices for a while, he's the reason Chad thinks I'm cheating on him, and he's the reason I needed to cheat on my history test in the first place. Still, I couldn't help but hover my fingers over typing a new message.

Before I could type one word, I was interrupted by a knock on the door. I lay on the couch for a second before turning my screen off and looking toward the kitchen. It would not do me much good to just stare so I forced myself to sit up and breathed in and out. It was still hard for me to breathe since I just had the chest tubes removed so that I could transition to home life, but I needed to take everything I did slowly. Any abnormal amount of breathing or physical exercise made my lungs ache and feel like they were on fire. It was hard to speak too loud or for too long as well so most of my conversations, I did more of the listening. People didn't seem to mind this, but I loved to talk so I felt out of sorts. As if anticipating that I wasn't able to hear, the person on the porch decided to use the bell that was beside the door. I huffed because I couldn't yell that I was coming nor could I move much faster. All I could do was huff and puff as I made my way over. I felt like a grandma.

As soon as I fully stood up and began walking, I felt like I was out of breath. I would definitely have to rebuild my tolerance to cardio activities when I was done. How else was I going to be able to participate in soccer again? I leaned myself against the doorframe that was to the kitchen and tried to calm down how hard I was breathing. I saw the door from where I was standing and watched as the person on the other side jiggled the door handle. I was surprised to see this and immediately felt uneasy as I watched the door being pushed open. Was I being robbed? I didn't have anything to fend myself off with and I definitely didn't have a car to show that anyone was home. When they knocked, they didn't hear any barking dogs either so they probably thought it was okay to rob. I looked around, but by the time I was able to see something that could possibly be a weapon, I saw the figure in my doorway.

"Oh hey."

"Uh? Hey?"

"You didn't answer the door."

"I was trying to." I stopped leaning against the door and walked forward to get closer. However, this bit of movement proved to be too much for me and I needed to steady myself on the door. "What are you doing here?" I panted out. I gripped hard and leaned without taking my eyes off of him.

"Chad wasn't in school today so I was told to give you your classwork and homework." He eyed his backpack and invited himself in further. I looked strangely at him as he placed the backpack on my table and began rifling through it. I closed the door behind him, looked at the clock on the oven, and stood puzzled for a second.

"Two questions," I stated. "School didn't even let out yet." I pointed to the time and Miguel just shrugged his shoulders. When I waited for him to answer, it was clear that he wasn't going to. I guess it wasn't that important of a question. He probably just ditched. It wasn't that hard at our school - you just leave. There aren't any alarms that go off or cameras in that area. The only way the staff knew you missed was if that teacher took attendance that day. Sometimes, they didn't even do that during class. Even if you did ditch, there wasn't anything to do. We lived in a rural area where it took us thirty minutes to get anywhere interesting - even home! We didn't have any fast food places nor did we have any hangout spots. Most students were athletes so you couldn't smoke weed because we get drug tested every month while our sport is in session. Most students didn't drink either because their parents were part of a church that forbade it. "Second question I guess," I whispered as I watched him bring all of the textbooks out of his bag. When he was done, he looked at them and then at me. "How do you know where I live?"

There was silence for a moment.

"The school gave me your address." He immediately went back to reshuffling the books and I just nodded my head. I wasn't sure if he was telling the truth or not, but I wasn't getting a creepy vibe from him. I just nodded my head and sat myself down at the table. He looked at me from the corner of his eye and I saw a smile play on his lips. "So did you want me to show you we did so it's not as confusing?" He stretched his arms on the table and leaned across them as he scanned the books.

"I haven't even done any of this week's homework," I admitted. He cocked his eyebrows and looked down at one of the books. "You know, Chad usually just drops them off on the porch and leaves." I pointed at the door and Miguel nodded his head. He seemed to contemplate for a moment but eventually grabbed his bag off of the table. He nodded his head again and without another word, tried to leave. "Thank you for dropping these off."

"Don't worry about it, I'm sure anybody would do it for you." He stood in the doorway for a moment before turning back around and looking at me. "Do you have a bathroom I can use before I go?" I nodded my head and slowly rose from my chair. I must've had a pained expression on my face because as soon as I did that, Miguel rushed over and steadied my body with his. "You okay?" He placed one arm around my back and one arm on my stomach and I jolted at the contact. He smiled at me to show he meant no cruel intention and when I was straightened, he moved away.

I was surprised for a second when I felt myself getting goosebumps. I don't normally like to have my stomach touched because it makes me insecure that I might have extra pudge on me, but when his hand left my shirt, I felt cold. His body and his presence were very warm. His hand placements also made me feel like he was truly just trying to help me and maybe doesn't know what personal space is.

"Uh, it's right down here." I walked a little bit, but as soon as I got out of the kitchen, I felt myself not being able to breathe well. I forced myself to walk a longer distance than I have been and began panting.

"If you just want to tell me where it is, I can try to find it." Miguel instantly wrapped his arm around my back again and placed his hand on my stomach. I felt a bit more insecure with his hand placement now than I did before because of how fast my stomach was going in and out. As soon as he saw the couch, he sat me down on it. He wouldn't have known, but the couch that he sat us on happened to be the couch that was broken in the corner. As we both sat down, I felt the cushion starting to sink in where he was sitting. We both instantly tipped over and I fell onto the side of him. He laughed a bit and I felt myself get embarrassed as I felt my own hand placement wasn't appropriate. Once I steadied myself on his knees, I sat back up and felt myself blush.

"If you go into the other room and there's another room, the bathroom is on the right." Miguel looked at me and just blinked his eyes for a second. "I know that was confusing." I laughed a bit and Miguel instantly joined in. He smiled along and I was able to see that his smile was beautiful. I was envious of it and at the same time, I made myself feel super self-conscious.

"What?" Miguel asked. His smile faded as well and he looked at me. I watched as his eyes darted between looking at both of mine. "Why'd you stop smiling?" I instantly shook my head and licked my lips as I pointed to the other room again.

"Go into this next room." I stared at him again and he nodded his head. "Once you enter, you'll see a doorway to the other room - which would be our laundry room. When you get into the laundry room, the bathroom will be on the right."

"Are you sure you want me to go?" Miguel asked. I nodded my head and his right eyebrow rose as if he was challenging me. "You can remove your hands then." I instantly blushed as I removed my hand from his knee. He got up without another word and I heard him walking.

I stayed sitting on the broken couch while he was gone, but I couldn't help but keep blushing. I felt so embarrassed. Why did I keep putting my hands on him? And why did he keep putting his hands on me? It felt weird since I was only used to being with Chad and he didn't like to touch me unless he was jealous. I am also surprised that Chad had missed school. It was Friday which meant there was a football game. If you missed a day of school, you were not able to go to your athletic events that day. So if Chad wasn't there today, he wouldn't be able to go to his football game tonight. Everything that I know about Chad told me this was wrong - Chad would be at school. This didn't sit right with me so I pulled out my phone and was ready to text him when I got distracted.

My app opened up to Miguel's messages and my fingers fluttered over the letters without typing anything. I looked at the couple of messages I had and sat there wondering. I never found out how he got my number because I was always distracted by finding out. In fact, I have to remember to ask him a lot of questions. Why did he disappear on me when that weight fell on me? I needed to ask him about both of these questions. Does he realize that I am hurt because he left me there to die?

I attempted to get up from the couch, but movement from the corner of my eye stopped me from standing up. I leaned over the couch and watched as a car stopped in my driveway. This car was instantly recognizable as the one that Chad drives and I froze in my spot. I watched intently as he got out of his car and put my school books on the porch where he normally had. I slowly watched as he waited on the porch for a second before taking off back into his car. When the car left my driveway, I was puzzled for a second before I heard the flush of the toilet and found myself getting up from the couch.

Why was Chad just here with my books? Whose books were Miguel's? Why was Miguel here if Chad was in school? How did Miguel get my address if the school didn't send him? How did Miguel get my number? How did Miguel find me in the work out room and then leave when the weight was crushing my chest? How did Miguel get my history book? All of these questions were racing through my mind and when Miguel came out of the bathroom and met me, he smiled sweetly at me.

"I'm back." I nodded my head and when Miguel saw that I wasn't joking around, his smile faded from his face. "What's wrong?" He instantly grabbed onto the sleeves of my shirt and was ready to steady me as if I needed it. I forced myself to stay stiff and despite wavering a bit under his touch, my body felt cold against his now.

I didn't know this guy and he was showing up in all aspects of my life. He was messing everything up in my life too - my soccer dreams, my relationship, and my grades. I didn't know him. Why was he in my house when no one else was home? When nobody answered the door, why did he come inside? What were his true intentions? When I looked back up in his eyes, he was concerned and searching for an answer. He acted like I was the problem when, in fact, he was.

"Why did you lie about the school sending you to my house?" I asked desperately.

"Why would I lie about that?" he chuckled. He grabbed my elbow now instead of the sleeve of my shirt, but when I didn't move he sensed it was even more serious now. He still had a smile on his face and shook his

                                    AMY KULP

head as if I was delusional.

"I just saw Chad on my porch putting my school supplies on my porch."

I spoke crystal clear and it was obvious that Miguel heard. There was no denying what I had seen and if I had actually seen what I had thought I did. Miguel could try to deny it, but we could easily go to the porch and find the evidence there. I think he knew he was caught because before I had said anything, he was bright, charming, and his body was warm. The mood in the room instantly changed to a dark and cold atmosphere. The creepy vibes that I hadn't sensed before made me want to crawl away from this guy in my room. In an instant, the safety and comfort I had always felt in my home was gone. Did my family and I not lock our doors? Did we need to start locking our doors? I have never locked our doors because of how small our community is. The one thing that chilled me to the bone, however, wasn't any of that.

It was when Miguel's smile instantly turned down and his face became stone cold.

Chapter 7--------

"How does it feel to be back?" Bri asked as she met up with me in the hallway. I shrugged my shoulders to answer her question. I wasn't used to the attention that I was getting today. For example, Bri never greeted me when I came to school. We only sat together if none of our closer friends were in the class. We still talked if we were together in the same class, but once the bell rang, she would rather sit with those other friends. I was the same way; if I didn't have Chad in my class, I would sit with her. I didn't really know what I was going to do now that we weren't together. It's not like he would even discuss it with me though. Every day, I would hear or see him drop my assignments off on my porch. If I had tried to get to the porch, he would be in his car already. "Also I heard about Chad and Holli, I'm sorry babe." I looked over at her and scrunched my eyebrows down. I stopped walking so that I could make sure I was comprehending what she said correctly, but also because I needed a break for a second. "You didn't hear?" Bri asked. I shook my head and I watched as regret showed on her face. "They've been hooking up."

I stared at her for a second before I shook my head and began walking toward our lockers. This must be why Chad has been avoiding me. It hurt to hear, but I'm glad that Bri told me about it. I could feel her nervous energy next to me as I opened my locker, but I tried not to acknowledge her. As soon as I opened my locker door, a note came flying out of it and I swiftly bent down and picked it up. She raised her eyebrows and I shrugged my shoulders and tucked it away in one of my notebooks. I would read it later. Obviously, if it was written on a piece of paper and not texted to me, it wasn't urgent enough for me to read right now. Although my curiosity piqued

"I do feel bad," Bri whispered beside me. "I'll text you and we'll hang out now that you're feeling better."

"You don't have to," I mentioned, shaking my head. I tried to walk toward my homeroom, but Bri stopped me.

"Well, then we can practice together or work out together." She immediately looked guilty and I couldn't help but wonder why. She stared at me and the longer I didn't say anything, the more it looked like she would break and tell me what she was talking about. "I feel bad that you were in that weight room alone. You could've gotten a lot more hurt than you did."

"I wasn't alone." I looked around us to see if there was a place for privacy, but there wasn't. People were interested in me like I was the main exhibit. Almost as if I was a refurbished gallery piece at a museum; I was the same old Emily, but I was better than before so I was more interesting. I didn't know what they could hear and what they couldn't, but I wanted someone to talk to. Being at home for three weeks was really, really boring when you didn't have any friends who checked in on you. "Miguel was with me, but he vanished before anyone could come and help get the weight off of me."

"Why were you two even hanging out?"

"He came to work out." I shrugged my shoulders. How was I supposed to know his intentions? "Listen, all I know is one minute he was there and one minute he wasn't." I shrugged my shoulders again, but I could see the judgmental face on Bri.

As soon as the bell rang, we both took our seats in homeroom. She went off to her end and I went off to my end. I was usually surrounded by Chad and all of his football friends, but today I was only surrounded by the people who were assigned to sit next to me. I felt like this was the perfect opportunity for me to look at the note that was left in my locker. I opened my notebook up a little to try and read what the note said, but a hand slapped down on it and distracted me.

"Miss me?" Chad asked. He climbed up onto the table to try and distract me. While I tried to not give in, I looked over at him anyway. I had a lot going through my mind, but as he smiled innocently at me, I couldn't help but smile back. "There's my girl." He pecked me on the cheek and slid into the empty seat next to me. I looked over to where Bri was and when we made eye contact, she made sure that she made a disapproving face at me. I would have to talk to him later about everything. "Are you okay?" he asked as the teacher began taking attendance. He snuck his arms around me and pulled me closer to him. His voice got lower as he got closer to my ear and I could tell that he was looking at everyone around us as he spoke. "I've been hearing a lot of things about you recently."

"Like what?" I turned my head quickly and broke his hold on me. He loosened his grip and stared into my eyes.

"Can we talk after school? I'll take you home." I stared at him for a minute before I felt myself nod my head. He smiled and kissed the top of my head before getting out of the seat to sit where he was supposed to.

I made eye contact with Bri again and she shrugged her shoulders. I tried to communicate that I want to speak with her after class, but I wasn't sure if she got the memo. Before I could even think about the letter that was in my notebook, the bell rang and I found myself floating to my first class. Bri managed to catch up to me and I felt her presence, but I didn't turn to talk to her. Everything was out of whack today and I was unsure if I should trust Bri or Chad. Why would Bri lie to me though? Chad was pleasant and acted as if nothing happened between us. I wasn't even sure if we were girlfriend and boyfriend. Although, he was acting differently now that I was physically in the school. When I was home, he wouldn't even talk to me while I was in the house. What's with his change in attitude all of a sudden?

"What was that about?" Bri asked as she sat down next to me. I was stunned that she sat next to me because she usually next to Miguel in history. I eyed the seat that he would normally be in,and when the bell rang, I knew he wasn't at school today.. "He hasn't been in school for about a week," Bri whispered to me.

I nodded my head and let myself get stuck in my thoughts for a moment. That day in my house when I confronted him, he had acted so strangely. His face had gotten so dark and, for a second, I was afraid of him. His face quickly changed and he laughed it off with some excuse I can't remember. I wasn't sure if I should have believed him, but it definitely sent shivers down my spine just thinking about it. Until today, I had let the incident slip to the back of my mind because I had just been cleared to start going back to school. That made me more nervous than anything and I found myself anticipating the first day again. It felt like she was restarting.. You have those butterflies in your stomach and you can't tell if you are excited or want to throw up.

In reality, it was both.

When I felt a nudge in my side, I looked over at Bri and she whispered softly to me about the note. I shook my head and glanced over at the teacher. He was too busy fiddling with his projector to pay attention to what anyone else may have been doing in class. I slowly opened my notebook to find the note and slid it in the middle of Bri and me. I slowly unfolded the note while keeping my eyes on the teacher. I did not want him to find this note and then have to read it out to the class, especially since I didn't know what it contained or who it was from. As soon as I opened it in my lap, my eyes crinkled in confusion and I let Bri see it before sliding it back into the notebook.

As soon as I shut my notebook, the teacher perked up with his projector and started teaching the class again. I couldn't concentrate though, and as soon as the bell rang, I grabbed my things and slid out of the classroom. I waited patiently for Bri to catch up by rifling through my locker. When she appeared at my side, she commented on exactly what I was thinking about.

"Unless you have a secret admirer, that had to be from Chad," Bri mentioned. I shook my head and brought the note into view again. I stared at the thin letters of the words and how bold they were and my stomach felt slightly queasy on the inside. "It's so cute."

"What about what you told me earlier?" I asked. I folded the note delicately and placed it back in the notebook that had been concealing it. I shut my locker door quickly and grabbed some books that I needed for the next couple of classes. "About him and Holli?" I looked at her as I asked the question and she shrugged her shoulders.

"I haven't caught them in the act or anything, but people talk," Bri quipped. She shrugged her shoulders again and smiled. "Maybe it's an apology note." She rolled her eyes and abruptly stopped at a teacher's door. "I'm in this class, but I would definitely talk to him after school." I nodded my head, because that was exactly what I had been planning to do.

I felt uneasy about bringing the note up to Chad because I didn't think he wrote it. I knew Chad's writing. He wrote with tall, fat letters. This was different as the letters seemed to be tall and thin. Who else would write me a note? I blinked and attempted to focus on whatever lesson was being taught, but as the note was in my notebook, I couldn't help but stare at it instead of taking notes.

I can't wait to see you again.

****

"Are you ready to go home?" Chad asked as he met up with me as I was packing stuff away at my locker. I nodded my head as I unzipped my bookbag and pondered what I should keep and what I should take home. He stared at me as I made my decision and pointed to a book that I had in my locker. "You'll need that. We have that vocabulary we need to do." I paused for a second before realizing that he was right and I silently pulled the book from the stack that it was under. I felt myself stumble with my bookbag and watched as it fell clumsily to the floor. "Are you okay?" I nodded my head as I bent down to pick my stuff up. Chad met me as I kneeled and made eye contact. He stopped my hand from grabbing at the papers on the ground and I felt myself flinch as he unknowingly grabbed the mystery note. He shoved it into a folder I had in there and smiled. He helped me up and closed my locker as he brought me into a side hug. "We'll talk in the car."

I nodded my head and he moved my body along with his. I could feel a couple of stares at me as we walked toward the entrance. He silently waved to people who called out a greeting, but he didn't say anything else to them. That was quite unusual for him since most of the time he loves social interaction. He truly was a very likable person even with his flaws. He was the type of person who would thrive going to a social event where he didn't know anyone. On the other hand, I would be the girl who would sit at the table the entire time trying to avoid conversation. We were complete opposites and I often wondered how we had gotten together. How were we compatible?

"I know what people are saying," he said once we were in the car. I looked over at him and blinked for a second. He had never addressed any rumors before when we had been dating; I was always the one who had to bring anything like that up. Of course, everyone wanted to date Chad, but I never actually suspected him of cheating on me. This was the first time I speculated the rumors might be true. "For the sake of us, I am choosing to believe that these rumors are false." I blinked a second before my mind could comprehend what he was insinuating.

"What are you talking about?" I asked once he started the car. "I wanted to talk about you and Holli." His face started to turn pale for a second, but he recovered nicely. He looked like his attention was caught by something else as he backed up his car. "Well?" I asked as he looked in the rearview mirror.

"There's nothing to talk about there." His eyes darted at the rearview mirror again and I briefly looked at the car behind us. "We are in a school play together." He paused and drove a bit slower. "We're the leads. We need to rehearse." He shook his head and I watched as his eyes darted at the mirror again. I looked at the car that was tailgating us and rolled my eyes. He hated cars that did that and he had road rage himself, so I was surprised that he didn't yell at the car or flip him off. "What about you and Miguel?"

"What about us?" I asked. I tore my eyes from the road and looked over at him and felt myself getting red. "You know that there is nothing going on with us. He's the reason that I got hurt in the first place."

"You keep saying that, but there was no one in that weight room with you." He started raising his voice at me and I felt my body shrinking against the door. This was not how I expected this conversation to go. "I want to know why he was at your house when I was the one in charge of dropping off your school materials."

He took his eyes off of the road and looked at me. I felt uneasy about that since I knew the students in our parking lot. I knew how fast and wild they drove. They didn't care. It was their mommy and daddy's car - not theirs. As quick as he was to look at me, his eyes focused back to driving. However, every time I spoke, he seemed to lose his focus on driving and direct it towards me. He needed to pay attention and I wanted to remind him of that but I was flabbergasted. I didn't know what to say. I was confused, but it made me feel better that he was watching out for me. He noticed the additional car when I was by myself. When I was stuck at home, I was upset that he wouldn't talk to me. Even now, I still do not understand why he wouldn't help me.

"He said-"

"Shit!" Chad immediately slammed on the brakes and turned his caution lights on all in one motion. His arm flew across my body protectively and I felt my body slide into his. The seatbelt yanked me back and I gasped for air as I realized that the car behind us had rear-ended us. I looked over at Chad to make sure that he was okay and to make sure that he wasn't going to hurt anyone, but he seemed calm. "Are you okay?" Chad mumbled. He looked over at me and I just shook my head as I saw that he wasn't mad. "Give me a moment, okay?" I nodded again and watched as he unbuckled his seatbelt and got out of the car. He closed the car door behind him gently and I crinkled my eyebrows.

I looked in the mirror to see Chad knock on this person's door. They talked for a few minutes, but because of the tint on the windows, I couldn't see who it was. I squinted to try and get a better look, but it was of no use for me. I patiently waited for Chad to come back. When he did, he sat still for a second. I didn't want to break the silence, but the air felt eerie. Why was he acting so calm about this car accident? When the car behind us left, I finally spoke.

"You okay?" Chad nodded his head and smiled slightly at me. "You're acting strange. Usually, you would be angry." Chad nodded his head and his grip on the steering wheel tightened. His knuckles turned white and he just kept nodding his head. "Chad?" I placed my hand on his arm and he calmed down for a second before looking at me. "You know this is really great luck," I smiled. "Ever since that note you left me, I thought we would immediately be making out and-"

"Okay first off," Chad interrupted. "I would love that." I smiled and was glad to see that he was out of his thoughts. "Secondly, what note?" I blinked for a second and thought he was joking. I explained the note that was left in my locker but he shook his head. "I didn't write you a note." I smiled again and rummaged through my book bag for a second to find the note. When I couldn't find it, I sat perplexed in my seat. "That's not funny, Em."

"I'm not joking. I must've dropped it in the hallway and-"

I stopped talking as soon as I felt a sting across my face. When I registered that Chad had taken his anger out on me instead of the driver, I saw a flash of guilt on his face before it went back to anger. I was stunned into silence.

                                          AMY KULP

Chapter 8 ---------

I looked at him and then back at the road and right back at him. My eyes kept darting around and I didn't know what to think. Did he just actually slap me? It was hard too, so it wasn't an accident. I stared at him and took his appearance in. His knuckles were white from gripping the steering wheel so hard, but his face seemed somber. My eyes darted towards his leg that was now bouncing up and down and my eyebrows furrowed. He only ever did that if he was nervous. I looked up at his face again but my eyes went back to the knuckles gripped on the wheel.

Without another word, I unbuckled my seatbelt and opened the car door. As soon as it slammed shut, I watched as Chad shifted to drive. His tires spun out and rocks flew at me as he drove out of the dirt lot. A couple pebbles managed to hit my face since I wasn't quick enough to shield myself. I stood still as I watched his car drive away until I was alone. The sun was setting and it seemed too dark for the time. I looked around and instinctively reached for my phone that was usually in my back pocket. I patted empty space though, and realized that I had left my bag and phone in his car. I silently scolded myself. How stupid could I be? I was going to end up like one of those girls dead on the side of the road.

I shook my head as if that would erase the thoughts from coming into my mind. I had to think positively. We were in a small town where nothing exciting happened except us winning our hometown football games. Nobody had ever gotten kidnapped. Nobody had ever gotten killed. I smiled slightly, but still felt uneasy about the entire situation. It was suspicious. Chad was hot-headed, but he had never laid a hand on me. Why didn't he yell at the guy who hit his car? Why did he hit me?

As it became darker outside, I scolded myself and forced my legs to begin moving. We were on our way to my house, and although it would have taken me about fifteen minutes to get home if I were driving, it would take a lot longer now that I was walking. I was wearing dark clothes,too,so I was conscious that someone could hit me by accident because they were not able to see me. I had to walk on the road–there weren't any sidewalks. As I started down the stretch of road, there were very few cars driving around. It made my life easier since I was freely able to walk without having to trip on the side of the road where grass, roots, and litter were scattered.

About ten minutes into my walk, I knew there was a car behind me. When you're in the middle of nowhere, there are not a lot of sounds. I moved over to give it as much room as I was able to, but I could hear it begin to slow down. I looked behind me, ready to signal that they could drive, but their car was crawling alongside me. I squinted my eyes to make sure it wasn't someone I knew, but the tint on the windows was so dark that I was unable to see through it. When I looked even closer, I was able to see that this was the car from earlier. This was the car that had hit Chad's car. I immediately stopped and the car pulled up next to me.

Was I going to have to fight?

I cursed myself again as I realized that I had nothing to use to defend myself. I had my fingernails, but they were bitten short yesterday. I'm uncoordinated, so I wasn't able to throw a punch or kick without injuring myself. As the car began to roll down its windows, I felt my heart skip a beat but still put a friendly smile on my face. Maybe I would be able to lie and say that I lived just up the road. They would not know.

"Emily?" I blinked as I saw light coming from the car and recognized Miguel's face. My fake smile became a genuine smile and I walked toward the car. "What are you doing out in the dark? I could have hit you if I was speeding." I shook my head and shrugged my shoulders. Before I even got a word out to answer his question, he asked another . "Do you want a ride back to your house?" I shook my head enthusiastically and immediately tried the door handle. Miguel blushed and unlocked it for me so that I was able to get in.

"Thank you so much." I grabbed the seatbelt to click in and patiently waited for him to start moving again. I had so many questions in my head, but I didn't start talking until he moved the car. "Why haven't you been in school?" I asked. He grinned goofily and made brief eye contact with me before turning his eyes back to the road.

"Are you a cop?"

"No." I tried to play it off just as goofily as he did, but it sounded strained. I cleared my throat and looked back to the road. Truthfully, I didn't like to hold conversations in cars. The car was where I was able to blissfully daydream and be alone with my thoughts. I had to force myself to stay engaged in conversations, and I would be more focused on staying focused so that I wouldn't listen to what they were saying anyway. It seemed like Miguel was the same way, because he didn't try to talk anymore. I was able to think, but that just made me think about what he could have been doing.

Was it something illegal? What else could he mean by "are you a cop?" The most that anybody did around here was pot, but since a lot of students were athletes, they weren't able to because of the drug tests. He could have also just been messing with me. I peeked over at him and he was still focused on the road. There was no hint of playfulness or grouchiness in his expression so I still couldn't tell. I used to think that I was good at reading people, but maybe I wasn't anymore.

Or maybe I just couldn't read Miguel. I barely even knew him, but he was always showing up in my life. Sometimes it was good, sometimes it was bad, and sometimes it was unusual. I was starting to think that maybe Miguel didn't have good social cues because he never articulated what he was doing, why he was with me,

                    AMY KULP

or anything else when I had questions. I also was unable to place him with a friend group yet. I never saw him hanging out with people, but whenever he was in one of my classes, he always seemed to be friendly with everyone. It was like he was that bad boy in teen movies that was so mysterious and was only needed for the plot. I also wasn't sure if he was trying to be my friend or if he liked me as a girlfriend. Maybe there were language barriers. I'm sure he grew up learning Spanish. Although that was a stereotype in and of itself.

"What are you thinking about?" Miguel asked. I shook my head to snap out of my thoughts and looked at him. He kept darting his eyes between me and the road. I appreciated that he was being safe while driving, but it also reminded me that he had crashed into Chad earlier. If he was so careful, how did he manage to hit Chad's car? Now that I think of it, I didn't even see a dent on his car. I didn't remember what Chad's looked like since I never looked at the back of it. I was more worried about walking home in the dark. "Emily?"

"Yeah?" I asked. I looked at him and as he slowed for a stop light, he looked at me carefully. He reached his hand over and placed it on my thigh for a second. He squeezed it and when the light turned green, it started sliding up my thigh. I stared at the hand hard and when I looked back at Miguel, it didn't look unnatural to him. I moved my legs over to my side of the car, but because of how tall Miguel was, it didn't bother him at all. I shook my leg briefly and when he still didn't move his hand, I felt myself gulp. Was he expecting me to do something for him? Was I expected to pay him for driving me home? "You know I have a boyfriend, right?"

"Chad?" Miguel asked and had a playful smile on his face. It looked like he knew something that I didn't. "Is it an open relationship?" I shook my head and furrowed my eyebrows.

I didn't have time to think about what he was trying to say. I was so uncomfortable as he slid his hand further up my thigh that I forced my hands on his. When I tried to force it off, his hand didn't budge, but his grip tightened. He angled his nails into my skin and as I tried moving his fingers, I felt him claw at my skin. My heart began to race as I realized that I didn't have a choice but to leave his hand on my thigh. I let go and grabbed at my seatbelt. I wasn't going to unbuckle it since there was no way I would survive jumping out of the car, but I needed to feel safe. I clamped my thighs as tight as they could go and he didn't try moving it up anymore, but his hand stayed where it was. I looked over at the lock for an option if we did slow down, but was frightened to see that it was locked and I wasn't able to unlock it.

I immediately turned my face away from him at this realization and felt myself begin to shake. I didn't want him to see my face if I began crying. I didn't want him to think that he had a chance at doing anything with me or to me. If Chad had been trying to have sex with me for this long unsuccessfully, Miguel wouldn't get it just because he gave me a ride. As a single tear fell out of my

                                         AMY KULP

eye, I immediately wiped at it and pulled down my seatbelt as if that would be good enough to block his hand from going up any further.

It stayed put.

As he pulled up to my house, I tried the door handle, but it was still locked. I let my hand straddle the handle and I couldn't wait for the clicks to come up. No way would he expect me to do anything in front of my house. I felt relief fly through me as the doors unlocked and I hurried out of the car. I looked back once as I slammed the door and Miguel was smiling at me as if nothing happened. As soon as the door shut, his face seemed confused and he waved. I didn't wave back and forced myself to turn to my house.

I didn't look to see what he was doing as I walked up the stairs to my porch and attempted to open the door. It was locked; I knew that my family always locked the door. I stared over at Miguel and saw that he was peering out the opposite window. It looked like he was trying to pull out of my driveway, so I quickly grabbed the hidden key and unlocked my door, slamming it shut. I turned to look out the window and watched as Miguel stayed where he was. I quietly locked the door, as I was still freaked out about what had happened, and tried the handle just in case. When I turned around I noticed how empty my house felt.

I looked around and forced myself to sit down. I was a bit shaky from what had happened and because of the temperature drop outside. My house was quiet, which usually wasn't the case if anyone from my family was home. When I looked at the clock, I was surprised to see that it was only six. For how dark it was, I expected it to be eight or nine. Maybe they were all sleeping? I doubted it, but because of the turn of events of being hit by Chad, Miguel feeling me up, and the quietness of the house, I wasn't sure what was normal for that day. I immediately went upstairs with my thoughts and knocked on my parents' door.

Nothing.

I tried the handle, but that door was also locked. This was weird. My parents never locked their bedroom door. I tried again to be sure, but it was definitely locked. I knocked once and listened for an answer, but didn't hear anything on the other side.

As I turned around to go back down the stairs, I came face to face with someone I had not expected. I immediately jumped in surprise and clutched at my chest. I made some type of noise, but it caught in my throat so only a horrible sound was heard. I grasped at my chest for a second before my emotions went from scared to angry.

"What the hell are you doing in my house?" I asked. My voice was loud from the quietness of the house and I felt like it bounced off of the hallway walls. I couldn't see that well in the dark and I didn't think that I would need to turn the lights on if I was just going from one room to another. Clearly, I was wrong. "How did you get in? I locked that door!" I pointed downstairs and he stood there looking at me. "How did you come up those

                                    AMY KULP

steps without me hearing you?" I asked when he didn't answer. I stepped closer to him and yelled louder. "Why are you always showing up when you aren't supposed to be here?" He opened up his mouth to talk, but that infuriated me so I spoke over him. "How come there are rumors going around that we're a couple?" He wrinkled his eyebrows and I realized as soon as it left my mouth that it may have just been something Chad had said to get me vulnerable so he wouldn't be held accountable for something. "Why'd you come to give me my homework when Chad was in school? You lied to me! I saw Chad at my door."

"Calm down."

"Don't tell me to calm down in my own house. Why are you here?"

"I'm here because-"

"Why did you hit Chad's car today? Then miraculously you come to save the day when I was kicked out of his car?" I asked. I was overwhelmed and I couldn't keep my mind on one task. It seemed like he was trying to think of answers to my questions and that infuriated me. He should automatically say what comes to his mind.

"Will you let me talk?" he shouted. I instantly shut up and stared at him. I felt my eyes blink a couple of times as if I didn't hear him correctly, but I remained silent. He closed his eyes and breathed in and out. When he felt ready to talk, he reached into his pocket and something lit up. "I have your phone." He threw it at me and I was able to catch it. I was dazed for a second. "You left it in my car."

"No, I didn't." I blinked and waved the phone in his face. "My phone is in Chad's car." I tossed it back and he lit the screen up. He showed me the wallpaper without saying a word and tossed it back to me.

"It must have slipped out of your back pocket."

I caught it and felt myself flinch for a second. "Thanks." I felt dazed and looked up at Miguel as he stood in the dark with me. "Are you sure-"

"That's your phone, right?" he asked. I nodded my head and he shrugged his shoulders. "How else would I have gotten it?" I shook my head because I honestly did not know. "Can you help me leave? I only knew how to come up because I heard the noise coming from up here, but I don't know the layout of your house and it's dark." I shook my head silently and placed my phone in my back pocket again. Miguel eyed me for a second before I made a "hmph" noise and admitted that it was viable that it could have fallen out of my pocket.

I just shook my head and searched the wall for the light. When I felt it, I clicked it on and we were instantly blinded by it. I had to squint for a moment before I was able to see anything. I didn't say anything as I led him down the stairs and into my kitchen. I led him straight to the door and when I opened it he immediately stepped out without a word. I looked at the lock on my door and noticed that it was never locked.

"Miguel." He turned around and I looked up at him. "How did you get into my house?"

                                    AMY KULP

"It wasn't locked," he answered as if he could see into my head. "Goodnight."

"Night."

As I closed the door, I locked it. I looked at it for a second before doing a double take and shaking the knob. I looked again and breathed silently through my mouth.

Was I losing my mind?

Chapter 9----------

"I didn't hear from you at all last night," Bri said as she slumped down next to me. I nodded my head but kept my face in my notebook. She brought her phone out without any worry that she would get caught and scrolled through her messages. "I don't even think you read them." She scrolled more and I saw her give me the side-eye before she continued to talk. "Unless you don't have that setting on?"

"I got busy last night."

The answer was enough for her and she nodded her head before putting her phone away. Truth was, I did get busy once Miguel left. My thoughts preoccupied my mind as I scrolled through my phone. I had messages from my parents explaining their absence, and when I woke up, they were exactly where they were supposed to be. Everything was where it was supposed to be. The kitchen door was locked. My parents' room was unlocked. I had my phone and when I stepped out on the porch, Chad had brought my backpack to my door. I appreciated the gesture, but it would've been better if he hadn't hit me in the first place–I would've never left it otherwise.

"You okay?" Bri asked beside me.

I managed to make an "mhm" sound come from my lips and she took the hint that I wanted to be alone. I felt alone too. I felt like I couldn't trust Chad. The things that Bri had told me and him hitting me made me unsure of who to actually trust. Was he sleeping with Holli? Did he actually think I was sleeping with Miguel? I also couldn't trust Miguel. He creeped me out.. I also wasn't even sure if I could trust Bri. She was telling me all of these things, but what if she just wanted to gossip? I also felt like I couldn't trust myself. What if I don't know my limits like I thought I did?

Bri and I were going to work out after school since I was better suited for it. We were going to start slow with minor cardio, but I knew that I would try pushing my limits.

"Alright, you are being too quiet now." Bri nudged my arm and I looked at her. She had a friendly smile on her face and she put down her phone to show that she was interested in talking to me. "What gives?" I opened my mouth, but I guess my face was showing my emotions because she interrupted me before I even had a chance to speak. "Don't lie to me, Emily."

I thought for a second and decided that it would probably be a good idea if I talked to someone. Bri was the closest thing I had to a friend, so it made sense for me to talk to her. Besides, it seemed as if she genuinely wanted to be my friend as well. I never had someone who tried to talk to me even when I pushed them away. I never had someone who constantly talked to me or sat next to me in each class. I wasn't sure what had happened with her and her normal friends, but I was okay with it. I needed someone if Chad and I were going to split. That day seemed closer and closer.

"Emily, what's wrong?" She laughed a little to herself and grabbed my arm. I sat up and looked at her. Once again, she spoke before I could. "You look like shit." I nodded my head in agreement.

"I feel like shit." I smiled a bit and realized that talking to her made me feel better. "Chad hit me yesterday." I waited for her response, but she just sat there. Her smile seemed to disappear and her mouth became a straight line.

"Are you serious?" I nodded my head and she stared for a second. "Are you sure?" I nodded my head again and suddenly felt uncomfortable. Normally, I would believe that she was in disbelief. However, it sounded more as if she was accusing me of lying. "He doesn't seem like the type to do that." I nodded my head and immediately felt myself beginning to rant.

"I know. I was so surprised that he did that. I stormed out of his car." I nodded my head and felt my anger bubbling. "I was forced to walk home." I rolled my eyes a bit and felt details slip off of my tongue before I was able to catch them. "Thankfully Miguel picked me up. He was weird too-"

"Miguel?" Bri asked. She arched her eyebrow and I nodded my head. I felt myself begin to blush at her implications, but I let her say them out loud before I commented on them. "I know you're worried that Chad's cheating on you, but it sounds like he should be more worried about you cheating on him." I was offended.

                                    AMY KULP

There was no way she said that to my face. "Nobody around here has even seen Miguel." She paused. "He's been absent for the past week. Then he suddenly comes and saves the day for you? Very likely." I paused to think about my next choice of words as she grabbed her phone and wrote a quick text to someone. When she pressed send, she put her phone back in her bag and she looked back at me. It was like she was trying to read how I felt.

"I am very faithful." I straightened my back and furrowed my eyebrows. "You don't think I'd actually cheat, right?" She contemplated it for a second before answering.

"I don't think you're capable of cheating, but him saving you sounds very unrealistic."

I nodded my head because I also agreed. It *did* seem very unrealistic for me to be saved by someone I know. Someone who has not been in school for the past week. He also was the one to hit Chad's car. Yet there was no damage to his car. Everything was suspicious. Why was everyone around me suspicious?

I didn't have time to think about it further because the bell rang. Bri and I gathered our stuff before we headed over to our lockers. We were both quiet as we walked, but I knew that our conversation was still hanging between us. I hope she didn't think I was mad at her. I turned to her to speak, but she ran into me as if it was urgent I went to my locker. She instructed me to just get my books because we were running out of time in the hall. I turned back around and did as she instructed, but was confused because our warning bell didn't even ring yet. As soon as I opened my locker, a letter fell to my feet.

"Wow, you're popular this week."

I looked at her as she smirked for a second before her expression turned to curiosity. I scrunched my eyebrows in confusion and as soon as I finished grabbing my books I reached down. She inched towards me as I opened it. Instead of the puffy bubble letters that were on my first note, this one was thin jagged letters. The letters were written hastily and there was clearly a lot of pressure used. It kind of looked like some of the markers snapped off while they were writing. When I actually read what it said, I stood there for a second in shock.

LIAR

"Who'd you piss off?" Bri asked me as she read over my shoulder. I shrugged my shoulders and just crumpled the note up. I threw it in my locker and listened for the warning bell. I looked at Bri, expecting her to push further, but she didn't acknowledge it. When we began walking alongside each other, I could see Chad coming from down the hall. He was coming straight for us. "This is my cue to leave," she whispered. Before I even had time to stop her, Chad grabbed my arm and forced me into the back of the auditorium.

It hurt as he dragged me and I felt his fingers tightening the more we moved. As soon as he let go, I readjusted my clothes and was about to yell at him. He kissed me hard and I pushed away from him. He looked hurt for a second before resuming his angry stance.

"Why are you going around spreading rumors about me?" Chad whisper-yelled. I didn't even register what he said before I felt my mouth starting to answer. He immediately talked over me. "You need to be quiet. We are in the back of the auditorium. The chorus class can't see us, but we don't want to get in trouble." I nodded my head but didn't talk regardless. He had explaining to do. "There are rumors going around that you are telling people I hit you."

"Because you did."

"When?"

"Yesterday after school."

"I didn't see you after school yesterday." His voice rose in volume and I just frantically nodded my head. "I was at football practice!" I shook my head again but was at a loss for words. "What the hell did I do to you that you want to ruin my career?" he asked frantically, grabbing me by the shoulders so that he towered over me. My mind was still reeling from his denial. I was not crazy and I knew what happened. I was not going to be pressured or bullied into silence. Besides, the only person I had told was Bri. Bri was with me the whole time though, so how did it spread so fast? "You're a liar."

I flinched when he said that. I looked up at him and he put more pressure on my shoulders. Was he the one who was secretly writing those notes? I refused to meet his eyes as I thought about it. If he had just found out about the rumor, he would not have had time to put those notes in my locker. Who could have done it?

"There's only one thing I can think of to let me forgive you," he said as he applied more pressure to my arms. I looked up at him once again and watched in slow motion as he leaned down to kiss me. I felt coerced to be compliant as his mouth kissed mine harder. His arms started moving to my waist and my instant reaction was to push him away. It took a lot of effort, but between kisses, I was able to express my disdain.

"Stop it, Chad."

He backed up and his eyes were full of disgust for a second. "You make up lies about me and won't even let me get some action?" he asked. "You are such a tease." I looked at him, confused, and suddenly found my voice.

"*You* need to stop lying about yesterday." I lowered my voice to a whisper when he gave me a sharp look. "I was with you in the car when you hit me. It was after Miguel hit your car." I saw a slight twitch in his face before he looked at me again in confusion

"My car doesn't have any dents, bumps, or paint chipped from it. I don't know what you're smoking, but you're acting crazy." He looked at me again and I saw him smirk for a second. "You need help." I squinted my eyes at him and realized he wasn't insulting me, but just making fun of me. He smiled at me and came closer, this time more gently. "You don't actually think I'd hit you, right?" I didn't say anything as he brought me closer to him. His mouth was so close to mine and it made me want to kiss him. Despite this entire situation. I looked at him

                                        AMY KULP

again and closed my eyes before exhaling the breath I was holding. "Are you sure you didn't just have a realistic dream?" I didn't say anything, but I felt his weight shift. He brought my body into him and I was able to smell his scent. I sniffed into his shoulders as he hugged me and I thought for a second.

Was I just hallucinating? I didn't think so. We were in that car together. Miguel picked me up. Miguel came into my house. My parents had their door locked. I was not making this up. Chad hit me yesterday. He lost all of my trust yesterday, but…now I was confused. I would have to ask Bri, because surely she saw me leave with him the other day. Although, Chad's excuse of having football practice was valid. Chad had practice five days a week and would even practice by himself on the weekends. He would never miss it, even if it *was* for us to reconcile our relationship.

I opened my eyes when Chad released me from the hug and brought his hand up to my chin. He lifted it and kissed me delicately on the lips. His mouth was soft against mine, and for once I didn't feel that horny hunger from him. It felt like he was sincere about it. It felt like an emotional bond was formed and I felt myself kiss back. Was I really kissing someone that I was 90% sure hit me? I stepped away from him and looked into his eyes. He seemed to register the frustration on my face because he whispered to me before kissing me again.

"I would never hurt you, Em."

I wanted to believe him. How could he expect me

to choose him over my own memory? There was no way that I was imagining anything that had happened yesterday. I stepped away from him again and licked my lips gently before darting my eyes to the hallway. Maybe his hand accidentally slipped? Maybe he didn't mean to hit me.

"Yeah, we should get to class," Chad said when he noticed my gaze. I nodded my head and he put his hand on the small of my back. He ushered me towards the doors but stopped me before he turned to go to the stage. "Meet me after school. We have to get you back to training for soccer." I nodded my head because I had honestly forgotten all about soccer this week. That really said something since I loved soccer. "We'll start with your training. I'll make sure that we are in the weight room." He paused for a second, and I realized it was because of the last time I was in there. "We'll start you off with cardio and maybe work our way to the weights." I nodded my head and he turned to me again. Instead of kissing me on my lips, he tried for the cheek and smiled at me delicately.

I was so confused.

I watched as he ran to the stage and was greeted by his classmates. Holli greeted him with a hug and brought him up to where they were practicing. I watched as they began singing and Holli turned to me for a second and winked. Had she seen the whole thing? Had they all witnessed it? I felt my cheeks flush at the possibility and scooted out of the room.

I knew that I should have gone to class straight

                                          AMY KULP

away, but I needed to think about everything that had just happened. I snuck my way into the bathroom and stared at myself in the mirror. It was a bit cliché, but I needed to weigh out my possibilities. I needed to figure out if I was lying, if Chad was lying, who started these rumors that I was starting rumors, and who was putting those notes in my locker.

I guess I could start by asking Bri if I had gone with Chad yesterday in the car. That was the only solution I could figure out in order to get an answer to any of the questions I had.

"Emily Washington, please report to your classroom," I heard over the intercom. I groaned and grabbed my stuff before hurrying out. I had never been one to get in trouble with anybody. I knew that if I didn't immediately go to the room they would send someone to look for me, and then I would probably get detention.

I rolled my eyes and immediately ran up the stairs to my next class.

Once I gained my breath, I walked briskly to the next classroom. I knocked on the door when I realized that it was locked and waited patiently for someone to open it. I heard shoes near the door and when I saw a pair of eyes peek out from behind the curtain I knew it was Bri. It took her a minute to open the door and without a second thought I gave her the "I need to talk to you" face. However, she gave me a different face of "be prepared" in response I immediately furrowed my brows and walked in.

In the front of the room was my teacher, who I was expecting. Joining him at the front was one of the guidance counselors, Mr. Barnett. I looked at him for a second and he made eye contact with me but didn't say anything. Bri tapped me on the back and it jolted me enough to grab a seat in front of her. I didn't listen to what they were saying, but I did find it the perfect opportunity to ask Bri my question.

"Did I go with Chad yesterday after school?" I asked. She didn't respond at first because she was pretending to pay attention to what Mr. Barnett was saying. When I faced her she shook her head no, but I wasn't sure if I believed her.

Maybe she didn't hear me correctly.

"With that being said," Mr. Barnett finished, "I would like Emily to come with me to my office." I immediately looked up and when I glanced back at Bri she shrugged her shoulders again. I nodded my head and grabbed my stuff before following behind Mr. Barnett. "If you need to drop off anything at your locker please do. We might be in my office for a while."

I nodded and immediately walked to my locker. I opened it, and once again there was another note. I instantly reached down to grab it and took a sharp intake of breath.

TEASE

Chapter 10 ----------

"Mr. Barnett wanted to see me," I said as I eyed the secretary. She looked up at me through her glasses and smirked. She asked for my name and I just blinked for a moment. Shouldn't she know? *He* wanted to speak with *me.* "Emily Washington." She nodded and her fingers typed fast and hard against the keyboard. It relaxed me a bit as I waited impatiently. When she stopped typing, I looked back at her and she kept darting her eyes between the screen and me. I tried to see what was on the screen through the reflection of her glasses, but I was unable to read what was so interesting. She popped her lips and smiled kindly at me.

"Do you have an appointment?" I stared at her for a second before shaking my head no. I was so confused. *He* wanted to meet with *me.* Why would I need an appointment? She nodded her head and typed more with her long fingers. I waited patiently and looked around the office. Her space was small, but the little walkway led to two guidance counselors' offices. "You may sit in the waiting room. An emergency came up and he had to talk with another student." She smiled sweetly at me. "He will be right with you."

I nodded my head and snuck through the hallway into the waiting room. Despite having never been there before, the room felt small, comfortable, and familiar.

There wasn't a strong scent to the room, but it smelt neutral–not disgusting like I expected. It looked how I thought it would. There were pamphlets for different problems splayed out, self-help books on the shelves, and a flier with different academic courses. Despite how small of a school it was, I had never needed to talk to the guidance counselors. Why would Mr. Barnett even want to see me? Maybe he heard the rumors that Chad heard.

I also wonder what he was saying when I first entered the room. Obviously, he had been there for some time for Bri to look at me with those warning eyes. Would what they were talking about be relevant to me? Or did he just want to talk to me about what I missed in class? Or why was I late to class? My mind felt like it was swirling, but I pulled myself out of the thought cycle when I saw an Anonymous Star Report box. The Anonymous Star Report was a box in which anonymous notes could be left for the counselors about a concern someone might have about someone. It was a neat idea, but people often took it upon themselves to start drama between people with it. The report box made me think of the note that was left in my locker.

Why was I getting these notes? *I can't wait to see you again.*, **LIAR**, **TEASE.** They came out of nowhere, starting out flirty before becoming mean. They all somehow related to my life though. The first note appeared when I came back to school. That could have been from anyone who may have not been able to see me while I was at home. Everyone I cared about knew that

                                     AMY KULP

they could visit me though. The note that called me a liar was something that Chad had said right before he hit me. I still wasn't convinced that I was lying. I was definitely with Chad last night.The only people who have ever called me a tease were Chad's friends. Chad never said it himself to me. He never belittled me for not having sex, he would just groan and moan about it. There was no correlated timing to anything either. These all happened so fast after one another that it would mean that someone had to keep very close tabs on me.

Or it may have been a group of people.

"Mr. Barnett will see you now," the secretary called. I nodded my head when she looked back at me, but I don't think she was very interested. I took my time in getting my bag and made sure that everything I needed was tucked safely away. I tried to peek at who was coming out of his office, but by the time that I got down the hall his office door was wide open.

"Sorry about that," he said after I knocked on the door to get his attention. I nodded my head and politely smiled. It was a waste of my time to be waiting out there, but it was better than having to go back to that class. I took it upon myself to sit in one of the chairs he had across from him, and when I sat he got up to close the door. If he had wanted me to close it, he could have just asked.

While he was getting all of his paperwork situated, I set my bag down in the chair beside me and took notice of his room. It was the typical guidance counselor's office from every teen movie. There was a filing cabinet with tons of student files, tons of motivational posters around the room, a computer taking up most of his desk, and unorganized stacks of papers and files scattered around.

"Are you done taking inventory?" he asked me. I made sure to whirl my eyes around the room once more. I nodded my head with significant force and turned forward to meet his eyes. "I have two things that I want to talk to you about." He held up his fingers like I didn't know how to count and waited until I shook my head before finding a notepad and jotting notes down. "Let me list them off and then I'll go through it in more detail with you." He paused but looked down at what he had written before looking back up. "We'll be skipping the lecture on your attendance in class but we will be focusing on how you are doing since you have been out and concerns I have." I eyed him but nodded anyway. "So first up, how are you doing back in school?" he whispered. He looked up at me with a pleasant smile on his face. He knew that I heard the question so he did not need to repeat himself.

"I'm working my body to regain my physical strength."

I paused. Mr. Barnett just sat up from his chair a little to look my body over. It sent chills down my spine and made me shiver. I grabbed my bag and immediately pulled it over my body. I tried to not make it obvious, but I'm not sure how I couldn't. I'm sure seeing me snuggling a huge backpack couldn't have looked comfortable.

"What about mentally and socially?" he asked as

he cleared his throat. I scrunched my eyebrows at his question.

It made me think. How was I socially and mentally? Before I left, I didn't have any friends. Now that I'm back, I have Bri. Before I left, my relationship with Chad was strained. Now that I'm back, I've been hit and rumors are being spread about us, but it feels like brand new love. The notes were also new. Did they impact me socially? I felt like I couldn't speak out without someone hearing about it and going to my locker. I also didn't understand what the person had to gain from me getting these notes. Like yes, it's making me more self-conscious, but that's it. I'm not crying and going off to feel bad for myself. They're notes.

"I have more friends than I ever had before." I look up and smile. It felt genuine too.

"Oh, who are they?" he asked.

"The co-captain of the soccer team, Bri." His eyes arched and he seemed interested in what I had to say about her. "You would think it's weird that we are friends."

"Why's that?"

"Well," I stuttered. I looked at him and was slightly confused. What does he mean? "We're both the co-captains, you would think we would be competing against each other."

Mr. Barnett paused as we both listened to the bell ring from outside of his room. He hesitated a moment and lifted a finger to signal me to wait. He turned his attention to his phone before calling my teacher and telling them that I would not be there for class today. He said I was excused, and as I glanced at the clock on the wall, I noticed that this was my last period. I felt relieved and the weight instantly dropped from my shoulders. I knew that everyone would want to know what I and the guidance counselor were talking about.

"Now," he said as the final bell rang. I wasn't sure if he was patiently waiting for the bell or if he was waiting for me to stop daydreaming. Either way, he grabbed my attention and I forced myself to refocus on what he was saying. "There have been rumors going around the school." He paused strategically and I felt myself shift in my seat. What rumors was he talking about? "I have to get involved because another student has brought them to my attention." I stared at him innocently. I felt like every pause he did was purposeful. Maybe he wanted me to spill my guts and then I would accidentally spill the wrong secrets. "We need to talk about how lies can hurt people and their reputation." My eyebrows instantly sunk down in confusion, but I tried to keep my face still and emotionless. "There have been rumors that you have been telling people that Chad hit you."

I immediately felt outrage course through my veins. What does he mean that I am spreading rumors? Why is he being so biased? Shouldn't a guidance counselor ask me about the situation instead of trying to silence me for something that happened?

"We need to talk about the consequences that your actions may have caused." I remained silent, but wasn't even sure if I was listening to him at this point. "Rumors about abuse will have consequences for his future. He might be denied football positions from colleges, he will lose credibility, and he may lose social standing." He continued to rattle off other things, but my mind was still swirling.

"Why are you already accusing me of these actions?" I asked. "You didn't even ask me if they were true." I listened to my voice shake, but I couldn't help it. Mr. Barnett didn't like that I was speaking out of turn. However, I was enraged that they were thinking more about Chad than they were about me. I was the one who actually got hurt. "Chad hit me while I was in his car. Miguel picked me up after the incident. Why aren't you worried about me?"

"I would be," he stated as if it was a fact. I'm sure my face showed disgust as he continued to talk to me in his tone. Could I report him to someone? Would someone even believe me about his attitude? "However, Chad was at his football practice yesterday. Therefore, he would not have been able to take you home as you claim." I was about to argue, but instead, I listened to what he was saying.

I was with Chad yesterday. Miguel was also with me. Why does everyone think I'm lying? Chad did not go to his football practice yesterday. I'm not sure if everyone was covering for him or what, but I know that I was with

Chad yesterday. Right? Could I have possibly imagined it? It would explain a lot. Chad's car wasn't wrecked and neither was Miguel's.

"The thing with lying is that once you make a lie, you have to remember that lie." I looked up at him. "I can tell that you are trying to backtrack to what you have been saying." He put a comforting hand on his desk, but I just stared at it. "Why would you begin this lie?" he asked me sympathetically. The way that he looked at me annoyed me, but I'm sure that he just wanted to help. "Did you want attention?" I stayed silent as he began rattling off other ideas. "Did you feel unfulfilled in your social life? With Chad? Were you tired of people feeling sympathetic to you since you got hurt?" I was sure that my face remained cold, but as he continued listing reasons, something in it must've changed. He stopped short and looked at me. When I looked up, he nodded his head and jotted some notes down. He hummed to himself for a second before putting his pen down on the clipboard. "I feel like we made progress." I raised my eyebrow to show that I had no idea what he was talking about, but I think he was too proud in thinking that I confided in him to notice. "Now, what we can do instead of spreading these rumors is ignore the issue. If you want to spread rumors, do not spread them about other people." He grabbed a piece of paper from his desk and held it towards me.

It was colorful enough that it caught my eye. I reached for the paper and brought it over to my lap. Whatever Mr. Barnett was saying I tuned out as I read the flier. It was a support group for pathological liars–basically people who like to start drama for no reason. I wasn't like the people that this flier was geared toward, but I wasn't sure how to prove this to my counselor. He thought that I was lying. I think he's lying. Who am I supposed to trust in this circumstance? Normally I would trust myself, but how can everyone but me be wrong? It didn't seem plausible.

"Can I see the video evidence?" I asked, interrupting Mr. Barnett. He paused for a second and I knew that he didn't know what I was referring to. I continued, "From yesterday? I really don't think I'm lying, but if I can see the footage that I did not go home with Chad, I will take whatever classes I need to take. I will come talk to you every week." I paused. Slowly, Mr. Barnett nodded his head and he excused himself from the room.

At that moment, I froze. Clearly, if he was going to get the video, I was wrong. Why would he voluntarily prove himself wrong? I gulped and instantly moved my eyes to his pamphlets that were on the wall. I was too distracted to read any of them. As the minutes passed by, my palms got sweatier, my legs shook faster, and my pulse increased. What was taking him so long? I felt myself beginning to tear off any loose hangnails I had. I didn't have to worry for too long because Mr. Barnett came back empty-handed.

"It is the last period of the day," he said as he sat down. "I do not have access to the video footage, but can look tomorrow and call you back when I have it." I nodded my head and he looked at me. "I want to schedule another wellness visit." He scribbled a date and time on his notepad and I graciously accepted it so that I could leave as fast as I could.

I didn't know who to believe anymore.

Chapter 11 -----------

As soon as I exited the office, I looked around at the bare halls. A couple of students were milling about, but mostly everyone had left the school to go home or for sports. I scratched my head though because while I was in that room it did not seem like it lasted a whole class period. I shook any worry from my head away to throw my schoolwork in the locker and grab my gym clothes. I would have to change in the locker room, but it wasn't usually too packed in there. I skipped over and as soon as I flung the door open, I started removing clothing.

I couldn't wait to exercise. I felt like I hadn't tried to work out since my accident with Miguel. I still had trouble going up and down the stairs so I wasn't sure how much cardio I could actually do either. Maybe I would surprise myself and be able to do more than what I had before. I smirked at the idea but knew not to get my hopes up because of it. I was also delighted that I would be working out with Chad today. He has been kicking me in the butt trying to get me to work out, but I've been making every excuse in the book about it. It wasn't until Bri started commenting on it that I decided I would want to work out again.

I missed soccer, but when you're in pain, you don't remember to like your favorite sport.

I threw my hair into a raggedy ponytail before I dodged out of the locker room. I wasn't going to bring any music with me this time just because I knew that Chad would be commenting on everything I'm doing. My posture is wrong, my breathing is wrong, my butt looks good, my sweat is gross, and probably other things as well. I needed to listen though because his critiquing of me would help me in the long run. I knew that I would be offended at first, but I've grown used to taking criticism. That's how I found out that I run with a hunched back instead of with perfect posture. If my posture is good that means it'll help me lose calories faster.

"Chad?" I asked as I peeked in. I looked around the cardio part of the gym but didn't see him. I swished my ponytail behind me as I hopped onto a treadmill. I was almost confident that we were starting with cardio and he should have been here by now. He wouldn't leave if I hadn't shown up. I would expect him to just be working out with the football team or possibly working out by himself. I looked around again but decided to just start with a light jog.

Within a couple of seconds of running, I was too exhausted to try anymore. I shut the machine off and put my hands on my knees to pant. I focused on looking at my shoes and when I came up, I was contemplating what to do now. Maybe I should try weights instead? I thought about it for a second and ultimately decided that that is what I was going to do.

I went down a narrow hallway and heard an

unfamiliar noise. Usually, when you were walking into the weight room, you could hear the clacking of metal against metal, grunts from the athletes, or the weights hitting the ground. This noise was more sloppy and sounded a bit wet. As I walked in, I curved my eyebrow up as I saw two people practically throwing themselves on top of each other. I cleared my throat and instantly watched as the two people turned around.

Chad.

And Bri.

****

I shivered as I looked at the freezer portion of the grocery store. I didn't know what I wanted, but I definitely wanted something sweet to calm my nerves. I know it was cliche, but I really wanted something chocolate. I looked through the foggy glass to see what flavors and brands of ice creams they had. While I loved chocolate, I was not a fan of caramel. Almost all of the remaining flavors had chocolate in them, but they also had some sort of caramel. I also wasn't trying to spend loads of money on ice cream so certain brands were out. I just wanted the store brand name, but they didn't have chocolate.

"Oops sorry."

I felt a bump against my back and squeezed closer to the refrigerator doors. I mumbled a response under my breath and barely looked at the passer-by. I saw their reflection of long, black hair, but was only mildly annoyed until I looked back at the ice cream. What did I want? I tapped my foot against the floor until I finally just grabbed a chocolate marshmallow. I sighed a bit as I held it between my fingers. I kept my eyes down as I worked my way towards the front of the store and eventually bought the ice cream.

I kept it in the bag as I sat in my car, but put the heat on anyway. I felt the tears start to swell up in my eyes and put my forehead on the steering wheel. While I wanted to wail, I didn't make noise, but my back heaved as I silently cried. While I knew Chad and I were on the rocks, I never expected it to end by cheating. Yeah, I did assume he cheated on me with Holli, but there was no proof of that.

I can't believe it was with Bri.

I shuddered as I heard a knock on my window. I peeked up from my arms and cleared my blurry vision. I wiped my eyes on my sleeves once again and when I looked at my foggy window, I rolled it down. The first thing I saw was that long black hair again. I didn't smile until I saw who the hair belonged to.

"Are you okay?"

"Miguel," I sighed. I smiled faintly and rolled my window down the rest of the way. It was nice to see someone familiar even though the last time we interacted it was weird. "I didn't realize it was you in the grocery store." He shook his head and smiled slightly at me. My eyes darted toward the grocery cart near him and I found it weird that he didn't have any bags or grocery items with him. Did he put them in his car already?

"Are you okay?" he repeated as his eyes darted to both of my eyes. I shook my head no and felt my chin beginning to tremble again. "Can I help?" he asked. I contemplated for a second, but him just being here made me feel better. Maybe anyone who would've checked on me made me feel better. I nodded my head because I realized that I wanted company and I didn't want to go home yet. "What can I do?"

I instantly unlocked my door and it was a noise that I knew he would be able to hear. It took him a second to register what I had done. He nodded his head and looked away from me for a second. He nodded his head to the back of my car, but before I was able to look back, he started moving towards the front of my car. He walked to the passenger side and as he did that, I looked in my rearview mirror to see who he could have possibly been nodding at. All I was able to see were cars parked behind me, but they didn't have anybody in them.

That was odd, right?

I rolled my window back up until he got into my car. He delicately moved the ice cream from the seat and handed it off to me so that he could sit down. I felt its slimy water coming from being heated up and opened it up. Miguel looked at it and then at me before he said anything.

"I have spoons at my house." I smiled faintly and put the lid back on the ice cream. "I don't live that far away." I looked at him and for a second, I was unsure if I wanted to go to his house. However, my heart was still stinging and I didn't want to face my battles at home. I didn't want to go home. I didn't want to tell my mom. I didn't want to tell my dad. My dad would kill Chad.

"Okay," I weakly said. "Can you just move the cart so I don't hit it when we move?" I asked. I looked back between our cars, but when I looked at where the cart was, it wasn't there anymore. "Oh." I stared for a second longer before looking at Miguel. "Never mind then."

"I can drive you to my house," Miguel comments. I look at him again and contemplate this for a second. Did he have any ill intentions? Miguel was a little weird. I couldn't tell if that was from cultural differences or not though. "I can drive you back as well." He shrugged his shoulders. "No use in having us both drive." I thought for a moment but ended up shaking my head.

"We can both drive, okay?" I asked. Miguel looked hesitant but nodded yes anyway. I nodded my head too and watched as he made his way to his car. He started it up and I instantly began following him. My heart raced as we traveled further and further from what I was familiar with, but before I could think too much of anything, we were already pulling into a driveway.

Miguel's house wasn't what I was expecting. It was huge. It was also isolated and I felt a little uncomfortable. Although there were different cars in the house, it looked dark and ominous. It seemed sad. There weren't any lights on in the house. He didn't have neighbors. It just seemed lonely.

Before Miguel could hop out of his car, I hopped out of mine and instantly sat in his. He looked at me confused and I confessed.

"I don't want to go in." My eyes darted around his face and I eventually just bit my lip. "Can you run your groceries in and grab spoons to come back out?" I wondered. He nodded yes and took his car keys out of the ignition. Instead of going to the trunk or the back of the car, he instantly just went inside. I immediately turned my body to look but didn't see any groceries. Why was he at the grocery store, but didn't get anything?

I started getting antsy when Miguel didn't come out right away and I felt the ice cream start to melt even more than it already had been. Why was it taking him so long? As I tried to find where he was in the house, I realized that he didn't turn any lights on. There were no lights on in the house and there were no porch lights on. Even both of our cars were now dark and cold.

It was starting to freak me out.

Thankfully, I heard a door slam and a figure walked up to our cars. I was relieved that it was Miguel but knew it probably would not have been anyone else. He opened his car door and with the car door came a bright flash of light. I had to shield my eyes from the sudden blindness that I had received, but that only made Miguel chuckle a bit. By the time I was able to open them, it was dark again and I could only make out an outline of Miguel. I huffed for a second, but it was like he read my mind. He turned his car back on and we were illuminated by the dashboard lights. I immediately opened up the lid and dug a spoon in. While I put some ice cream in my mouth, Miguel shoved his spoon in. We took turns for a couple of minutes before I felt my body begin to shiver. I wrapped my arms tightly around myself and Miguel must have been paying attention because he put the heat on low for me.

"What's up?" Miguel asked. I shoved some more ice cream in my mouth and looked at him questionably. "Why are we in my car just eating ice cream?" he asked. I shoved another spoonful in my mouth and looked at him. "Why were you crying in the freezer section?" he asked again.

"I..." I droned on as I felt my throat tighten and heard my voice quiver. Miguel looked alarmed, but he shoved more ice cream in his mouth. "Chad." The one word was enough to make tears flow from my eyes and Miguel seemed freaked out for a second. He didn't know how to comfort me and that made me feel welcome there. He was trying to be there for me and that's what mattered. I shook my head to tell him that I didn't want to talk about it and he shook his head that he understood. We waited in silence for a second before I felt myself shivering again.

"Are you still cold?" Miguel asked. I nodded my head and looked at his temperature in his car. I was surprised to see that he had his heat blasting. Why was I so cold? "Maybe ice cream wasn't the best option," he mentioned as he looked at the small carton. "Come here," he instructed. I looked at him with wild accusations as he opened up his arms and he huffed. "I'm not making a pass at you when you just found out that your boyfriend cheated on you." He rolled his eyes and I looked skeptical at him. I said nothing to him about being cheated on. "Just come here, I'm naturally a warm person."

I darted my eyes between him to see if I could sense any ill intention on his part, but I wasn't able to. I slowly lifted up the armrest that separated us and plopped down next to him. He wrapped his arms around me and I instantly felt warmer with him. His skin even seemed a little clammy. I looked at the temperature gauge and realized that he was probably dying under this temperature. Why was I so cold though?

"You are warm," I said as I sniffled back any tears. He nodded his head and rubbed my arms with his hands. Normally I would think this is a loving gesture, but it seemed more like he wanted me to say warm.

"Are you okay?" he asked once we got comfortable in each other's arms. "I know we ate ice cream, but it feels like you're getting a temperature." He placed the back of his hand on my forehead and confirmed his suspicions. "Maybe that's why you're so cold?"

I shook my head and felt myself close my eyes. I was just a little sleepy. I could hear that Miguel was still talking, but as he continued I felt myself slowly drifting off to sleep. His voice sounded like it was going further and further into the distance until I could no longer hear

him.

It was the best sleep I have gotten in a while.

****

My eyes flashed open as soon as I heard my alarm. I instantly shot out of bed with a dull headache. I managed to hit the snooze button and looked at my surroundings. I was in the clothes that I wore the night before, but I wasn't sure how I had gotten home. I instantly searched the bed for my phone but wasn't able to find it. As I got out of the bed, I felt groggy and groaned as I made my way toward the bathroom.

It wasn't until I got in and looked in the mirror that I was able to see how bad I looked. My eyes were bloodshot red and pink around the lids. My hair was knotted in the front and back. I ran cold water out of the faucet and splashed some on my face before realizing that it would not help. I pressed the back of my hand to my forehead and realized that Miguel was right, I did have a fever.

I instantly crawled back into bed and didn't think about anything else before I fell back asleep.

****

"Where were you yesterday?" Chad asked as I approached him near my locker. I shrugged my shoulders and felt my face sag at the realization that we were broken up. "Why

                              AMY KULP

haven't you answered any of my calls or texts?" I didn't answer and found my way towards my locker. I still wasn't feeling too well but didn't want to stay home another day. "Hey, answer me." Chad grabbed at my elbow and I instantly dropped all of the books that I was holding. I lost my balance as a result of the sudden weight distribution change. He tried to steady me and concern flashed across his face before it became blank again. "Are you okay?" I nodded my head and bent down to pick up my books. "Em?"

"Can you just leave me alone?" I asked. He looked hurt for a second but ended up nodding his head. He instantly left my locker and I found that I was exhausted already. I opened up the combination and instead of a letter daringly left for me, it was a photo. I picked it up as it fell to the ground and looked at a picture of me and Miguel in his car. My eyebrows went down my face and I rolled my eyes. I didn't feel like dealing with this right now. I threw the photo in my locker with the rest of my unneeded books and closed it back up to reveal Bri's face.

"You aren't going to tell anyone right?" she asked. I looked right through her and said nothing. "Earth to Emily?"

"I'm not feeling good right now, Bri." I stared straight ahead, but she didn't seem too worried about me. She wanted to know if her reputation was safe. "I'm half-tempted to tell your boyfriend though." Bri pursed her lips for a second and huffed.

"I don't think you should."

"Why not?" I asked.

"You are already receiving notes in your locker." She motioned towards my locker and I nodded very delicately. "Someone obviously has it out for you. I would watch your back. You mess with the wrong people and it could be social suicide." I looked at her because I knew she was threatening me. It didn't matter though because I was a nobody to begin with. The only thing I had going for me was soccer and right now, not even soccer. I haven't built that strength up. "Emily, I'm asking as your friend."

That immediately infuriated me. A friend would not help my boyfriend cheat on me with themselves. A friend wouldn't even think like that. Granted, I wanted her to be my friend, but if it meant that she was doing things like this, I didn't want it. I immediately rushed past her and started walking through the herds of students. Thankfully, they all parted ways as I made my path through them. Nobody tripped me and I tried not to hit them.

"You okay?" I heard as I passed a familiar body. I was already past the person who said anything, but it immediately made me slow down. They caught up to me and I felt a smile form on my face. "You wanna ditch?" he asked. I looked around to see if anybody was listening, but they all seemed bustling to get to their next class. I shook my head and knew that it was wrong to ditch, but what was stopping me? Two minutes in and I'm already having a terrible time.

"I'm assuming you've done this before?" I asked. Miguel smirked at me as we went out the double doors and I instantly felt like I was going to be yelled at. There were no sirens and there wasn't anybody chasing me down and asking me to come back inside.

"I see you haven't," Miguel noted as we were in the parking lot. He smiled at me and turned toward me. The smile that was on my face instantly vanished as I took note of Miguel's face. I instantly lunged toward him and while he flinched, he let me take hold of his face. There was a red scratch going from his eye down to his chin.

"What happened?" I asked. Miguel instantly shook his head and shrugged his shoulders. Did I do this? I have no recollection of last night so what happens if I did this? Oh my gosh. Did Miguel try something on me and I reacted badly last night? "Did I do this?"

"I don't think you would hurt a fly," he mentioned. He chuckled a bit and we both found the doors to his car with ease. I instantly sat myself down and was relieved to see the ice cream spoons still there. Okay. That meant I was here last night like I thought I was. My memory was not failing me. "What do you want to do?"

"You're the ditching expert," I mentioned. I instantly began coughing and felt my throat getting tight. It sounded bad, but it was because of the phlegm in my throat.

"Hmmm," Miguel thought. "What if we take it easy and go back to your house?" he asked. "I make a mean chicken noodle soup."

"How?" I asked.

"Straight from the can."

* *

"That was nice of him to help you throughout the day," my mom said as she came up to my room. Her eyebrow was cocked and I had a feeling she would be lecturing me for something. She sat on the edge of my bed and felt my forehead with her palm. "Do you think I should call the doctor?" she asked. I instantly shook my head no, but a cough appeared as my response. "You have had months without anything happening, what could possibly have happened that made you this sick?"

I shrugged my shoulders but was curious as to why I was randomly getting sick. The only thing I could think about was if my ice cream was somehow spoiled. It was heated when it shouldn't have been and more thawed out than I would have liked, but if I were sick, shouldn't Miguel be sick? Was the news about Chad and Bri the reason I was sick? Mental sickness is just as great as physical sickness.

"Emily, did I lose you?" my mom asked. I zoned back in and she looked at me. "I was saying that you just need to stay warm, okay?" My mom looked at me for a second and sighed. "Emily, were you high the other day when you came home?"

"What do you mean?" I asked.

"You were acting strange when you came home." She didn't say anything else as she looked at me. "Is something going on that you need to tell me?" I shook my head no, but she seemed disappointed in my answer to her. "Emily, I will always support and love you, okay?"

"Yes, mom, I know." I crunched my eyebrows down once again and she watched me intently. "Are you dying?" I asked. My mom instantly broke into a smile and shook her head no. "Mom, I think it's just a common cold or flu." She didn't seem sure, but she nodded her head.

"Can I pry?" my mom asked. I immediately shook my head and watched as she got giddy. "Are you and Miguel more than friends?" She raised her eyebrows suggestively and I shook my head no. "Why not? He treats you better than Chad and he's the one to help you in the house the other day."

"Wait, what?" I asked. My mom froze for a second and she sensed that she said something wrong. "Mom, I can't remember what happened the other night." I licked my lips and tried to sit myself up, but it wasn't working very well as she had me under so many blankets. "Is that why you think I was high?" I asked. She shook her head and darted between looking at both of my eyes.

"You could barely walk Emily. It was like you were loopy or drunk. Miguel had called me and I met up with you guys to get the car." She paused. "Miguel said you were freezing, but burning up at the same time. If he hadn't brought you home when he did..." She trailed off with her thoughts and looked at me again. "I fully believe that Miguel saved you."

Chapter 12 ------------

"How are you feeling?" my mom asked as she turned the lights on. I squinted under the light and tried to wave her off. She was being overprotective since her confession about me being sick, but my mom was an over-dramatic person in general. I know that I probably wasn't in any real danger of dying. My mom just worries too much. I shrugged my shoulders in response to her and she nodded her head. "If you need anything, just call me. I told the school you weren't coming in today." She shut my light off and I was finally able to look over at her.

I gave her a thumbs-up as she closed my door to leave my room. I listened to her start the car and listened as it drove off. I gave myself about five minutes before I forced myself to sit up from my bed. My head was still groggy and everything was a little blurry until I fixed my eyes. I blinked a couple of times and felt my body head downstairs before my mental capacity was able to comprehend what it was doing.

When I opened the fridge, I wasn't sure what I wanted to eat. I wasn't even sure that I was hungry. but when I scanned the shelves and saw my ice cream container, I smiled. Attached to it was a little note from Miguel and the spoon from the other night.

Since you weren't feeling well, I got you another ice cream. Enjoy :) Mig

I looked at the note as I read it again and a smile blossomed on my face. Was it sad to say that this was one of the nicest things someone has given me? Chad had never gotten me anything but lingerie. Good it did him because he never saw me in any of it either. I looked at the spoon for a second as well. I wasn't sure if I needed to use it since I was now at home and could just use a spoon in my kitchen. It was the thought that counted, but he wouldn't know if I used it or not. I set the plastic spoon on the counter and made sure that I grabbed one from my kitchen.

My biggest flaw is that I do not know how to sit down and only enjoy a portion of the food. I will mindlessly be doing something else and keep scooping ice cream into my mouth. Sometimes I can eat an entire half-gallon of ice cream in one sitting because of my scrolling. That was exactly how I planned to spend this day as well.

I put a TV show on in the background, got into a comfy spot on the couch, and grabbed my phone so that I can scroll through my social media. I mostly enjoyed scrolling and watching videos, but there comes a point where you scroll through it so much that you keep getting the same kind of videos over and over again. It annoys me, but I'll probably be back on it within two minutes. I opted to look at other media instead. I wasn't very popular so I didn't get texts, videos, or chats too often. In fact, when I scrolled, it showed that I had no messages. I swiftly swiped left and made my way to the stories page. I have so many friends, teammates, and mutuals blocked from having me see their stories because they either post too much or they are annoying. So I was able to scroll through the stories with a breeze.

Chad.

Some girl from the soccer team.

Some girl from my grade.

Bri's boyfriend.

Holli.

Chad's teammate.

Bri.

Miguel.

Some teammates.

I paused once my brain processed what I had just seen. I scrolled back two stories and looked at what Bri had posted. It was a picture of her and Chad together. While that bothered and stung me, I chose to screenshot the picture immediately. When I looked in my camera roll, I zoomed in and saw a scratch going from his eye right down to his chin. I placed my ice cream on a table beside me and looked at the picture longer. I had to make sure that I was not making this up. I stood up, rubbed my eyes, stretched, and sat back down before looking back at the picture. This was the same scratch that Miguel had.

I felt my phone vibrate in my hand and I scanned

it briefly to see that it was a notification from Bri. I was too lost in my thoughts to open her message. It was probably just asking why I had screenshotted that picture. For all she knew, it was just because I was mad that she and Chad were spending time with each other. Granted, it looked like a party that most of the students were invited to, but it didn't matter to me. That was not the reason I screenshotted that picture. I had proof that I was not crazy with this picture so now all I had to see was Miguel in person. It wasn't like it was hard to get him here, he was always around me. He was always there when I needed and didn't need him near me. He was there when I was sad. He was there when I was lonely. He was there when I was happy. Sometimes he was in the background, but it seems that he has been more prominent in my life.

"Hello?" a groggy voice sounded on the other side. I looked at my phone to make sure that I had called the right number. When I verified that, I looked at the time. If this was Miguel, he should not be this tired from answering the phone. Was he up all night at that party too? "Emily?" He yawned on the other end and it made me smile. It felt like I had butterflies in my stomach because it was cute. I could picture him being in bed and waking up just from me. His hair would be wild, but frame his face at the same time. I heard a thump on the other end that startled me and I remembered that I needed to get him to my house.

"Are you not at school?" I asked instead.

"Am I ever at school?" he teased on the other side.

"Why did you wake me up so early?" he asked after a beat. I looked at the time again and scrunched my eyebrows together. "While you were resting up, I was out partying last night. So I'm a bit hungover."

"Don't say that too loud," I responded. I looked around the room as if I wasn't home alone. "Anyway, I was wondering if you could do me a favor." I drew out the last word of my sentence to try and make it sound convincing. He didn't respond though and waited patiently for me to continue. When I was tired of waiting for him to ask, I decided to just roll it out. "Can you come to my house?" There was no noise on the other end and I felt my nerves start to worry.

"Why?" He sounded skeptical and I felt my palms beginning to sweat.

"I, uh... just want company." I looked around the room and realized that it was true. I wanted to hang out with Miguel. Does this mean I like him? I bit my lip as I tried to figure it out, but was caught off guard by him being loud on the phone. I think I heard a groan on the other end. "Please?"

"Sure." I instantly smiled and waited for him to end the phone call. I heard rustling and assumed he was getting out of bed when I heard him talking to someone else in the room instead. I pressed my ear closer to the phone to listen because let's be real, who wouldn't want to hear things they're not supposed to? I love gossip. I liked drama too, I just did not like being a part of gossip or drama. "Yeah, I'm going over guys. Give me an hour?"

With that, I ended the call. It wasn't drama or gossip. Although I am curious as to who he was talking to, I would just be able to ask him when he comes here. Personally, I couldn't wait because I wanted to see the scratch comparisons, but I also did like spending time with Miguel.

Maybe I did like him.

He's cute.

He's tall.

He's funny.

He's caring.

There is a connection there.

He buys me stuff without me asking.

Maybe I should try? There was the thing with Chad though. We haven't talked yet. I don't even know if I want to talk to him though. He has tried. He sent me chats, called me, and texted me for the entire day after it happened. How can someone willingly cheat on someone else though? I don't get it. I liked Chad. I knew we probably wouldn't last but I would have never guessed he would cheat on me with Bri.

Bri!

Bri had a boyfriend! She was off-limits too. I wonder if her boyfriend knew about them together. I instantly went onto my chats and looked to see if he had any stories. It didn't look like he was at the party because if he was, he usually always posts it on his story. I searched his name and instantly scrolled over to start a message. How do you start a text saying your girlfriend is cheating on you? I began typing, but as my fingers hovered over the keys, I couldn't think about what to write. While I was thinking, I saw his face popup and I watched it. It felt wrong to betray Bri, but she betrayed me.

Instead of me typing, I watched as a picture popped up in the chat. It was the same screenshot that I had taken to show him. He typed a message and I watched as his character left the chat.

ollie_124: I thought you should know about this.

I looked at it for a second before closing out the app. How do I even respond to that? I had already known about it and I've kept it from him. It seems like he was just finding out about it and he immediately sent me something. I bit my lip and thought about a response before deciding to ask him the dying question.

Me: How long have you known?

I waited a beat for him to respond, but I watched as he opened it. It didn't seem as if he was typing so I swiped out of the chat and looked down at Bri's. I hadn't opened it yet, but I know what would be coming if I had. She would ask why I had screenshotted the message. I tried to peek over, but ultimately, I failed at that and it opened by itself.

I honestly wasn't expecting that response. I wanted to type back how furious I was and how I felt betrayed by her, but I heard a knock at the door and knew it was Miguel. I placed my phone down and started walking over, but before I even made it into the kitchen I heard him open the door. He closed it behind him and I met him at the doorway of the kitchen and the living room.

"You should really learn not to enter without permission," I teased.

"You should really learn to lock the door," he spat back. He smiled at me as he looked back at the door and I made a small motion to look at it. He hadn't locked it so I went over and did it myself.

"Happy?" I asked. He nodded and I pushed his body gently towards the living room. "Thank you for the ice cream." I nodded towards the carton and picked it up. It was soft so I imagine that it was beginning to melt. "Want to share?" I plopped on the couch and it took a second for Miguel to join me. He sat upright and near the edge of the seat so that he wouldn't intrude on my personal space. I appreciated that, but I was relaxed and I wanted him to join the relaxation. I sat upright with him and handed him the carton.

"You didn't use my spoon?" he asked.

"Oh no," I immediately said. I watched his facial expressions and realized that I had somehow offended him. "It's just that I'm at home so I prefer using the spoons I have here." He nodded his head, but wouldn't look at me. "I'm pretty full anyway. Maybe in a little bit, we can enjoy some?" I asked. He looked over and I saw a small smile appear on his face. "Can you put this back in the freezer for me so it doesn't completely melt?" He looked over at me and immediately nodded his head.

As he went to put it back in the kitchen, I couldn't help but grab my phone again. It wasn't like I was obsessed with it, but I wanted to compare the scar on Chad's face to Miguel's face. Thankfully, when he came back in he didn't question why I had my phone in my hands. Although, he looked a bit weirded out. He kept glancing out my window and looking behind him. I immediately thought this was odd - even for him.

"You okay?" I asked as I put my phone to the side. He nodded yes and joined me back on the couch. His posture was too perfect and it was slightly annoying me. "Mig?" He immediately smirked at me and looked at me. His posture relaxed a bit and it felt better to know he was getting more comfortable with me. "Where did that come from?"

"Everyone I'm close to calls me that." I watched as a vivid blush crept along his cheeks as he realized what he had said.

"So does this mean we're close?" I asked questionably.

"I like to think so," he answered quickly. I looked at him and watched as he started to straighten his posture again. He picked at his fingers and I immediately put my hand over his.

"It's okay, I like to think we've become closer too." I smiled at him and looked into his eyes. He made short eye contact with me before I looked at the scratch along his cheek. "What happened again?" I traced my finger down the scratch and rested it on his neck. He put his hand on top of mine and closed his eyes. His breathing was normal and I realized that he wasn't going to answer me. "Why does Chad have the same scratch as you?" I asked. Instantly his eyes opened and he swatted my hands off of him. He stood up and looked down at me with a confused expression. It looked like it was changing from disgust to confusion.

"I'm going to the bathroom."

I nodded my head and watched as he walked out of the room. I waited a beat before stretching my legs and going back to the kitchen. Dessert could help ease the tension that I was feeling. I grabbed the small carton from my freezer and looked at my dirty spoon in the sink. I kept staring at it before I grabbed that spoon and the spoon that Miguel had gotten me. What was with him and spoons? I shook my head and on my way out of the kitchen, I stopped in my tracks. I could have sworn that I locked the front door. Miguel and I were joking about it so I locked it. I stared at it for a minute and really tried to play back the events of the door.

"You okay?" Miguel asked as he stared at me. His eyes darted from my hands to my face and back down to the ice cream and spoons. I nodded my head and smiled at him as if I wasn't losing my mind completely. I relocked the door quickly and followed Miguel back into the living room. "Couldn't resist the ice cream?" he asked.

"I figured it would ease the tension?" I said. I looked at him and he raised his eyebrows. I handed him the plastic spoon that he wanted and dug my regular spoon into the ice cream. "I got your spoon for you."

"Actually, I wanted you to have this spoon," he stated. He gave it back to me and I looked at him oddly. This was weird, right? Why does he want me to have this spoon? It made me a little uneasy, especially with his mood swing about the scratch. "Here."

"I'll make a deal with you." I scooted closer to him and he looked at me as if he were ready for my challenge. "If you tell me how you got that scratch, I will use your spoon." I sensed a lot of hesitation from him and put on my best smile. "Please?" I asked.

"Why do you want to know so bad?" he asked.

"Because I care about you." I paused for a second and now it felt like it was my turn to blush. "Listen, you said that we were close and I also feel that way." I put my spoon in the ice cream and looked out into the empty space. "I know that Chad and I just broke up, but I feel a connection with you that I didn't have with him." I looked at Miguel to see if I could read any emotions on his face, but for once, he looked like a blank slate. I was going to feel foolish if he thought we were close like sister and brother instead of boyfriend and girlfriend. Hell, I didn't even think of us as boyfriend and girlfriend until recently. "And if we go back to the day that you picked me up off the side of the road, you think of me at least sexually." I paused and waited for his response. "I like you, Mig and I don't know why." I felt desperate for him to respond, but all I got was a smile.

He leaned in and my instincts took over and I kissed him back. He leaned into me and despite all of my fears, they seemed to evaporate as his lips touched mine. I wasn't sure if this was a romantic attraction or a sexual attraction, but it did feel like my feelings were being validated. He didn't argue with me and he didn't pick me up. He didn't argue with me that he didn't touch my thighs. He didn't argue with me that he wasn't attracted to me. Maybe I was just lusting after him as well. I didn't have a lot of experience and the only boy I've dated was Chad.

"Y'know," he said in between kisses. "Being the new kid in school is hard." He leaned further into me until I had to start retracting back on the couch. Eventually, he had gotten on top of me and I felt tingles shooting through my body. "You see all of the pretty girls and you realize everyone thinks you're weird." He looked down at me and smiled. "I thought you did for the longest time." I didn't say anything and I realized that I probably should have. It felt awkward, but he kept going. "I'm glad I wasn't overthinking us." He placed his mouth back on mine and didn't let me answer. He slowly added his tongue into the mix and his hands took hold of my throat. He didn't choke me nor was he hard with his hands. Instead, they were lightly placed and soon they traveled down my body. I let him touch me, but when he got to the waistband of my pants, I broke from the kiss and shoved his body back a bit. He seemed taken back, but his body froze for a second.

It felt like this was lust.

"I-I'm a virgin," I confessed. His pause lasted longer than I would like and it made me feel terrible. I heard about boys not being interested in someone because of them being a virgin and my fear was that that was how Miguel was going to react. "Mig, are you okay?"

"You're a virgin?" he asked. He blinked his eyes at me and I nodded my head. He slowly got off of me and he ran his fingers through his hair. "You're not messing with me, right?"

"Are you okay?" I asked again.

"You're a virgin?" he asked. He looked angry for a second and then looked at me. "What about Chad?"

"What about Chad?" I yelled back at him. Was he just going to use me? Did I just confess feelings for someone who wouldn't even like me back? "I've never felt comfortable enough to have it yet. Chad understood." Miguel immediately got up off of the couch and started pacing. "Mig, you're freaking me out." I got up to stand next to him and kicked the ice cream container on the floor. Oh shoot, I would have to clean that up before my mom got home. I instantly bent over and started cleaning it up when Miguel grabbed my arm.

"We have to go," he said. I clumsily threw the items on the table and tried to stabilize myself as he kept pulling me. "Emily, now!" he yelled.

"Stop, you're hurting me," I said. Instantly he stopped and looked back at me. He helped me get up and put his hands on my shoulders. I saw fear and anger in his eyes and I immediately started panicking. "What's going on?"

"I care about you a lot, Emily." He sniffled and looked around. "I care about you more than I should." He looked at me and in a second I watched as his eyes got watery. "We need to leave this house right now."

"Why?"

"Please, trust me." He looked at me again and I nodded my head. He smiled and pecked me on the lips for a brief second before we heard cars pull up outside of my house. "Shit!" He grasped my arm harder than he did last time and I winced, but he didn't seem to notice. "We're too late."

"Too late?" I asked. I peeked my head outside and saw three vans pulled into my driveway. "What's going on?" I watched as men and women of different shapes, sizes, and ethnicities got out. They all looked super creepy in their black outfits. "Were you going to rob me?" I asked. Miguel shook his head and in an instant started pacing again. "Miguel, what the fuck is going on?"

"Do you have a place to hide?" Miguel asked. I shrugged my shoulders and when I watched all of the figures starting to run towards my door I began panicking.

"You relocked the door?" he asked. I nodded my head and he grabbed my wrist. He led me up the stairs and I immediately had no idea where we were going in my house. "We need to hide."

"Who are those people?" I asked. Miguel instantly shushed me and I listened as they began kicking the door to my kitchen in. My heart began thumping through my chest and I felt my hand beginning to get sweaty. One minute, I'm making out with this hot guy and the next minute I'm running for my life. I feel like I'm part of a bad sitcom. Miguel didn't talk as he led me to my room. He put me on the bed and closed my bedroom door. I heard them get into my house and I immediately began crying.

There was no way anything good could come out of what was about to happen.

"You need to be quiet," Miguel instructed. He joined me on my bed and instantly began hugging me. His arms felt warm, but as I wrapped my arms around him, I realized that his posture was too straight. I looked up at him as he was reciting relaxing sayings and saw that he was looking at the door. He didn't have any emotions on his face and as I tried to get up, I felt his arms struggle against me. "We need to stay quiet."

"We're in plain sight," I whisper. He immediately looks at me and I feel his posture relax a bit. I looked at him for a second and all he did was shake his head. I felt my forehead crinkle as a new onset of emotions were starting to bubble up. Whatever was being planned to happen, is going to happen and it's too late for Miguel to stop it. I instantly feel myself try to shush just in case they wouldn't find me, but I doubt there was any chance for me. "My bedroom door doesn't lock," I whisper to Miguel.

"I know." He started stroking my hair and I instantly hugged him. I needed this false sense of security. "I really do care about you," he whispered right as I heard footsteps outside my door. He kissed the top of my head and I felt a little drop. When I looked up, I saw Miguel wipe one tear out of the corner of his eyes before facing forward.

"I'll be honest, Emmanuel," a voice boomed. He opened the door and as he came in, I saw three other men behind him. "Everything almost went according to plan." He stepped in and looked at both of us. I felt Miguel beginning to retract from me, but I forced my arms around him. It was like I was hugging a mannequin. "You got her to trust you," he stated. He looked at my arms around his waist and I immediately let go. I sat back and looked at him. "Did he use the nickname trick?" He paused before crouching down to my eye level. "Mig?" I immediately revolted as I looked at Miguel. His face stayed blank. "The only two things that were off book were the kitchen door being locked."

"The subject is very observant and has taken notice that I had unlocked the door. I could not unlock it again without raising suspicion." The subject?

"And she is awake."

"She wouldn't eat off of the spoon I gave her." He

said it authoritatively and it sounded so different than what I was used to. There wasn't an accent either. After the initial hit of his speech being different and that his name wasn't actually Miguel, I froze as to what they were implying.

"Were you going to roofie me?" I asked. My voice was shaky and it made the man laugh. He grabbed at my chin and smiled evilly at me.

"He's been doing it the past couple of days to test how fast your reaction is."

Chapter 13 --------------

My first instinct when I wake up usually is to open my eyes and stretch. However, I knew I wasn't in my bedroom, the living room, or somewhere where I could feel safe, so I kept my eyes closed. It was difficult to keep them shut without falling back to sleep. My head was pounding from where I was hit, my eyes hurt from how much I'd been crying, and my throat was sore from yelling for help. I knew I wouldn't get pain reliever from any of these guys. I wasn't even sure what they wanted from me yet. All I knew was that they kidnapped me.

Why me? What did I do? I don't have a lot of friends, I play soccer, and I haven't been mean to anyone. I'm usually by myself or with Chad or Bri. Nobody is going to cry if they find out I'm dead. Nobody is going to offer a one billion dollar reward for me–my family doesn't have that much. Maybe that was it though. Maybe because I don't have a lot of friends I was a perfect target. Maybe they don't want to get caught and that's why they didn't pick someone who had money. Maybe these guys are smarter than that.

If they're smart, I just have to be smarter.

"Is she up yet?" I heard a voice ask. It sounded like the guy who came to my house.

"No," Miguel answered. "You're lucky you didn't

kill her with that swing." I accidentally groaned at the thought of it, but immediately shut up. What was I doing? I'm in danger. "Sounds like she'll be up any second though."

Nobody can say I didn't try to get out of this situation. As soon as I realized that Miguel–or Emmanuel, whatever his name is–had no good intentions for me, I swung. Granted, I'm weak because I haven't been working out nor have I been doing soccer. Instead, I've been getting cuddly with Miguel. I swung hard though. It surprised the main guy and while Miguel tried to pin me down, I managed to grab my lamp and hit him with it. I don't remember everything that happened, but from what they are saying it sounds like he swung on me to get me to stop thrashing. It definitely worked.

"Alright hot shot, you completed another successful mission." Was it just them two in the car? I didn't hear anybody else. "I had my doubts when you wouldn't bring her in the house."

Was he talking about that first night we were eating ice cream? They were inside his house? I'm glad that my gut told me not to go in there. I think that was when I started to realize that I liked Miguel. Yes, he was weird, but I liked that air of mystery about him. Now that I found out what that air of mystery was, I didn't want anything to do with him. He didn't care about me. He just wanted to put me in danger. He just wanted to complete his mission, whatever that was.

"Sorry about that cut, but it had to be done. We

didn't know your motives," another voice said. I listened and counted in my head. So there was me, Miguel, the driver, and this lady. I can't beat three. I couldn't even beat two.

I wondered if they meant the cut that ran down his eye to his chin. It was oddly placed, so it didn't look like it could have been an accident. While it did look like it had hurt, he wouldn't tell me why he had gotten it. This lady could be referring to any cut on his body, but there was a very slim chance that he had cuts anywhere. They had to be talking about that cut. If they were talking about that cut, then that means Miguel had gotten it because of me. Did he try protecting me? Did he actually care about me?

I couldn't think like that though. I was going to get my hopes up and I was going to trust him again. I could not trust him again. He made me believe him. I believed that he didn't mean any harm to me. That was all lies. I was just a "subject" to him. I was just a target for him. I meant nothing to him. It always ends the same. I mean nothing to anyone.

Is it too early for my mom and my dad to be worried about me? I don't even know how much time has passed since I have been taken. I believe it was one or two when Miguel came over. My parents wouldn't start worrying about me until the next day. Although, my mom was already worried about me from how ill I had been so she might think that I'm in a hospital somewhere. That would start the search, right? Or would the scene throw them off? I'm sure that the kitchen door was broken after

                    AMY KULP

they were done kicking it in. I spilled ice cream all over the floor, which would make my mom mad, but she would know that I wouldn't have left it like that. I never leave home without my phone and I'm certain that I left it on the table. My room is a wreck too! My lamp is busted. This may not be the best situation, but at least there's a scene to tell my parents that I am not alright and they need to search for me immediately.

"She's awake!" someone yelled.

I immediately felt two bodies on me and forced my eyes open. I couldn't see because of how dark the van was so that gave me an indication of the time. I felt ropes being tied to my hands and I began to thrash about. However, I quickly gave up the fight when I found it was a lost cause and let them finish tying up my hands. At least they placed them in a comfortable position.

"What were you doing, feeling yourself up?" the one man asked. I looked at him with a sneer but didn't answer. "Guys, I think she's horny. Her hands were grabbing at her body." Even in the dark, I could feel his eyes traveling up and down. "We can still touch, right?" He tried to touch my body and I immediately scratched at him. He recoiled and I heard a laugh come from up front.

"That will teach you a lesson, Reggie." I shrunk myself into the corner of the van as Reggie looked angrily at me. He wouldn't try anything with other people here, right? "You all know the rules. Nobody can touch her until after she gets transported."

"At least she's a looker," Reggie commented. It

felt like his eyes could see through my clothes. I shrunk further into the corner. "Emmanuel, how much fun did you have with her?"

"Get your head out of the gutter," Miguel responded. It is so weird to hear him answer to another name. Although I guess his other name was Miguel. He is Emmanuel. Emmanuel and Miguel are two different people. If this is how I have to separate them so I don't fall for him, this is how it's going to be. Miguel and Emmanuel are two different people.

"Welcome to what it's like being the only girl around, Emily," the woman up front said. "You'll get used to them and put them in their place."

"Yeah, maybe if she was being trained as one of us," the guy in the back said. I looked at him but was unable to see him as well as the rest of them since he sat all the way in the back near the door. They all mumbled in agreement, which resulted in the end of the conversation.

I took this time to look around. In the rear of the van, there was me, Reggie, and the guy in the back. I wasn't sure if he didn't want me to see his face or what, but he stayed hidden. When he had gotten on top of me to help Reggie tie the knots, he seemed inexperienced. He readjusted the ropes afterwards so that they weren't too constricting and so that I wasn't in pain every time I had to move. To be honest, I think if I had a little time by myself I would be able to get out of the bound. He was a weak point.

Reggie seemed experienced. He wasn't too old nor

                    AMY KULP

was he young. He was probably one of those guys at a bar who would wait to see which girls were alone and drunk at the end of the night. I would not doubt that he had some charges filed against him. Just the way he looked at me freaked me out. Maybe I could use that against him. I would have to get over him giving me the ick though.

I turned my body to look toward the seats of the van and saw Miguel –Emmanuel–in the back seat. He was by himself and he was looking out the window. I wanted to spit at him, I was so angry. I felt so betrayed. I wonder how many people he's done this to. They said it was another successful mission. Did he do this to other girls? Did he like these other girls? Miguel and Emmanuel are not the same person.

In the front seats were the girl and the guy who had confronted me at my house. How can a girl be part of this? Does she not have a mom? Or a sister? Or a daughter? The guy seems so professional, but I feel like he treats his team as his family. I wasn't even sure if he was the leader, but the power bouncing off of him told me otherwise. I wonder how long they've all been doing this. This can't be the life to live. They're going to get caught eventually. Hopefully, they'll get caught while I am still alive.

"We are coming up on our pit stop. Analee, would you like to prep her?" the driver asked. I heard movement from the front before I saw a leg come down to my right. She hopped down from the backseat and sat down next to me.

"Go up front Reggie, he needs a navigator." Her voice was not what I expected. When she talked to me, she used a smooth and motherly voice. However, when she talked to them it was stern and direct. "I'm sure you have to go to the bathroom." She didn't wait for me to nod my head or answer and kept going. "Let's talk about appropriate behaviors. You walk out and you go to the bathroom. That's it. Don't talk to the clerk or anybody passing by. Don't talk to us. Don't try to buy anything." She paused and smiled. "If you do not follow these rules, you will be paying the price when we get you back in this van. Let me be clear, you will be getting back in the van regardless. How comfortable you are depends on how you behave." She started nodding her head at me and I immediately nodded back. It was accidental, but she just commanded respect. "Murphy will pull these ropes off of you when it is time to exit the van. If there is any misbehavior, the same rules apply. Am I clear?"

I once again nodded and she patted me on the head like I was a good dog. I rolled my eyes as she climbed back into the front and found myself staring at the boy in the back. I could see very little of his face as we passed by the lights overhead. He looked really young. I want to say he was younger than me, but I couldn't be fully certain. He wouldn't make eye contact with me. Every time his eyes darted around the back of the van and landed on me, he would notice that I was looking and quickly avert his gaze. I couldn't tell if he was making sure that I wasn't moving,if he was checking the perimeter, or if he was just

                                      AMY KULP

nervous.

I bet that he was nervous. If he was the one who was going to be pulling the ropes off me, I bet that I would be able to throw him off guard. I was a soccer player, and even though I hadn't worked out in a bit, my calves were like steel. I could kick him and escape out the back. I just had to make sure that they opened the back first. I can't underestimate how smart they are. The back is most likely locked. These are not dumb people. They've done this before. They've probably done this a dozen times. Maybe hundreds.

"We're here." I felt a jolt and knew that we had parked. "Listen up, here's the plan," the driver called. Murphy reappeared from the shadows and paid attention to the commands that were about to be given. "I and Analee will go out first. Give five to ten minutes, and Murphy and Reggie will guard the front doors. Don't make it obvious," he warned. "Lastly, Emmanuel and Emily. When they come out and back into the van, you two can go to the bathroom. Analee will buy snacks and drinks for us and I will pump the gas." I watched as Murphy nodded his head and heard everyone else mutter their okays. "Alright, everybody can stretch their legs for a few seconds and then pull her ropes, okay?" I heard multiple people get out of the car.

I looked around; it seemed as if we were alone. Murphy looked at me and waited a few moments before inching closer and sitting next to me. I didn't say anything, but the air felt comfortable. It felt like I could truly tell he did not want to be here in this van with me. I could definitely use this as a weakness.

"I'm going to wait a little longer to get your ropes off," he whispered. "Analee and Cyrus usually like to go at it for a few minutes before they actually go to the bathroom." He smirked a little bit before grabbing at my hands. I willingly placed them in his and he fumbled with the ropes for a minute. "They're not too tight, right?" I looked at him and shook my head. "Good." He smiled a bit and I watched as he turned my wrists over to undo them. I looked at the door and was surprised to see that he hadn't opened it nor had someone opened it for us.

When he finished taking the ropes off of me, I smiled at him. I instantly followed that up with a kick to the back of his leg and got up and tried to run. My balance was completely off and I smashed into the wall, but I was able to make my way toward the back door. As I pushed the button to try and escape, I realized that it was indeed locked. I turned back around to look at Murphy and he just looked at me with an amused grin on his face.

"You would not be the first person to try that," he said. He pulled a key out of his pocket and dangled it towards my face. "My, my you have a kick to you though." He limped a bit as he walked over to me and smiled sweetly. "So one thing you should know about me..." He grabbed the back of my hair and pushed me towards the door. I felt his fingers grip harder as I struggled against following his orders. He looped them around each strand multiple times and put his fist tight

                                    AMY KULP

against my scalp. Any trying to pull away would definitely tear a clump or two out. As he pushed me harder into the door, my breath became ragged. I didn't expect this fight from him. I thought he was the weak link.

"While I do feel bad about the situation you are in, I was born and raised in this business." He came closer to me and whispered into my ear. "I know how to do my job." He yanked at the hair again before relieving the pressure on my head. I continued not to say anything as he let go and smiled at me again. "Do it again and I'll be more violent." I nodded my head and watched as he opened the trunk.

"What took you guys so long?"' Reggie asked as Murphy exited the van.

"The usual," Murphy said, shrugging his shoulders. He high-fived Reggie and then took his place behind me. I was ushered in the middle of all three of them, but I refused to even look at Miguel. "Can I bum a cig?" said Murphy. Without a word, Emmanuel threw him the cigarette and lighter.

I didn't know Miguel smoked.

"Let's go," he said as he tried to grab my arm. I immediately shifted my body away from him and watched as he held open the other door for me to go through. I rolled my eyes and purposely went through the door that he wasn't holding. I heard him scoff at me, but knew he was close behind.

I looked around the store for a second and noticed

only one employee at the register. There weren't any customers in the store either. What time was it? I slowly walked around to try and build the distance between us, but he was right on my tail. There was no way this looked natural to the cashier, right? As soon as I found the bathrooms, I briskly walked to them. As I was about to close the door, Emmanuel put his foot in the door.

"The other one is occupied." He smiled at me and I still tried to close the door on him. He rolled his eyes and easily applied more weight to the other side of the door so that he could give himself room to come in. As soon as he was in, he closed and locked the door behind us. He kept his back to me and left his hands on the door. It was like he was pondering what to do or say to me.

"Are you going to go?" he asked. I stared at him and felt myself take a step away from him.

It was a single bathroom, and despite it being small, I felt like I was able to put some space between us. There was no way I could escape with him being by the door though. I couldn't even hide. It was a simple restroom—a toilet, sink, hand dryer, toilet paper holder, and trash can. I couldn't use any of this to my advantage to get away from him. Besides, after underestimating Murphy, I didn't want to underestimate him. He was the entire reason I was here. He manipulated me to the point where I thought he had caught feelings. I thought he was trying to save me in my room, but now I was angry at him. I wanted to get revenge on him. Most importantly, I didn't even know him.

I know Miguel; not Emmanuel. I know the new kid who was slightly awkward when he arrived at school; not the kid who could play different parts. I know the kid that made me soup when I was sick; not the kid who roofied me. There had to be a time where I realized that these two kids were the same person though.

"Are you crying?" he asked. He turned around and looked at me as I sniffled. I instantly wiped the tears that were forming in the corners of my eyes, but it was no use. As my view got blurrier, I saw his figure come closer to me. I backed up into the wall across from Emmanuel, and when I couldn't go anymore, I fell down into a squat. "Emily." He crouched down with me and tried to hug me. I instantly wailed and pushed him away.

"Don't touch me." It was evident that I was crying and Miguel instantly put his finger to my lips and looked at the door. He shushed me and watched as the light moved from underneath. I grabbed his finger off of me and forced him away from me. "I trusted you," I whispered.

"And you still can," he whispered back. "I want to get you out."

"I don't believe you."

"All we have is each other," he whispered. He looked at me and smiled a bit. It was comforting, but I tried not to let him know that. "I need to know if there's anything else you are hiding from me." I didn't say anything and refused to look at him. "Okay." He stood up and nodded. "I really need to pee." I nodded my head and stared straight ahead as I heard him unzip his pants.

Right now would be a good time to leave. He couldn't really leave the restroom with his pants undone, could he? I know that he's smart by the way he tricked me into being here. However, I hoped he knew that I was smart as well. I couldn't possibly believe that all we had was each other. He's probably said this multiple times to other girls and they've believed him. Unlike them, I refuse to be part of this scheme. I will come back home to my mom and dad. I will go back to school. I will see Bri. I will see Chad. I will love them both again because they are the only two I have left. I need to think about them.

"Actually, I do have a question." I heard him zip up his pants again and cursed myself. I lost my chance because I forgot boys take shorter time to go to the bathroom than girls. Screw him. "Why did Reggie believe you were feeling yourself up?" He was washing his hands, so I don't think he saw the panic that had flashed through my face. "Emily?"

As soon as I heard the hand dryer start to go off, I tried to run. However, because the bathroom was so small, he was able to get his hands on me before I could get to the door. He left wet prints on my shirt as he pushed me against the wall. With the pressure on my body, I found it useless to struggle against him. I needed to save my strength for when I could actually escape. He started doing a pat-down, and with each pat, there was less and less water on him and more water on me. He did the sides of my shirt and pants, but when he couldn't find anything, he knew he would have to get a little more intimate. He looked at me as if to ask for my consent, and when he didn't get it he continued on. He started with my breasts and as soon as he couldn't feel anything there, he started pulling down my pants. As soon as he slid a little bit of the pants, he gasped. He grabbed the phone and stared at it admiringly.

"You could get us killed," he whispered. I tried to grab it and he instantly put his arm on my throat. I felt myself gag. He pressed harder and his face began to get redder. "Do you realize the danger you could've put us in?" He threw the phone on the ground and started stomping on it. Each time he stomped he put more pressure on my throat. I felt like I couldn't breathe. I brought my hands up to his arm to try and remove it, but he was pressing much too hard. I sunk my nails into his arms and he reacted by hitting me. He released the pressure on my throat as the realization hit him . I started gasping for air.

"Shit," he whispered. He crouched beside me and tried to get me to hush, but I couldn't catch my breath. "Emily, you have to shut up. You don't want to get them worked up next door."

"They're too involved with each other," I whispered between breaths. I laughed quietly to myself and watched as Miguel smiled with me too. I stared at his eyes for a second and felt myself beginning to frown. The joy that was on Miguel's face started to disappear and he got closer to my face. We kept our eyes locked together before he placed his lips on mine again. His lips were cracked and rough since the last time I had touched them. It didn't feel like a good kiss, but when he retracted, I pushed his face closer to mine.

Maybe if I got him distracted enough I could escape. I would have to deal with Reggie and Murphy outside, but it was worth it if I could just get away for a moment. When I felt him beginning to retract again, I added my tongue to mesh with his and he once again showed interest in me. I opened my eyes to see if he had his closed and was delighted to see that he did. I looked at the door behind me and the trash beside me. Would I be able to do this? I huffed once and moved my hands to his back. I slowly started lifting his shirt and he got the hint and started lifting it the rest of the way for me. As soon as he had it above his head, I grabbed the trashcan and knocked him over with it. I got up and reached for the door but was only able to grab the handle before I felt his hand on my ankle. I tripped and came crashing down on my elbows.

That didn't feel good.

He started huffing and grabbed me by the back of the hair. He got on top of my back and leaned down close to my ears. "I am the only chance you have at surviving this." He got so close that I could now smell his breath. "I wouldn't ruin this chance." He nibbled on my ear for a second before getting up. He hoisted me up by my arms and looked at me for a second before pushing me against the wall. "Give me a second."

He placed his lips on my neck and I felt him suck on the skin. That was the last thing I expected him to do. It felt slimy and creepy. Almost as if he did it for his own pleasure instead of helping me. I didn't see how that would help me. I wanted to shove him away from me in disgust but knew that it was a losing cause. Every time I tried to run, he was always there to catch up. Every time I was caught, I was winded and had to take breathers. He seemed perfectly fine and ready for more. I would never win this fight here.

When he backed up, he looked down at his work and smiled, winking. "You'll thank me for that.When we walk out, we need to be hand-in-hand." He grabbed at my elbow and I winced. "When I get out with the boys, I have to be in control."

"What does that-"

Before I could even finish my sentence, he opened the door and pulled me out. I noticed that Analee was still in the store and she made direct eye contact with him. He smiled and we pretended to browse the aisles. When he felt like we did a good enough job, he started walking toward the exit. I instinctively looked toward the cashier and when I realized that I had his attention, I calmly pulled away from Emmanuel and walked toward a possible escape.

"Hi, I was here earlier and was wondering if you had found a black wallet." As the cashier went to the back, I caught Analee's attention and could sense that Miguel was behind me. Not wanting to cause a scene, all he could do was stare at me.

"We have nothing in the back."

"Do you mind if I leave my name and number just in case someone turns it in?" I asked. Miguel stepped closer to me as I leaned down to put a name and number.

"Don't you remember, honey, we found it while retracing our steps earlier?" Miguel placed a hand on my arm and I felt his grip. He tried to get my hand off of the pen and only managed it after I wrote my first name. "I think you're getting tired. We should go."

As I was dragged out of the convenience store, I made eye contact with the cashier and mouthed "help." He looked like he didn't care though. At least getting my first name on that piece of paper was better than nothing.

As we walked out of the convenience store, Miguel's loving attitude changed and he grabbed the back of my hair. He held control in his palm and I felt myself following along. Mostly because it hurt if I didn't.

"About time you guys are out," Murphy squawked as he put his cigarette out and ran inside the store. Reggie noticed our reappearance right away.."If that cashier sees you holding her hair like that, they'll call-" He stopped abruptly as he approached us and looked at my neck. He looked between me and Miguel and scoffed. "Serious?" He groaned and looked at me again. "You're lucky." He looked me up and down and I felt my skin crawl under his stare. "I see you two were busy. Couldn't keep your hands off of her?" He pointed at one of the handprints on my shirt and I felt Emmanuel tense until he moved away. "I wonder how Cyrus would react if I told him you touched our prize."

"Cyrus would only know from someone who snitches," he snarled back. Reggie looked between us again and rolled his eyes. He pointed at me again and poked the hickey on my neck.

"Just remember, hickies only last so long. If she's still with us, I'll make sure I'm the next mark."

With that, he walked into the store and we made our way towards the van. The grip loosened on my hair and we started walking as if everything was normal. However, as soon as we approached the doors to the van, Cyrus shouted to us. Miguel immediately grabbed my arm and walked tentatively towards him. I trailed behind him and Cyrus looked at both of us with a smirk.

"How old do you think I am?" He motioned towards the door to imply that he heard everything that was said. "You guys still have hormones running through your bodies." He shrugged his shoulders. "We're used to this, Emmanuel. You do it every single time you're the main tracker with a subject. Just remember, once that hickey wears off, you will be temporarily moved until she is not on our caseload again."

I instantly furrowed my eyebrows at the thought that he does this to everyone. Too bad he is underestimating me and thinking that I am falling for him. I am smarter than he thinks, but maybe being dumb is the move I need to make.

I'm Emily Washington. I have a mom and a dad

who love me and are looking for me. I like to play soccer and I like to work out. I have reasons to try and stay alive.

AMY KULP

Chapter 14 ---------------

My mind couldn't stop thinking about how everything Migue-Emmanuel does is calculated. His loving attitude to getting me into my room was calculated. Him constantly telling me to trust him is calculated. Whatever he just did in the bathroom was calculated. His hickey was calculated. According to Cyrus and the other members of this group, he always does this with all of the other girls. I am not special. However, I don't think that he suspects that I am also taking advantage of his feelings. I let him make out with me in the bathroom. I let him give me that hickey. He probably thinks that I am just some dumb chick that can't think for herself. He will find out that that is just the angle I am playing.

    As he pushed me towards the van, I felt his anger beginning to boil over. He grabbed my arm and showed me to the side door of the van. I looked at him and he opened it further for me to go in. I hesitated but went in anyway. As soon as the door slammed shut, he exploded with anger. He had to quickly sizzle out to avoid raising Cyrus's suspicions though.

    "What was that?" he asked. "I can't protect you if you do something stupid like that again." Without responding to him, he breathed a sigh of relief and looked at me. He moved the hair from my neck to look at the hickey and I found myself flinching away from him. "That means I am in charge of you," he said. I looked at him but didn't say anything. "You have to be with me at all times which will protect you from Reggie." He paused as if I should be thanking him, but I didn't say anything. "However, since I disobeyed the command, I will have to leave once that is gone." I nodded my head and pressed my lips together as I thought about that. "Which means if I don't get you out before that disappears, you are most likely stuck."

"What is-"

I was immediately silenced as I heard the back of the van open. Migue-Emmanuel wrapped his arm around me and put me closer to him. I thought it was so I would be closer to him, but instead, he leaned down and whispered to me. It repeated in my head since this was the second time he has warned me about this.

"Don't tell anyone you're a virgin."

"I bought snacks and drinks!" Analee chimed in as she got back into the front seat. The rest of the gang cheered and I silently watched as they were dispersed between people. I saw chips, candy bars, meat sticks, seeds, soda, water, iced tea, and energy drinks being passed back and given to everybody. "Now, since Miss Emily wants to disobey rules, she will starve." She looked me square in the face as she said that. She smirked at me and I felt ashamed as I looked down at the ground.

"What did you do?"

I didn't answer as I stared down at the ground. She

was definitely more observant than I gave her credit for. She switched back in her seat and I found myself listening to them chew on their various snacks. I put my hand on my stomach to silence the grumbling that would come from me thinking about the food. You could definitely hear it against everyone else being so quiet, but nobody mentioned it. Quietly, Migue-Emmanuel broke apart some of his candy bar and handed it to me. I reached it with my pinky finger and scooted it in my hands. There was no way that I could get this in my mouth without someone noticing. I looked behind me to see what Murphy and Reggie were doing, but they were both too consumed in what they were eating. When I looked at Cyrus and Analee, they seemed too focused on directions and driving to notice.

When I thought the coast was clear, I bent down and popped it into my mouth.

"Get a hold of your subject," Cyrus warned.

I looked over at Emmanuel and watched as his face showed recognition that he was caught. He immediately looked at me and swung at my face. He didn't even hesitate when he did it which caught me off guard. The candy bar popped out of my mouth as a result and I clutched at my face. I groaned a bit and felt his posture beginning to straighten. He was uncomfortable with hitting me which was a good sign.

When I stopped feeling the pain from the blow, I let my hands drop and felt my lip begin to swell slightly from the impact. I looked over at him and he grimaced as he looked at me. He didn't say anything as he popped a piece of his candy bar in his mouth and looked out the window. Within ten minutes of him staring out the window, he wrapped up his bar and slid it to me on the seat. I placed my thigh over the nice gesture and scooted closer to him. I could tuck this in my yoga pants where I had my cell phone. Nobody checked me for it so it seemed like a good place.

"We won't make it to the transportation spot," Analee announced. "We're going to go to an off-location. Reggie, Emmanuel, and Emily will be in one location and the rest of us will be in the other one." She looked back at all of us. "Play nice. We don't want to disfigure her before the evaluation." She looked at me again but didn't smile this time as if she was joking. "In the morning, we will come back and get you. Remember to take shifts and keep her awake at all times. Don't underestimate her, she's smart and observant."

"Do we have the blindfold?" Reggie asked from behind me. There was movement in the back, but I was too nervous to look behind me. I didn't have to wait long before something was wrapped around my eyes and tied to the back of my head.

I immediately grabbed Migue-Emmanuel's arm as I tried to find my place and he let me, but he didn't offer any additional support. I looked down at my feet and was surprised to see that I could see very little if I looked straight down. I can't let them know I can see through it.

****

"Here's where you're sleeping," Reggie announced as he turned the lights to the room on. I immediately reached for my blindfold but felt swats on my arms. I wasn't sure if that was him or Emmanuel. "There are only two beds so you get to pick which one to be a part of." He paused for a second. "Of course, you won't know who's sleeping with who."

I didn't say anything until I was coaxed to one of the beds and put all of my body weight on it. I instantly laid flat on my back as the softness felt great as it surrounded my body. I felt the others walk around the room and put their stuff where they needed it to go. As I got a little comfortable, I felt a shake on my bed and a pull at my arm.

"You can't sleep," Emmanuel announced. I picked my head up and sat up on the bed. I crisscrossed my legs and sat up straight as I was waiting for someone to talk to me. I assumed that once they weren't in front of their supervisors, they would relax a bit, but I was mistaken. It seemed they were trying to prove who was the bigger boss around here. "What did you want for dinner?"

I remained quiet as I assumed that this question was aimed at Reggie. Although, it didn't hurt to contemplate what they may have had. Would they even feed me? I was beyond hungry and thirsty. They couldn't dehydrate me, right? I would eventually die if they decided to do that.

"I just want to sleep," Reggie said. He pounced on one of the beds and I felt the movement from the bed I was staying on. "You want to take the first shift?" he asked. I didn't hear a reply, but I assumed that Emmanuel had agreed to it. I tried to peek down from my blindfold but was only able to see my body and the bed. It was super hard to see anything.

Now that I didn't know where I was, there was no way I could escape. I understand that was the reason for the blindfold, but if Emmanuel was really trying to help and protect me, why didn't he take it off of me? We would have to escape together so that he wasn't killed if I left, but I was okay with just thinking about me right now. After all, he was the reason I was in this mess.

I felt a body come next to me and I immediately tensed. When the hands were smaller and gentle on my shoulders, I relaxed a bit knowing it wasn't Reggie. He placed his lips next to my ear to whisper, but I wasn't able to hear him over Reggie's screams of disapproval.

"Wait until I go to bed first!" He turned over in his bed and I knew that Emmanuel's posture was straight up. He waited a moment before breathing in my ear again to talk to me.

"Sleep while you can. I'll wake you before his shift."

****

I felt fingers dancing along my thighs and stomach. I

immediately tried to move them away, but they came back. I smiled into the blankets as I pressed my face closer to the fabric. I took a huge whiff before I realized that I was sleeping on Emmanuel. I traced my hands along his arms. I went down one and then went up it before moving across his chest. I went down with that one and back up again before I stopped. His fingers were not on my body. I froze for a second before I went to whack the other fingers that were on me. I was immediately caught and a hand pressed over my mouth.

"Surprise, it's my shift," he whispered. He pulled me up by my arm and I clumsily followed him. I lost my footing immediately as I wasn't sure where the bed ended and the floor started. I grabbed onto his arm and he made some inappropriate joke to me. I immediately straightened myself out before telling him I had to use the bathroom. He walked me to the restroom and warned me, "don't close the door all of the way."

I nodded my head and made my way inside. I closed the door enough to where I thought there was a crack. I had to feel around for the sink, toilet, and lights. As I switched the lights on, I realized that they wouldn't do me any good and quickly turned them back off. I did actually have to go this time so I quickly went before washing my hands. I heard my stomach growl and knew that I had the candy bar in the front pocket of my yoga pants. Did I want to risk eating in the bathroom with Reggie? I looked underneath my blindfold to see exactly how big the bathroom was, but was not able to see much.

The bathroom had a shower in it so it was bigger than the one in the convenience store. I looked around to find where the mirror was and knew that I would have to eat this candy bar with my back facing the mirror. I positioned myself away and quietly tried to pull the chocolate out of my pants. With the rustling, I could just say I was on my period and excuse it as a pad. I just had to hide the actual candy bar evidence. I would have to pop this quickly into my mouth. I snapped the one bar off of it and popped it in my mouth. Unfortunately for me, when there is no noise in a house, any noise is loud noise.

I heard footsteps coming to the bathroom and the slam of the door. The lights were flicked on in an instant and I was shoved into the shower. The blindfold slipped off of my one eye and I saw just how angry Reggie was. He slapped his hand over my mouth once again and grabbed at my pants. He pulled them down just enough to see the wrapper and took it from me.

"You'll want to stay quiet for this sweetie," he growled. He grabbed the blindfold from my face and it took me a couple of blinks to be able to see properly. "Your sugarplum is asleep. He broke his shift." I was too afraid to move from the uncomfortable position on the tub. "If anybody finds out, he can be killed." I didn't say anything as I watched him start to crumple up the rest of the candy bar. "He's not who you think he is." I raised my eyebrow at him and he chuckled at me. "Let me guess." He kept his body on mine, but he kept most of the pressure on my body. "He started off as a new weird kid

                                        AMY KULP

who happened to be everywhere you were." He paused. "He was always there when you needed him to be and surprisingly, you started to long for him." He pretended to beg for him. "You realize you caught feelings and invited him over. He told you to trust him and you ended up in our van. We purposely didn't do a body check on you so that you would have your phone." He paused and I felt myself beginning to look around the bathroom. "In that convenience store, he told you to trust him. You guys fucked in there and all of your trust was restored because he didn't tell anyone about the phone in your pocket." He paused again and poked my hickey again. "Then he gave you that and told you he would protect you from me." I nodded my head and slowly started wrapping my head around what he was doing. "Then he snuck you some candy on the car ride here and gave you the rest of the candy bar. Once I went to sleep, he told you he would let you sleep until it was my shift." I nodded my head and felt myself stop struggling with him. "All of his moves are calculated." He paused again and he let go of me. He put his hands around my hands and squeezed. "He has done this with every girl." He shook his head and looked at me again. "He will betray you."

"And you won't?" I asked. I knew what he was doing. He was going to have me be very skeptical of him. I was already skeptical of him. I was skeptical of everyone here. Reggie didn't like that answer though and squeezed my hips harder. "My family doesn't have any money so I don't know what you guys are kidnapping me for."

"Kidnapping?" he asked. He began to maniacally laugh. My eyebrows furrowed and I found myself giving him the hardest glare I could muster. He went along with the charade of laughing and it took too long before I realized that he was actually laughing. Tears were pouring out of the corner of his eyes and I felt very uncomfortable. "Honey, we aren't kidnapping you for ransom."

"So why am I kidnapped?" I asked. Reggie smiled at me and put his finger on my lips. I think he was going to be seductive, but it didn't work. I immediately bit his finger and he slapped me across the face. I groaned in pain and he got up from me. He threw the blindfold at me and spit in my direction.

"I can't do anything to you right now, but just wait until that hickey starts disappearing." He shook his head and grabbed my arm. He yanked me up and slowly we walked towards the little kitchen area that there was.

Without my blindfold on, I was able to see that this place was not that much bigger than a little motel room. There were two beds, a little kitchen area, and a bathroom. I was able to pinpoint only one window and one door to the outside world. The only thing that made me refocus back on the guy who had my arm was the fact that he pressed a cold ice cube to my neck.

"Here's to helping it disappear quicker." He grabbed another ice cube and licked it before putting it on my neck. I winced from the coldness of it against my skin and winced again when he pulled it from my neck. He smiled at himself as if he enjoyed seeing my pain.

"What are you doing?" Emmanuel asked as he came into the kitchen. He looked between us and arched his eyebrows when he realized I wasn't wearing a blindfold. "Are you warming up to her?" he asked. He walked to the bathroom to retrieve it and place it on the table. "Not even I remove blindfolds."

"Why are you up?"

"I got cold." He shrugged his shoulders and sat down at the table between us. "My shift doesn't start for ten minutes, but I'll take those extra hours if you want." Reggie didn't miss a beat before he jumped back to the bed. "I'm too tired to play any games truthfully," he said. "Do you want anything to eat? From the mess in the bathroom, I'm assuming he stopped you from eating the candy bar." I shook my head and watched as he registered that I didn't want to eat. "I won't roofie it," he tried to joke. I didn't answer. "Too soon?"

"How do you plan on getting me out of here?" I asked. He looked at me and shrugged his shoulders. "Were you going to plan to get me out of here?" He stopped in his tracks and looked at me as if I did something bad by questioning his motives. "Reggie said-"

"Reggie said!" he yelled. "I'm trying to build you up. We can't just leave." He came closer to me until our noses were touching. It scared me a bit. "You need to get some sleep. You need to get food to have energy. I'm trying to help you." He crouched down to me and kept the eye contact he made. I wouldn't back down from him though. "You think the sleazebag wants to help you? He was putting ice cubes on your neck so that he can take advantage of you sooner." He grabbed the ice cube tray and looked at me like I was stupid. He moved quickly and out of reaction, I kicked my foot out to him to stop him. He ran into it and I watched a variation of emotions on his face. "Let me look at the hickey." I tilted my chin up for him to see and when he moved closer, I put my chin back so that I could see him. "Let me create another one." He moved closer and I immediately kicked at him again.

"No."

He looked at me with amazement. He actually had to take a step back and look at me before deciding to come near me again. Was he going to try anyway? I immediately kicked at him and when he tried to catch my feet, I fell out of the chair that I was in. He put his body weight on my back and wrapped his hands around my throat. He squeezed hard and I felt myself gasp for air. He put more pressure on it when he felt me trying to buck off. He only let go when I stopped fighting. I laid my body flat on the floor and closed my eyes. What would he do if he thought I was passed out?

I listened to him walk around my body for a second. When he finally stopped pacing, he went into the bathroom and I heard the faucet start to turn on. I listened for a few more seconds before I realized that it was the shower head going and not the sink. I looked behind me for a second and when I was able to, I began to crouch down. I saw one exit and that is my only chance to leave.

I crawled past Reggie's bed and listened to the water in the shower continue to go. As soon as I got near the door, I looked at the locking mechanisms and undid each one. I had to be ready to bolt.

As I opened the door, a piercing siren started wailing. Before I could even react, I looked back and saw Reggie running toward me. The impact of him alone was enough to knock me off of my feet. The beating I got from both of them was enough to convince myself again that I couldn't trust either of them.

* *

"Wow, guys, I said don't do too much damage to her," Analee said as she circled around me. She looked at my face and saw a cut lip, bruised eyes, a cut that ran from my eye to my cheek, and could see hair was pulled, small cuts were on my stomach, and multiple bruises on my leg. "Nice touch with the duct tape," she pointed out.

After they had caught me, they had thought that ropes on my hands, feet, and duct tape on my mouth were what would probably work best. They kept me up all night with each shift and I have never been so appreciative of what he was trying to do before when I was sleeping. Whenever it was Reggie's shift, I had to put up with a bit of groping, but he was mostly too tired to do too much. Emmanuel didn't even look at me. He made sure I stayed up, but he didn't hurt me. I guess that was better than nothing.

"Well, we have to get ready for transportation in a couple of hours."

Emmanuel grabbed my body and we both shimmied our way toward the van. I was too tired to jump into the van so he was nice enough to lift me into the seat. I instantly fell over and found myself closing my eyes to try and catch some sleep. He pushed his way in and jostled me awake. I groaned a bit and heard a laugh from upfront. Everybody looked so restless compared to the first night.

"Sit her up."

I felt my body move against my will, but as soon as I sat straight, I felt my body lean towards the seat again. I was placed again and again until finally, he had gotten the idea to wrap my tied hands around his neck. I leaned into him and even though I'm mad at him, I'm too tired to think about it. I felt my eyes close and realized that as long as I look like I'm awake, they can't tell I'm sleeping because of the blindfold. I positioned my body in a way that would make it seem as if I was awake and relaxed a bit. I stayed awake for most of the ride because every so often I would feel Emmanuel's taps on my thighs. This would make me flinch enough to wake up and listen for a few seconds.

I appreciated the thought.

"We're here."

I felt the van pull to a stop and my body lunged forward. I would be on the floor if it wasn't for Emmanuel so I appreciated it. I had my own plans to get out of here.

When you are in this situation, you don't just stop thinking about an escape because you're tired. I started kicking my shoes off and felt the rope loosen instantly. I smiled underneath the duct tape and began licking at it continuously. Within seconds, I felt a piece of it lifting from my mouth. I tried to keep from taking it all off. I wasn't sure who was in the van still and didn't want my plan to go awry.

I felt Emmanuel's hands take my arms away from him and I cursed myself as I felt another set of arms. I didn't account for the blindfold being on. I wasn't able to see who to attack and how to get help. As I was lifted out of the first van, I felt the cold air ooze into my skin. I shivered immediately and felt another pair of arms grab my body. Was this a third person? I wasn't sure, but I immediately swung my arms over his head, kicked my feet out of the rope and at all of the people, and lunged my body into the person that had a hold of me. We went crashing down from the sudden impact of weight and I was able to swiftly remove my arms from around their neck. I immediately removed my blindfold and looked around for a second.

I didn't have too much time but I was able to notice that I was in an alleyway. I immediately bolted towards the clearing where I saw the hustle and bustle of people. I began yelling but found that my throat couldn't support the yelling I needed. I tried anyway. I heard the vans start to run up after me, but all I needed was to get into that crowd and I was good as gone. I heard the yells from everyone behind me and hoped that they were secretly rooting for me, but as I saw the van pull up alongside me, I knew that that wasn't the option.

There was an unfamiliar face driving the van and I knew that these were the second set of the groups. I ran so fast and hard and I hoped that all of my training as a soccer player would catch up with me. There was no one to save me and help me in this group. Maybe Emmanuel wasn't trying to help me, but at times it felt like he was. Nobody would be looking out for me in this second van. I would just be shipped off to my doom with the other van. I couldn't let this be.

As soon as I made it into the crowd of people, they all stared at the van that was about to run them over. However, I was able to slip into the masses of them. I'm sure I was noticeable with the marks on my face and the way I limped, but now that I was in the public eye, I felt safe. If I were to guess where we were, I would have to guess New York City. However, I am just someone who would guess that because of the amount of traffic there is. There is no traffic where I live. This is unusual for me.

However, I felt like we traveled further than New York City. I feel like we should be halfway around the globe at this point. I didn't even know what day it was. I had to look around to figure out that it was daytime, but that didn't help me know how much time had passed. Were my parents looking for me? Were the police notified that I was missing? Would anybody miss Miguel? What would everyone at school think?

I slunk my way into an open store and noticed how it wasn't too busy. I looked around for a bit before I saw a set of newspapers ready to be purchased. The date. It had been three days since the initial day I was captured. How could it have been three days? It felt like one day. I grabbed at the paper and looked at the articles before flipping to the page with missing children's faces. Was I considered a child? I looked through them and was unable to find one for me. Were we even in my home state?

"You have to buy that if you want to continue reading it," a voice said as they plucked the newspaper from my hand. I slowly turned to see if it was someone that wanted to hurt me but was pleasantly surprised.

"Chad?" I immediately brought him into a hug and he hugged me back. His hug was firm and it hurt a little bit, but I was so relieved to see him. "What are you doing here?"

"I work here." He smiled at me and I took notice of his uniform. There was a name badge and apron to match it. I stifled a laugh for a second, but he immediately played it back. "Where have you been? You have your mom and dad worried about you, y'know." I immediately felt relief shoot through my body. "When I go on break, I can take you back to them." I nodded my head enthusiastically. "They have a whole search party looking for you." I sighed again since I knew that they wouldn't stop looking for me.

"How far away from home are we?" I asked.

"About an hour."

"And you work an hour from home?" I asked. He nodded his head and stopped smiling at me. "Why?"

"You know my mom lives up here," he answered. He shrugged his shoulders and looked me up and down. "I want to spend more time with her and it pays well." I nodded my head and looked out the window. For a split second, I saw Miguel and I crouched down. He seemed to look right through me though before he nodded his head. "Are you okay?" he asked. He looked me up and down again. Before I could even answer, he continued to comment on my appearance. "You're all bloodied and bruised up." He took me by the shoulders and I felt comfort in collapsing in them. "You know what?" he asked. He steadied himself as I leaned into him. "I'm sure that my boss would be okay with me going on break now." He immediately took his apron off and grabbed his keys from the back.

He grabbed me by the arm and I couldn't help but grab onto his arm. As we walked outside, I couldn't help but duck between people. I just felt so scared that they would catch me after I thought I was safe. As we continued to walk further and further from the shop, I started getting an icy feeling in my gut again.

"Where did you park again?" I asked.

"Not too far away. All employees of these shops have to park a little away. It's such a hassle." He rolled his eyes and I felt him tighten his grip on my arm.

"I'm getting a little cold, do you mind if I wait in one of these stores and you can pull up?" I asked. I stopped him in his tracks and he looked at me. He looked around at the environment and with the sun hitting his face, I was able to see the faint line going from his eye to his chin. "I want to go to the store," I said urgently. He nodded his head and pointed to one of the stores.

I briskly walked there, but at the last minute he tightened his grip on me and we went down the alleyway. I immediately started bartering him with questions until I saw a very familiar van parked in the alleyway. I looked back up at him and tried to remove my arm from his, but he had too good of a grip on it.

"Chad?" I felt my chin beginning to quiver and as I looked at him, he refused to look at me. I heard the van starting up and the doors opening, but I couldn't keep my eyes off of Chad. It didn't matter though.

"Promise me that you won't tell anyone you're a virgin."

I'm Emily Washington. I have a mom and a dad who love me and are looking for me. I like to play soccer and I like to work out. I have reasons to stay alive.

Chapter 15 ----------------

Was I able to fake like I was asleep again? Would it last longer if I remained perfectly still? Would they talk around me if I was still passed out? I wasn't sure, but I forced my eyes to stay shut and listen to what was around me. I knew that I was in a van from how my body was shaking from the unsteadiness of the driver. With my eyes closed, I tried to sense maybe where we were, but all I could tell was that there were a lot of potholes which meant that we were still in Pennsylvania. Were they just driving around in circles to confuse me? That's what it felt like. I could be wrong though since Chad was the one who had told me we were only an hour away from my house. He was somehow involved in this, but I wasn't sure how yet.

All I know is that I cannot trust him.

Or Miguel.

Or anyone.

Maybe I could trust myself, but I still wasn't sure of that one. My eyes and mind play tricks on me. I didn't know if I was recalling things correctly at this point because Migu-Emmanuel may have manipulated me into thinking something else. I couldn't think of either of them as friends anymore either. They were here to send me off. They had to get close to me because of their assignment.

Why me though?

As I kept my eyes closed, I could not hear anybody talking. This van was much quieter than the previous one. I wasn't even sure how many people were in the van with me. Was this van like the one I was in previously? I was not willing to compromise my situation though. I didn't want them to know I was awake. It seemed as if I was passed out or if I was asleep, they left me alone. Who knows what would happen if they thought I was awake?

I felt the van start to slow down and while my initial reaction was to stop my body from sliding across the van floor, I couldn't give myself up. I slid from one side to another and knew that I had plowed into someone. They roughly pushed me away from them and I whimpered slightly. I felt hesitation in their movements, but they didn't say anything to anyone. I breathed out slowly but had a new realization hit me.

I was bound. My arms were wrapped tightly and so were my legs. Even if I wanted to brace myself for impact, I was not able to move an inch. This was different from the other van that I was in. They made sure I was comfortable and had empathy towards me. I also had tape around my mouth. Fortunately, I have mastered getting this off. I needed it since I felt like I couldn't properly breathe with the tape on. My nose was usually too stuffy to just breathe through my nostrils. I was, unfortunately, a mouth breather. I licked the tape on the edges and grimaced at the taste. It still stuck to my tongue a bit, but I found that it was slightly coming off. I just needed one corner.

Something else that made me uncomfortable was the environment I was in. Nobody was saying a word. In the last van I was in, they chatted. Even Reggie's sleazy comments towards me were better than this complete silence. Against better judgment, I popped open one of my eyes. Another difference in this van was that they had their overhead light on. I was able to see every speck of dirt on the floor. I could see that the color of the seats was beige. I moved my head slightly and was able to see that only the driver was in the seats, which meant the other Agents were with me in the back. I felt someone latch onto my ankle and I immediately squealed out of fear.

When he got up to tower over me, all I was able to see was the black of his clothing and a black ski mask he had chosen to wear. He had his hand on his belt with what looked to be a Taser. My eyes got huge and he looked at what I was looking at. Through the ski mask, I was able to see him grin evilly at me. He grabbed me by my hair and I immediately broke the corner of the tape off to make contact with his skin. I bit down softly at first, but when he didn't let go of my hair, I bit as hard as I could. His reaction was to push me away and hit me in the face. I groaned out from it and stayed laying on my side.

When I felt another hand grab the back of my shirt, I shrieked again. I turned around to see that there was someone else looking at me now. He firmly gripped my arms and walked me towards the other two who were in the back. I was tripping over my own feet as they were tied together and the van was moving at what felt like a faster pace, but every time my legs gave out, he supported my body with his hands on my arms. I tried to shove past him by shouldering into him, but he had too good of a grip on my body.

"She's a handful," he stated as he repositioned his fingers on my arms. I felt his nails starting to sink in and felt myself whimper. I couldn't let them win, but their attitude was so much different than the other van.

"She's a biter," the one I bit said. I looked over at him and felt myself bare my teeth at him. If it was any other situation, I would laugh at myself. If it was what it took to get him to stay away from me, then that is what it took. He came closer to me and I felt myself begin to cower into the man who was holding my arms.

I managed to buckle my body into his knees while eventually squeezing between them. He tried to grip me hard, but I shot myself back into the corner. I was able to see him grab for his belt and see that he had a gun holster on him. I immediately squinted my eyes closed thinking that maybe that would be the worst of it. Maybe he would shoot me right then and there. Unfortunately, it wasn't going to be that easy for me to get out of this situation.

"If you touch me, I will pee on myself!" I yelled. Growing up with the Amber alert precautions and stranger danger programs going around elementary school, I always took away that if you peed on yourself that they would be too disgusted to try and deal with you. While I did have to go to the bathroom, I would only resort to that as a last piece of measure. However, I saw both of the Agents share a passing glance at each other before looking at the third Agent. He wasn't looking at them though.

He wasn't even interested in looking at me. He stared out the window as if what was happening inside the van wasn't fascinating and thrilling. To me, it wasn't, but I'm sure these sick perverts get off on this sort of thing. What did they want with grabbing me like that anyway? The other van had other rules. Did these guys not have rules? Why couldn't they do things to me while I was unconscious? At least then I wouldn't know about it even if it was disgusting to think about it.

The other two grabbed at me and I immediately started shrieking and trying to kick or shoulder them. When the first one had a hold of my shoulders, the other grabbed my legs. I tried to buck and kick him off of me as hard as I could, but he wouldn't let go. He slowly slid the rope off of my legs, which burned like hell. The scream I left out was one I had never thought I could produce. It pierced the air and eventually I had a hand clamped over my mouth. I screamed into it and found myself biting down from the pain. While the guy was gloved, I'm sure that he could still feel it. I didn't even take the opportunity to try and shoulder my way out of him dropping me. It was too painful. It felt like sandpaper was rubbing against my legs. When he eventually got the rope off of me entirely, I began kicking at him.

"We need help," the guy with my feet yelled. They looked over to their third unit, but he didn't seem to try and help them. "Agent F, can you pull over and help us?" he asked. I felt the van lurge to a stop and I immediately continued to try and kick the guy. He managed to grab one of my feet, but the loose one I couldn't stabilize my body with. I would not let them win. I heard the back of the van open and while the other two were distracted, I managed to take my loose foot and kick the guy holding me with it. He let go of both of my feet and I immediately tried to kick the guy who was holding my arms and mouth. I wasn't flexible enough to kick, but when Agent F stomped on my leg, I was able to wince enough for them to grab ahold of me.

"We do things a little differently here," he mumbled. I grimaced as he continued to smash his foot into the skin on my leg. "We don't care how you get to the facility. We don't care how broken you are. As long as you have a heartbeat when you leave this van." He bent down to me as the other two grabbed my arms and legs again. This voice was so scary that it had me frozen in place. "Threatening to pee on yourself, gets you humiliated." He got up from his crouch and immediately grabbed at my pants. "Yoga pants," he noted. "Easily rippable." Before I even had a chance to think about it, I heard the fabric shred.

I instantly tried to move my arms down to my legs, but they were now holding me with so much force. They had complete control. He tore at my pants until most of it was scraps on the van floor or would be able to fall off if I tried anything else. I kept struggling to cover myself up, but it didn't matter to them. My arms were removed as the knife was taken to my underwear. I immediately started blubbering and when I was about to speak, the hand resurfaced onto my mouth. Tears were falling down my cheeks as I imagined the worst to happen. I felt the fabric break underneath the knife's blade and flinched to try and cover myself more. It was a struggle and the guys were grunting to try and keep me still. As the other side of the knife was pressed into the side of my thigh, I felt myself get cut from my movement. I looked down to see a small slice of blood and was surprised. The cut didn't hurt that much to make me bleed. He quickly did the other side and looked at me. He smiled a sinister smile before hopping out of the van.

He slammed the door shut and made his way back into the front. I was too stunned to say anything, but when I was dropped to the floor, I found myself curling into a ball. They were still hovering over me and I watched as they tried to corner me off. However, I wasn't going to move. I was too embarrassed. I hadn't let anyone ever see my lower half. Hell, I never let anyone see my upper half either. They were able to touch, but nobody was able to see.

"Enough!" the third Agent yelled. I shuttered as I saw him grow from his sitting position into a standing position. He walked towards the other Agents and sprayed the one in the face with whatever he had. I'm assuming pepper spray or mace? Wouldn't that make all of us choke in a few seconds though? He groaned and coughed before backing down. The third Agent only had to look at the other before he backed down as well. I moved to the corner as he walked closer to me. I covered myself with my arms, but the third Agent plopped down beside me. He turned my body non-threateningly so that the other two would have less of a view. As he continued to stare at me, I looked into his eyes and realized that this was Chad.

I smiled a little bit at the gesture. He brought his arm out to shield my body and angled his so that he was slightly on top of me. I couldn't help but wrap my arms into one of his and felt myself push my face into his shoulder blade. I looked down at the floor and listened to his breathing. It usually calmed me down, but with it being uneven and fast-paced, I knew that it would make me more anxious. He tried to seem like he didn't care about the situation, but this small act of covering me up helped me understand that he had his duties he had to follow, but he also had a small loyalty to me. Why wouldn't he? He's the reason I got captured the second time. He should feel a little guilty about that. If something bad happens to me, it's in his hands now.

My family would kill him.

I wonder how they were doing. He said that my mom and dad were looking for me. I knew this had to be true, but my gut was telling me that something was wrong with him saying that. Why would he start telling the truth now? Why would he get my hopes up? Maybe he thought that it would stop me from fighting him if I had the peace that my family was looking for me. It worked. I didn't fight him when he got me into the alleyway. Why didn't I try to escape?

I tried to wipe the tears that were falling down my face but was met with resistance. My gaze fell back on my hands being tied together and looped around Chad's arm. His head made a motion to look down, but his gaze fell right back out the window. My chin began quivering harder as I thought about how I only survived this far because I grew attached to Migu-Emmanuel and Chad. They had to have formed some sort of bond with me too, right? Why else would they be protecting me? I forced my face into Chad's shoulder blade so that the other Agents couldn't see me cry. I didn't need them to know I was weak. With everyone remaining quiet, I knew that they could hear me. I felt snot starting to come out of my nose and onto his shirt, but I just wiped my nose on him to get it out.

This was pathetic.

I needed to stop feeling sorry for myself. I needed to get out alive. What would a badass character from my books do? Would I be able to get out of this? I could try to outwit them, but I wasn't even sure of this van's intelligence. There was Chad. While I initially thought he was dumb, I couldn't be more wrong. He outwitted me. He moved here when he was seven and there was this plan in place ever since. He had waited for me to get close to him and we started dating. I trusted him completely. I

                    AMY KULP

still trusted him. Obviously, I had to keep my guard up, but if he was protecting my body, he knew how uncomfortable I was with showing it. What if this was his ruse? What if they were just planning this so I would start to trust him again.

I just needed to keep my guard up.

"Your new name is Y," Chad whispered beside me. I looked up at him and saw his eyes look back down to me. He kept his posture perfectly straight and he didn't bend into me caringly. This felt wrong. "Don't answer to anything else." He swallowed hard and I continued to stare at him. "You will be hurt otherwise." He looked out the window again and I gave this my chance to look at the other two men in the back with us.

The first guy looked older than Chad and I, but he still looked like maybe he was in his mid-twenties. He was staring at me. He had a blank expression on his face so I couldn't tell if he was more like Reggie or if he just wanted to hurt me. I was cooperative. I didn't know his strengths or weaknesses yet. I knew that he was okay with asking for help though. So I needed to be wary of him. He wouldn't struggle with me if he knew he was going to lose. While I didn't have the training that they probably had, I had the will to live.

The next Agent gave me odd vibes. I felt like he wasn't good at taking control or doing anything mean to me. However, he was able to hold me down so that other people could do things to me. Was he too scared? Why was I trying to look for good things in these men? They were monsters.

"Pit stop," Agent F shouted. The van stopped and I looked around as none of the other Agents moved yet. "Agent C, you are staying with the subject." With that being said, the two other Agents immediately got up and left through the back door.

I counted to sixty seconds before I unraveled my arms from Chad's. He looked at me through his ski mask, but when he realized I was going for the door, he grabbed my ankle. I was embarrassed that he was seeing my lower half-naked, but I just wanted to leave. I tripped as he grabbed the ankle, but I still tried to crawl towards the door. Chad instantly pinned my arms down and looked down at me. I felt my chin quivering again and tried to force myself to kick him. All of my power was in my legs. He placed his whole body weight on top of me to where I was barely able to move.

"Let me go!" I screamed. I tried to get out of his grip again, but he wasn't having it. He held me down with such force that no matter what I tried, I was unable to move. "Please!" I was able to see his facial expression fumble for a second before it went back to being stone cold. "What did I ever do to you?"

"You think I want to do this?" he asked. I froze as his voice began getting louder. He had never yelled at me before. "You don't think I've tried getting out of this?" He removed one of his hands for a split second to remove his mask. He motioned towards his scar once and put his hand back on my wrist. "Did you ever think that maybe I

                    AMY KULP

was just desperate and needed money?" he wondered. Spit came flying from his mouth, but I didn't say anything because I could tell he was a tyrant. "I have been involved with this for ten fucking years, Emily." He looked around the van for a second, but I just stayed there stunned. He started this when he was seven? "I was doing fine. I was moving up the ranks." My eyes got big as I realized that he was insinuating he held rank here. No wonder the other guys listened to him. "Then your assignment comes along and I forget all of my training." He shook his head and pressed harder into my body and wrists. I flinched for a second, but he was too busy yelling at me to notice. "I tried to get them to switch my assignment." He moved his face closer to me and it was in such a fast movement, that I flinched. He immediately backed up. "That's why Emmanuel was coming in. That kid's good. He was an up and comer." He shook his head. "I got hurt because I was trying to protect you." With every word, he pounded his body into my wrists and I couldn't help but feel the pain in them. "I tried to hurt you so that you wouldn't want to be with me." He paused. "Even after I cheated on you, you still were so excited to see me in that shop." He shook his head. "Why couldn't you use your brain? I know you're smart. Something had to tell you something was wrong with me being in that shop."

"Stop, you're hurting me."

"Shut up!" he yelled. I felt a drop land on my face and realized that he was crying. Was he frustrated or was he sad? "Emily, I can't help you anymore." He readjusted his body so that his knees were on either side of me and he reached for his belt. "God, I wish we weren't in this situation." He shook his head and I watched as he brought out his spray can. I immediately shook my head and tried to beg for him to stop, but he shook his head. "I need the money."

"Please, don't," I begged. I began crying as I saw him hold the can right up to my face. He was shaking. "Please." His face broke and I saw the discomfort in his face. "Chad," I whined his name and I saw the movement his finger made as he pressed the trigger. I shrieked in pain and he rolled off of me. I instantly brought my hands to my eyes to try and get all of the spray out of them, but I just felt it getting further and further in there. Along with the pain in my eyes, I felt my chest gasping for air. "I can't breathe," I mumbled out.

I opened my eyes for a second but was unable to find where Chad was in the van. I heard the van door open from the other Agents to get in, but I didn't care. My palms were back in my eyes and I was left gasping on the floor. I felt like my chest was going to explode. I could not breathe. The pain in my eyes was no longer the main issue for me. I found myself gasping and gasping for air that wouldn't come. When I opened my eyes again, everything was a blur. I looked around to see if I could pinpoint Chad, but I couldn't tell the difference between any of them. They all sat around towards the edge of the van like this was normal.

This was not normal.

Was this part of the torture?

"That's not a normal reaction," someone mentioned. I crawled in desperation towards the voice and held my hand to my throat. I could not breathe. Shouldn't I be dead already? How long did it take to die? "Agent C, what did you do?"

I closed my eyes again and felt the Agent put a gloved hand on my throat. I wheezed out for help, but it didn't sound like any words. I was getting tired. My chest stopped heaving so much and I felt my body going lax. Even my eyes that were burning, didn't feel like they were stinging too much.

"We have an emergency back here!" The one I wasn't near yelled. I felt movement from all over the van that I could not possibly dictate what was happening and who was touching me where.

I heard different levels of commotion, but I felt very light. I felt like air. I felt my body begin to tingle a little bit and all of the pressure left my body. I heard disgusted shouts from around me about how I was peeing on them, but I wasn't embarrassed. I couldn't feel it. There was a small burning sensation in my lungs, but it was mild to what it had been before. I opened my eyes now to see a blurry vision around me. There were three people by me, but they all had their ski masks on. No Chad.

"We cannot let her die!" one of them yelled. "Flush her eyes."

Water was poured on my head and body and I blinked multiple times. It was still blurry and I felt a little tinge of irritation in my eyes, but I felt myself beginning to breathe again. I took one massive inhale at the same time that they had poured another bucket on me. The inhalation of water had me gagging and gasping for more air. The pain was coming back and I wasn't able to breathe and I realized that I was slowly being revived. Whatever was in that spray bottle was not having a good reaction on me. I laid motionless on the floor when the command to stop pouring water on me was given. Maybe they would think I was dead and leave me alone. I instantly tried to hold my breath but knew it would be a lost cause. I coughed crazily and fell back to the floor. My chest was heaving and I felt like I was going to spray my lungs if that was even possible.

"Is she alive?" one of them asked. I kept my eyes closed as I rolled off to the side. "I don't think she's dead," he answered. I felt a kick to my leg, but I didn't react to it. I was tired and exhausted. There was movement from around me as I felt them crouch down. "See if tasing her will get her to move."

I knew that I probably should have moved once I heard them say that, but I didn't want to. I wanted to keep my eyes closed and just sleep. If I slept for eternity that would be great. However, I felt the initial pain of the shock and wanted to cry out when they did it. I felt frozen in place though. Why couldn't I move? I tried to talk, but my mouth was permanently open in an 'o'. When the initial shock was over and they were done experimenting on me, I opened my eyes.

"Fucking shit," I whispered. I heard a chuckle and immediately I watched them all stand-up.

"I can see why you wanted to be switched out," Agent F mentioned. I stayed frozen in place from the pain I was in, but I moved my eyes to look over at Chad. He smiled solemnly. "What were you spraying her with? We try not to use our weapons unless it's an emergency."

"She tried to escape," Chad said. I looked back up at the ceiling. "I am trying to separate experience with professionalism," he added.

"Remove the ropes on her arms," he instructed. As I was pulled into a sitting position, I groaned in pain. "I'm not worried about her trying to escape anymore. The Taser will probably leave her sore for the rest of the day." As soon as the rope was removed from my arms, I immediately let my back hit the floor again. It was followed by another groan. "What went wrong with the pepper spray?" he asked. From the far corner, I knew that Chad was shrugging his shoulders. "Agent K, you're our brains."

I looked up to see exactly who Agent K was. He was the one who held onto my arms before. I knew that he wasn't the fighter or leader of the group. The nerd makes more sense, but he is still capable of kicking ass. Maybe not my ass, but someone else's ass.

"The only thing I know is she might be allergic to the pepper spray," he mentioned. "Or she has lung problems. Maybe asthma?" I closed my eyes again as the light began to be too much for my mind to look at. I was in too much pain and felt woozy to watch them talk. I could easily just listen.

"Look at her file again," Agent F commanded. I heard rustling and am assuming that they brought my file out.

"She can't be asthmatic," the last Agent said. "She's a soccer player - oh!" He paused for a moment and I felt like that was a true indication of his personality. For a second, he sounded like a normal person. "Sorry." He cleared his throat and continued. "That explains her strength in those legs." He placed a hand on my leg and I winced. He immediately removed it and went back to his paper file. "I guess she's a good soccer player though." He looked through the files again and suddenly brought them down on his lap. "She has a collapsed lung."

"Did you know about this?" Agent F asked.

"Absolutely not," Chad answered too quickly. "I wouldn't jeopardize the mission if I had known she had lung problems."

They continued to talk, but I kept to myself. Chad did know I had a collapsed lung. He was the one who was trying to design an exercise plan for me to try and heal that. He was the one who was always trying to convince me to go back into cardio and start working out again. He was convinced that that would help me with gaining the strength back to be able to breathe better. Kind of like how runners have to start slow and build their endurance up.

The fact that Chad had lied about knowing made

me wonder so many things. Did he know I could possibly die from inhaling that? Was that the goal? I thought about it more and more and as I just laid there, I realized that Chad had to have known that I would die. Dying would be the easiest choice from what I'm about to face. It scared me to think about what I was about to face, but I felt comfort in what had happened.

Chad was trying to save me.

"I cannot exactly tell where your loyalties lie right now," Agent F mentioned. "I will be asking to keep your contact with her minimal. As a result of the mess, I would like you to clean up the pee that is still in the back.'

"Yes, sir."

"I am getting a little tired from driving. Agent K, are you up for it?" I didn't hear an answer, but I heard movement and knew that he was going to drive us the rest of the way. "We should arrive in about a day. In the meantime, we do have to prepare the subject. We will start when the area is clean. Let us know Agent C."

I heard a 'hmph' noise back in response to them and kept my eyes closed. What did he mean to prepare me? It didn't matter though because I was too weak to try and figure it out. I remained laid down in the position I was in. I listened to Chad clean the area around me until it was inevitable that he would have to clean me. He touched me tentatively and wiped off my legs. I grimaced in pain as he drug the sponge down my legs.

Why were my legs hurting? I opened up my eyes and tried to sit up to see, but the soreness in my abdomen was too strong. I laid back down and stared at the ceiling. My vision was still a little hazy and stung just a bit, but I stared at the ceiling. Without any resistance, I let Chad clean me to the point where I felt embarrassed again. It is true that when you're in pain you forget that you are embarrassed. I wasn't wearing pants or underwear. The whole crew probably saw my undercarriage and more. As Chad finished cleaning up, he moved my body and I groaned in protest.

"I'm sorry," he whispered as he cleaned near my head. My eyes looked over at him and for a second, we made eye contact. He did look sorry, but I wouldn't let myself fall for that. He might just be playing with me.

He's done this before.

He's done this since he was seven.

Why would I suddenly be the one he cared about?

He bent down next to me and lifted my leg again. I felt scribbling on my inner thigh and looked to see what he had written. Once again, I was in too much pain to look so I let it flop back. I moved my eyes down my body and looked to see that I had rope burn all up and down my shins. No wonder it was so painful. I moved my thigh a bit, but when I realized it was too much movement and could cause a stir, I put it back down.

"Don't forget your name," he whispered to me as he looked around. He smiled delicately and kissed the top of my head before getting back up. "She's ready for prep." He looked down at me again and I saw the concern scrawled on his face. It was too late though because they hopped in the back and he went back to his corner to look out the window. I would take his advice now. I don't know what was in store for me, but I did know who I was.

I'm Emily Washington. I have a mom and a dad who love me and are looking for me. I like to play soccer. I have reasons to stay alive.

Chapter 16 ------------------

I felt something slam into my back and sobbed louder as the tears fell down my face. I attempted to move, but was in so much pain already that it was a struggle. They beat me for what felt like hours. They didn't need anything to restrain me because I was too sore to move. I was stubborn and was not going to give them what they wanted from me.

"What is your name?" Agent F asked me.

I tried not answering, but it only ended up hurting me more. They pulled my hair to force me to look at them, and when they knew they had my full attention, they would either hit me in the face or bite me. At least when they whacked me, it was always on my back. The entire thing was probably busted and swollen from the hard and constant beating. It was only in one spot though. I would rather one spot be aching than my entire body.

"Don't make me ask again," he whispered, grabbing my hair. I stared straight at him and although my vision was a little blurry, it wasn't because of the pepper spray anymore. My tears were clogging up my eyes and, despite my best efforts to keep them in, they spilled out from the pain. He glared at me as I squinted to let tears fall down my face. I waited too long and I watched as the ski mask exposed his teeth and they bit into my shoulder.

I cried out in pain and he threw me back on the floor. "What is your name?"

I felt helpless as I lay there. I wanted to fight, but my body was past the point where I could move it willingly. If I was close to being transported again, I wouldn't be able to run if I wanted to. I don't even know if I would be able to walk with support. My legs felt like jello.

I cried out as he grabbed my hair again.

"Emily!" I yelled. He let go of my hair and I dropped back onto the floor. Before I even had a chance to brace, my back was hit again. I cried out and felt a snot bubble burst in my nose. "Stop!"

"What is your name?" I was asked again. I stuttered out my response and felt another whack on my back. I let out a small cry as I let my body take the beating again. "What is your name?" I hesitated for a second before replying again. I braced my back as best as I could and cried out again. "What is your name?"

I didn't have time to react before my hair was pulled and I got hit in the face. I felt blood spew from my nose and my body fell back down on the ground. I felt the warm liquid spread on the side of my face and down my neck. It was a lot, but I couldn't feel the pain because of how sore my back was. I wished I was dead.

"This isn't working," one Agent acknowledged. I closed my eyes and tried to relax. I needed to save my energy. Maybe I could take a quick nap. "I have an idea though." I kept my eyes shut as the two Agents collaborated. Once they seemed to come to an agreement, I opened my eyes and watched as they turned away from me. "Agent C, come here."

Chad had been silent throughout the ordeal. He was following orders as best as he could by staying away from me. He was still in the back so he was able to see what was happening, but he chose to focus his attention on the window. He kept his mask off so every time I rolled near him and had my eyes open, I would look over at him. He grimaced any time he heard a whack or I cried out. We made eye contact at one point and I have never seen fear so prominent in someone's eyes.

He hesitated before slowly walking toward all of us. They watched him carefully as they handed him the wooden bat. He took it as they offered it, turning it over in his hands and staring at it for a moment. He looked up at both of the Agents and they nodded their heads in confirmation. He nodded his head in return and walked towards me. He stayed motionless for a second before Agent F and the other one grabbed me by my arms. Each held onto an arm and one of them grabbed my hair so that I was forced to look at Chad.

"What's your name?" Chad asked uncertainly. I felt the blood beginning to drip from my nose and sniffed it back up. My hair was pulled tighter and I grimaced. A hand slowly brought up my shirt and I knew that was their new mark. It was the only place on my body that had yet to be touched. It was sore from the tasing earlier, but it wasn't abused. "Please, what is your name?"

"Emily."

He didn't hesitate for a moment before hitting me in the stomach. I immediately felt like I was going to vomit and was stunned at how hard he had hit me. It felt like he did it harder than Agent F. I let out a cry and he grimaced and looked away for a moment before returning his attention to me. I saw a single tear fall down his cheek. I hoped I wouldn't cave in. I know what he wanted me to say, but I refused to say it.

"What... is your name?" he asked again. I locked eyes with him and knew he was begging me to just say what he wanted. I shook my head no and refused to answer. He slammed the bat into my stomach again and I couldn't help but let out another shout for help. "What is your name?"

"E-Emily."

"What is your name?" he asked again. I shook my head and felt myself start to cry again. He hit me once more without giving me a chance to respond. Without another second, I felt vomit leave my mouth and spray everywhere. While the other Agents were distracted by the mess I was making, he showed me that the bat was beginning to crack. "What is your name?" he continued flawlessly.

"Please, don't," I whimpered. "It's Em-"

"What's your name?"

"Agent C, I think we can take a break."

Whack.

"What's your name?"

"It's... Y," I finally admitted.

****

I felt a shift in the van and forced myself awake. After I finally said what my name was they let me go. Chad was forced to clean off me and the van since he was the one that made me vomit everywhere. For the entirety of the ride, it was only us two in the back. We didn't talk. We didn't act like we knew each other. I stayed in one position on the floor to try and ease the pain I was feeling everywhere. I think Chad broke some of my ribs. He stayed in his usual spot and stared out the window. He didn't explain to me why he hit me hard, so I was only able to guess.

He was trying to break the bat.

That sounded reasonable to me. If the bat was broken, he couldn't hurt me anymore. I wasn't sure if it was an excuse I had invented or not, but I needed to believe in someone. I couldn't count on myself because my judgment was so clouded. I didn't want to give up so easily either. I wanted them to know that I would be fighting my way out of this situation. I was not an easy target. Even if it did seem easier to just give up.

"Wake her," Agent F announced.

I opened my eyes so that when Chad was going to touch me, he didn't. He looked at me sadly and slowly started to help me up. He took his time so that I was able to get used to standing, but he had to support me. He

                                    AMY KULP

leaned my body on his before looking towards the front of the van.

"There's no way she's walking," he stated. Agent F shrugged.

"You're the strongest of us. We'll go up ahead and Agent K will stay with the van in case she decides to try and bolt."

I heard doors open and close, but I was leaning too much into Chad to see them walk out. He adjusted my body for a second before slinging me over his shoulder. I immediately winced and started blubbering from the pain and he muttered something I couldn't quite hear. He should have just talked normally, but I guess he wanted to make sure that nobody could hear him.

We seemed to be in the middle of nowhere and there was not a house in sight. Even if I managed to escape, I would not be able to run somewhere to get rescued. At this point, I might as well just go into the house they had for me. Maybe it would be nice? I rolled my eyes at that thought. I was someone they kidnapped, this was not going to be a fairytale princess story where I get locked in a tower and left alone with food and a comfy bed. Just think about what they did to me in that van. Wherever I was going had to be worse.

"I'll keep trying to get you home," Chad whispered to me when we were far enough away from the van. "I always knew you were stubborn, but I didn't realize they would have to destroy your back." He paused. "Keep that fire in you. That is how you will escape." He had a grip on my legs so I wasn't able to kick him, but I was able to hit him in the back. "I deserved that."

He didn't say anything else until we were where we needed to be. He set me down on my feet, but I instantly fell to my knees. I heard the annoyance in his sighs as he picked me up by my arms to try and get me to stand. He walked forward with me and kept my head up by grabbing onto my throat. He wanted me to see who was there with me as we entered.

Analee.

Cyrus.

No Reggie.

No Murphy.

No Emmanuel.

They both looked over my body and I saw the horror that was depicted on their faces. I wanted to see what I looked like, but I was too scared to even look down. Analee shared a glance with Cyrus before she followed me and Chad in the house. I was brought into a small room with a chair and a table. Chad sat me down and lingered before getting a dismissing nod from Analee. She looked me up and down and I slumped in the chair from the pain. I could see the pity in her eyes.

"What did they do to you?" she wondered. She stuck her skinny hand into her jean pocket to pull out a white little pill. She handed it to me immediately. "It might help with your pain." I forced myself to move and wrap the pill between my fingers. I squeezed the pill tight but knew that the chalky dust wasn't going to be that easy.

I stuck it in my mouth and instantly felt the pill turn into mush. Without a second thought, I bit down hard and when I felt my teeth snap through it, I spit it out. After the after taste was gone, I looked up at her in defiance. "Glad to see the spirit hasn't gone away." I wasn't sure if she was being sarcastic or not. "I have never seen this many marks on someone." She looked me up and down before coming closer. She took a pen and paper and wrote down all of my injuries.

Van A - bruise on head from Cyrus, bruise on shoulder from Murphy

Van B - skinned shins, broken nose, small cut near pelvis, taser marks, irritated eyes, bruises and cuts over back and stomach. Possible broken ribs. No pants, no underwear.

She continued to examine my body and I let her. I winced whenever she touched me. At one point, she crouched down to my level and nonverbally asked if she could examine closer. I knew I didn't have a choice so I didn't say anything. She made her lips into a thin line before spreading my legs to see if I was hurt there. It was quick and painless and she didn't spend too much time there. She stood back up and stared at me.

"I need you to tell me your name," she commented. She had her pencil ready with what I was about to say and I thought about it. She looked at me with eyes that were pleading and I looked at the door to see if someone would come bursting through at any moment. I looked around the room a bit longer before meeting her eyes. She was pleading with me to say the wrong answer.

"Em..ily?" I asked.

"I really wish you hadn't said that," she whispered. She wrote down on her paper my answer and sighed. "The other Agents are being briefed right now." She looked at me again and sighed. "You can try to escape if you want, but that door will be locked from the outside. I suggest regaining your energy before Cyrus comes in." With that, she left the room without hesitation.

I'm not sure what rest she was talking about because as soon as she left Cyrus came right in. The briefings could not have been that long. I had to assume Cyrus and Analee were not the only ones here and that Reggie, Emmanuel, and Murphy were the three that were doing the briefing sessions. How long would it take three Agents to interview four of the others? Not long in my book. Especially since Agent F was so professional. He would know exactly what to say and what he shouldn't to avoid wasting time.

Cyrus brought in a pitcher of water and I instantly felt my mouth begin to drool for it. I hadn't even noticed how dry my mouth was because of the pain I was in. He placed the pitcher of water next to me and watched me with a smug look. I arched my eyebrows and he nodded his head for a second. I grabbed the pitcher without hesitation and instantly started downing the water.

Until I actually tasted it.

I immediately started spewing it out of my mouth and he chuckled to himself. It was salt water, which only made my dehydration worse.

"You can have this water and this pitcher," Cyrus mumbled to himself. "Until you learn your name, you will not be getting fresh water. Analee will try with you again tomorrow." I didn't say anything to him.

In frustration, I hit the water container and it flew to the other side of the room. The water went everywhere and the container bounced against the floors and walls. I sat, satisfied with myself, until I looked over at Cyrus.

He immediately grabbed my hair and kicked the chair out from under me . The aches and pains from the constant tugging were beginning to loosen the hair that was attached. It felt like I shouldn't have any hair left and that it was all being ripped out. I was sure my head was bleeding but when I saw part of his hand, there was no residue.. Realizing that it was just sore, I rolled my eyes. Boy did I hate having my hair grabbed and pulled. When I get out of here, I'm definitely going to make sure I cut my hair off. It's easily a weapon for everyone to use against me and all their tugging hurt the back of my scalp.

"You need to learn to be thankful for what we give you." He let go of my hair and my head smacked into the floor. "We can make this a much more miserable experience, but my wife has a little soft spot for you." Cyrus stomped on my hand and I winced. He rolled my fingers under his shoes and I heard them crack. "I'm here to torture you," he spoke again. "The things I've done to past girls would not compare to the horrors that I would do to you after the other Agents' reports of your behavior." I could see the fury in his eyes, but then he closed them and took a step back from me. When he reopened them, the anger was gone. "However, to keep my promise, I have agreed that I would do more psychological torturing than physical. Let the games begin." He looked at me one last time before looking over at my container. "I suggest grabbing that water container."

He closed the door and as soon as he left, I followed his advice. I didn't know what it could do for me, but if he wanted me to take it, I would.

I was completely shocked that he had a wife. I assumed it was Analee. It made sense, but why would someone bring their significant other into this business? Unless...she was forced to like him? It wouldn't surprise me if she was one of the other women who had gone through this. I can see her manipulating someone into liking her to get out of a dangerous situation. However, now she has to do evil things too. And if those two are husband and wife…

Is Murphy their son? That made sense to me as well. They were always grouping up together. He did say he was born and raised in this business. I feel even worse for him. I could tell that he's a nice kid and has a heart. Why would you bring your son into this? I would purposely try to get out if I knew I was pregnant with a kid. Granted, I don't think I would ever join this group in the first place. It doesn't matter if I'm desperate for money like Chad claims he is. I would never be a part of this. This is sick.

When I heard a knock at the door, I quickly put the water container in my lap and stared at attention. The person waited a couple of seconds before coming into the room. It was the Agent whose name I didn't know. He smiled slightly at me and took his ski mask off. He had scars all over his face. They were identical to the ones that Chad and Miguel, er, Emmanuel had.

He threw me a sack and I looked at him with my eyebrows arched.

"You need to put this on."

I still couldn't pinpoint anything about him. Was he good? Did he have a soft spot? Was he bad? Did he think he was doing good? Was he pressured to be here? Did he willingly join? Should I be afraid of him? I looked at the sack that was in my lap again and looked back up at him. He arched his eyebrows and I sat there just staring at him. I didn't even know what his first name started with and I haven't heard anyone call him an Agent.

He grew impatient and opened the sack for me. While initially I wasn't sure what he wanted me to do, I had a pretty good guess when he started holding it up to my face. I clung to the water container that was in my hands and gasped for air. I assumed he was going to try and suffocate me, but in reality it was just something to place on my head.

Being completely blind was new to me. I was

always able to see something even if it was dark. When I had that blindfold, I was able to see underneath it so I could see where I was walking. This was pure black and let in no light whatsoever. I would have to trust the guy I was with, but he had to know that every instinct in my body told me not to trust him. I didn't even know him!

He grabbed my wrist and forced me to stand up. I felt dizzy as I walked, but he quickly took notice and started to support me from the back. He knew exactly where to press to make me ache, which in turn made me walk faster. I tried to gauge exactly where I was going, but all I knew was a long, cold corridor. When we stopped, he whispered we were going down some stairs and I clumsily made my way down beside him. Right when I got my footing, I felt how damp and cold the floor was and realized that I was probably underground somewhere. It kind of felt like a cellar or garage. My feet felt like they were becoming increasingly dirty as I walked, but I wasn't sure how I could tell. My shoes have been off for a while now. Why did they suddenly feel like they were becoming dirty?

"Stop," he instructed. I stopped moving and heard a slew of metal objects clang together. He placed his hand on my back and pushed me forward. I tripped on something on the floor and felt myself fall before I could catch myself. I heard the door slam and heard what must have been the keys. I listened to his footsteps walk away and eventually go up the stairs. I counted to sixty before I decided to move.

I wasn't bound anymore so I felt the area on the floor around me and couldn't find anything. This floor was definitely dirty though. I felt it in my hands! I crawled a little bit before deciding to take off my sack first. It was knotted around my neck to the point that I couldn't push it up past my chin. I twiddled with the knot for a second before realizing that it was much harder to get it out when I couldn't see it. I tried to sink my nails into the rope but slowly realized that most of them were busted.

"Here," a voice said. I heard something being slid across the floor and groped around to try and find where it may have landed. The voice gave me directions to find it,and when I did, I pricked my finger. I flinched underneath the sack but was able to untie the knots with the object. I immediately tore it off my head and my eyes slowly adjusted to the low light in the room.

The first thing I noticed was that I was trapped in a cell. It looked like it could have been a jail cell at one point. It was small and there was one bucket in the corner. I crawled over to it to immediately find out how I would be going to the bathroom. I grimaced in disgust before looking down at my knees and feet. They were already dirty, but as I crawled around in my cell they became muddy. I looked around the floor and saw a small puddle forming in the dirt. When I looked up, I saw a small leak in the roof. I immediately held my mouth open to try and catch the drops. I wasn't sure if this was good water or not, but I was desperate.

"Use your container," the voice said again. I immediately looked around the room to see who could possibly be talking to me. My eyes focused on a girl in another cell to my right. She was further away from the light so I wasn't able to see her too well, but I knew who it was. "Collect the water with your container." I stared at her for a couple of seconds to try and wrap my head around what I was seeing.

"Bri?" I wondered.

"Shut up," she immediately hollered at me. She flinched and went to her mattress as she looked up at the ceiling. I heard footsteps, but within a couple of seconds, it was silent again. "My name is X." I shook my head and kept looking at her as if she were a ghost. "What the fuck happened to you?" I looked down at myself and was able to see the various bruises all over my body. When I looked at Bri, she seemed to be in her normal soccer attire. When I looked off of the clothes and onto her skin, I saw that it was mostly flawless; no cuts, bruises, or blemishes."Why are you naked?" she wondered.

"Uh..." I said. I didn't know how to answer her. Was her van ride not the same as my van ride? I shook my head in disbelief and looked at her again. Squinting through the dark, I could tell that her hair was still in the perfect ponytail that it was always in. "How do we get out of here?" I asked finally.

She shook her head at me. "I have no idea." She shook it again and sat on the floor. "I can't even escape the cell." She kicked at one of the bars and it clanged loudly in the empty space between us. "We can talk more tomorrow, okay?" she asked. I nodded my head. "Can you collect water with your container?" I nodded my head and placed it under the leaky roof. "Slide it to me when it gets full. I haven't drunk anything for a while now."

"How did you end up here?" I wondered.

"I'm assuming the same way you did." I nodded my head and listened to the pitter-patter of the water collecting in the container. It was going too slow. "How did you get that?"

"One of the Agents gave it to me," I whispered. It felt wrong to disclose this. Why didn't they let her have a container? I tried to slide the container out of my cell and into hers, but it didn't seem to work too well. It tipped over and the rest of the water came gushing toward her. "Sorry."

"It's fine, I can drink with my hands."

I watched as she savagely tried to render her thirst that way. I wasn't sure if it was working, but I didn't even think I could reach the container to get it back. When I tried to stick my arm through the holes, it was too far to reach. I immediately felt my lip quiver but tried to convince myself that it wasn't that big of a deal. I could just open my mouth and drink from the roof. Bri could not.

"Do you even know what this place is?" I asked once my neck was sore from drinking. Bri looked up from her hands to stare at me. "We need to think of a way to escape."

"If you can find a way to get us out of the cell, I will totally help you. I have tried finding every way out without getting myself hurt." She looked down at me. "Exactly how do you get yourself hurt like that?" I shrugged my shoulders.

"I was trying to escape." I looked at her for a second and knew that there was judgment on my face. "Did you not even try?" I asked.

"No," she admitted. Even in the low light of the cellar, I could tell that I had struck a nerve. "I was too scared."

"How long have you been down here?" I asked. She shook her head and I listened to her sniffle. "Whatever happens, we will find our way out of this, okay?" A hopeful expression crossed her face. "I am not giving up, and we're smart!" I bit my lip and I contemplated telling her the next part before deciding that it couldn't hurt. "Chad and Miguel are here somewhere." Her head perked up at the sound of their names. "They both told me they were going to try and help me out of this. So we just need to rely on them, okay?" She nodded her head and I smiled.

If I had Bri, I would be able to hold on. We could do this together. With Bri's help, we would have two brains working together. We could sabotage Chad and Miguel. I wasn't sure how, but it just felt better to have her here. It was a little weird that she wouldn't try to escape though. Bri was not someone to just give up.

"Get in the corner of your cell. Don't say a word."

I looked at her confused, but saw her rush towards her side of the cell. "Put your sack back on!" she whispered to me.

I looked around on the floor for it and immediately pulled it over my head. I tried to tie it like it was before but was unsuccessful; my fingers seemed like they didn't know what they were doing and got tied up with each other. I did a simple knot before laying down on the floor and listening for what she was freaked out about. Footsteps were coming down the stairs slowly and I felt my breath hitch. I wouldn't be able to defend myself if they came toward me.

"Here you go, X, eat up." A loud clatter was dropped onto the floor as I listened to the gruff voice mock her. The sounds of her eating sounded like a wild animal. When she was done slurping, she said her thanks and moved away.. Should I act like that? I wasn't going to thank them for imprisoning me here. "Here you go, Y." I heard the food drop to the floor in my cell, but I didn't react. I couldn't see. No way was I going to trust that he wouldn't do something to me. "You have to eat or I have to force-feed you." I still didn't move and heard him mumble under his breath. He unlocked my cell and I heard him come toward me. Until he stopped. "What's this?" he asked. I moved my head slightly to see if I could possibly see what he was talking about, but still couldn't. He took a few more seconds contemplating the item before moving towards me again. He took my sack off and looked surprised. "Have you been tampering with your sack?" I just stared at him. "Cyrus will not be happy to learn that you are messing with his psychological torture." He grabbed me by my hair and showed me the object he found in my cell. The needle Bri gave me to get the sack off. "Were you planning on using this as a weapon?" I didn't respond. He looked off into the distance for a second before a smile grew on his face. He brought his lips close to my ear. "Stay still or else this will hurt."

He let go of me and I stared into his eyes for a second too long. He grabbed my arm and flipped it over so that my veins were showing in my wrist. He toyed with the needle on my wrist for a second before sliding it in. I grunted and bit down so I wouldn't scare Bri, but it hurt. The poke felt like a searing pain into that part of my wrist. Couldn't scare Bri though. I continued to bite down on my tongue until I could taste a metallic flavor in my mouth. That did not compare to what my wrist was going through. I felt ill. However, I tried to convince myself I was just getting blood drawn or my ears pierced. Bri didn't need to know the amount of pain I was in. *He* did not need to know the amount of pain I was in. As soon as he realized I wasn't giving him much more of a reaction, he took it out.

He tossed my food onto the floor without a care in the world and stared at me as he locked my cell up again. In his hands was the pin and the sack. I didn't dare move until I heard him go up the stairs and I counted to thirty. Rushing over, I tried to find a piece of food that wasn't covered in dirt; I didn't get the luxury of having a tray.

                    AMY KULP

However, I was so desperate and hungry that I ate all of it anyway.

"The roofies will kick in soon," Bri mentioned in her cell. "I would just lay down so you don't hit your head." I paused and sat down. I might as well take her advice. I knew there was something wrong with them giving us food. "I'm sorry that he did that to you with my needle." She paused, becoming drowsy. Did she get a double dose? Why did it take her so little time to be affected by the drug? "It should've been me."

I didn't answer. There was no point. What I thought didn't matter. Instead, I laid my head on the dirty floor and found my memory to be a bit cloudy . I wasn't sure how long it had been since I was kidnapped nor how long I was going to be in this cell . I knew they wanted me to forget my name to dehumanize me, but I refused to forget it. Bri still knew her name, but she chose to outsmart them and pretend she didn't know it.

I probably should have done that. I wouldn't have sustained all these injuries. I wouldn't have to be in constant pain if I just cooperated. However, I was worried that she was just cooperating. What could have happened that made her want to stay? Why would she want to be away from her family, school, and friends? Why wasn't she fighting? I have not seen Bri play soccer without yelling at the referees. She was stubborn and that's why we got along.

Chad was the main guy on the football team.

Bri and I were co-captains of our team.

Bri had a boyfriend who played baseball.

Chad did music and choir because he loved it.

I looked up at the roof and thought to myself. What were little things that I could remember? What were the little things that would sustain me to try to break free and get back to my life? I didn't want to give up like Bri. Why was Bri giving up? What did they do to Bri? She had to have been tortured or something. I got punched for trying to run away. Nobody could convince me that Bri didn't try to run.

Although she didn't even mention how she got abducted. I looked over at her to see if she was passed out and was surprised to see that she didn't move a muscle. She looked so serene too.

As I looked at her cell I noticed that she had a dirty mattress on the floor. I looked around to see if I had one but to no avail. My head was starting to get loopy, so I laid down and said my usual mantra.

I'm Emily Washington. I have a mom and a dad who love me and are looking for me. I have reasons to stay alive.

Chapter 17 --------------------

"Emily."

Analee shook her head as she wrote down my answer. She looked at me with sorrow in her eyes and looked at her list of what she might still need to do. She examined my body and gasped as she turned over my wrist. Her fingers grazed the small hole in my wrist before her eyebrows crinkled. She wrote down the new mark on her paper and looked at me confused. She wanted me to tell her how I had gotten that mark. Did I want to tell her? I didn't so I just shook my head.

"I'm trying to help you," Analee said firmly to me

"Then get me out of here," I mumbled to her. She stared at me for a couple of seconds and it was the longest I had held someone's gaze in this place. She slowly backed down and shook her head. When she left, I sighed and immediately put my head on the table. I was beyond tired.

"So..." The door slammed open and Cyrus came barreling through. I barely picked my head up to acknowledge him. "You didn't want to keep the hood on." He threw it on the table and I just stared at it. "Welcome to phase two of your psychological torture." I looked up at him through my drowsy eyes and he smiled evilly at me. "There are only three phases I have planned. The second one is lack of sleep."

"I already have a lack of sleep," I mumbled under my breath.

"Would you like to just skip to the third then?" he asked. I nodded my head and he stared at me stunned for a second. Without saying a word, he turned around and looked at the mirror. Probably wondering who the hell I was to want such a thing. When he turned back around, he gritted his teeth and ushered me along. I was too tired to fight right now so they knew that I didn't need to be bound anymore. It was such a relief as my body was still healing from everything else. I think the only thing that had improved since the day before was the irritated eyes. They were no longer bright red with irritation.

I was brought back down the stairs and into my dirty area. I looked over to see if X was still in her cell, but she wasn't. I watched as Cyrus locked me back in and he stared at me for a second. He shook his head and huffed before going over to the other cages and grabbing my water container. He fit it through the bars and handed it to me while he was crouching down. I looked at him for a second to see if he was trying to play a trick on me, but ultimately, I was too thirsty to care. I grabbed onto the container and he roughly grabbed my wrist and hair. He pulled my head towards the bars and whispered so softly that I wouldn't have been able to hear him if he hadn't pulled me close.

"Stop making this so difficult."

As soon as he released my hair, I looked at him

and tried to hit him with the container. He put his arms up in self-defense and fell backward from lack of balance. I grinned smugly at him before he tried to come close to the cell again. Out of the corner of my eye, I saw the Agent with the scars and immediately moved to the center of my cell so no one could touch me. Cyrus turned around at my sudden posture and he also seemed surprised to see the Agent.

"What are you doing down here?" he asked. The Agent froze in his spot and looked between both of us. He moved closer to the light and smiled at us. He saluted Cyrus and briefly turned his eyes towards me. I immediately downcasted my gaze so that I wouldn't be punished for eye contact later.

"Just checking in."

"On? Neither of the girls was down here."

"Right," he mumbled. "I didn't know that."

Cyrus nodded his head and turned back to me. With a short-expression on his face, he and the other Agent soon went up the stairs. I knew that whatever Cyrus was planning, it was going to happen later today. I needed to rest up for it though and seeing as I haven't had decent amounts of sleep since coming here, I knew that it was now or never. The only thing that made me feel better was knowing that people were starting to feel sorry for me. I saw it in their eyes as they talked to me. Analee, Emmanuel, Chad, and Cyrus.

This was how I could possibly get out.

I jumped as I felt the water splash all over my body. When I opened my eyes to look around me, I saw the Agent with the scars and Chad with me. I immediately kicked at both of them but was quickly handled as they held onto me. I couldn't struggle too much - I didn't have enough energy to keep up the good fight. Chad steadied me with my arms behind my back and I slowly walked up the stairs with both of them. I felt Chad dig his nails into my arms a bit and I tensed up because I knew I wasn't doing anything wrong. I felt like I was lagging a bit, but I kept up with both of them before they placed me in the other room. The Agent stood outside of the door and Chad entered with me as I sat in the seat.

He stood and stared at me for what felt like ages. I didn't say anything to him as I looked at my arms from where he was holding them. Instead of him digging into my arms, it seemed as if he was playing with the hole he had made in my wrist. Just running his finger over the empty part. I covered it with my fingers and stared at the table until he cleared his throat.

"What's your name?" he asked. I looked up at him and it was clear that I was confused. He cleared his throat again and seemed uncertain of himself. He looked over at the other side of the mirror and for once, I wanted to know who was on that other side. "What's your name?" I stared at him intently for a second, but it seemed that I had made the wrong choice. Chad immediately seized and grabbed at his neck. For the first time, I noticed that it seemed to be some sort of shock collar for dogs. "What's your name?" he asked.

"Emily."

He fell to his knees with this shock and I watched as his neck began bulging from where it was hurting him. This question-and-answer kept cycling through until he started crawling toward me. He pleaded with me to stop the torture of him and I felt tears beginning to well up in my eyes. I could not be attached to him. He was the person who was doing this to me. I wasn't doing anything to him. Whoever was controlling that collar, was controlling his pain. He crawled up my legs and into my lap, pleading with me. I accidentally made eye contact with him and felt myself tearing up as he pleaded for me to say the right answer.

"What is your name?"

"Em-Emily." I stuttered it out and couldn't look at him as the pain that was inflicted on him, made him squeal. He fell in a heap to the floor and I felt myself kick at him. It was a slight nudge, but his body did not react to it. I tried once more, but all he did was grunt. "Chad?" I asked as tears welled up in my eyes. I crouched down to his body and looked at him as he laid there. He was motionless, but his eyes were open and he was aware of what was going on.

"Lie," he whispered. I flinched as he grabbed at my thigh and I revolted back. He looked at me with sorrow in his eyes again, but he didn't ask the question again. He remained motionless and very slowly, I started going back to the seat in the middle of the room.

I sat there for what felt like an eternity and kept my gaze at the table. I normally sit with my legs spread a little apart because of how toned my thighs are. It was inconvenient since I was naked on my lower half, but as I stared at the reflection of the table, I saw my legs. I saw the thigh that Chad was pointing at and finally remembered that he had drawn on this thigh. I had never looked at what it was before because I had completely forgotten it, but with the reflection of the table, I could see it drawn out.

Emily

While the black writing looked familiar, I wasn't too worried about the notes that were in my locker anymore. This was a reminder to me about who I was. I looked at Chad on the floor and knew that this was not what he had intended for me when he had written my name on my thigh. He wanted me to comply and it was a lesson for me to never forget. However, it showed that Analee cared. She never reported this in any of her paperwork and there was no way she missed it. She had to take a daily roll on how my body was doing.

"Emily, Emily, Emily, Emily," I sang to myself. I forced a smile on my face and watched as Chad's body began twitching from the shocks. Maybe it was voice-activated? Could someone who worked so closely with Chad, do this to him? They were criminals after all.

I stopped singing to myself and stared at Chad's body. It felt weird that we were in here alone. What if I made my escape to the next room? It was probably locked. Right? I slowly stood up and tiptoed my way to the door. As soon as I grabbed for the door's handle, it opened and I got whacked in my face. I yelped back in pain and immediately ran back over to the table and chair. This is where I was expected to be when someone entered the room.

Or else they would hurt me.

"Are you okay?" Emmanuel asked as he closed the door behind him. I looked up as soon as he spoke and stared at him for what felt like hours. In reality, it was probably ten seconds. I suddenly felt self-conscious without having any pants on and found myself covering up for him. He looked down at me and pressed his lips into a smile. "Wish we were meeting under better circumstances." He walked towards me and showed me his neck which had the same contraption on it that Chad did. He lowered his body so that his face was at eye level with me and I could see the red lines in his eyes and a faint bruise on his forehead. Without thinking, I stroked his hair back to better look at it and he pushed his head into my palm. "The others got it worse."

"How come?" I asked.

"I need to keep up my appearances," he motioned. He smiled again and looked towards the ground for a second. "What's your name?" he asked. I shook my head as he waited to be shocked and I shook it again. Without me saying a word, it shocked him and I listened to his grunt the pain. He wheezed his breath out when it was done and smiled a bit. "It gets worse as I go."

He just wanted me to believe that.

"Emily," I finally answered. I squinted as I watched him wince. Was he acting or did it actually hurt? He looked over at me and let his hair fall into his face. "Emily." I watched again as he struggled and tried to pry it off of his neck. His balance was starting to waver and he slowly fell to his knees as I said my name again. He closed his eyes now and he refused to even look at me. I kept saying his name though and he started crawling over to me like Chad did. I kept saying my name, but as I did this, I noticed that Chad's body was still twitching. Was he still getting shocked?

"Why are you willingly hurting me?" Emmanuel asked as he sunk his nails into my knees. I felt myself wince and tried to remove his hands. "You're just as bad as us."

I stopped moving and looked at him. With one final breath, he looked at me and his body fell to the side. I stared at the ground at the two of them. I couldn't hear any noise and didn't see any movements from their bodies besides their breathing. I suddenly stared into my hands and felt my eyebrows crinkle.

Was I as bad as them? I was willingly hurting both of them. However, they were the reason that I was in this place. Did that justify it though? I wanted to say yes, but I wasn't sure. I won't lie and say I didn't find enjoyment in them being shocked. I finally had the power over them and it felt good. I was finally able to hurt them as they had hurt me and I was excited about it. My name finally held power and status here and I was able to control whether they had gotten hurt from it. Yes, I didn't like seeing them get hurt, but I wasn't going to say the name they wanted me to say. I was never going to be Y. I was never going to be who they wanted me to be.

I couldn't ever be like X. I don't know why she didn't fight to get out of here. Although being left alone at night felt amazing. I was sleeping constantly or I was looking for a way out of here. While I have dulled down on giving the Agents a hard time, I haven't given up completely. I don't know why they thought that I would give up my name so easily just because of two stupid boys I fell head over heels for. I can't trust either of them. I cared more about myself than I did for either of them.

Did that make me evil?

I looked up as I heard clapping from outside of the door. In walked Cyrus and he had a smug look on his face. He walked over to Chad and slowly took the necklace off that he had around his neck and I gasped. His neck was mutilated. It was red on the outside of the cut, but it was oozing liquids and it looked like his neck was melted off. Tears immediately welled up in my eyes and came streaming down.

I was a monster.

I immediately crouched down against my better

judgment and crawled to Chad. I examined his injury but pulled his head into my lap. I couldn't stop crying as this boy continued to sleep. I had known him since I was little and to see him so hurt, hurt me. I still cared about him, I don't think I could stop. I hate him a little bit, but I could never hurt him like this. Seeing his injuries made me feel like a monster. Emmanuel was right.

"Please, don't," I whisper as Cyrus goes over to take Emmanuel's necklace off. Cyrus didn't say anything as he disobeyed me. I wouldn't blame him though. He had orders to do and they were to scar me. I continued to play with Chad's hair as I watched Emmanuel's collar come off. While his neck was gross as well, it wasn't as bad as Chad's. This meant that his was going off when I was torturing Emmanuel. I squinted my eyes closed and pressed my forehead onto Chad's. "I'm so sorry." I let my forehead off of his but kept it close. I saw a slight movement on his face and felt myself giggling a bit. I didn't kill him!

I flinched when Cyrus moved toward me. He grabbed me by my hair and sat me back down in my chair. I immediately felt my butt smack against the chair and let out a little yelp. When Cyrus looked at me intently, I quickly covered up again. He arched his eyebrow and came towards me again. I felt my body shrink into a ball and he placed both of his hands on the table.

"These two boys are part of my team." He looked at me until I made eye contact. Even though it was only brief, he was able to grab my chin to make me look longer. "You better hope that they make it out okay or I'll-"

Cyrus was interrupted by the lights turning off. I felt his hand let go of my chin for a bit and I took the opportunity to take in a breath of fresh air. I felt like I was going to die if he hadn't been released soon. I had to keep blinking my eyes, but I was able to see the environment around me. While Cyrus was searching the walls for a switch, I could see the door. I started quietly walking across it, but as I continued, a hand latched around my ankle.

My chance was gone.

The lights turned back on and my body was tossed against Chad's and Emmanuel's. Who grabbed my ankle? I don't know that answer, but Cyrus didn't give me a chance to try and figure it out. He grabbed me and we immediately started heading downstairs. The lights were now constantly flickering and I felt a sense of panic in him as we hurried downstairs. As soon as I was in my cage and the gate locked behind me, I immediately went to my container and grabbed some water.

"What's going on?"

I whipped my head around as I saw X in her cage. A smile played on my lips from seeing the relief of someone familiar to me. Someone I knew I could trust. She got up and I pushed my water container toward her. She nodded appreciatively, but only took a sip of water from the jug before sliding it back. She wiped at her mouth and looked over at me for confirmation.

"Lights are flickering." I shrugged my shoulders and looked at her. "This is a perfect diversion to escape." X looked over at me and I nodded my head.

"We're locked in," she stated. I smiled smugly at her and immediately reached into my shirt. When I managed to get into my bra, I grabbed what was underneath and pulled it out. I showed it to her, but in the darkness, I don't think she was able to see it. "What is that?"

"I'm not exactly sure," I whispered. I went over to my lock and immediately started fiddling with it. Lock picking can't be too hard right? I stuck the object in the end and immediately started twiddling with it. I felt it bend and immediately cursed under my breath. "I saw that Chad had it on his shirt. I think they all do, but it signifies rank."

"Do you know how to do that?"

"No," I stated. I immediately started banging the locker with my water container as I continued to fiddle with the pin. I listened to the floor above me as I continued to bang. However, no shoes seemed to be coming toward us. "What punishment were they torturing you with?" I asked as I hit the lock again with my water container.

"You need to be quiet," she shouted towards me as I banged again. I looked above me to try and hear if there was anybody coming down, but I couldn't hear anybody. I immediately started banging again but stopped myself for a moment.

What I was doing was not working. Instead of just banging the lock, I decided to bang the pin into the lock. I timed it so it didn't sound like I was banging, but it was taking too long. How long does a possible power outage take? I hit it hard with all of my might and the recoil hit my body so bad, that I fell onto the dirty floor again. I heard a gasp from X's cage and looked over at her. She was pointing to me though and when I looked back over, my lock was open. I immediately started fiddling with it to get it off of the edge and opened the gate. I skipped through it and tried to salvage the pin, but it was too broken to do anything with it. I heard footsteps coming from upstairs and immediately looked over at X. I listened intently but ran over to her cage anyway. I handed her the container and she shook her head for a moment. I saw the fear in it.

"Try," I whimpered out. I looked around me on the floor to see if I could find anything with a point, but wasn't able to do so. "Hit it!" I shouted towards her. She shook her head and immediately I heard the uncertain banging coming from her. I heard the door open to come down here and I immediately started shaking the lock as she hit it with my container. Multiple boots and footsteps were heard and I immediately looked at X for a second. I gave her a face and my lips quivered for a second before she knew what my decision was. She shook her head no and I whispered to her as I chose to hide. "I'm sorry."

I ran off to a corner away from the door and

watched as the lights went dark. I crouched my body as small as it could get to be in the corner of a mess and listened. Emergency blue lights came on in the dark and I was now able to see X in her cage. Two Agents came running down the steps and only one of them stopped to look at my cage. He quickly joined the other one and went to X's cage. I tried to look at the faces of the two that were near X, but the lighting was so poor that I wasn't able to tell. I couldn't hear anything that they talked about, but I was stunned that they were just talking. No hitting? No abuse? What was up with that? They quickly opened the cell for her and she willingly went with them upstairs. I waited patiently and although that didn't sit right with me, I quickly forgot it.

I needed to get out of here. I knew that wasn't the only exit because of that one Agent with the scars. He hadn't come down that way and he was down here. I just had to find it without hurting myself. I got up from where I was crouched down and felt the walls. There wasn't too much lighting as I moved further away from the door, but maybe that could help me in the long run. My eyes were adjusted better to the darkness than any of the Agents. They were barely ever downstairs with us.

As I crept along the walls, I started hearing a small buzzing noise. I crept silently over to it - despite my better judgment - and saw an Agent crouched near the breaker system. I bit my lip and slowly walked past him. He didn't look like he would turn around and hurt me because he was so focused on fixing the problem. However, what I didn't notice was the other Agent with him. At this Agent's shout, I immediately started hustling to get out of there but was caught far too quickly. He turned me around to look at him, but I was blinded by the flashlight on his uniform to glance at him.

I followed along with little resistance and we stood patiently with the other Agent as he finished with the breakers. I saw the sweat starting to drip down his forehead, but had to close my eyes when he let out a victory sigh. The lights came back on and I was temporarily blinded. When I reopened my eyes, Agent K was fixing the breaker panel. I smiled softly at him, but it was short-lived as I was tugged up at a different entrance. This was good because now I could see different points of entry.

As the door opened to go to the new level, it was still pitch dark up there. I heard Agent K curse to himself and he excused himself to go back down the stairs. The Agent who had me held on roughly and started walking forward. There weren't even blue emergency lights up here. I couldn't see where we were going and neither could the Agent because I felt my body slam into a wall.

"Sorry."

Did he just apologize to me? This wasn't Chad's voice. This wasn't Emmanuel's voice. This wasn't Analee's or Cyrus's voice either. I wanted to say it was the Agent with the scars who had me. I tried to look behind me but was still unable to see because of his light. I tried to brace my hands against the wall, but my arms were once again pinned to my sides by this Agent. I could try to make a move, but I had no idea where I was. With that stupid light, I wasn't sure if I'd lose him either.

"I got her!" he yelled.

****

"Where's X?" I asked as Analee checked my body again. She didn't say anything as she noted the new bruises, cuts, and other injuries on my body. I haven't seen her since the power went out. Analee didn't say anything, but her eyebrows rose in suspicion.

"X?" she wondered as she jotted a note down. I shook my head, but couldn't quite remember why that didn't sound right to me. She didn't say anything else as she continued her body check on me. She sighed as she watched me flinch under the light tapping on my ribs. "They were supposed to let you heal." It was more of a note to herself, but she didn't whisper it so that I wouldn't hear it. Did she want me to hear her? She tapped on my thighs for a second and I held my usual resistance for her to check me there. She tapped me again and I opened slowly. She made her usual judgments and raised her eyebrows. She didn't write anything down or say anything to me. "What's your name?"

Here we go again.

"And before you answer," she said. "I want you to think about your comfort." I didn't say anything as she stood at her full height and looked down at me. I felt like I

                              AMY KULP

was being yelled at. "What is your name?"

"You know how I'm going to answer this. Bring in Cyrus," I taunted. She nodded her head and tucked her clipboard into her arm. She said goodbye to me and briskly walked out the door. I waited a couple of seconds before looking at the door in preparation for Cyrus. He always came a couple of seconds behind when Analee was done. However, I just waited.

And waited.

And waited.

"Better late than never, right?" I heard. I looked at the door as Agent F came through the door. He looked at me thoughtfully and threw what was in his hands on the table. I looked at it carefully before grabbing it immediately. He chuckled, but before I could put it on, he grabbed it for me. "You just have to answer something for me before you get it." He walked close to me and put one of his legs between mine. I felt myself blush. I tried to clamp my thighs together, but he just moved his leg closer to me and made me spread my legs. "What's your name?"

"Emily."

"Are you sure?" he asked as he grabbed the underwear off of the table. I bit my lip as he waved them in my face. "You know, none of us really got to play with you yet." He looked at me for a second before stooping to my level. He placed his hands on my thighs and I felt revolted. This wasn't his usual behavior. This was Reggie's usual behavior. "What's your name?" He pushed his nails into my thighs and I felt tears well up in my eyes.

"It's... Y-Y."

He immediately stood up and tossed me the underwear. Without another note to me, he walked out the door and I hurried to put the underwear on. It felt so weird but so fresh to put them on. I could sit down without feeling the cold or dirt on myself. I smiled to myself and immediately sat back on the chair. It felt comfier to be separated by this thin piece of cloth. I hugged my knees to my chest and smiled as I knew I wasn't flashing anyone right now.

I wasn't even scared when the door opened and now I saw Cyrus walk in. He walked closer to me and smiled down at me. His smile didn't seem fake or scary either. He seemed like he was genuinely happy.

"What's your name?" he asked.

"Y," I said without hesitation. He couldn't take this bliss away from me.

"Are you sure?" he asked. I nodded my head at him and he turned around to face the mirrors. He nodded his head and walked to the door. "Congratulations, you are ready."

"For what?" I asked.

"The auction."

****

I haven't been touched, talked to, or moved since I had gotten the underwear back. While this made me feel good and I felt like I was properly healing, it was lonesome. I haven't seen X since the day the power went down and my thoughts went to the worst thing that they could possibly go to. Was she dead? I at least got her cell which was a plus. She had a mattress in here which helped my back feel better. The only thing her cell didn't have was the water. So I was, unfortunately, always thirsty. They started feeding me better too. I'll wake up and see larger portions of food.

Maybe complying was better for me. It's not like I could actually forget my name just because they call me something else. I could start to fight again when I heal all up. I have been able to see more and more of the building because they trust me more. I'm always accompanied by someone, but nobody makes me feel uncomfortable. I haven't had my hands or feet bound in a little bit. I felt like a princess.

I haven't yet seen Chad or Emmanuel since I shocked them. I wasn't concerned though because even though they both promised that they would help me out of here, neither of them has lived up to it. Neither of them has come down here to help me. Neither of them has even checked up on me. I was alone.

I still don't even know what the power outage was about. Not like anybody would tell me, but I could speculate. It's all I could do to pass the time. I had a lot of outlandish ideas. Maybe we were in someone's house and they didn't know. When they realized that they needed to pay bills for a house they didn't live in anymore, they turned it off. Maybe it was sabotage. Maybe it was my willpower that they turned off.

I heard the door open and listened to multiple feet coming down the stairs. I watched intently as a girlish figure popped down with a hood on her face. She was struggling with them and they eventually put her into the cell right next to me. I stayed on the mattress as she bucked wildly to get the ropes off of her, but I didn't say anything. The guards locked her back up and then came over to me. I stared at the girl as the physical struggle was becoming too much and I listened to her pant.

"Here."

I looked up as I saw a pair of pants being thrown at me. I flinched and grabbed them when they landed on the floor. I heard my door lock again and watched as Murphy looked back at me. He did a double-take to make sure it was me and I watched as the light in his eyes seemed to dull. When he noticed me looking, he whipped his body back around and I heard him and Reggie talking as they headed up the stairs.

That's where they were.

I put the pants on and immediately felt a sense of relief. I didn't even pay attention to the struggling girl as I sat back down on the mattress fully clothed. When her squirming and gasping became enough, I huffed and walked to the edge. Our cells were connected with the slight barrier of a wall between us. However, I would be able to squeeze my hand through anything else that I needed.

"Stop struggling," I whisper. I moved closer to her

and watched as she listened to my instructions. "Come here and I can help you take them off." She moved her body slowly over to my voice. I was able to grab at the rope near her feet but wasn't able to get the knot off. Damn Murphy. I started working on her head ones so then she would at least be able to see. When I managed to slide it over her head, I was able to see a mess of hair before seeing her face. She immediately grabbed at her face to pull the duct tape off of her mouth. With that, she also kicked at me. "Hey!" I yelled. I immediately backed up and stared at her. "I was just trying to help."

"How do I know that you aren't working with them?" she hissed at me. I blinked a couple of times to make sure she knew what she was accusing me of. Her face softened a bit, but she remained firm.

"Why would I put myself in this situation?" I asked. I found myself giggling a little bit, but stopped myself because what I was thinking was not funny. "I would be the boss if anything." Her eyebrows rose in suspicion, but I resigned myself. "To make it here, you are not going to want to fight. You will need to save that energy."

She was dressed in yoga shorts and a crop top. She must have been freezing down here with that on. While her legs and arms were bound, she didn't seem to have too much bruising on her body. My eyes traveled up to her body and that's when I noticed her thighs. There were bruises, nail marks, and bite marks on her thighs and my mind only thought the worst. I had Emmanuel and Chad protecting me, she didn't. Who knows how many Agents were with her?

"Just let me help," I whisper. She struggled against me, but after a second, she agreed. She scooted towards me again and I undid her arm binding. When I tried to get her legs, I still couldn't do it. She thanked me and tried it herself. When she got them undone, I smiled politely at her. "What's your name?" I asked. She squinted at me for a second before answering.

"Z."

"No," I groaned. I shook my head and looked at her intensely. She could not forget her name. "What's your actual name?"

"Z."

"Your real name," I whined. "You cannot forget it. Do not let this place get to you. What is your name?"

"That's enough." I immediately flinched when I heard Analee's voice. I went back to the mattress and she calmly walked toward me. She unlocked my door and opened it for me. "Come with me." I looked at the girl next to me, but she wouldn't stare at me. She was crying. I made her cry. I looked at Analee again, but she just nodded her head for me to come. I obeyed and walked with her.

She calmly walked me up the stairs and we started heading towards an area I am not familiar with. Right before she entered the door, she stopped me. She looked at me and smiled and carefully brushed my hair from my face.

"Inside, you will see a fresh change of clothes, a brush, toothpaste and toothbrush, and other necessities you might need. Clean yourself up." She smiled at me again. "I'm so proud of your achievements."

She opened the door for me and I hesitantly walked inside. It was a small bathroom, but there was a toilet, shower, and sink. I felt my eyes beginning to water and immediately turned on the shower. It was too hot for my skin, but I jumped in anyway. This felt great. I haven't had a shower in what felt like months. Who knows how long I was in this place? I slept every chance I got.

I slowly grew accustomed to the temperature of the water and started combing back my hair so that I could get all of the dirt out of it. I slathered some shampoo on before doing everything I needed to. I felt so happy. I felt so clean. I found myself smiling and I felt myself beginning to hum. As I continued throughout the rest of my shower, I redid all of my cleaning because it made me feel so good. My skin was burning, but it had a nice little tinge to it. I felt so refreshed.

I grabbed the towel that was laid out for me and twisted my hair into it. When I reached for the other towel, I gently patted my skin dry and wrapped it around me. I shivered as I stepped out of the shower and pulled the curtain back. It was breezy.

"Oh my God, you scared me!" As I lost my balance from having the shock of someone in the room with me, I reached out to steady myself. They quickly grabbed a hold of me and I couldn't stop staring at his neck. "Does it hurt?" I asked as I straightened up. I laid my hand gently near the gash and watched as he flinched. Here was my answer. "I'm sorry." I stepped away from him out of embarrassment and looked into the mirror.

"I'll wait outside for you, okay?" I nodded my head and smiled slightly. "Remember to make yourself as pretty as possible for the auction."

"Emmanuel," I started as he opened the door. "Am I going to be okay?" He nodded his head but didn't say anything as he slipped out. I looked back into the mirror and dropped the towel that I was wearing. Now that I had taken a shower, the marker was very faint against my leg, but I was still able to see it. "I am Emily Washington. I have a mom and a dad who love me. I have reasons to stay alive."

Chapter 18 -------------------------------

I have now upgraded from ropes to handcuffs on my arms, duct tape on my legs, and the sack was back over my head. I was once again thrown into the back of the van with Emmanuel. I could hear that there were other people in the van, but I wasn't sure how many. Without being able to see, I had almost zero chance of running out of here. I was going to comply until this was removed from my head. I feel like duct tape wouldn't be too hard to remove from my legs either so I wasn't worried about that. The handcuffs were not an obstacle for me so I knew that I could easily bonk someone on the head or carry something if I needed to.

I listened carefully to the space around us and knew from the little potholes that the van hit, that there were three other people in here. Mostly I heard feet being replaced as they repositioned, but I could hear a little clanking too. I tried to look under and through my hood to try and see how many other people were in here, but these were fully blacked out. I knew that Emmanuel was next to me because he constantly kept a hand or thigh plastered to me. Was it Reggie? Was it Murphy? Was it anybody else I knew?

I readjusted my hand position for a second and

listened to the noise the handcuffs made. I immediately froze and made the noise again. I heard a very similar noise from across the van and started sweating with anticipation. Emmanuel put his hand on my wrists to stop me from making the noise again, but I knew. There was another girl in this van. Was it the girl who called herself Z? I moved my legs out from under me so that I would have a better stance. Emmanuel constantly let me be affectionate toward him so I casually placed my hands on his chest and leaned into him. I let my hands roam his chest, but I was truly trying to find the pin that they all have on their chests. It was somewhere, but as I roamed Emmanuel's chest, I couldn't find it.

"Stop, that tickles me," he whispered through gritted teeth.

I put my hands on my lap and I made the metal noise again. I listened carefully and this time I heard it from two different locations. Emmanuel's hand immediately flew back to my hands and I stopped for a second. I started to breathe heavily at the implications and opened my mouth for a second. If there were other girls, did this mean there were other Agents? Would I get in more trouble by doing this? Hell, I had to do it.

"How many of us are there?" I asked confidently. I heard clinks before hearing another girl talk and someone else. Emmanuel tensed up beside me and while I couldn't fight him, I could talk to these other girls while he was trying to silence me. "We can fight back if there are more of us."

"Shut her up, Emmanuel!" I heard from the front.

My hood was taken off of me and for a split second, I pushed my hands against Emmanuel's chest. While searching, I realized that there was no pin on his uniform. I looked around too and saw while there were other girls here, there were also other Agents. None of them had pins in their uniforms either. I turned back to Emmanuel to ask him a question, but it was too late because he taped my mouth shut. I pushed harder against his chest as he tried getting the hood back on. He applied all of his body pressure before he could get it back on.

I felt like I couldn't breathe.

I stayed on my back and as we rode longer, I knew that Emmanuel was getting relaxed. I could try to flip him? Was I even capable of that? The other girls were starting to become uneasy too, but I slowly heard them being corrected into submission. Was this what I was becoming? Was I submitting to what was happening? Was I becoming brainwashed?

A new fire was in me. I had to be smart though. I couldn't escape with all of these Agents. I had to get these girls out of here. Would I be able to save all of us? Would I even be able to save myself? I began licking the duct tape that was on my lips and knew it would fall off if I kept doing this.

You think they would learn by now.

"Behave," Emmanuel whispered to me. I paused for a second before realizing that was probably my best bet. I relaxed underneath his body weight and he eventually eased up. He sat me back up and I leaned my body against him. He eventually wrapped his arms around me and in any other situation, this would have been romantic. Right now, I knew this was so he could have better control of me.

I was surprised to feel the van beginning to slow down. When it stopped, I felt my anxiety start to go through the roof and I held onto Emmanuel. He held onto me as well and as I heard different things happening, I couldn't pinpoint any of them. Eventually, Emmanuel lifted me up so that we could start walking, but I refused to move my legs. He huffed for a second before I felt him lean down and cut the tape on my legs. As if that was the problem with this situation. I pretended it was though.

He kept his hand in the middle of my back and slowly he led me into different places. I could see that some of the rooms were of different lighting because my hood kept becoming different shades. However, I was not able to see out of it. Eventually, I was told to sit and I obeyed. The handcuffs were taken off of me and I was tied to the arms of the chair that I was sitting in and my hood came off.

"Seriously?" Emmanuel asked as he noticed the duct tape came off of my mouth.

He continued to talk to me, but I couldn't concentrate on him. There were three other girls with me in the room. They were all cuffed to their seats and remained immobile. However, they didn't have duct tape on their mouths. While they remained obedient, they still stared at each other. Emmanuel grabbed more duct tape, but instead of taping it only on my mouth, he taped it around my head and hair. When he was done, I could see the small smile on his lips as he was satisfied with his job. He patted my legs and left the room.

There were more than three girls in the van. What happened to them? What happened to the other girls? Why was I being paired with these girls? All of these girls were beautiful and none of them had blemishes, cuts, or bruises on their bodies. Why was I with them?

"What happened?" one of the girls finally asked. I looked over at her and she was staring at me. Does she not see that I have duct tape that I cannot get off? "Keep licking it and stretching your mouth," she advised. She smiled gently at me and I started doing that. I knew about the licking part, but I have never tried stretching my mouth. Slowly, I felt it start to tear away from my skin. She smiled and looked around her for a second. "They're supposed to let us heal before we come here." I shrugged my shoulders as I continued licking the duct tape, but other girls started to join in.

"Where are the other girls?"

"They are probably sold already," the last girl replied. She shrugged her shoulders and I saw tears welling up in her eyes. "This is a human trafficking ring." She didn't say anything else and it looked like she was giving up.

"Why?" I asked as I tried to puff out some of the tape from my lips. "Are... you... giving up?"

"Do you not see the predicament we're in?" one of the girls asked. "I fought and fought, but I had a breaking point." She closed her eyes and smiled a bit. "I'm just hoping whoever buys me is better than this crew." I shook my head at her.

"We need... to leave."

"How?"

I shrugged my shoulders and looked around the room. There was only one exit point - the doorway to and from. There were no windows. There wasn't a closet. There were only our chairs in the room and nothing else. How do we get out of this? How can I get out of this? Emmanuel and Chad both told me they would try to get me out of this. Where are they?

"D!"

One of the girls winced as her name was called. My eyes grew big and an unfamiliar Agent came in to get rid of her bindings. They put the hood back on her and I watched as she clutched onto their arm. Is that what I looked like when I did it to Chad and Emmanuel? It looked so pathetic. As they were leaving, the Agent pointed to the camera that was mounted in the corner and we all knew that we were caught. They could see us and they could probably hear us.

That stopped the interaction between all of us. Slowly and one-by-one each girl was called. I wish I knew the time intervals between them so that I could prepare for my turn. However, I watched as Emmanuel came in with a sympathetic smile. He undid my arms first and I immediately swung at him. I hit him in the head, but he didn't seem phased at all. He looked at me and pointed to the cameras. Within seconds, there were more Agents standing by the doors. I knew that this battle was lost immediately.

He made eye contact with me and mouthed 'sorry' before putting my hood over my face. I tried to stay in the chair that I was in, but I felt more hands on me trying to pry it off of me. With a hit to my knuckles, my immediate reaction was to let go and I was then grouped into one pair of arms. I was hoping it was Emmanuel's, but I was not able to tell at the moment. As we were walking down what felt like a very long hallway, I was set down and my wrist was grabbed. I felt my hands beginning to get sweaty because I wasn't sure what to expect.

I could hear doors being opened and heard people turning in their seats. The squeaks made it obvious. I walked slowly down the aisle with the Agent I was with and tripped on the first step. I heard some chuckles, but how was I supposed to know there were stairs? I stayed frozen when I lost track of the body by my side until I was moved to another chair with ropes tying me to the chair by my arms and legs.

"Welcome back for our grand prize." My eyebrows scrunched underneath my hood. I knew that voice, but it couldn't possibly be. "This girl was our hardest case yet. As you can see, she is not fully healed." She paused as she spoke. "She is a fighter, but she is also beautiful. Known for playing soccer at home and being captain of her team, she is not that used." She paused again and I felt my hood being untied. "Only having one boyfriend her entire life, she is almost in pristine condition. That boyfriend - Agent C - will now lift the hood from her face." With that, it was lifted and I saw what felt like hundreds of faces staring back at me.

We were somewhere that had a stage. All of these seats were filled with different people. Old men, old women, young men, rich women, white men, black women, Hispanic women, kids, teens, Asian women, every possible combination you could think about. I could see some of their slimy smiles as they licked their lips looking at me. I could feel the stares as they tried to get a good look at my body. My attention wasn't held by the audience though.

My attention was held by the announcer. While still standing at the podium, her smile was dazzling and she knew how to play the audience. She kept motioning towards the slideshow that was playing behind me and while I only caught glimpses of it, I could see that they were different pictures from our soccer games, study halls, and different photos during my capture. I didn't even know they took pictures in the van. However, no picture showed that I didn't have clothes on. I could thank Bri for that later.

"Give a warm round of applause to Y. This girl was my best friend for the past two years and it took a lot to get her to trust me." The crowd laughed at that and I immediately felt my skin beginning to boil. "With that

                                    AMY KULP

being said, we are starting her off unusually high - one million dollars!"

There was a gasp in the air, but I saw someone's number flicker. Bri continued to announce higher and higher numbers until they started to wade themselves out. She smiled as she rang the bell to end the sale and I stared at her longer. While I felt that Emmanuel was undoing my ties and people were starting to leave, I couldn't control the rage that I had for Bri.

I trusted her.

"What is your problem?" I yelled as I lunged for her. She took a step away from me, but I could see there were more Agents flocking toward the stage. I could also see that the sellers were intrigued by this. "I trusted you!" I dove for her and while I was able to grab a chunk of hair, I was immediately yanked back. "Why are you doing this to me?" I held onto the hair that was in my hand and felt tears beginning to drop down my cheeks. "You coward!" I finally yelled as she walked off of the stage. I felt myself being dragged away and just let my body be dragged away.

This made sense. Why else would she have a mattress? Why else would she not try to fight when they kidnapped her? They never actually kidnapped her! She was part of this! Was everyone I knew a part of this? Where were my mom and dad? Is everything I know a lie? That's why the Agents no longer have pins on their uniforms. That explains so much to me. To think about how much I had confided in her when we had those cages.

I even tried to help her out of it and she wasn't actively trying to get out of it. Everything made so much sense now.

"She is one of the highest ranks," Chad whispered as he carried me away. "Please don't cry."

I just needed something familiar at this point. I felt myself clutch onto Chad and cry into him. I had gotten over Chad's betrayal a little bit ago because I needed to in order to survive. At this point, it just felt like I was born to do this. How many people did I know that was a part of this? Were my teachers a part of this? How about my family? Why was I a target for these people?

I cried so much that I didn't even bother fighting anymore. Chad was forced to carry me back into the basement and it was to the point that nobody even gave me a hood, nobody put duct tape on me, and nobody put ropes on me. My spirit was far too broken to need any of those things. They wanted to break me this whole time, but it was finally Bri who succeeded in doing it.

"I tried so hard to get you out of here," Chad whispered to me as he laid me down on the mattress. I turned to look at him and he kissed me on the forehead. "The thing is, I can't leave this." His smile faltered and he kneeled next to me. "They'll kill my mom. I'm so sorry, Y. I was never supposed to actually catch feelings." Tears started welling up in his eyes and I found myself stroking his cheeks to keep them away.

"Say my name," I whispered. Chad looked at me and shook his head no. My chin started quivering and I

turned away from him. I felt myself beginning to cry
again and I listened to him lock my door and leave. His
footsteps soon disappeared and all I could do was listen to
myself cry.

I don't know why I needed him to say my name. I
wanted comfort and it would make me feel better if he
said my name. It would take me back to when I thought
the world was a much better place. When I didn't know
that things like this happened. It would take me back to
when I had a loving boyfriend and friends. I would
choose to relive my life better if I was able to. I would
make more friends and hang out with people. I wouldn't
just be focusing on soccer. I would focus on the people
around me and tell them how much I loved them. I missed
my mom. I missed my dad. I missed my boyfriend Chad
who was sometimes a jerk. I missed Bri as my friend. I
missed school. I missed everything about my old life.

I eventually calmed myself down to just whimper
instead of cry out loud. However, I couldn't force myself
to sleep. How could I sleep knowing that I didn't know
where I was going? I wasn't even paying attention to who
had bought me. Who knows what kind of things they
were going to try to make me do? Obviously, they were a
multi-millionaire if they could start the prices at one
million. What did you want to have to do that girls weren't
willing to do for you for a multi-millionaire?

I listened as I heard Chad's footsteps come back
down the stairs. I smiled to myself as if I knew he could
protect me. Maybe this was his idea of a last-minute

escape plan. I didn't turn toward him as he unlocked my door. I just let him come in and listened as he stepped closer to me. When he relocked the door as he stepped in, I felt suspicious though. Why would he do that?

"Surprise," Reggie said as I turned over. I immediately shot back and hit the bars of the bed. Reggie plopped onto the mattress with me and smirked at me. "I figured since you're going somewhere else tomorrow, I'll give you a lasting impression of me." He immediately started kissing my lips and although I tried to make my lips disappear, it didn't seem to phase him. He pressed harder onto my lips and I felt as his hand began traveling down my body. He played with the waistband of my pants before digging his hands into my underwear.

"Stop!" I beg.

"You have it too easy," he said. With his other hand, he raised my chin to examine my neck. "You are free territory and I've been on assignment so long that I need a break." He smiled again and even in the dim light, I am able to see just how yellow and nasty his teeth were. "It's not fair that Chad and Emmanuel get to have all of the fun." He caressed my chin with his thumb before I felt his other hand trying to maneuver below my underwear. "I've been thinking about this ever since I laid my eyes on you."

I managed to free one of my arms and I started hitting him with it. He laughed as I struggled with him and I heard him unzip his pants. I pleaded again with him and found myself trying to roll out of bed with him. He put his arm to steady himself and slowly brought my underwear and pants down. I pleaded once more with him and he distracted me by biting on my ear gently.

"Please, don't do this."

"Why shouldn't I?" he asked. He started kissing my neck and laying little kisses down as he went. It was so creepy and I felt myself trying to slap and kick him. "The more you struggle, the more turned on I get."

"I'm a virgin!" I yelled when I felt his hand going back down below. He immediately paused and for a second he alleviated the pressure on my body. I was too scared to escape though and found myself beginning to cry. Hysterically cry. Ugly cry. Whatever you wanted to call it. I wailed with him on top of me, but he wasn't moving.

"Are you serious?" he asked. He zipped his pants back up and looked at me as if I was cursed. He quickly ran towards the other end of the door and started unlocking it. He shook his head and I listened to his footsteps run up those stairs. I'm not sure where they ran to, but I listened until they disappeared.

As I continued to cry, I felt a hand trying to comfort me while petting my hair. Through the darkness of the downstairs and blurriness of my tears, I was able to see that it was Z. She had a black and blue eye and I saw a hickey on her neck, but I didn't comment on either. I wasn't humiliated that she has seen me crying since Chad left and I wasn't humiliated that she almost saw me raped by this man.

I was scared because I was warned not to tell anyone I was a virgin. I was warned multiple times by different people. What was going to happen to me now that they found out?

****

Nobody talked to me as I walked out to the waiting van. I'm sure that they had all heard the news of me being a virgin was out and about. Chad and Emmanuel were conveniently absent as everyone said goodbye to me. Nobody would meet my eye though. I walked past Cyrus, Analee, Murphy, Agent K, and Reggie, but only Reggie looked at me. He smirked as I passed and slapped my ass. If I didn't have the Agent with the scars behind me, I would've hit him back. However, I was being pushed along and how everyone was acting, I knew that I should be afraid too.

The Agent opened the van doors and I was surprised to see Emmanuel and Chad in handcuffs in the back. My eyes grew big and both of them looked up at me but didn't say a word. I looked at the Agent beside me and he just nodded his head. I got in and he closed the doors behind me. I was able to see that Bri would be driving with us and instantly gulped. If she was so high in power, what was going to happen?

"You all cost us over twenty-two million dollars," she announced. I immediately sat down in the middle of Emmanuel and Chad. Neither of them said anything as the van started to drive. Should I say anything to them?

A pothole in the road made the van jump and I found my body leaning into Chad's. He didn't say a word to me, but he did put his hand on top of my hand. I grabbed onto Emmanuel's as well and he did look at me. He took it as an invitation to slide closer to me and suddenly I felt cramped. It felt like a love triangle where I didn't love either of them. However, I had to make them think I did. What if they were my only way out? Then again, they were in handcuffs in the back of the van with me. Were they even acting anymore? They seemed scared too and you can't fake the level of fear that we all are having.

Chad squeezed my hand and I held onto him as I felt the van starting to slow down. Were we here already? I always felt like these rides took multiple hours or days. Hell, I didn't even know what month we were in let alone day or time. It felt like I had been trapped there for months, but I highly doubt they would keep me for months. I know my parents were searching for me so if they were to keep me somewhere for months, they were most likely going to find me at that place. How long was I there?

"Let's go, Emmanuel." Bri opened the back of the van and she sneered at all of us together. Emmanuel looked back at us once before going along with Bri. "I'll be back for the rest of you. My most trustworthy Agent will be watching the doors so don't think about anything." Bri said it so condescending that even I shivered from the anticipation of what was going to happen to them.

We were shrouded in darkness when she closed the van doors behind Emmanuel. I didn't dare to move until I counted to sixty. I looked at Chad and he looked back at me too. His pupils were so big that I knew he could not be faking how afraid he was. He sat up with me and tried to envelop me in his arms. With him being handcuffed, he couldn't spread his hands out. I rolled my eyes at him and knew that he was not the one who was used to being handcuffed.

"Did you ever think I was going to make it out of this?" I asked quietly to him. I put his hands into mine and looked at him for a split second. He bit his lip at me and I saw his tears beginning to collect in the corner of his eyes. He shook his head no and it felt like I had a second before my entire face reacted. I was tired of crying, but hearing that come from him crushed me.

"That doesn't mean I never stopped trying," Chad whispered as he forced his body closer to me. He put his chin on top of my head and breathed in for a second. I couldn't tell if he was trying to make me feel better or not. "I will die trying to figure out how to get you out of here. You have my word on that." He reached out his hand and although it felt silly to do something like this, I shook it.

"What should I expect?" I asked. He didn't respond to me but instead brought me closer to him. I wasn't even sure if that was possible. "Thank you for trying." He shook his head and I closed my eyes as I was glad he was familiar to me. "I'm sorry I couldn't keep it a secret."

"Don't apologize," Chad said. He abruptly moved away from me and put one hand on my shoulder. "I was trying to protect you. I don't know what to expect from him."

"Who's him?"

"Our leader and organizer." Chad blinked a couple of times before smiling small. "He's recruited everyone here. He's not afraid to do anything to get what he wants." Chad licked his lips. "If you lie to him, make sure you lie to him well."

"I'll take Chad now," Bri said as the van doors opened again. We immediately jolted away from each other and I couldn't help but feel like Bri was listening in on the other side of the doors. She was waiting for the perfect opportunity to split us up. Bri waved at me teasingly as she took Chad away and gave the instructions to the Agent to come into the van.

The comfortable air that was in here before quickly turned into awkward silence. Especially since now, I knew that this was Bri's favorite Agent. I was having trouble figuring out the hierarchy of these operations though. Whoever I was about to meet was the leader. I knew that. Then did it go to Bri, Agent, everybody else? Or how did this go? It seemed to be that Cyrus and Agent F were the leaders of their groups so why would he be more trusted than Cyrus?

He stayed pretty aloof to me too. I don't remember him hurting me too much or initiating any painful memories. He never tried to make a pass on me and he never offered to help me. He was just always there with someone else or following orders. I guess I could see why he was Bri's favorite. He was obedient and didn't form attachments to anybody he wasn't supposed to. It was alien-like, to be honest. It didn't even seem that he had a good relationship with the other Agents here. How can someone refrain from talking to everybody? It wasn't possible unless he was hiding something. Was he hiding something?

"How did you get your scars?" I asked. I didn't mean to ask it and I found it kind of rude that I asked it. Why would I care about being rude though? I was literally their hostage! I need to stop feeling bad about things like that. He didn't react as I asked my question and simply averted his eyes to me and then back to what he was staring at. He was stone cold.

"For disobeying orders," he murmured.

I nodded my head and knew that was all I was going to get out of him. I couldn't imagine him disobeying orders though. I also couldn't imagine what kind of fiend would make scars that bad. It couldn't have been Cyrus. He was more about mental torture than physical torture. Was it the leader that I was going to meet? Was it Bri? She seemed to tease that he was her favorite, but only because Emmanuel and Chad lied to everyone about me being a virgin. What was so bad about me being a virgin anyway?

It wasn't long before the van doors opened again

and Bri smirked as it was now my turn. The Agent followed behind us and I made sure to take note of what side he was on. Bri's betrayal is the worst for me and I'm still not sure how she is okay with doing it. We really only became really good friends this year and I guess now that made sense since she really needed to up her game so that I would trust her while we were both prisoners. Before I knew of the deception.

"In here," she ordered.

She led me into a room and quickly shut it when I entered. I looked around to take note of any possible exit points and was surprised to see a huge window. I walked towards it and looked to see what was outside of it. It was too close to another building for anybody to escape from it. Why would someone build a building and put a window there? It seemed pretty useless to me. I turned around when I was bored with the window and took notice of the mirror that was in here. It was probably a two-way mirror. I waved at it just in case someone was watching me, but I felt silly as soon as I did it. Unlike all of the other rooms I have been in, this one wasn't as dark as the other ones. The walls were painted white and the floor was a creamy color. It feels eerie to be here.

It didn't help that there was blood splattered all over the walls, floor, and chair. The chair contained most of the blood splatter so I was nervous to think about what had occurred here. Was it Chad's? Was it Emmanuel's? Was it someone else's? Maybe one of the boys had fought back and it was actually the leader's blood. I couldn't see

Chad fighting though because I knew how close to his mom he was. He wouldn't want her to be harmed in any way. Was it Emmanuel's though? What happens if this was another calculated move? Like they planned it.

"I'm ready," I announced as I stopped staring at the blood. I looked through the two-way mirror as if I can see the people on the other side. I couldn't see a thing, but maybe I could trick them into believing I could. Would it be Bri who was going to talk to me first? Or was it their leader?

"I've heard about the fire in you," Bri said as she entered the room. "I never saw it and I definitely thought Cyrus would have killed the flame." She closed the door behind her and casually motioned for me to sit in the chair. I refused though and she just smirked. "I am not afraid to hurt you," she threatened. I could see a sadistic interest in her face as she thought about the possibilities of what she could do to me. "You see the blood splatter from previous participants so I would listen well." She stepped closer to me and it took every urge in my body to not step away from her. She was a little scary. "Chad and Emmanuel can take the beatings and torture. They were trained for this. You were not." She took another step closer to me and I couldn't resist taking a step back. Her eyes took note of my movement and I immediately cursed myself. She doesn't know that she scares me. "We run a pretty tight ship around here so I want you to listen. My leader is a very important man so he can't squeeze you in for two days."

　　　　　　　　　　　　　AMY KULP

"So what does that mean?"

"That means that I am in charge of you until then. I am going to make sure you don't have contact with anyone, but my trusted allies." I immediately knew that she meant the Agent with the scars. I rolled my eyes and wondered if she had a thing for him. Could evil people fall in love? "If you do not cooperate, I will break a bone for every command you do not follow." I scrunch my eyebrows and she immediately began snickering at me. "I see that you don't believe me." She took a step closer to me. "Unlike Chad and Emmanuel, I don't grow attached to my missions." She shrugged her shoulders and pursed her lips for a minute. She took another step closer to me and I knew that she was tempted to break something on me. Would it be a bone? What bone could she break that wouldn't be detrimental to me?

"Why are you like this?" I asked her. Her smile didn't falter as she lunged toward me. My feet slipped from the blood that I was standing on and I immediately lost my balance. She had quick reflexes and I knew that she was better than any of the other Agents I had dealt with. She showed no mercy to me. Was she soulless?

She contemplated what to tell me, but instead, she grabbed me by my hair and yanked it back. Maybe this was payback from pulling some of her hair out at the auction. She dragged a sharp object to my neck and for a second I was petrified. It was just used to tease me and I felt my heart beginning to race. It really didn't seem like she had any attachments to me.

A sharp pain came shooting down my leg as she pressed onto my leg. Did she break it? Or was she just torturing me at this point? She immediately got off of me and I let out a sound from my throat that I hadn't expected. It felt worse when she lifted the pressure off of my body. I looked up at her through blurry vision and saw her smiling down at me. It infuriated me, but I couldn't do anything. She was stronger and she was trained. I was weaker and I was not skilled in fighting. I could only kick, but with one of my legs burning, I wasn't sure I had much of an advantage.

"I was told you were a runner," she mumbled. "It makes sense, but now you don't have that option." She shrugged her shoulders as she walked towards the door. "Stand up." I looked over at her as if she was stupid. She just hurt my leg and expected me to stand up? "Stand up!" She shouted it this time and I flinched so hard that I had no choice but to stand up. I put all of the pressure on my good leg, but it still hurt to even touch the other one to the ground. She smiled as she exited and gave orders to the Agent. "Take her to where she's sleeping." She turned to me. "You'll find that it's a lot cozier."

I wasn't sure I believed her.

"I can't walk," I whispered as the Agent ushered me to follow him. He looked at me for a second, but I wasn't able to read his face. "I think she broke my leg." He moved his face so that he didn't look at me as he continued his stance to have me walk behind him. I crinkled my eyebrows, but he didn't seem mad or

                                    AMY KULP

impatient with me. Instead, he seemed like he was stuck on what to do. He wasn't told to help me, but he should know that it wasn't his job to help me. I grumbled under my breath as I slowly began to hop on one leg. I winced every single hop and I was sure I was making noises as I did so.

Thankfully, we only had to go three doors down before I saw my room. When he opened it up, I was shocked to see a plain room. There were no windows. There wasn't anything besides the door and the long mirror covering the wall. The floor was bare and I looked at the Agent to make sure he led me into the right room. When he closed it behind me, I knew he did because of the little space there was carved out of the door. Almost as if that was how he was going to feed me.

How was I supposed to go to the bathroom here?

"You will be fed tomorrow morning. You will have a bathroom break after breakfast. I will be standing out here for the rest of the night."

He mumbled other unimportant details for me, but I wasn't paying attention. I was in too much agony to listen to him read off the directions he memorized for me. My leg was in pain and every time I moved it, the fire was shooting up my entire body now. I felt desperate to get out of here, but I felt myself giving up hope. They had transported me so many times and I still wasn't able to get out. I was starting to think that I was in here for the pure enjoyment of them torturing me.

"Make sure to be well-rested for tomorrow," he

said as he finished up his mantra. I nodded my head but didn't meet his eyes. As he promised, he stood outside of my door all night. I didn't hear him move at all, but I could see his shadow underneath the door and see him in the slot of the door.

I decided to take his advice and tried to fall asleep. I huffed since I knew that if I closed my eyes at all, I would immediately fall asleep. I forced them open and looked at the ceiling before saying my mantra.

"I'm Emily Washington. I have a mom and a dad who love me."

"Oops."

I heard the Agent drop the granola bar he was eating onto the ground. He looked around him for a second before picking it up and dropping it through the slot of my door. I cautiously watched him before realizing that he was giving me the food to eat. It didn't look like a trap. I crawled quietly to the piece that was on the floor and rushed back to the corner I liked. When I turned it over, I noticed that he hadn't even opened it. I immediately chowed down on the item since it seemed that I had been lied to about being fed. My stomach immediately growled as I ate and I felt my cheeks blush. Now I just wanted more.

"Do you need your bathroom break?" he asked me. I pondered for a second. Last night I definitely needed to go to the bathroom but was forced to hold it in. It seemed as if I didn't anymore. I shook my head before realizing that he wasn't facing me as we talked.

"Yes, please." I watched as he shifted around to look at me through the little slot in the door. I wasn't sure what to expect from him - he was unpredictable. He coaxed me over so I walked cautiously towards him. He held his hands down so that I could see he had a rope on him and I knew he wanted me to stick my hands through the slot. It felt like I was in prison. What if I was in an old jail cell?

It made sense. The other room that I was in could have been an interrogation room. The room I was currently in looked like I was in a solitary confinement cell. Maybe that's how their leader started. He could have been a criminal or maybe he was a guard. This couldn't have been someone's house because it was too big of a building. Just from seeing how many rooms there were and how long the hallways were, I knew.

As soon as my hands were tied, the door opened and I was able to follow the Agent. His shoes squeaked loud against the clean floor. It also felt way too loud since there was no other noise. Even the noise of my feet slapping against the tiles made me feel uneasy. It felt like we weren't supposed to be doing this. I wasn't sure if I was picking up some anxiety that the Agent was having, but that's what it felt like to me. His back was straighter than what it usually was and I saw that he had his hand on his belt the whole time. Who was he preparing to fight?

"What's your name?" I asked. His pace slowed for a moment before he quickened his pace again. Sometimes he seemed like I could crack him and other times he was the perfect pet for Bri. Why couldn't I crack this man? He brought me around the corner and I wasn't sure he was going to answer. He took an unusually long time to answer me and for a second, I thought that he was going to lie. Maybe he was. I wouldn't know.

"Ellis."

I was shocked that he gave me his whole first name. I didn't even know some of the other guards' names. They only referred to them as Agent C, Agent K, Agent F, or it would be Agent E for him. He didn't look like an Ellis though. That felt like a weird name for him. I pictured him as Thomas. The scars covering his face made him seem like he was older than he was. Ellis felt like a juvenile name compared to him. He seemed stoic versus what a normal person was like. Maybe his name was Ellis before he became an Agent here, but he wasn't an Ellis to me. I didn't want to get to know him on that personal level because what if he used it against me?

"And yours?" he asked me. I immediately squinted at his question. Was this a test? Was he asking me what my actual name was? Did I even want to tempt fate that he actually wanted my real answer? I bit my lip as I thought about how I should answer, but since he was walking ahead of me, I wasn't able to read his face. I also had to think about if I wanted to fight him. I was really tired and I was just healing from all of the cuts, bruises, and pain from the other Agents. I also had to expect that when I met the leader, he would hurt me too.

"Y," I finally answered. The Agent didn't say anything or even change his pace as we walked. Was that the answer he expected? Was that the answer he wanted? Regardless of the answer, I didn't say anything else to him. I felt like maybe I could open up more to him as we progressed, but he seemed cold. Like he knew he shouldn't talk to me, but he was for the benefit of him.

Maybe he really did like working here.

As we rounded another corner, I was growing skeptical about finding a bathroom. I felt like we were walking far too long for there not to be a bathroom close by. What was he doing? I put myself on high alert just in case he wanted to attack me. I had to be ready to fight, but it would make it harder because my arms were tied together. It would help if I remembered what his weapon was. I know it wasn't the pepper spray because that was Chad's weapon, but what were the other options? I stared down at his belt and watched as he kept his hand protectively over it. Even when he moved it slightly, his shirt was untucked and covered that portion.

I knew that my best bet was to behave.

He looked behind him to see if I was still there and opened a door for me. I stared at him confused. He wanted me to go first? I stepped foot in the smaller hallway first and slowly walked. The hall was different from the ones I was used to seeing. This one had little rooms attached where you can see inside. It looked like a tiny prison and that's when I confirmed that this had to be jail at one point. We walked down the hallway slowly and eventually, I saw movement on the right side of my eyes.

It was a figure. He had bindings to the floor and wasn't able to move from how he was sitting on the floor. His hair seemed to be ripped from his scalp by how patchy it was. Some hair was longer than his shoulders and some hair was buzzed to his scalp. While looking at his face, he had two swollen eyes and a bloodied lip. He probably wasn't even able to talk through the damage. Probably couldn't see either. As my eyes traveled down his body, I looked at his arms. Both wrists seemed like they were sawed by a chainsaw. Over and over and over again. It looked to be from struggling against the wrist constraints, but it could've been something that was done intentionally. I grimaced as we passed him. He didn't make a noise and didn't even acknowledge that we were there. I don't think he could even see us.

I looked through the rest of the separate rooms before I saw another figure. This room was different. While it seemed to take up the same area space, there was a bed in there. Not just a mattress, but a bed. The figure wasn't even restrained either. The hair was swept off to the side in a fashionable style and I was able to pinpoint it was Chad. The only similarity between the two was that he was also sleeping. The only real disfiguring I could see on him was his foot seemed to be twisted or broken. Just from him sleeping in his bed, I could see that he would have a hard time walking for the rest of his life.

I must've slowed down because I felt a tug on my arms from the Agent. He didn't face me as he tugged and I knew I would have to catch up to him. Why was he showing me this? I followed him down another long hallway before coming to a stop in front of another door. He turned toward me and it made me jump for a second. My mind immediately went to him attacking me, but it was clear that he was just about to give me directions. I stared at the door behind him and wished that it would be a bathroom.

"You have to leave the door open a crack for safety measures," he instructed me. It was a bathroom. "I will loosen your hands, but I cannot take them completely off." I flinched when he brought his hands to mine and he flinched as well. As if he didn't realize that him being an Agent would affect me. He put them back on the ropes and tugged them softly so that they were a bit looser on me.

I didn't even notice that my hands were hurting until he did that. With them being looser, I could also see the bright pink that was surrounding my wrists. My skin was so dry that I even saw little flakes around the knots that were rubbing against the skin. It looked gnarly and I couldn't help but grimace about it. Now that I had noticed it and he had let it breathe, it would hurt a lot more now. My senses were tuned into it now.

I opened the door to find a tiny room with just a toilet in there. There wasn't a sink. There wasn't a trash can. There wasn't even toilet paper. I looked around the room for a minute to verify that it was a working toilet. I immediately blushed as I usually had a shy bladder, but seeing that had made me want to go immediately. It was like I couldn't hold it any longer.

"Do not flush when you are done," the Agent instructed.

That was gross. As soon as I was done, I turned back and looked at it. I'm not sure why. I think I was so used to just throwing toilet paper behind me that it was natural to look. I felt my cheeks burn pink as I noticed the discoloration of the liquid in the toilet. Maybe they had toilet bowl cleaner in it before I went? I coughed to let him know that I was done and he scooted into the bathroom. I felt a tug on my ropes as he looked in the bowl before flushing. He didn't say anything about the color change.

When we both walked out, we took a slow stroll the other way. We didn't go back through the rooms with the two boys in them and I tried to figure out why he had shown them to me in the first place.

Was it to scare me? I feel like if he wanted to scare me, all he had to do was hurt me. I have been very compliant though so he would not have had an opportunity to hurt me. Although, now that I'm thinking about it, he's a criminal. He did not need a reason to hurt me. He could just hurt me because he wanted to. This Agent was the only one that hasn't really hurt me too much. Yeah, he hurt me in the beginning when he was with the rest of his group, but he hasn't touched me since. I'm actually surprised that he tried to be friendly toward me and ask me my name. I still feel like he asked that so I would say the wrong answer. Everything this Agent did was so calculated.

Maybe he just showed them so I knew that Chad was still alive. This meant that the unrecognizable person in that cell had to be Emmanuel. Why was he hurt worse than Chad? Why was Chad barely injured? I had so many questions that I wanted to ask both of them. Emmanuel must have put up a fight to be so badly beaten that he was unrecognizable. What did Chad offer if he was barely touched? Did he spill anything about me?

I felt my palms begin to sweat as I thought about these things. I couldn't tell who I could trust. I thought that I could trust Chad to get me out, but now I was concerned that he gave all the information away. However, they were all criminals. I couldn't trust any of them.

"I am going to have to inform the bosses about the current situation," he whispered. When he turned around, he was ready to change the rope on my arms. I let him and scurried back to my room. That little bit of movement had exhausted me - mentally and physically. Maybe it was because I had to keep thinking about Chad and Emmanuel. Maybe it was because I started my period.

I wasn't sure.

I did know that that was the most peaceful night of sleep I have had in a while though.

****

At least when the Agents wake me up, they try to wake me up nicely. Today's morning routine was far more bizarre than what I was used to. I woke up when pressure was added to my body and I felt like I couldn't breathe. When my eyes fluttered open, I saw Bri's face smirking down at me. Her hands let go of my neck and she looked down at me pleased. I stopped fighting when I was trying

                                        AMY KULP

to breathe and she smirked at me. She got off of me and stared at me from a distance. My eyes darted towards the open door, but I had to assume that someone was there waiting for me. She wasn't stupid.

"If you would like to, you can," she announced. She smiled at me and I just shook my head. "I like the chase." I didn't move or make any motion. She just liked it when I talked back. It excited her. If I was compliant, I could fool her and she wouldn't get as much enjoyment out of it. Maybe she would leave me alone. "I see that my Agent wasn't lying to me about your period." She kicked at my leg and I was able to see a blood stain on the floor. I immediately blushed red and knew that it had run through my pants overnight. "Clean it up," she instructed. My eyebrows crinkled, but with my moment of hesitation, she reacted. "I said to clean it up." She grabbed me by my hair and immediately pushed my face to the ground. I groaned a little and I regretted it. She would like to hear me struggle and I didn't want to give her that satisfaction.

How did she expect me to clean this up? She didn't provide me with any cleaning materials. With my body immobile, I won't be able to clean it up anyway. Did she want me to fight her so that I can clean it? I don't think I even cleaned when I was at home. It doesn't seem like I would. Or would I?

"Do I have to tell you more than once?"

I cried out in pain when I felt her nails scratch my back. I couldn't imagine the skin under my nails from doing that, but I also couldn't imagine seeing what these scratches look like. She dug in at the top of my back and slowly sank them in until she was dragging them to my lower back. I grunted, but it was better than me screaming. I wanted to, but I couldn't give her what she wanted me to do. I didn't want to satisfy her, but how could I?

I brushed my hands over the blood spot on the floor. It was gross and felt gross to do it, but she eased the tension on my back. I immediately wiped my hands onto my pants and felt her release more pressure on me. When I saw more of the blood on the floor, I wiped at it again and when it was finally cleaned up, she got off of me. I stayed on the ground, though, because my back was stinging from her nails. She may not be as strong as some of the male Agents, but she knew how to use what she had.

I will give her that point.

"We have a little different procedure when girls get their periods," she mentioned. She walked around the perimeter of the room and I watched her. She wasn't moving toward me so I felt my body relax a bit. I know I shouldn't have, but I've been liking the peacefulness I've had with Ellis. I shouldn't trust anybody here. I had to keep reminding myself that they were criminals.

My mom was probably looking for me.

Right?

I didn't have time to react when I heard Bri run toward me. She already had my pants halfway down my legs before ripping them off of me and before I could react. I immediately crawled back to get them from her, but she waved them above her head like she was waving a flag. I felt the anger in me boil as I tried to get them back. She taunted me with them by waving them in my face and then reaching them up high. I didn't want to waste my energy, but the clothing I wear makes me feel safe. This was the one thing that I needed. I would not let her take them away from me.

"Do you want these back?" she teased. I looked up at her for a second and as she lowered them, I jumped up. I grabbed them by the pant leg and she tried grabbing them back. She wrapped her hand around it to try and get a better grip on it, but she struggled. Every time she opened her hand, that was my chance to get them off of her. "Give up now," she warned me.

I immediately kicked at the back of her knees and she stumbled down. She put her arms out to stop her and she cried out in pain. I whipped the pants off of her and immediately brought them up to my chest. She turned around and I saw fire in her eyes. However, I also saw that her one hand was weak. She clutched it to her chest and she winced whenever she thought about it. These pants were going to be the death of one of us. She charged at me to grab them from me, but I protected it with my body. She slammed against me and threw both of our bodies against the wall. My face smacked the side and I was dizzy for a second, but I was not letting her get these pants.

"Leave me alone!" I yelled.

She struggled with me and I could tell that she was losing grip because of her weak hand. With her body pressed against me, she managed to get her knee on the back of my legs so that I couldn't move them. I winced in pain, but she shoved her body harder against mine. She attempted to grab the pants by clawing at my hands, but I wasn't giving up. I felt the burn and sting from her scratches, but I didn't want to let go. She fought me for a second before pausing. I didn't let my guard down though.

Instead, she yanked at my underwear. I started yelling and lashed out at her. I turned around and my fist hit her across the face. She was stunned for a minute, but now that I was facing her, she pinned me against the wall by my throat. It was just to hold me there, but when I was still fighting her for my pants and underwear, she applied pressure to it. I felt myself beginning to loosen my grip on my underwear and my pants. I dropped them from my hands and she smirked at me. She loosened her pressure just a bit so that I could breathe, but not enough that I could breathe well. My movements started getting groggy and I brought my hand up to her arm. I started scratching her back, but it didn't seem to have an effect on her.

"Give up now," she warned. I nodded my head for a second and she laughed at me. Once released, I fell to the ground and gasped for air. I needed to know how to defend myself against her. I needed to know how to defend myself against being choked. She laughed again and I watched as Ellis came into the room as well. Bri handed him my pants and underwear, but I wasn't listening to what else she said. He took her by the arm and escorted her out of there. I felt the vibration of the door being slammed shut and allowed myself to cry.

I felt so naked.

I was naked.

My lower half was naked.

I immediately turned my back to my door. If anybody tried to open it, I would be able to hear it. The door creaked open and scraped against the top. It was a loud noise which is why I'm surprised I didn't wake up when she came into my room this morning. I was too comfortable before. Maybe that was Ellis's job. He needed to make me feel safe and comfortable so I would be caught off-guard when Bri or the leader came around. So that I would be weak.

I was weak regardless. I didn't have the training they did. I was fit at one point, but that was when I was getting regular exercise in, eating normally, and having a sleep schedule. At my prime, I may have been able to take down Bri, but since I have been abused and treated like a rat, I would never win against her. Now that I'm having my period, I am even weaker. The insides of my uterus were killing me and I was constantly wanting to throw up. I wanted to lay in my bed all day with a heating pad, pain reliever, and some blankets surrounding me. Instead, I was naked with blood dripping on me, on a cold surface, and anybody could come and see me.

When I listened to the door open again, I immediately flung around so I could see the door. I tried my best to stretch out the shirt I was in so it covered me, but I wasn't sure how well that was working. When Ellis popped his head in, I kept my guard up as he walked closer to me. I could see that he kept eye contact with me as he moved closer and I appreciated it. That didn't stop me from having my doubts though. I was becoming soft again because of him. He showed me that he had a rope for my arms and I nodded my head no. I kept my hands holding on tightly to my shirt and refused to let them move. He shook his head at me and wrapped his fingers around my wrist. He tugged gently and I immediately swung at him. He grabbed at the wrist and I felt myself beginning to panic. He shushed me and I felt tears brimming in the corner of my eyes.

"It's okay," he whispered. He focused on the rope on my arm and when he let go of me, I brought it back to pull my shirt down. He gently grabbed the other wrist, but I smacked him across the face. He blinked for a second and looked at me with a gentle expression. Through the tears in my eyes, I could see that he wasn't mad at me. In fact, he looked like he pitied me. "Please?" He tried again and although I didn't hit him, he had a harder time getting my fingers off of my shirt. He pressed on multiple knuckles until there was too much pain. I winced for a second, but he managed to get my hands tied together.

I tried holding my shirt down, but he lifted me up by the rope around my wrists. My arms widened at the motion and I realized that he could kill me if he wanted to. He was strong enough to lift me like a doll. What else was he capable of? I didn't have time to think before he started walking me outside of the door. I eventually started walking too and within a few seconds, we were outside of the bathroom that I had used previously.

It only took me a few seconds.

Before it had taken about ten minutes.

What was this guy's ploy?

I closed the door as much as I was allowed before rushing to the toilet. I could use this time to clean myself up, but I knew I needed this time to think. I needed to start noting the other doors; were they open or closed, if it looked like a door to the outside world, where the stairs were, and how long the hallways were. I needed to start thinking about the route to get out of here. The longer I was here, the more I was forgetting. I was getting used to being in here and I was starting to not want to leave. They were treating me far better than my other two other groups - besides Bri. There were fewer guards. Less surveillance. I wasn't as tortured here. Or was I?

"You have five minutes," Ellis told me. I watched him, but he didn't turn back to take a peek. Something was off about him. I couldn't put my finger on it though. His demeanor changed when nobody else was around. When Bri was around, he obeyed her orders, but he didn't take joy in doing them. He showed himself to be more of a person when I was alone with him. I couldn't tell if that was his ploy or not. Why did he show me Chad and Emmanuel? Why did he tell me his name?

I stopped my thoughts and forced myself to clean

up. This was my one chance to get clean and I shouldn't waste it. This was disgusting and it was so humiliating. I knew that me being humiliated was the entire point. I knew, if given the chance, I would beg to get underwear, pants, tampons, or pads. It was humiliating and while I have never thought about it before, I realized just how lucky I was to be able to have those things before. I was so desperate for them now that I would do whatever it took. I would steal them. I would hurt someone for them. I would do anything to stop being humiliated.

I tapped the guard on the shoulder to let him know that I was finished and ready. He started walking without looking at me and I walked slowly along too. I tugged at my shirt again as we walked, but he didn't look at me during the short trip. When I got into my room, he closed the door and I put my hands through the hole for him. He fiddled with the rope until my wrists were undone and I quickly put them back in my room. He stood a distance away from the door and I moved my body to the little corner that I liked. I turned my back to it again and laid down.

My back hurt from the scratches I had endured from Bri, but the coldness of the ground helped soothe them. I could only imagine what I had looked like. From what the scratches felt like, I assumed that most of them were bright pink and inflamed. However, I knew that some had dug too deep in my skin and probably looked like actual cuts instead. Those were the ones that were making it hard for me to move. They stung and I felt

                    AMY KULP

myself wince every time I moved. I had to settle for laying on my side. It still hurt, but it didn't feel nearly as bad as my back did.

After a while, I even found it comfortable enough to fall asleep in that position. It was a restless sleep though. I woke up every hour to my back crying out in pain and then I would try to turn over, but feel the excruciating stings from the scratches. It was like I couldn't win where I was sleeping. I eventually woke up for good when I heard a harsh knock on my door. I panted from the nightmare that I was having and it took me a couple of minutes to see that my door was about to be open.

I now had to worry about who was coming in that door. I still wanted to be prepared for anyone, but if it was Ellis, I wouldn't have to worry too much. If it was Bri, I would need to prepare to fight. I immediately looked at the ground I was on and started wiping away any blood that was on the floor. She would not hurt me for the cleanliness of my room now. I was even one second ahead of them as they opened the door. While Bri was in my room, I didn't expect Chad to be too. I saw Ellis still standing in the doorway and was confused for a minute.

Chad's eyes flickered down to my body, but immediately back up. I felt myself tug at my shirt again to try to keep it down past my thighs, but it didn't work. He looked at Bri and then back at me. There seemed to be some sort of disconnect because he stared straight ahead. He didn't try to talk to me or signal me about anything. I could see that he was walking with a limp now, but every other part of his body seemed to be normal. His face was recognizable. His hair was recognizable. He still looked like the boy I knew a couple of months ago.

Bri was different though. Her attitude was a little lower than it was yesterday and it was because of the sling and cast she had on her hand. I stared at the bright green thing and saw a couple of signatures on it. As I looked closer, I noticed that they were names from people in our school. She still went to school? Does that mean we are close to school?

"I see you did some cleaning," Bri noted as she looked at the floor around me. I didn't nod my head in case this was a test. I understood why she had Chad with her now. Since she had that cast on her, she would not be able to grip me as much as yesterday. Yesterday she was even struggling with it. "Do you see any blood on the floor?" She turned to Chad and he hesitated a moment. Bri adjusted her footing and I watched him flinch. It was so severe that I was able to notice it.

What did she do to him? He looked around the ground and his eyes stayed focused on a spot for more than a second. I reacted by looking at it as well and if Bri hadn't noticed his stare, she did see me stare. Her eyes locked on a smear on the ground and when I looked back at Chad, his eyes were trained on the wall. When I looked at Bri, I only had enough time to see the smirk on her face. She clonked me with the cast and put her full body weight on me.

                    AMY KULP

"I'm sorry!" I yelled as my face was pressed to the floor. "I'll clean it up!" I started crying as she pressed my face harder into the floor. She mumbled under her breath how she wanted me to clean it up, but I started screaming and yelling for her to stop. "Don't make me do this!" She pressed my face harder into the floor and I had to turn my head so that my nose wasn't cracked from the pressure. I cried as she pressed harder and kept telling me she knew what I wanted. "Please!" I yelled as she put more pressure on the back of my neck. I felt like I could throw up from the pressure she had on my head and neck.

"Help me!" Bri demanded. I attempted to hit her off of me but felt hands wrapping around anything that was hitting her. She smeared my face on the floor and I felt myself continue to cry. "It will do for now," she growled at me. The pressure was let off of me, but I stayed on the floor. "Next time, you will do as you are ordered, Y." She kicked my legs and I tried to listen if she was still in the room. "Take her to her new assignment. Let's go Chad."

I listened for a few minutes while shoes were shuffling around. When a few minutes had passed in silence, I felt a slight tap on my shoulders. I refused to get up as I felt the tears still running down my cheeks. Maybe it mixed with the blood that was on the floor and it washed off. I could wish that, right? Ellis steadied my body and gently flipped me over so that I was laying on my back. He came close to my face and I watched as he grimaced for a second. He carefully and gently wiped the tears and blood off with his gloved hands. I forced myself to stop crying from the humiliation and he placed the glove in his pocket. He smiled at me before putting the ropes around my wrists. He tugged gently for me to get going and had to tug hard to get me moving.

He took me to the stairwell and I immediately started fearing for my safety as he walked me downwards. He didn't flinch or say anything to me and I could tell that he was frazzled. His body posture was straight once again and although he showed compassion to me by cleaning me up, his face was rigid. He didn't show any caring towards me as he led me down the stairs. Were there cameras here? Why were his emotions suddenly changing again?

I looked at the ceilings as we passed and tried searching for anything that might be a camera. What if it was disguised as something else? I have never seen a security camera that I can remember. What if it looked like an everyday item? I immediately put my head down as we were walking because I didn't want my face to be on those cameras. But maybe I did. Would people be able to hack into a camera?

I shook my head at the thought. I had to be close to home if Bri was constantly going to school to get enough signatures. I recognized some of them - besides Chad's and Emmanuel's. I saw Oliver's name. I saw Holli's name. I saw some girls' names that seemed familiar to me. I couldn't pinpoint where I knew the names from though, but they seemed familiar. If I was close to home, that would give me more courage to actually try and get home. I could possibly escape this nightmare.

However, now that I was going somewhere I wasn't familiar with, I had to start all over again. I had to think about exits, entrances, and how to get out. As I looked around, there weren't any windows. There weren't any doors either. It was a long hallway and Ellis stopped sooner than I thought he would. I bumped into him and he just let out a slight sigh. I heard a buzzer and then the door in front of us slid open.

This was new.

I felt the strain on my wrists as I refused to move forward. Ellis looked back at me, but he motioned me forward. He had a job to do even if he didn't want to. The tug on my wrists wasn't malicious, but it was hard. I winced at the pain and eventually kept up with him. He stopped at the end of the hall and waited until I came up behind him. He stared into the room and I felt self-conscious as the door was clear. I could see clearly in there and there didn't look like any hiding spots. As Ellis took the ropes off of my arms, he didn't have to fight me from running. The door that we had come through had already closed. He looked at me from the corners of his eyes before shielding the keypad to insert his code. When the door opened, I stood mesmerized.

This was technology I haven't encountered yet.

Ellis stepped foot in the room first, but I refused to. I didn't know how to get out of a room like this. There wasn't a window except for the door itself. If I even got out of the door, I wouldn't be able to get out of this hallway. I should've looked in the other rooms to see if there were other people waiting like me. I just stared at the ground when coming in. I was surprised. By now, Ellis was staring at me and this was the first time he had looked me in the eyes. His jaw was set in a line and I knew that he was getting upset with me.

He patted his legs as if that would encourage me to come into the cell. I shook my head and backed away from him. He put a finger up to his mouth to indicate to me to be quiet. I watched intently as he pointed up to something mounted on the wall. I tried not to stare too long at it, but I was curious. It wasn't something I have ever seen before. He motioned towards his eyes and his ears and I knew that someone was watching and listening. He patted his knees again for me to come closer, but why would I want to be trapped in that room with him? He was the nicest out of the Agents, but he was still an Agent. I couldn't trust him. I stepped away again and he looked up at the camera again.

"I don't want to hurt you," he whispered.

I had to try.

I immediately started running towards where the door was. I knew that it was locked, but maybe I could type in his passcode and escape. As I ran towards the door from which we came from, I looked for a keypad on the wall but couldn't find one. I heard Ellis huff under his breath and I knew that he would be with me at any moment. I touched every part of the door to see if there was a trick to it but knew that there wasn't. It was probably controlled by whoever was watching and listening to us. I turned around and stared at the camera for a moment before Ellis grabbed me by my arms. He was a lot rougher this time and I didn't blame him.

He typed the passcode in on the keypad and when it opened this time, he shoved both of us in there. While I wasn't afraid of him before, I was afraid of him now. He shoved me to the floor and he towered over me. When the door closed behind us, I cursed under my breath and stared up at him. Was he trapped in here with me? I didn't see anything to let him out of here either. His face started turning purple from holding his breath and he let out a monstrous yell. My eyes grew big and I felt myself cowering in the corner. I would not be able to take him if he hurt me here. My best bet was to just listen and do as he asked.

"Listen to me," he whispered. His face looked like it was in pain as he continued to come closer to me. "With that door closed, they cannot hear us." He subtly made a gesture toward the camera and I was able to see a light shining from it now. Was it purposely pointing towards this room? "They can see us though."

"Why are you telling me this?" I asked fearfully. My chin began quivering and I knew that I might cry. He was scaring me. This is why I don't trust anyone here. They may seem like they are on my side, but I have to remember that he is not. He is a bad guy. I cannot trust

him.

I cannot trust Chad.

I cannot trust Emmanuel.

I don't even know if I could trust myself at this point.

"I am going to be the only interaction you see until you are off your period." He paused and hit the wall beside me. "Unless Bri decides to make an appearance." He paused again and kicked at the air. "When you are off your period, you will meet the leader." He shook his head and I saw the fear in his eyes. He kicked in the air again and even though he hasn't touched me yet, I still flinched. "You will be by yourself most of the day." He straightened his back and turned away from me. "Do something to keep yourself sane."

"And if I don't?" I wondered. He shook his head and I listened to the door open. He walked out and the camera stopped pointing towards my room. He shook his head again and walked away. I couldn't hear if he had left the entire hallway, but I felt my nerves get the better of me.

I wanted to know what this leader did that had everyone so scared. I wanted to know what Ellis was doing when he was punching the air next to me and kicking nothing. I wanted to know why I needed to keep myself sane. I am left alone most of the day regardless. I think I could manage another day.

Besides, I watched as he had put in the passcode to get out of my room. I knew how to get out of my room.

I just needed to know how to get out of the hallway. I needed to know how to avoid that camera as well. There had to be blind spots. All cameras had them, right?

I just hoped that I would remember that passcode. I barely remembered my mantra anymore. All I know is that my name is Emily Washington and I think I have a mom that loves me.

Right?

Chapter 20 --------------------------------

When I heard creaking from outside of my room, my eyes shot open. I picked the crust from my eyelashes and whipped my body around. I immediately regretted that as I felt some of the skin rip open from the scratches on my back. I flinched, but I had to react. Without thinking about who it might be, I scoured the floor for any bloodstains. When I saw some, I immediately took my shirt sleeves and wiped them off. I was not going to be forced to try and lick it up. Her torture was repulsive. When my door opened, I pulled my shirt down to try and cover my lower half before recognizing who it was.

Ellis looked at me as I stared back. He kept his back to the camera and I watched as the light scanned the entire room - not just my cell. Was it possible that nobody was there today and it was automated? As the lights left us, he dropped something on the ground for me, quickly turning around afterwards and leaving the door open. I waited a couple of minutes and saw the light scan my room again before switching back. I listened carefully to see if Ellis was out there, but when I heard the hallway door slide closed, I knew he had left.

I looked at the item on the ground, but I wasn't able to see what it was. I looked over at the camera as it did another rotation and waited for it to turn away from my room. I darted for the object when the camera's light swiveled away from me, but made sure to go back to my original position when it swung back around. I put the item underneath my thighs so that nobody could see it. If he was trying to keep it secret, it had to be a secret, right? I slowly slumped my posture so I could turn away from the light. They wouldn't be able to see it if I was blocking the view with my body.

I pulled the item from my thighs and inspected it for a second. I was surprised as I unwrapped the item and noticed that it was a tampon. I had never used one before, but I knew the basics of how to insert it. How would I do that without the light seeing me do it? I quickly placed the tampon inside of my bra and rolled back around.

My door was still open. Was that a coincidence? I got on my feet and peeked my head around my wall. I forgot about the light for a second before it blinded my eyes. If I was already going to get in trouble, I might as well make it worth it. Peeking in the hallway, I saw that the door to be let out was still secure. As I looked around, however, I noticed that one of the other rooms was open.

Was this a trap?

I slowly walked over to it and saw that there was a very small bathroom in there. The light still shined in from the camera, but I could clean myself up and put the tampon in in a short amount of time. I took the opportunity, and, when I was ready, I opened the wrapper. Where would I stash this now? I crumpled it into a ball and hoped that nobody would clean the area until I was out of there. I didn't want to get myself in trouble. The scratches on my back were still healing.

My thoughts turned to Ellis.. Was this a trap? Or was he trying to help me? If he was trying to help me, that would mean that I am not supposed to have this. If it was a trap, I already used it and the harm was done. I quickly hid the string so that it wouldn't be seen and turned around to flush the toilet.

I had no idea how to flush this toilet. I looked around for a handle or pedal before giving up. I was their prisoner. If anything, they could have the authority to flush it themselves. As I stood in the doorway to the small bathroom, I watched as the light took a couple of seconds to turn around and scan each room before coming back to the one I was in.

One second.
Two seconds.
Three seconds.
Four seconds.
Five seconds.
Six seconds.
Seven seconds.
Eight seconds.
Nine seconds.
Ten seconds.

It took ten seconds for it to come back to the start. I would have to remember that. I exited the bathroom and took my time getting back to my room. What were in these other rooms? The two near the bathroom seemed similar to the room I was in. However, other rooms had different things in them. I tried the code that I watched Ellis punch in and was relieved when it worked for these rooms as well. The door unlocked and I slowly made my way in to look around.

The first room had a filing cabinet hidden in the corner. I tried all of the drawers, but unfortunately they were all locked. I wasn't sure how to break into one either. I tried rocking it, but it felt too heavy for me to move. I slammed my body against it to see if I could sway it, but knew my luck was up. I didn't have any strength for it. I scurried out of the room but was stunned to see Bri standing there with Emmanuel.

She had a smirk on her face.

He stood with a blank expression and was staring at the wall. He wouldn't make eye contact with me, but I couldn't stop staring at him. His hair was growing in, but it was patchy. Why wouldn't they just shave it off? He looked better, but I could still see the bruises that covered his eyes and I could still see some scars from the cuts he had. This was confirmation that the person I had seen before, the person I couldn't recognize, was Emmanuel.

"I'm getting bored of yelling and hurting you," Bri mentioned. I looked at her in surprise, but she looked at Emmanuel. "I want him to do it." As Emmanuel stepped closer to me, I saw the fear on his face. His eyes looked like he didn't want to do it, but he didn't try to disobey his orders. "Do what you want, but I want her crying."

I immediately ran from him as he started charging

toward me. All of the clear doors that were open before were now shut. I only had this hallway to run around in. Was there any point in me trying to escape what was going to come? Maybe if I just faked my crying, I would be let off the hook. As I ran to the end of the hall, I turned around and faced him. He shoved into me and we both hit the wall. The breath was knocked out of me, but Emmanuel was still raring to go. I immediately started blubbering as he put pressure on my back. While it did hurt, it wasn't enough to make me wail as much as I was. I wasn't sure what he was doing at first, but I slowly began to realize that he was opening old wounds. The scratches that were healing were now being nicked open with his fingernails. It stung and I felt something oozing out of the scratches. Blood? Puss maybe?

"Get her steady!" Bri yelled. I wasn't sure where she was placed in the room, but it sounded more distant than I was used to. Emmanuel stopped scraping my back and laid his entire body onto mine. "This should be fun," she said as she got closer to us. I attempted to hit and kick, but he weighed most of me down. My knees were locked from kicking up and he pressed his shoes into them so they were digging into the ground. I could see her in the corner of my eye now and she crouched down so that she could see me. "Layout her hand." I fought with Emmanuel on this, but he was eventually able to claw my fingers open. He applied pressure onto my hand to stay flat and I hesitantly watched as Bri came closer to me. "You have her under control?" she asked.

                                   AMY KULP

"Yes ma'am."

That didn't sound like Emmanuel. His voice was flat and quiet as he spoke to her. It sounded like he was now afraid of her unlike before. Instead of being loud and jolly, it was now quiet and stern. He sounded like he was trying to gain attention from the surrounding areas or like he was about to announce that I was being pranked. What happened to him that he was scared of her?

I heard a small clicking from her hands and I was able to move my head far enough to my side to see that she was carrying nail clippers. I was confused at first, but once she started applying pressure to my nail, I knew she wasn't just giving me a trim. I immediately started fighting Emmanuel off of me, but my efforts didn't do me any good. She stuck the end of the nail clip underneath my fingernail and started pulling it up. I tried to fidget my hand from underneath Emmanuel's, but he was strong. I could see that he was fighting over whether to let me go, but his loyalties were to Bri. I shrieked louder as I felt the tearing of my fingernail.

The pulling.

Tears were streaming down my face as I begged for her to stop. As I begged for Emmanuel to let me go. I shrieked for forgiveness and caved to give them whatever they wanted. The pain didn't stop though. She kept pulling. She kept tearing my fingernail away from my finger until it was gone. She twisted and broke it as she pulled and I could feel the blood. I could feel it being ripped out of me. I have never felt so much pain before.

"Please!" I begged. When she finally got the nail off of me, I collapsed. I let my body lay underneath Emmanuel's without trying to fight him or her. I was happy because my torture was done. At least that's what I thought until she went for another finger. I immediately tried to knock the clippers out of her hand, but she only laughed at me. "Please stop. I'll do anything!" I begged. She stuck the clippers under my fingernail again and I cried once more for her to stop. As she began tugging at it, my crying began again. I started blubbering and was hoping that Emmanuel would come to his senses and get off of me. Or help me.

"What are you doing down here?"

I immediately felt the tug of my nail stop and felt Emmanuel's bodyweight lift off of me. I stayed on the ground and closed my eyes as I held onto the finger that was missing the nail. I didn't want to look at it. I could feel the blood on it and knew that it had bled quite a bit. It was sensitive to movement and it stung against the air. What could I do for it though? I closed my eyes and tried to apply pressure to it. It was throbbing and so was the other finger that was starting to be pulled by Bri. What kind of monster was she?

"You know our orders." I listened to the chaos around me and hoped that nobody would touch me. "Only you and I are to see her. Take Emmanuel back to his cell before someone in the control room reports back that you brought him in here."

"Change your codes," Bri ordered back. "She has

access to all of these rooms because of your careless mistakes." I heard a thump and without warning, I was being pulled by my hair.

I let out more cries and with my good hand, I tried to stop the hand from pulling any hair out of my head. I was dragged across the room until I heard the keypad. I knew that I was being placed back into my cell so I started crying from relief. Maybe I would be left alone now. I was placed in there and immediately opened my eyes when I heard the door close again. I was in here by myself. However, I saw another tampon on the ground and quickly grabbed it to hide it away from Bri and Emmanuel. As I looked out, I saw Ellis, Bri, and Emmanuel. I couldn't hear what was being said, but I could tell that Ellis and Bri were arguing. Emmanuel stayed distant, but when I realized he saw the tampon, he focused his eyes on the wall.

I didn't understand the dynamic here. Was Bri or Ellis in charge? While she has been giving him the orders in the past, he was the one to yell at her today. Were they equal in their leadership? I wasn't sure, but when he was yelling, he seemed like he was afraid for himself. Was he in charge of making sure he and Bri only had contact with me? What was going to happen if he failed his mission? There was no way that he was above Bri. Back when I was being transported, he didn't hold any rank there. Chad held more rank there.

How did he gain it so quickly?

When my door opened again, I started yelling for

help. I started pleading for someone not to hurt me and cried out when I watched them step closer to me. Why can't they just leave me alone? What did I do to deserve this? I was immediately hushed as he kneeled closer to me. I heard him whispering and shushing and I found that I was getting quieter, but I was still in pain. I was still crying. I was still going to be left without the marks.

"Let me help you." I felt his hand start pushing up my shirt and I instinctively moved away from him. "Let me see." I shook my head no and turned around to face him. He grimaced for a second as I slapped his hands away. He flinched slightly and got off the ground when the security camera started spinning towards my room. Someone was now in the control room. "I will be back with food." He got up without touching me again but kept eye contact with me. "I have orders to feed you once a day and you may use the bathroom once a day." He eyed the tampon I had under my hand but didn't say anything else about it.

Once he was gone, I watched as the light began to swivel around the room again. I counted to ten seconds before breathing out. If it was spinning, did that mean nobody was there? Or did they only focus it when an Agent was in my room? Did they not trust them? I wouldn't. Chad and Emmanuel are on my side. They were two trusted Agents and now they're here being tortured like me. Although I guess now Emmanuel is on their side again. I don't know about Chad though.

As it became darker in my room, every time the

light passed me, I looked at my finger again. It was still bleeding. Although the amount of blood had gone down since it first was ripped off. It was becoming increasingly irritated from the dirtiness of my environment and my body. Every time I rolled over, I could feel that the scratches that Emmanuel reopened were swelling too. Maybe they would get infected and I would die. That would be so much better than having to stay here.

I heard my door open again and turned back around to face Ellis. He had a styrofoam bowl in his hand and tried to hand it to me. I flinched at how he was rapidly moving around me and when he noticed, he slowed down. He put the bowl on the floor and stepped away. I stared at him for a minute before reaching for it. I was too starved and hungry to refuse it. I just had to make sure he wasn't going to harm me while I was eating. When I grabbed the bowl, I moved it hastily to my corner and watched as some of the contents spilled out of it. I grimaced at my carelessness.

It was soup. Cold soup, but still soup. I watched Ellis out of the corner of my eye as I brought the bowl up to my mouth. I slurped it down quickly and felt my stomach turn. It started making uncontrollable noises and I found myself coughing. My throat felt like it was on fire and I couldn't get the itch out of my throat. I threw the bowl at Ellis so he wouldn't come near me and my coughs became so powerful that I had to get on my hands and knees so that I wouldn't lose my balance. My vision was starting to get blurry and I was dizzy. As the room spun around me, I closed my eyes so I didn't feel like I was twirling in a hurricane.

"What did you do to me?" I yelled at him. I felt the pressure building in my stomach and opened my mouth to let up the vile that was escaping up my throat. I felt my body begin to sweat as I continued throwing up the soup on the floor. After it was all out, I felt myself continuing to gag. I wanted it all out - my insides and outsides were hurting now. When my stomach calmed down, I felt my arms give out. I landed on the floor with a thud and felt the mushiness ooze into my hair. As if the physical torture wasn't enough. Now I had to be humiliated by the smell.

I looked around my room when I calmed down and noticed that Ellis was no longer in my room. I wasn't sure when he left, but he did it soundlessly. I closed my eyes to try and sleep, but as I lay there I started smelling my bile. Or was it me now? I couldn't just accept this. I tried to move but felt the stomachache that I was having and felt my dizziness appear once I stood up. I trudged towards my door and watched the camera.

One second.
Two seconds.
Three seconds.
Four seconds.
Five seconds.
Six seconds.
Seven seconds.
Eight seconds.

Nine seconds.

Ten seconds.

I hesitantly pushed on the top of the glass door until a keypad appeared. I punched in the code that I knew from earlier and exhaled gleefully when it was accepted. The door opened and I chased the light as fast as I could. From how it was constantly moving around the room, I knew that someone wasn't in the control room. If they were, they weren't paying attention and moving the camera to find me. They would have seen that I was out of my room already. I walked over to the room with the toilet and put the code in there as well.

They didn't have a sink in this room, but the toilet had water in it. Was I this desperate? I looked into it to see if it was previously flushed and was relieved to see it was. I bit my lip and bent down in front of it. This was it. Did I want to do this? I thought about it for an additional second before deciding that the smell was too much for me. I dunked my hair in the water and tried rinsing it as quietly as I could. When I felt like it was efficient, I rang out my hair so it wasn't dripping before grabbing my spare tampon that was in my bra. Once clean, I hobbled back to the hallway before noticing that the light was still just swiveling.

Did I just want to go back in? Or did I want to investigate again? I bit my lip and stared at the camera for a little too long before I went back to my room. I forced myself to lay down and felt the pain all around my body.

My back with the scratches.

My finger from the absence of a nail.

Past bodily harm.

My throat from the burn of the bile.

My stomach from whatever was in that soup.

Couldn't they just kill me at this point? I had nothing left. I didn't have any self-respect. I didn't know where I was. I didn't know what month it was. Hell, I didn't even know if it was the same year. The only thing I had was my name. They were still trying to take that away from me as well.

All I knew is that I was Emily Washington. I am Y.

****

"Just let me help you."

"Get the fuck away from me," I growled back. He stayed in the other corner of my room and stared at me as I glared daggers at him. "I don't want any help from you." I covered my arms around myself and stared at the ground. We remained quiet and motionless. After about five minutes, I watched as he pulled something from his pocket and tossed it on the ground towards me. My eyebrows raised and I swiped it with my foot. I placed it under my bra effortlessly but remained stone-faced to keep up my act. I was scared shitless right now so I'm glad that my terror was interpreted as an attitude instead. Ellis reached in his pocket again and slid a granola bar at me. I stared at it for a second before gliding it back to

                    AMY KULP

him.

"It's unopened." He slid it back and I crinkled the packaging under my hand before putting it behind my back. "I didn't know they poisoned the soup yesterday. I'm sorry."

Poison.

They poisoned me.

"I wouldn't have given it to you if I knew."

"Why?" I stared at him and he seemed shocked for a minute. "Why do you care if I'm poisoned or not?" I saw some emotion flash across his face, but when I looked again, it was gone. He looked over at the camera and sat down on the floor with me. Directly across from me.

"They would never put enough poison in to kill you." He shook his head and looked at me. "Just to torture you. I didn't join this place to play games. I want my hands dirty." I stared at him for a second before deciding that I didn't believe him. He barely did anything physical to me. I doubt that he would be the one to want to kill people. I honestly doubt he would have done this willingly. Nobody does this willingly.

"You want to kill people, but you're here with hydrogen peroxide to help my cuts?" I asked. He didn't answer except to question me.

"Can I?"

I stared at him again. He opened his jacket again to reveal his band-aids, wraps, and various skin ointments and sprays. I shook my head. What did I have to lose? I was already poisoned. I was already beaten. I was already tortured. I already lost my friends. I already lost my family. I already lost everything close to me. I agreed and he cautiously walked toward me. Not too fast, but not too slow. He knew that I didn't react well to fast-paced things.

"I need you to watch the cameras," he noted. He crouched down beside me and kept his back to it. It was just swiveling right now. "If it starts pointing towards us, I have to look like I'm hurting you." He set down his supplies on my legs and fake punched me. "Or else I'll be tortured too."

I wanted to give a snippy response but decided against it. Did he think I cared what happened to him? He did this to me. He was the reason I wasn't out of here. He was the reason I wasn't dead. He was the reason I couldn't remember anything about my past. He was the reason I was alive. He was the reason I didn't get tortured more. He was the reason I ate. He was the reason I didn't have to worry about blood getting everywhere. He stopped me from getting numerous beatings from Bri because of the tampons. He let me see Chad and Emmanuel when they were hurt. He was the reason I was able to stop worrying about them. He had done a lot of good for me, but I wasn't sure that they outweighed the bad.

At least I could finally understand why he was fake-punching the air when I was first placed in this room. He was doing it to give an illusion to the cameras. From their view, it probably looked like he was hitting and kicking me. He probably had them all fooled about it too. This guy was smarter than I thought he was. That

                    AMY KULP

scared me though. Was I falling into his trap? What if that wasn't hydrogen peroxide? What if it was some chemical to burn me even more?

"Wait," I whispered. I looked at the bottle he was holding and looked back at him. He stopped as I asked, but I wasn't sure if he was going to do the next task. "Pour that on one of your cuts first." He put the bottle down and raveled up his sleeve to show off a nasty, crusty scar. I shook my head for a second before he pointed to a smaller, deeper cut. I grimaced as he poured it over and watched as the white bubbles appeared. He pulled his sleeve back down and held up the bottle to me again. I nodded my head and he placed his hands on me.

They were tentative. He wasn't sure if he was allowed to touch me or if I would try to hurt him. I looked at him and did as he asked. I turned onto my stomach and moved my shirt up. I gave myself enough privacy to feel comfortable and he gasped as he took sight of it. I didn't want to know what was so reaction-worthy, but he let me know. My back was mutilated. Past beatings from Chad hadn't healed properly. Bri's scratches were on top of them and they were infected. When Emmanuel had opened them back up, the grime under his nails had gotten into those scratches. I couldn't imagine looking at them.

"This is going to burn."

He hesitated before pouring it on my back. I wasn't sure if he just doused me or if he was pouring the worst places, but I felt the pain. I knew not to scream. Instead, I bit my tongue and felt the metallic taste in my mouth. I couldn't help but make some sort of groan as he continued. I closed my eyes and waited for the sting to go down. I could hear the little sizzling from the back and stopped him from pouring anymore on my back.

"I can't continue," I whined. I shook my head at him and while he smiled, he didn't listen. I winced again and closed my eyes until the pain subsided.

"I'm not very good with this."

"Why are you helping me?" I ask as he applies slight pressure to my back. I have no idea what he's doing, but I let him continue. From what he just said, I doubt he knew what he was doing. I opened my eyes to look at what he was thinking, but his face was blank.

"I'm saving my ass," he mentioned. He shook his head and took his hands off of my back. "While you were in my care, only Bri and I were supposed to see you. We both knew that we could not harm you." He leaned in close to me and whispered, "I have never seen Bri torture someone." He shook his head again. "If the leader sees you harmed, I am going to be harmed."

"I'm not going to heal that fast," I mentioned. He shook his head.

"I know." He closed his eyes for a moment and opened them again in an instant. He immediately started pounding the air and that's when I realized that the light from the camera was now trained on us. I wasn't sure how long though because I was lost in my thoughts. I wasn't very helpful with this. "Pretend you're in pain," he whispered to me.

I immediately did as he asked and the light started swiveling again. Every ten seconds, I moved and pretended to cry so that the camera would pick up on me, but I wasn't sure if that was what was needed. When Ellis was done focusing on my back, he brought my fingernail so that he could see it. He grimaced and I felt the pain of it.

"Is it..?"

"It probably won't grow back to normal," he whispered. He shrugged his shoulders and dumped peroxide on it. I immediately grunted in response and he smiled at me. "I think we're all done here." I nodded my head and took my hand back into my own.

"Why are you doing this?" I asked.

"I told you, I'm saving my ass." He got away from me and stuffed everything he brought back into his pants.

"No." I shook my head and moved away from him again. Just like when he came in this morning. "A believable answer," I warned. He stood there for a minute before I heard him sigh. Was he going to tell me? Or was he going to just lie to me?

"Eat up."

He nodded at me before putting his code in the doorway. It was a different one this time, but I was still able to see it. I mentally took note of it before he left. I crinkled the granola bar before opening it up. Would this upset my stomach too? It was in the original packaging. I shook my head and ate it anyway. That seemed too genuine for him to just be helping me to save his ass.

Besides, he gave me tampons. He gave me food. He cleaned me up. He didn't need to do all of that - just one of those.

I took notice of the camera and saw how it was swiveling every ten seconds again. Was there someone there? Was that person paying attention? Did I want to take the chance? I closed my eyes for a couple of seconds before deciding to just bolt. My stomach was still a little queasy, but I was able to move around. I got on my feet before watching the light pass over me.

One second.

Two seconds.

Three seconds.

Four seconds.

Five seconds.

Six seconds.

Seven seconds.

Eight seconds.

Nine seconds.

Ten seconds.

As I emerged, I scoped out the other rooms before punching the code in for one I haven't seen before. Although I wanted to go to the filing cabinet room, I knew that I would never be able to move that thing. Unless Ellis, Bri, or Emmanuel left a key somewhere for me to get to, I would not see what was inside any of those. It was killing me to know, but I needed to check out the other rooms. Especially the room with the computer.

They couldn't be this stupid, right? They had to

know that I would have checked all of the rooms. They had to know that I would have been intrigued by a room with a computer in it. Or was this a trap? What if it wasn't a trap though? I couldn't take my chances. I plugged in the code and scattered it to the computer. The way the computer was set up meant that I was blocked from the camera light seeing me. This was a trap.

I moved the mouse and it immediately started up. The light was blinding my eyes, but it was working. It didn't seem to be a trap yet. I clicked to find the internet icon and was surprised at how easy this was. It booted up to a webpage I wasn't familiar with. I moved the cursor over the webpage button and immediately hit a mind block. What was a website I could use to tell people where I was? I sat there for one minute trying to figure out one I used to go to but was upset to realize I couldn't remember.

Maybe I could type my name in the search engine. I typed in 'missing persons' and typed Emily, but stopped. What was my last name? I hadn't thought about it for a while and if I did, I was tortured. What was my last name? At least I remembered my first name, right? Would that be enough? As I clicked enter on the computer, I watched as trillions of results appeared on the webpage. None of them looked like me.

Some of them were younger.

Some of them were older.

Where was my picture?

"Are you trying to get killed?" Bri asked. I turned

around in the chair and felt my breath leave my body. "Just restrain her." She rolled her eyes at me and Chad and Emmanuel grabbed me by my arms. "Your period should be over by now, but just in case, one of you check her tampon."

I chose not to struggle as they both grabbed ahold of my arms. I was a little stunned that Bri knew about the tampon and didn't say anything earlier. Neither of the boys was moving to look and she rolled her eyes as she came up to me. She had a little more attitude than yesterday so she must have gotten yelled at for something. Although, I didn't see a mark on her body.

"Do you think Agent E would know what a tampon was?" She sneered at me and reached herself. She inspected it before throwing it to the floor and turning away. "We're good. It's your lucky day, Y." She looked back at me with a smile and the boys brought me closer to her. "You're the first visitor in a while that the leader gets to see."

"Who was the last?" I wondered.

"Who else, but me?"

****

This was how I died. I was going through all of the torture before just to get here and meet the leader so he could personally kill me. When we walked up the flights of stairs and through useless rooms, I saw the torture devices. I saw random swords, knives, guns, and other weapons I wasn't aware of. Everything could be a weapon here. I wasn't aware of how well-equipped the place was. Why was it unprotected though? I could go into any of those rooms and just grab one of those to attack them with. Unless they were so confident in themselves that they knew I would never get to one of those rooms.

I was now placed in another dark, small room. This time, there was a table with five chairs. I was sitting in one with Emmanuel and Chad by my sides. Bri was sitting across from us and the empty chair was right next to her. I felt claustrophobic. This was the most people I had been around since I was kidnapped.

Emmanuel seemed brainwashed. He obeyed all orders Bri had given him and didn't question them. While I did see a little bit of his old personality, he never expressed it for long. His eyes wandered and his fists clenched, but he didn't do much else. I haven't heard him speak since his torture so I wasn't sure if he could speak. What if they destroyed his vocal cords? I could even see his physical torture still. His hair was still uneven, his eyes and nose were red, and there were still so many scars. He looked like Agent Ellis.

Chad seemed more human, but he didn't defer from his work. He obeyed most orders Bri had given him. He was still a little human. I saw the worry on his face and I heard it in his voice. I was still skeptical of him though. How did he get out of most of his torture? He only had a broken foot. It still wasn't fixed. It was still facing the wrong way. He would be injured for the rest of his life. He limped with me. He couldn't keep up with us as we walked. He lagged and I felt like I was dragging him. He seemed pretty useless to me.

Bri. How could she be so evil? I thought we were friends and she is fine with torturing me. How does someone become so desensitized to that stuff? Ellis has never seen her torture someone though. Was I first? Maybe she had something to prove. Why would she be at the top of the totem pole if she hadn't tortured anyone before? I had so many questions for her, but I was too afraid of her to ask. What did she mean when she said she was the last person to visit him? Did she mean in a victim sense or that she casually visits him?

What was the ranking here?

As soon as the lights turned off in the room, I grabbed at the arms of the chair I was in. Emmanuel and Chad each had a hold of my arms and I felt one of them pinch at the skin. I haven't looked at either of them since coming in here so I wasn't exactly sure who was sitting on what side of me. Why would they pinch my arm though? I didn't do anything bad.

I shook my head at the thought. These people were criminals. They did illegal things. They didn't need a reason to pinch at my arm. They didn't need a reason to do anything. If they wanted to, they could just kill me. I'm sure they would get punished, but they already broke the law. At this point, if they killed me, they would be doing me a favor. I would let them kill me.

A small glow started appearing out of the corner

of my eyes. I turned to look at a small TV set that was playing a black and white video on it from another room. I couldn't hear any audio from it and my vision was blurry, but I was able to see a distinct setting.

Our school parking lot.

As the video focused and the snow started disappearing from the sides, I was able to pinpoint myself and Chad. I looked so happy. I was smiling and holding his hand. He was smiling back at me. I looked at the sides of me to see which side was Chad and smiled innocently at him. He didn't react and kept his eyes trained on the TV. I felt a small pinch to my inner thigh and knew that it was him. I didn't know how I knew or what his pinch to my thigh meant, but I knew it was him. I watched the TV set again and watched as it transitioned into a different day.

"Do you remember when you were confused as to whether you went home with Chad?" Bri asked. I tried not to look at her, but the video was paused as she awaited my answer. I made eye contact and shook my head. "Want to know the truth?" she asked. I nodded my head again and she pressed play on the remote she had. How did I miss her having a remote? When did she get that remote? She didn't have it when we were walking the halls. Was I just oblivious to things?

The screen played as students filed out to the buses and their cars. Too many people for me to notice if Chad and I were in the mix. The scene kept replaying and as it replayed, I looked at a different student each time.

We weren't in this clip that she was playing. I looked over at Chad, but he was staring at the wall now. He squeezed my thigh again and I refocused my attention on the screen.

"Do you see it?" Bri asked. I didn't answer as I kept scouring the screen for us. I wasn't delusional. I know what Chad and I looked like. She fast-forwarded the scene to when no students were in school. Out walked Chad and me.

I did leave with him.

I knew I wasn't crazy.

"Congratulations," Bri whispered to me. She turned the TV off and sat staring at me for a few seconds. She turned the lights back on and I was temporarily blinded. "You can thank our leader for those tapes that you requested."

I immediately scrunched my eyebrows as she repeated her line. To be able to get those tapes, it would have to be someone from the school or a police officer. It was not a police officer. I haven't seen one in a long time. It was someone from the school. Someone I had requested those tapes from.

As soon as I realized the answer, I tried to get up from my chair. Chad immediately squeezed my thigh so that I couldn't escape and I sat back down. I will admit that I was painfully slow at realizing this answer and I wanted to kick myself for not realizing it first. Why was it everyone that I knew?

Was everyone I knew involved in this?

"I want you to welcome our esteemed leader into the room. We are all familiar with him and have personally worked with him on and off school premises. Y, I would like to reintroduce you to Mr. Barnett."

They must have rehearsed this because as she said his name, he pounded through the door. I remained sitting, but Bri, Emmanuel, and Chad all stood up. I felt like I was going to be ill. It was one thing for my friends and ex-boyfriends to be part of this, but now a school counselor? Specifically my school counselor?

What did I do to deserve this?

Chapter 21 ----------------------

"It's so nice to see you again, Y." I didn't move as he leaned down to hug me. Everyone's eyes were on me, but I stared straight ahead as I tried not to cry. "I still expect you to refer to me as Mr. Barnett." He sat down across from me and right next to Bri. "If I ever ask you to speak." He and Bri shared a laugh, but I could tell that Bri was more nervous than usual. "Sorry for the long wait, but I was not going to deal with all of that blood." He shuddered at the thought and looked at me more intensely. "First thing I want is a body check." He looked at Bri, Emmanuel, and Chad before zeroing on Chad. "Strip her down."

I didn't fight when Chad got up from his seat. He took me away from the table and took the rest of the clothing off of me. I didn't try to fight him and I didn't try to cover myself up. What was the point? I was supposed to be here for some reason. Everyone I knew was part of this scheme. My ex-boyfriend, my almost-was boyfriend, my best friend, and now my school counselor. Was anybody else a part of this? Was my family part of this? Was the entire student body population at school part of this?

As Chad removed my bra, I didn't think about the tampon that was underneath it until Mr. Barnett had gotten up. His creepy eyes slid up and down my body before picking it up. He inspected it for a minute before slapping me across the face. I didn't make a noise as I accepted the force against my cheek. I watched him and kept my eyes glued to him. I wasn't afraid of Chad. I wasn't afraid of Emmanuel. I wasn't even afraid of Bri at the moment. Something about Mr. Barnett had made everyone afraid of him. I was trying to figure out why.

He threw the tampon in Bri's direction and she flinched. While taking hold of the object, she put her eyes down to stare at the table and would not look at him. He hastily grabbed the back of her neck and forced her face onto the table. I watched as she struggled a bit so that she could breathe, but he didn't let up. I was afraid that her neck would snap from all of the tension he was putting on her. Eventually, she let her body take the punishment as he whispered in her ear. I couldn't hear what was said, but could only watch as she scuffled out of the room. Fear was in her eyes.

As he turned back to me, he made me spin around. I followed directions as they were given to me and when he stopped to touch my back, I couldn't help but wince. His fingers traced delicately along with my scars and I couldn't help but feel grossed out as I thought about how this was Mr. Barnett. Mr. Barnett that I had come to trust in that one session. He told me he would get the tapes and he fulfilled that promise. He fulfilled it in a sick, twisted way. I didn't care about those tapes anymore. I had honestly forgotten about wanting to see them.

"I see you let someone have fun with you," he whispered into my ear. I grimaced as his warm breath touched my ear. I never liked when people did it and even with him, it felt wrong. It was too warm and it made me feel like there was a bug crawling around in there. "Who did this to you?" he asked. I didn't answer him and I felt a slap against my back. I winced from the pain and immediately whimpered out the names. He shook his head and sat back down. I started going too, but Chad grabbed for my wrist absentmindedly. "I see we still have feelings for each other." He tsked in his seat and whisked Chad back to him. I felt myself beginning to cover up and felt insecure when his eyes flashed over my body. "I thought you said she was a fighter. It won't be fun if she doesn't put up a fight."

I was starting to get annoyed. I hate when people talk about you as if you aren't in the room. I was right here! Even if I didn't want to be. He could at least pretend to talk to me instead of to Emmanuel and Chad. They were like brainless zombies anyway. Emmanuel still hadn't talked to me. I could see that there was a part of him in there, but it was so small and fearful.

"So I'm going to tell you what's going to happen," he said, finally turning to me. He nudged his head towards the chair and I sat down as soon as I could. "You managed to break two of my best Agents into submission in favor of you." He gestured towards Emmanuel and Chad and they both put their heads down so that they were looking at the table.

"So sorry," Chad whispered under his breath.

"Yes, you'll be forgiven eventually." He looked back at me with a new gleam in his eye. "Unfortunately, I am not that forgiving to you, Y. I have had to give directions to others to brutally torture them back into submission." He gestured toward each of them and they nodded their heads in agreement. "So I expect something in return." He leaned forward in his chair and he whispered his words so slowly, that I couldn't tell if he was trying to seem powerful or if he was trying to be sexy. Either case, it didn't work. "Your virginity."

I immediately stared up at him and then at Chad and Emmanuel. Neither Chad nor Emmanuel made any movements to look at me. Mr. Barnett was smirking at me though. My eyes grew big and I felt the anger boil inside of me. This man that I was supposed to trust in a school setting was the leader of this sex trafficking ring. That was bad enough! Now I find out that he personally gets to see the girls who are virgins and takes their virginity for himself. What kind of perverted pedophile was he? How has he never gotten caught? Was he even going to school? Someone had to catch on that he was part of this. Someone had to know that he was twisted and demented like this.

"What kind of sick, perverted, pig are you?" I asked to get up. I slammed my hands on the table and he seemed shocked that I was reacting this way. He just watched me though. His demeanor didn't change when I climbed onto the table to yell in his face. He didn't react when I tried to take him by the throat. "How many girls have you done this to?"

He knew that he was protected. He knew that everyone would stand up for him because even though my hands were gripped around his throat, he remained unmoved. He looked behind me at Emmanuel and Chad and I knew that the stare he was giving was enough for them to save him. I felt their hands on my body and arms and I still tried to fight them off. I was going to die fighting him off. All of the energy that I had lost, was back with a vengeance. I wanted him to die. I wanted him to suffer as I had been. Like countless other girls had been.

"Millions," he whispered when my hands were forced off of his throat. I was forced back in the chair and Chad had his fingernails in me. I felt the burn that they were cutting into me, but I didn't want to stop. "Or are you talking about how many girls were special to me?" He hovered over the table and took his finger underneath my chin. "How many girls got their special treatment like you did?" I felt tears form in the corner of my eyes. "Five."

"You're disgusting!"

I squirmed from the boy's grip until I got in his face. I bit down hard on his nose and heard his terrible scream. As soon as he screamed, I felt arms wrap around my waist and another set at my jaw. I wasn't letting go. I bit down harder and felt him punch at me. It hurt. It all hurt, but it was better that I did this now. Maybe he would kill me instead. He would get so angry with me that he would kill me.

I could only hope.

When I let go, he clutched onto his nose and I saw the blood. I felt like I was losing my mind, but it was better than having to stay here for the rest of my life. Maybe if I acted crazy, he would leave me alone. Maybe if I acted crazy, he would let me out of here.

"Do you want to make your time here worse?"

"There's nothing you can do to me to make it worse! Just kill me already!" I yelled. I struggled against the boys' hold. I felt tears starting to roll down my cheeks and I let him see. "Somebody will find me! Somebody has to be looking for me!" I yelled. I felt my body begin to collapse against the table and the arms that were holding me suddenly relaxed. I fell to my knees and let my chin rest on the table.

Mr. Barnett started laughing. It was like a scene out of a horror movie. He took his hands away from his bloodied nose and he started laughing maniacally. The blood dripped down his face and into his mouth, but it didn't seem to affect him. I watched as it dripped onto his clothes and onto the floor. His laugh got louder and grew crazier the longer he drew it out.

"You think people are looking for you?" he asked. He got closer to me and I felt my body lurch away. Only I couldn't move from how the boys were holding me. "You think anybody cares about you after all of this time?" My eyebrows crinkled as he talked, but I tried not to make it known he had affected me. What was he talking about? "What year do you think it is?"

"20--"

"Wrong," he snarled at me. "It has been three years." He held up his fingers and ticked off fingers. I stared down at the table as I tried to think about what he was talking about.

There was no way he was telling me the truth. I couldn't have been hauled up in this place for three years. I looked at Chad and Emmanuel to see if they could give me a hint as to whether he was lying or not. Both boys kept their robot face on and stared straight ahead. Neither of them reacted to what he said. I waited to feel a pinch from Chad but didn't get one. The blood ran from my cheeks and I felt myself growing pale. What if he was telling the truth? I've seen the statistics: after the first year, most people give up hope of finding their loved ones. What happens if my family gives up on me? Did I have any family to care about me?

"Who would even be looking for you?" he asked. "Think long and hard. Do you remember who would possibly look for you?"

My forehead creased as I took up his challenge. There had to be someone. As I tried to think, my mind became blurry. It was like I knew I had someone, but I couldn't picture them. I jolted out of the haze and replied with a basic answer to cover my tracks. I couldn't let him think I had forgotten.

"My family."

"Anyone specific?"

"My mom," I answered bleakly.

"What's her name?"

I stuttered at his question. I closed my eyes hard and tried to remember. I willed myself to remember, but I just couldn't. My memory was failing me and maybe that was a true measure of how much time I had been here. Or that the torture they have been put me through is so traumatic I chose not to remember them.

"I do want to say that your family looked for you for a while." He got up from his chair and walked over to me. He placed his finger under my chin and forced me to look up at him. I was too busy thinking about my mom's name to pay attention to what he was saying though. "But they gave up their search." I shook my head and squeezed my eyes closed as if that would help me figure out her name. "I can show you the proof. Shall we show her the proof?"

"Yes." Bri walked into the room and had a gash across her cheek. My mouth fell open as I saw her, but she pretended not to notice. Instead, she looked astonished at how bloody the room was. She looked from my mouth to his nose and back again. "Do you want me to clean you up?" Bri asked him. He nodded his head and gave an evil look toward both of the boys. As he left, he dimmed the lights, and the TV set turned back on.

To the news channel.

"Breaking news, we are here with the parents of a teenage girl who has gone missing in our small town area.

FBI is said to now be involved as they believe this is the same organization that has taken dozens of others around the state as well." The news anchor turned to an older couple. Their eyes were red and the woman did not look like she had been sleeping. The man looked rough too. His overweight belly was hanging out of his shirt and his beard was uncombed.

Was Mr. Barnett insinuating that these were my parents?

I stared at the lady longer and while she had a darker complexion, everything else resembled me. Her hair was the same color. Although I could see that her roots were turning gray. Maybe she dyed her hair to be the same color as mine. Or maybe I had dyed my hair the same color as hers. She had a small nose and her eyes were the same colors as mine. Even the bags and under-eye circles looked like mine. But she didn't trigger a reaction from me. Was this my mom?

As I turned to the man, I wondered how they had ended up together. The lady looked well-kept and looked like she cared about her body. The man had a shirt a size too small with pants that had bleach stains up and down the legs. His hair was ruly and unbrushed but blended it with his untrimmed beard. I was growing pink from thinking about how this could be my dad. Was this my dad?

"We are pleading for whoever has my daughter to please," the mom begged. She cried as she said her next words. "Keep her safe." She put her face into her husband's shirt and cried. While I couldn't see her lips clearly, I heard her voice on the tape. "We can't afford to pay a ransom if there is one. Please keep her, but keep her safe." The woman shook her head again and the man began patting her hair.

"This is tough. Let our daughter know we love her and we will always be looking for her." He shook his head and closed his eyes. The screen started playing the white, black, and gray snow, but I could still see the images. Barely. "Keep our daughter safe in your hands. You have our blessing. We are no longer looking for her."

I felt tears in my eyes as I watched the unknown man and unknown woman cry over their lost daughter. This couldn't be about me, could it? Those were my parents? Was I poor? I couldn't remember, but their voices didn't match up to what they were saying. One would be high-pitched, and the other would be low like a baritone. I couldn't tell if this interview was real, but my heart felt like it was. It would explain so much. Why was I not found yet? We traveled so much at the beginning that I felt like there had to be an opportunity for someone to see me. The fact that Bri had a signed cast had told me that we were close enough to school for her to keep attending school. After all, it would look suspicious if both of us went missing. They might question people around her.

"Now you know the truth."

The TV screen went off and I heard Mr. Barnett's voice. I wasn't sure if he was on the other side of the mirrors or not, but I shuddered. I hated being watched. I liked watching others. I was good at taking notes of the surrounding areas and reading people's body language. If a random girl can just do that, a criminal should be able to as well.

He came through the door the next moment. In his hands was a phone and beside him was Bri. They sat down across from me and motioned toward the phone. I didn't touch it. I kept my gaze downcast and kept my mind occupied. Somewhere in my hazy mind had to be my mom and dad. I had a feeling that they weren't them.

"Make a phone call saying you ran away."

I stared up at him as if he was a lunatic. My eyebrows raised and I was questioning Bri, Emmanuel, and Chad's judgment. They fell under orders for this guy? There is no way that I would make a phone call saying I ran away. This guy had to be crazy. He would have to poison me until I was too weak to resist. At that point, I would just let him kill me.

"No." I crossed my arms over my chest since Emmanuel and Chad had let go of me. They tensed as I moved and I knew if I made a hint that I was going to explode, they would be on me again. "I would like to see you try and make me." I smirked at him to show him that I wasn't afraid. It was all an act though because I was petrified.

"I shouldn't have to make you. Your parents just admitted that they do not want you." He smirked as well and I felt mine falter. "Why would you want to be with a family that doesn't love you? We want you. I want you.

The person who bought you wants you." He motioned for the phone and I shook my head again. "You don't know who your mom and dad are. Why are you saying they aren't your family?"

"I have a gut feeling."

"Ask Chad. He's met your family, right?" I nodded my head, but I wasn't sure. I think he had met them. If he was my boyfriend, then there was a good chance that he had met them.

"Chad, are those my parents?"

Chad straightened his back as he was spoken to. His eyes darted from mine to Mr. Barnett's and back to mine. This would be where his loyalty would be tested. If he told me the truth, he could possibly die, but we'd go out fighting together. If he lied to me, I would never know. I could always try and tell, but I would never know for certain. He sighed and shook his head.

"Those are your parents, Y." He shook his head again and looked up at me. There were tears forming in his eyes, but he quickly blinked them away so that he could stare at the ground. I felt my face beginning to crumble and I let out a couple of tears too. "I'm so sorry. I never thought they would say that about you." I immediately started crying harder and let my body fall into Chad's. He wrapped his arms around me and let me cry. When he squeezed my inner thigh, it coaxed me out of my daze and I straightened my back.

"We love you, Y," Mr. Barnett insisted. He pushed the phone closer to me and I looked at it.

Maybe if I stopped fighting they would stop hurting me. Did they actually care about me? I looked at Bri's face, but her eyes were staring at the ground. I looked at the big cut on her face and winced when I saw it. When I looked at Mr. Barnett, he had hunger on his face. With bandages covering his nose, I couldn't see most of it though. He wanted me. He even wanted my body - nobody has ever really wanted that. Emmanuel's eyes were facing the ground too and I couldn't make out any emotion on his face. He had scars of cuts and bruises on his face as well. When I looked over at Chad, he was also staring at the ground. He had tears running down his face, but he wouldn't look up at me.

Did these guys want me more than my own family?

I reached out my shaky hand and took the phone. Mr. Barnett's smile grew and he handed me a slip with a number on it. I dialed it once and heard two rings before getting an automated hotline.

"Hi, mom?" I asked. I didn't hear anything back and knew it was being recorded. "This is..." I blanked on my name for a minute and immediately shook my head. "Y. I just wanted to let you know that I am safe. I didn't run from home. I-I just want to be left alone. I found people who care about me. I love you." I hung up the phone and Mr. Barnett immediately grabbed it from my hand. He played with it for a second before removing a little chip inside and breaking it in half. He threw it on the ground and he smiled.

"We have shown so much improvement in this little amount of time we have had together." He grabbed at my hands and I immediately revolted away from him. My hands were placed on my lap and I felt Chad try to grab for my inner thigh again. "I am going to let you go back to your room. I want you to be prepared: the next time we are seeing each other is when I am going to show you how much I care about you."

I nodded my head and Emmanuel tugged me up to leave the room. Chad followed behind quickly, but was stopped by Mr. Barnett. I looked back at him, but Emmanuel tugged me along. He let his fingers loosen on my wrist and I followed without a word. Once we traveled further down the hallway, he completely let go and turned around. He had pity on his face and hugged me. It hurt my back for him to squeeze, but I knew that he didn't mean to hurt me. He cared about me.

"We have to do something so that he doesn't steal your virginity." Emmanuel let go of me and looked around the hallway. He started whispering to me just in case, but I shook my head.

"He cares about me."

"He doesn't care about you," Emmanuel whispered to me. I nodded my head at him. He had to care about me. He said so. "He just wants to make a profit from you." He grabbed me roughly by my shoulders and stared at me until I made eye contact. "Listen to me. That video, those people, that family was-"

"What are you two doing down here?"

Emmanuel straightened his back and dug his nails into my arm. I squealed in pain for a second, but he grabbed me by my wrists again. He was a completely different person around his coworkers. I couldn't tell who he was playing. Why did he constantly want to hurt me? Telling me the wrong things? Why would he talk bad about Mr. Barnett? He cared about me.

"Taking her back to her room."

"I'll take it from here. She is mine to look after." Ellis nodded his head and I felt the uncertainty from Emmanuel. Reluctantly, my wrists were clasped with ropes from Ellis. He separated us and I was soon led back to my room. I felt peaceful as I saw the familiarity of the spinning camera. As soon as I got into my room, I sat down in my usual spot and stared at Ellis. He seemed to be hovering around. "How did your meeting go?" I shrugged my shoulders and sat still. As I watched Ellis, he seemed more nervous than usual. "Want to talk about it?"

"I found out you all truly care about me." I looked up at him and smiled. "You all kept me here because you care about me." As I continued talking, Ellis's face twisted into an emotion of pure terror. I didn't stop though. I ranted on about how my family didn't love me, but all of them did. He didn't stop me as I talked and he didn't try to interrupt me either. He let me continue onward with my small rant. I wasn't sure if I was trying to convince him or myself.

"And he told you that?" Ellis asked. I nodded my head and looked up at him. "And did he tell you his

                                    AMY KULP

name?"

"I already know him from school," I said. I blinked and noticed Ellis's shift in his body. "You don't know who you take orders from, do you?" I asked. He raised his eyebrows suspiciously at me but ended up nodding no. "Mr. Barnett is a wonderful man. He really cares about me. You should meet him."

He nodded his head and left. It was so abrupt and weird for him to do that. I just had to make sure that he wasn't playing a prank on me. I looked out the door and was surprised to see him leaving. When the door opened for him to step out, Bri was trying to step in. I immediately pretended that I didn't see her and sat farther away from the door. If I didn't see her, she wouldn't be here. I let out my breath when I saw her through my door. She put her combination in and allowed herself in.

"I'm here to prepare you," Bri started. She threw the items in her hands at me and I flinched as they clunked against me. I looked at the little bottles of shampoo, conditioner, body wash, and other things and realized that I would be taking a shower. I looked up hopeful and Bri nodded her head. "It's not that bad." She helped me up and took me to one of the extra rooms I hadn't been in.

There had been a shower here the entire time?

"It'll help if you relax when it is happening," Bri whispered. "He may taunt you and want you to fight back, but he likes a chase. Once he catches you, it will be worse for you." She started turning on the water and felt the temperature with her hand. She stared at me as I undressed, but I could see deadness behind her eyes. "He will torture you."

"How do you know?"

She looked at me but didn't answer. Instead, she pushed me gently into the water so that I could freshen up. I tried not to think about it, but I knew the answer. Bri was me. I was Bri. Did this mean that I would be part of their gang? I would never kidnap girls. I would never torture other people for the fun of it. I would not throw away anyone's trust like she had.

As I started finishing up, I turned off the water and got into the fresh clothes. I felt my body screaming from how clean I was. My pores were open and breathing while my hair was smooth from the cleansing ingredients. Any dirt that was on my face was now gone and replaced with delicate fresh skin. I could actually stand to smell myself. Although I felt a little itchy. My skin wasn't used to this treatment.

"Has it really been years?" I asked. I patted my body down with the towel to get any excess water off, but I could see Bri's shadow. She shook her head, yes, but I doubted it. I saw how frigid her stance was and how she wouldn't meet my eyes. I felt like even though it has only been a little bit here, everybody was already acting so much nicer to me.

"We're going to wait for you to dry. When you are..." She trailed off as she led me back to my room. I sat on the floor and as she left, I saw the glimpse in her eye again. Was Bri being real with me now? Or was just trying to play me again? Get me to trust her?

I couldn't keep up with everyone here. I was either being treated nicely or like trash. Sometimes I was okay with staying here and other times I was screaming to die. I was fighting with my inner self too. I couldn't comprehend what was real, what was my imagination, and who I was. Could I actually believe that they all cared about me? My own family doesn't love me, why would these guys?

I wondered how long it would take my hair to dry. Was I able to make it stay wet forever? Then I would not have to worry about anything. Why was everyone okay with this? I bet if I had more time with everyone that I would be able to get everyone to revolt. I felt like I had so many of them under my grip. Or maybe that was part of their ploy too. I wasn't sure what was real anymore. They had to be human though. Underneath, they had to know that living like this and stealing other people was wrong. Hell, they knew it was wrong, they hid from everyone. It was a secret mission.

As I stared at the ceiling, I couldn't help but wonder what would've happened to me if I was auctioned off. I would be rid of this place, but who knows if the person who bought me would be better? What happens if they were worse? Sure, they had to be rich, but that means they could buy more expensive torture devices. They could buy better security. They could kill me with finer techniques and items. They would be able to pay off someone to hide my body. I doubt there would be a chance for me to escape from there. At least here I could plot it out.

All of them had their weaknesses here. That weakness was me.

I listened to my door open up, but I didn't react. My hair was not yet dry so I didn't have to go up just yet. I didn't have to whisk my life away just yet. I truly wondered what it would be like. I wish I could have my first time be as I imagined it, but that seemed like a very far-fetched idea. From what Bri was telling me, this would be my worst nightmare. It had to have stripped something from her to make her such a black-hearted individual. If he knew what I was going through, why would she want me to go through the same thing?

"My hair is not dry yet," I said as I kept my back to the wall. Whoever it was, didn't take the hint and scooted closer to my room. I listened to their shuffle of the feet and realized that this wasn't Bri in my room. She was the only person here who didn't wear boots. Instead, she wore sneakers. While it may not seem like a huge difference to most people, it made a different sound. It was the reason I was able to tell who was in my room before turning over. I used to have to brace for impact when I heard the soft scuffles. "Agent Ellis?" I asked. I turned around to see him staring at me. He kept his distance though and stared down at me. "What do you want?"

"I'm here to prepare you," he said absentmindedly.

I looked at him confused and showed him my wet hair. I was already prepped. He looked over at the cameras that were now pointing in our direction. I immediately nodded my head and pretended to grimace. As long as I pretended, he didn't actually hurt me. I had to keep that in mind. He took a step toward me and I flinched backward. As soon as the cameras were off, he put his back to it and stumbled over his words. "I need you to trust me." He held out his hand to me and I felt my eyes go wider. I shook my head immediately and he seemed stunned for a second. "Do you trust me?"

"No." I couldn't tell if this was a test. If it was and I took his hand, Mr. Barnett would torture me if I disobeyed him. If this wasn't a test then I was confused as to what this meant. Why was he asking me that? He shifted his gaze down for a moment and started reaching into his pockets. When he came back empty-handed, he started putting his hands down his pants and I immediately started shouting. "Please don't do this!"

I backed my body into the corner of the room and immediately tried to hide. I pulled my shirt higher to my chin and pulled my shorts as low as they would go to cover my butt. When Ellis saw me doing this, he immediately took his hands out and put them up like he was being caught in the act. He moved carefully around me and pulled his shirt up a little. He pulled his pants down a little more and I saw something shiny underneath his layers of clothes. I didn't want to inspect it though so I stayed where I was and only darted my eyes to it occasionally. When the light stopped shining our way and started circling the room again, his demeanor changed. He let go of his shirt and pants and stepped closer to me as if he had permission. He knelt down beside me and I thought he was going to whisper in my ear. Instead, he wrapped his hands in my hair and started ringing it out.

"Don't do that!" I yelled. I forced myself away from him and looked at him with distrust. Why would he do that? He wanted me to trust him and then he was going to willingly send me off to Mr. Barnett? He was going to send me earlier to Mr. Barnett. I felt my hands slap at his and laid there shocked that I would touch him. I couldn't keep it straight in my mind as to whether I loved the people here or was so afraid that I had to convince myself I loved it here. What were my other options?

He didn't react when I slapped him though. There was no pushback to me defending myself. He wasn't mad that I had put my hands on him because he had done it to me first. In fact, I wasn't sure if he had noticed that I did it. While his hands were on my hair for a split second, he turned to look at the door. Something I hadn't noticed was another presence in my room.

"What are you doing here?" Bri asked as she took a step closer in here. Ellis backed off of me and I scrambled to my corner. The further I was away from everyone, the safer I felt. Bri's face was emotionless as she stepped closer to Ellis. I looked between them to see who wasn't supposed to be there, but neither of their faces gave it away. Bri's face stayed in her usual snobby pose and she kept her nose upturned in the air as if she was better than everyone else. Ellis kept his lips pressed in and his eyes remained cold.

"I was never taken off orders to watch over Y," he said. When Bri moved to touch me, he moved as well. He guarded every move she made until she gave up. Her nose was no longer in the air and she looked as if she was staring down Ellis. At this point, it was like I was a prize to be won.

"I am giving you orders to stop watching over Y."

"I am sorry, but I do not take orders from you." Bri's face crumbled in a second and turned into stone. I could see her sucking her cheeks in and clenching her jaw - she was mad. "Orders from the head."

"And who might that be?" Bri questioned. She stepped forward and smiled sinfully at Ellis. It was almost as if she knew he didn't know the answer. But I had told him the answer.

"Mr. Barnett."

Her smile faded and she seemed at a loss for words. She shook her head once, but her eyes darted back towards me. Ellis turned slightly to look at me, but he kept me guarded.

"I have orders to take her for more prep."

"I will be coming along then."

Bri seemed hesitant at first but nodded her head. Ellis hoisted me up on my feet and my legs buckled underneath me. He put his hands under my armpits and I felt myself trying not to leave. What was this second part of prep? Bri leaned out of the room and grabbed something to hand to Ellis. He stood paralyzed for a minute before turning to me and wrapping the rope around my wrists. Bri motioned towards the ground and Ellis hesitated for a moment. I looked between them but didn't understand what was happening. I stared at him as Bri pushed past him and unwound some of the rope so that she could wrap my ankles.

"So you can't run." As Bri tightened the knot, she made eye contact with me for a second and I saw the sorrow in her eyes. She kept her eyes on the ground when she straightened up and gave orders to Ellis. "You stay in front with her in the middle and I'll follow behind." She sneered for a second as she pushed Ellis out front. "I don't trust you."

"I am faithful to my orders, not to you." He held his head high as he marched out of the room first. I trudged behind as Bri poked her finger into my back. While it didn't hurt, it was uncomfortable. With how tight these ropes were, I knew that Bri meant business. There was no way I could easily get out of these. I was going to my destination whether Bri felt sorry for me or not. My ankles were definitely going to have a burn on them when I got out of them, but I didn't have to hurry as Ellis took his time.

We exited and came up into a hallway. I trudged along with them and felt Ellis slow down while Bri sped up. I was trapped between their bodies but Bri kept her finger poked into my back. She urged me to move forward until I was pushing into Ellis. Was he delaying this? Or was it unintentional?

"Keep up the pace," Bri warned.

He followed her orders and we slowly made our way into a staircase. Walking up the stairs was torturous with the rope, but Bri didn't show any sympathy. Nobody talked and I knew that I shouldn't either. When Ellis stopped next, we paused outside of a room I haven't been in. Bri instantly took her hands to my ankles and started to unwrap the rope. When she was done, she grabbed me by my hair and pushed me inside the room. Ellis followed after, but we stopped as soon as we stepped in.

Looking around, I would have thought I had stepped into a hospital. There was a bed with different constraints tied to it and then a surplus of surgical gear. While the smell outside would not have given it away, it smelled like bleach in this room. When I was done admiring this place, my eyes trained on Bri. Her back was to us and she noticeably shuddered. When she turned around, she opened her mouth to give instructions, but she stopped when the electricity shut off.

And the emergency lights came on.

Chapter 22 ----------------------------

I watched Ellis and Bri both freeze as they registered what was happening. I looked between them to see if I should be concerned as well, but they were masters at hiding their emotions. Bri kept looking around the room and I heard her breathing become rhythmic. Ellis stepped closer to the door and watched Bri. He wasn't going to let either of us try to escape. When he was done observing Bri's antics, he looked at me and zeroed in on my gaze. He smirked as if he knew this was going to happen, but played it off when Bri stopped spinning in circles.

"Okay that's sixty," Bri whispered. She walked close to Ellis and grabbed his arm. "Do you remember your training?" she asked. Ellis refused to back down from the door, but he did nod his head yes. Bri looked between all of us before nodding her head. She let go of him and he side-stepped away from the door. Now giving her enough room to leave, she looked at me before leaving and smiled. As if to congratulate me. "I'm going to check the perimeter and try to protect our leader." She paused for a moment and looked at me again. "Your job is to protect our most valuable asset."

As soon as she left, Ellis slammed the door behind her. He walked closer to me and put his hands back in his pockets. He walked closer to me and the fright that I had before seemed to come back. I didn't say anything as I shuffled to the back of the room. At least it was cluttered over here so I could hurt him by shoving things at him if I needed to. He didn't say anything as I moved but he did follow after me. Almost like he was my shadow.

"Stop moving," he instructed. His voice was shaky and I looked behind me to see that he was pulling out a knife. My eyes grew wide and I hurried away from him. Why are his mood swings so difficult to keep up with? One minute he is helping me and the next minute he is trying to carve my body. "We need to get out of here," he whisper-yelled at me. He looked back at the door and the red emergency lights before ducking down behind the bed.

The door smashed open and I found myself frightened far beyond what I was before. I looked over at Ellis and when he motioned for me to get down, I listened. I snuck behind one of the rolling trays they had to torture me with and now that I was close enough to it, I was able to see all of the sharp instruments that were there. Whatever they were planning to do to me seemed horrific. Those thoughts quickly escaped my mind as I watched a different body scour the area.

He didn't look like anyone I had seen before. He seemed to be in a suit of armor because as he moved, I heard how heavy his footsteps were. He had a helmet on that allowed him to see out, but I could not see him through. In his hands was a shield and what looked like a bat. He scanned the area quickly but didn't take time to look where Ellis or I were. He left the room just as quickly and Ellis breathed out. He turned to me and motioned for me to follow him.

I stayed put in the tiny corner I was in. He grabbed out his knife from before and came towards me again. I started whispering under my breath for my life, but he didn't seem to care. I closed my eyes as he came closer and I realized that I would not be able to run away this time. He grabbed my hands roughly and I felt the relief from the constraints. I peeked open one eye and got rid of the ropes all of the way. Once they were discarded on the floor, I turned my attention back to him. It seemed as if he was trying to give me the knife. I carefully took it from him but expected there to be a catch.

"Why are you giving me this?" I asked.

"We need to go," he whispered. He got up from the crouch that he was in and held out a hand to me. I looked over the knife again and then back at him. "Do you want to get out of here or not?" he asked. I looked up at him again and clutched the knife in my hand. I may not be understanding what was going on, but I definitely wanted to get out of here. I grabbed onto his hand and felt myself beginning to play with the knife. I constantly twirled it in my hand and was trying to decide what to do with it. Should I stab him? He walked towards the door and peeked outside to see if anyone was coming down the hall. "It seems safe," he whispered. He looked back and was surprised to see that I was still near the table of sharp objects.

"Why did you give me this?" I asked.

"Do you know how to shoot a gun?" he asked. I shook my head no and he pulled it out of the boot he was wearing. He cocked the gun and kept it by his side. He looked back at me with a smirk and tried to egg me to go. "I guess I'll be in charge of this then. I'll guard the front, you let me know if you see someone coming from the back?"

"Do I have a choice?" I asked.

"If you want to live," he whispered. He looked over at the door again and ushered me over. My feet seemed like stone though. I didn't want to move. I was too afraid of what was happening. Was I going to die? Who were those people?

"What is going on?" I asked. I twirled the knife in my hand again and when Ellis stepped closer to me, I held it at him. I probably didn't look threatening, but I felt like I was. I had never held one of these and now that I had one, I was going to use it on anyone who came near me. His only reaction was to put my hand down. Apparently, I wasn't scary especially since I didn't even attack him with it.

"You're being saved," he whispered. "I'm Special Agent Aaron Ellis Harmon from the FBI."

"I-I don't believe you." I raised my knife up again and he didn't react much.

"I showed you my badge already." He dug under his pants for a second to show me the shiny symbol again. I readjusted my eyes to be able to read it and felt a small blush appear on my cheeks.

"How do I know that's not fake?" I asked.

"You won't." He paused and looked out the door again. "I can explain everything to you as we go, but I need you to trust me." I looked at him again and he darted his eyes back to the hallway. I shook my head and followed behind him.

I felt giddy. I was being saved! I would be able to escape this awful place and then go home. Although I didn't know what my home was nor did I know if I had a place to call home. What about my parents? They said they didn't want me on national television. What would happen if I were to show up again? Would they pretend that nothing happened? Would their lives be better without me in them? Would our lives be strained?

I know that I would definitely need therapy. Everybody around me was living a double life - Emmanuel, Bri, Chad, Mr. Barnett, and now Ellis. Although I was grateful for him having a double life. I couldn't trust anyone though and I knew that was going to leave problems for me. Would I be able to trust my future partner? Would I be able to trust my future classmates? Was I even still at school or did I graduate? Could I have graduated?

If I did go into therapy, would I trust them? Someone I was supposed to trust - my guidance counselor - turned out to be the leader of this sex trafficking ring. I doubt that wouldn't leave an impression on my life. What if I went crazy after all of this? What if I am actually crazy now? After all, I am trusting this guard with my life. Who says that the badge was real at all? I wouldn't be able to tell if it was fake or not. Did they have some papers that went along with the badge? Should I ask him for his?

I'm confused though. If these were FBI Agents, why were we hiding from them? FBI Agents were good guys. We were the good guys. I was a victim. Why would they attack us? What happens if I accidentally charge at a good guy? Would I be shot instantly? Then I would never get my freedom.

Ellis did say that he would answer any of my questions as we went. So I asked him as we started descending the stairs. We listened carefully for any doors opening and closing, but it was just our footsteps making noise. When we got to the bottom floor, he held the door open for me and I walked into a black room. I couldn't see anything and Ellis took a moment to breathe out his response.

"I don't know which guys are Agents from the FBI or from here." He clicked a flashlight on and we scanned the area around us. Nothing but dirt, rats, and dust were down here. "I've been following this lead for so long and haven't had contact with my leads in so long." He shook his head but smiled at me. "It will be good to get you home. You are the reason no other girl will ever get into this situation." I felt my face pale at the thought. "You are the first girl that has ever met the boss."

"I don't feel that lucky," I whispered. I turned the

knife over in my hand and listened to footsteps above us. When I looked back at Ellis, I nodded to keep going. We started backing up as he watched the front and I tried to focus on the backside of us. I couldn't see without light and we were only fortunate to have one. "If you haven't had any contact with them, how do they know they are coming? How do they know who the leader is?"

"They don't." He paused as we listened to footsteps around us. I immediately ducked behind some dusty old cloth and Ellis crammed beside me. He pointed his gun at the entrance we came from and turned his light off. I hoped he wouldn't shoot someone in front of me. "When we get out of here, we are going back to headquarters and releasing all of the names we know." He shrugged his shoulders. "When you tapped into that computer downstairs, my friends had it wired to get notifications of use." He shushed as we heard people come around us. They scurried out without warning and he remained seated for a minute. "When you had your meeting with the big boss, I typed on a word document saying we finally caught the bastard." He started moving from the position we were in back over to the entrance. I followed suit and believed everything he said. I was hoping I wasn't falling into a trap. "I didn't know who he was until you told me."

I didn't have any other questions for him that I thought deserved to be said aloud. I wanted to leave this place and the longer we spent talking, the less chance we had of escaping. I followed him as he assessed every corner we came across. I wasn't sure if I should be doing the same thing so I copied it just in case. I felt silly and stupid because I technically didn't know what I was doing. I probably looked like a fraud.

As we passed through more rooms without interference, I was beginning to feel hopeful. The more we moved, the faster we were to leave this place. I felt like I had been walking miles but it didn't help that I didn't know the layout of this building. From looking around, I could tell that we were underground. There were no emergency lights down here and the ground was wet like compacted dirt or mud. As we traveled forward, the ceiling grew shorter and shorter. I wasn't that tall but even I had to crouch down a little so my hair wasn't touching the top. However, the spread of the rooms felt the same. There were always crates and furniture in here. Most of it was covered and all of it was coated in dust. I didn't know how long this ring had gone on but from the glimpses of furniture I could see, some of them were dated. Maybe it was an operation handed down from generation to generation. Maybe Mr. Barnett was brainwashed into this.

He was smart though. He had the social skills to pass as a guidance counselor. He helped students and never raised anyone's suspicions. I don't recall there ever being a scandal at our school. He also had to be book-smart as well. To be a guidance counselor, he would have to have a degree in psychology. Unless he made that up. I could see him being able to forge that somehow. I guess that could be a scandal if someone found out.

The only 'scandal' I really remember is when Emmanuel came to school. People in my school weren't used to seeing people different than them. Emmanuel was the first boy who wasn't white-passing in our school. Emmanuel was news to be talked about. I guess I should have listened to some of what they were saying because he was the entire reason I am a part of this mess. He was creepy. He stalked me. He followed me.

He was something new.

He was enticing to me. He was attractive. Of course, I would pay attention to him. That was the goal anyway. He showed up anytime I needed someone. He showed up when I didn't need anyone. He was always there and to me, that was comforting. Until it became creepy. I can't remember exactly what threw me off, but something made me feel off about him. I wish I trusted my instinct though.

Ellis took me out of my thoughts when he stopped abruptly. I slammed into him and lost my balance but he quickly repositioned me without much noise. I tried to listen to whatever he had heard but was unable to. I couldn't hear anything except the panting from me and him. We weren't running but we were definitely walking briskly. It was enough to knock me out of breath since for the last length of time I was here, I was hauled up in a small room. I never got to walk around unless it was to go to the bathroom which was rare. I'm not sure why Ellis was out of breath. Maybe he was nervous.

I'm sure if they found out he was a mole or a

double Agent he would be tortured. Thinking positively, he would be killed. However, I knew not to give anyone here the benefit of the doubt. Ellis would be tortured painfully. His life depended on it. What happens if nobody found out it was him though? Would that be possible? What happens if they accuse the wrong person?

Ellis flashed his light to the floor and with his quick flash, I was able to see pools of blood. He switched it off just as quickly though and I heard him gulp. Ellis timidly walked forward and when we got close enough, shined the light just enough so we could see. It didn't give away our position but it did let us see the crime scene.

A body was lying face down. I felt my stomach lurch as I tried to look at him. I looked away so that I wouldn't throw up as Ellis crouched closer. This person definitely wasn't alive. I could see that from the amount of blood that was covering the floor. He searched the body for a second to find a shield, another knife, and a badge. He examined it for a second before putting it on the body. He seemed sad for a moment before handing me the knife.

Did he know this man?

My body froze as I heard running footsteps towards us. Ellis immediately stood up, turned towards the noise, pointed his gun, and fired it. I heard a thud and closed my eyes shut. A groan escaped their lips and I immediately knew that raspy voice. I popped open my eyelids and looked towards the black figure opposite from the dead body. I felt tears prickle in my eyes as I registered the face and he smiled at me.

"Well, I'll be damned." He laughed a little and groaned as blood came out of his body. My feet were already covered from the other blood but I let myself step closer to him. He may be behind most of the torturing I had and maybe it was Stockholm syndrome, but I did not want to see him die. "I thought you would have died when you ended up here."

"Looks like you're the one dying, Cyrus." He laughed a bit and I saw blood appear on his teeth. He smiled at me as he held in his wound.

"I don't think I'm making it out of this." He eyed Ellis and I suppose he was trying to figure out who he was. I wouldn't tell him that though. "If you see Analee or Murphy, tell them I was trying to protect them." He closed his eyes for a second but reopened them in an instant. "Hopefully they've made it without me. We never thought this day would come." He shook his head but I could tell it was getting more difficult to talk and be awake. "Don't let me suffer." He shook his head and Ellis finally came over and put his hand on my shoulder. "You're a good shot but now I want to go." He didn't seem surprised when he saw Ellis's face and I wondered if maybe he was a part of this. Was he a good guy? He was stuck here trying to protect his family. Cyrus grabbed my hand as Ellis pointed his gun at him. He squeezed my palm at the same time the shot went off. Blood splattered onto my face and when I let go of his hand, it fell to his side.

I pressed my face into Ellis and he let me sob onto

his shoulder for a second. I never wanted to see anyone die. Especially for me to escape. I should have known it would be a huge possibility, but I didn't think it would happen without warning. I understand that we didn't know what was going to happen as we heard the footsteps. I understand that Ellis had to protect us. I understand that he didn't want Cyrus to suffer.

It was just hard.

I had blood in my mouth.

I had blood on my face.

I had blood between my toes.

I had blood everywhere there shouldn't be blood.

"We have to keep going." Ellis handed me the other flashlight that the other FBI Agent had and I turned back to them before we started sneaking again. He moved them so they were flat on their back and had their hands holding their badge. Kind of weird, but kind of angelic. "We're almost to the end." I nodded my head and felt like I was more enthusiastic about leaving now.

I followed closely behind him as we continued forward. I was so excited to get out of here that I wasn't bothering to check behind us. This entire time nobody had been following us. It had been to the side of us or from the front. Besides, I could probably hear someone if they came behind us. I kept my hand on Ellis's shoulder as we pressed onward. The ceiling stopped getting shorter but I felt colder. I was not prepared for how cold it was since I was only in a short-sleeve shirt and shorts.

They must have thought ahead. If I were to

somehow escape this place by myself, I would never survive the winter. I stopped for a second trying to process that. If it was winter, then I was roughly gone for a year. How had I survived this place for a year? Aren't statistics showing that anyone who is gone after a week is very likely dead? How did I beat those odds?

"I never thought I'd see that face again."

I immediately inserted my nail into Ellis's shoulder. He turned around and held out his arm to protect me. He flashed his light over the area we just passed but couldn't find where the voice was coming from. We heard a cough again and Ellis flashed it forward. I tapped on his shoulder and pointed to the very back of the room. There was furniture scattered around her and I could tell that there was a struggle. Ellis shined the light right on her face and it took him a second to move.

He ran towards her. I had to fight the urge to join him. I looked around me again to make sure nobody else was here and watched them from a distance. He grabbed her face and looked into her eyes. She laughed a little at the recognition and they both smiled. Her mouth had blood trickling down it and I traveled my light down her body to see a knife in her abdomen - similar to Cyrus's death. She sounded weak and when my light shined on her legs, I could see the rips in them.

The blood drained from my face as I thought of the implications.

"Ellie, I never thought I'd see you again." She smiled as she placed her hand on his cheek. Her eyes were dimming every second but I didn't want to ruin the moment. Although it would seem like a romantic fling, I knew better. They seemed to care for each other but not romantically. Maybe family. Or maybe just being close. Maybe they did have history. He seemed too old for her though. "Are these from the cuts I gave you?"

Ellis didn't say anything as he nodded his head. I stared at them for a second and cleared my throat so they knew I was still here.

"I didn't know anyone from my unit was working here."

"I wanted to welcome you back. A bit naive, I know." She laughed again but I heard the pain behind it. Her eyes flickered towards me and she smiled. "You're in safe hands, kid." She paused but only for her to breathe. "He saved me when I was being trafficked."

"She attacked me," he chuckled and shook his head. He turned towards me as he held onto her and now I understood their dynamic. "I cannot leave someone from my unit behind." He let go of her for a second and approached me. He handed me the gun and stared at me. "Just point and shoot. If you follow the way we were going, you don't have far to go."

"W-What?" I asked. I felt my chin tremble at the thought of having to walk the rest of the way by myself. "I can't shoot this." He shook his head. "What about you?"

"No man left behind," he whispered. "I have my inside guy at the end of the tunnel. If you are quick, you shouldn't have any problems." I shook my head in protest, but he raised his voice at me. "Go, now!"

I felt tears form in the corner of my eyes but I proceeded onward. I flashed my light towards them one last time and saw him press his lips on her forehead. His eyes shined towards me and I smiled at him. I put the flashlight in my mouth so that I could hold onto the gun and the two knives I had. I stuck them in between my knuckles so that I could stab someone with them if I needed to. Should I run? What if the person that attacked her was up here? Ellis wouldn't know.

Why would he give me his gun? What would he use to protect both of them? Was he planning to just die there? I stopped for a second and thought about turning around. I couldn't though. I needed to get out of here. This was my one chance. I didn't survive all of the torture, sexual abuse, kidnapping, being roofied, auctioned off, and sex trafficked to give it up for an FBI Agent who saw an old friend.

I felt my feet getting colder the more I traveled down the way. I shivered as the cold ripped through my shirt and shorts and saw the small goosebumps form on my thighs. I walked about five more steps before I was able to see my breath. I bit my lip but forced myself to trudge forward. Eventually, I was able to see the light at the end. I squinted my eyes and stopped to readjust for a second. I immediately smiled when I realized that it was the outside world.

I made it.

I dropped everything in my hands and sprinted

　　　　　　　　　　　　　　　　　　　　AMY KULP

outside. Even though it was light at the end, it was dark outside. I was better able to see out here than in the tunnel but I expected it to be daytime. I knelt on the ground and immediately started sobbing.

I made it.

When I was better able to control my emotions, I wiped the tears from my eyes and looked around. Where was this inside man that Ellis was talking about? Who was he working with? I looked around and clutched my arms around my body. I was so cold. There was snow on the ground and as I walked further into it, I saw the bloody footprints. I didn't want to know what I looked like.

When I heard footsteps, I immediately turned in the direction they were coming from. When my mind saw who it was, I smiled and brought them into a hug. I was picked up into the air and squeezed until I couldn't breathe. My tears started rolling down my cheeks again and I couldn't stop hugging them.

"Was it you all along?" I asked. He nodded his head and I brought him into another hug. He let go and brought his hands to my face. His eyes darkened as he looked at mine and I knew that he was being serious.

"We have to get out of here now. We don't know what's going on down there. We don't know who's alive. We don't know who's still after you." I nodded my head and grabbed onto his hands. He tried walking faster than me but I felt myself slipping on the ice. My feet were too cold. I grimaced but refused to give up. If he hadn't given up, why should I?

"Stop!"

I turned around as my arm was pulled in the other direction. When I saw Chad running up after us, my body froze. I looked at Emmanuel and he pulled me harder. I immediately lost my balance and stumbled onto the snow - freezing me to the core. Emmanuel still tried dragging me though. I had to scratch him to force him to let go of me.

"What are you doing?" Chad asked. He looked at me with pleading eyes and I retracted my hand from Emmanuel. "Don't trust him." Chad grabbed my hand and lurched me towards him. Emmanuel looked mad but only showed affection towards me. "He's still working for them."

"He's lying to you, Y." There was a growl in his throat that I have never heard before. It sounded predatory. "Come with me. He's the reason you are in this mess."

"You're the one who roofied her," Chad explained as he poked at Emmanuel's chest. He immediately punched him and I watched as Emmanuel immediately tried to guard me against Chad. I knew that I wasn't in the way of being hurt though. I felt my cheeks blush red at the thought of having to choose between them.

My ex-boyfriend or the guy who was supposed to replace my ex-boyfriend?

"You are the one who led her back to vans once she escaped," Emmanuel hissed. He knelt down next to

                                    AMY KULP

me and started wiping the snow off of me. Chad attempted to touch me but Emmanuel stopped him from coming closer.

"Emily, you have to trust me."

"Emily?"

"Y, I told you from the start that I would not stop until I got you out." He gestured towards the snow-covered environment. "This is your escape." I looked around and noticed how peaceful and quiet it was. It seemed suspicious to me. I didn't know who to trust but I did know that one of them was lying to me. If only there was a way I could know.

I searched both of their eyes but it didn't help me. One of them was a good actor. I knew that Chad couldn't be a good actor though. He had to take himself away from this project. That's what brought Emmanuel to me. I turned to Chad to speak but Emmanuel hurried and gave me his coat for a second. I took the chance and put it on to warm myself. I was freezing. He brought me closer to him so that I could stop shivering and felt thankful for his warm body.

"I was beaten and kept all of your secrets," Emmanuel urged. He motioned towards the haircut he was still growing out and I could see where the hair was tugged out of him.

"We were both tortured," Chad mentioned.

"However I didn't beat you when Bri instructed me to." He motioned towards my back and I winced. While it didn't hurt anymore from all of the help that Ellis had given me, the memory of it gave me chills. Chad reached for me and when he got the opportunity to, he squeezed my inner thigh.

It sent a pang of relaxation through me. I wasn't sure why though. I looked down at his hand and then back at him. He smiled at me and I found myself smiling back. I forced myself off of the snow and dusted myself off. Emmanuel and Chad both tried to block each other from me but I stayed quiet in my decision. They weren't going to need to know because I wasn't sure who I wanted to pick.

On one hand, Chad was the initial reason I was here. He was here because of the money he wanted. Everything between us was fake. How was I supposed to believe him now that he wanted to get me to safety? I did have to admit that him pulling out of this mission was a big indicator to me that he felt sorry for all of the actions he did. I looked at him but he was too focused on Emmanuel. He was also tortured less than Emmanuel was. I felt like there was a reason for that. Did he spill something about me to whoever had tortured him? I couldn't reject him though. Something about the thigh grab felt familiar to me.

On the other hand, Emmanuel was the actual reason I was here. He roofied me. I didn't know his backstory and I didn't need to know it to know that he was good at his job. He played his playbook as he wrote it. He knew how to get into my feelings and he knew how I would react to things. Maybe him being beaten more was an indicator that he knew this would come down to my final decision. However, whenever Bri gave him orders, he followed through with it. It was like he was a drone without any feelings. A robot. I worried that he was born into this and that he didn't know life outside of it. He never told me his life story. I never asked.

I never asked Chad either. He just gave it up to me. That was the difference between him and Chad. Everything Emmanuel did was calculated. Reggie told me what was planned. It was like he planned his emotions and my reactions. I refused to let my reactions be played by a robot.

I opened my mouth to give an answer but was ricocheted to the ground from the explosion that happened. Emmanuel dove to protect me and when I came to my senses and realized what happened, I watched the fire spread throughout the building. I immediately screamed and shoved Emmanuel off of me.

"Ellis!" I pushed Emmanuel to the ground and shakily tried to run towards the building. I didn't see Ellis get out. My eyes darted across the landscape but I didn't see any bodies. Only me, Chad, and Emmanuel. My body was wobbly from the blast that knocked me over and I knew something hit my head but I still attempted to run towards it. My movement was unbalanced and I slipped on the snow but I didn't stop until Chad pulled me down.

"Emily stop, we have to go!" He grabbed me by the shoulders and I immediately started crying.

Ellis didn't make it.

Cyrus didn't make it.

Who else didn't make it?

I felt tears and blood trickle down my cheeks and I screamed once more. Chad shook me and told me to focus. I couldn't concentrate. I darted my eyes back and forth between them but shook my head. What did Ellis tell me? Who should I trust? Why couldn't he just tell me the name of the person who was supposed to be here? I hit my forehead and tried to remember but got distracted by the sirens in the distance.

"Let's go!" one of them yelled. I wasn't even sure who. I felt myself getting tugged by both of them and hit my forehead again. I cried out as I remembered his advice.

Now I had to pick. Who was I going with?

I steadied myself as I stood up and felt tears falling down my cheeks again. I was wobbly and my vision was beginning to blur. I wasn't going to give up. I didn't make it this far to just give up. I made it this far and I knew who had good intentions for me. I wiped my tears and blood, I looked back at the building, cursed under my breath, and turned back to my boys.

They both looked frightened - one of their expressions met their eyes and one of their eyes was dead inside. They both looked like they wanted me to come with them - one I trusted and one I didn't. They both were someone I used to care for - I still do, but one a little more. They were both great actors - one I was able to see through.

Was I ready to make this decision though? If I made the wrong choice, I was probably going to die. If I made the wrong choice, Ellis died for nothing. If I made the wrong choice, Cyrus died because of me. If I made the wrong choice, more girls were going to be trafficked. If I made the wrong choice, I would be stuck here forever. If I made the wrong choice, I would never see my family again. If I made the wrong choice, I could never be me again. If I made the wrong choice, I would hope they would kill me somehow. There have been way too many chances given to me to escape. Why am I messing up so much?

The sound of sirens pulled me out of my thoughts. I watched as ambulances, fire trucks, and police cars pulled up to the building. I immediately started running with the boys and found myself growing colder and colder. The part of my head that was bleeding felt like it was gushing more and I knew that I didn't have another chance to make my decision. It was now or never.

Ellis's words spoke to me first.

I put my hand in his palm and we ran off.

Chapter 23 ------------------------------

"Welcome back everybody." He leaned his arms on the back of the rolling chair with excitement. If someone were to kick it out from under him, he would lose his balance and fall. He had too much confidence in this room though. I looked around the rectangular table but nobody looked in my direction. The air in here was stale and if you breathed in wrong, it could hurt you. Or maybe the people in here would hurt you. "Our numbers are smaller but I know that you are my most loyal." Mr. Barnett stared at the crowd and slowly made eye contact with everyone so that they knew they were valued.

Agent F. I haven't seen this man in quite some time. I knew that he was a great getaway driver but I wasn't sure if he would be moving up in positions. Someone had to. Someone had to fill in Ellis's shoes, right? His eyes stayed on the table but I could see him actively resisting the urge to make eye contact with Mr. Barnett. He was afraid of him.

Reggie. Somehow it didn't surprise me that this pervert had managed to survive despite how low the probability was. He kept his gaze in my direction but he didn't lift it to meet mine. I felt chilled under the impression that he was delighted to see me. I was repulsed by the thought he would probably move up in positions as well. He would have more access to hurt innocent girls. He would have more access to vulnerable girls. He would love that position. It was disgusting. He was probably the best for the job since he didn't include emotion in it.

Murphy. He looked so much older now. His undereye circles were darker and there was a pink cut starting at his wrist and going up to his neck. It looked cool but it made me wonder how he had gotten it. Was he fighting for his life? Or was he fighting to ruin someone else's? I hoped he still had his childlike innocence to him but the longer I studied him, I already knew that it was lost. His leg bounced up and down and I was able to read him like a book - he was nervous. Did he know his family was trying to get out? Did he know his dad was dead? Was Analee okay? Why was Murphy left behind?

Mr. Barnett. He didn't seem sad about the loss of his other Agents and that scared me. Were they just pawns to him? Or were these people dedicated to him to the point that they were willing to sacrifice themselves to him? He didn't seem worried about how he would manage with only this much crew left. He could probably exchange for more men in a different circle. How many other circles were there? He didn't act like he missed anyone.

Bri was gone.

Cyrus was gone.

Agent K was gone.

Ellis was gone.

Chad was gone.

I turned my attention to the last person in the room. The boy who I mistakenly trusted. I have never felt so betrayed. When I took his hand and ran with him, I let my hopes skyrocket. I thought I had made the right choice until I heard a van. My blood instantly ran cold and I tried to plant my feet on the ground. I was woozy though and kept tripping over my own feet. I was fully supported by the boy I was with and felt my tears starting to freeze on my face. I was dragged along the rest of the way and when I was put in the back of the van, he smirked.

It was Emmanuel's mission all along and I wasn't going to tarnish his perfect record.

I wish that I had screamed for Chad. I wish I could say that. I didn't though. I accepted my fate. How many times was it that I was so close to escaping? I knew that I was going to be killed when I got to see Mr. Barnett's face again. I knew too much.

I just wish I had chosen Chad.

What would life be like if I had chosen him? I would not be here anymore. I would be with the FBI or police officer or at home. I would be with people who cared about me. I would be somewhere that I could bathe. I would be able to eat meals. I would be able to do all of the things that I couldn't do here. I would be able to learn. I would be able to grow. I would be able to thrive. I would be able to get the help that I needed.

Emmanuel grabbed my inner thigh and I

immediately shot him a glare. I moved my legs away from his hand and turned my body so that it wasn't directly next to his. I still think that Chad was trying to signal to me something by holding it. I should have known he was on my side with that thigh squeeze. What did it mean though? Why couldn't I remember? Emmanuel tried to squeeze it again but I realized the second time, I needed to answer what Mr. Barnett was saying.

"We are all so delighted to see you again, Y." He smirked as he leaned more of his weight on the back of the chair. His smile made his lips curl up to show his teeth. I guess it was supposed to look malicious but instead it looked awkward. He was trying too hard. He had to realize that he was losing the trust of his crew to me. I wanted to be the pin that loosened all of his structure. "In honor of you choosing us," he paused. He darted his eyes towards Emmanuel and I could not help but get angry. I lowered my eyes to my lap and allowed Emmanuel to squeeze my inner thigh again. "We would like to offer you a position on our team."

I stared up at him and cocked my head to the side. He couldn't be serious, right? I wasn't going to harm girls as they harmed me. I wasn't going to allow him to control me as he did with Bri. I wasn't going to be hypnotized into thinking what they were doing was good. They weren't saving anyone. They were killing these girls. They were murderers. I opened my mouth to protest but was quickly interrupted.

"Before you make your final decision, I want you to know the repercussions." Reggie slid a remote control across the table and perfectly into Mr. Barnett's grip. I stared down at him but he only smirked at me. He really was scum. "First repercussion is that you will consistently be tortured day in and day out." I wanted to shrug my shoulders. They have been doing that to me the entire time I was here. "During these trial days, we will be practicing new techniques to break the girls we bring in. You will be fed the bare minimum but enough to keep you alive." He paused and I already knew that he did it strategically. "I cannot promise you what will happen if any of these men have free time and need some enjoyment." He smiled evilly at me and this smile was much scarier than his actual smile.

Was he insinuating that they would try to have sex with me? I looked around the table at each of them. Reggie, I could definitely believe he would force himself on me. I didn't know Agent F well enough to know if he would or not. When I turned my gaze to Emmanuel, I knew the answer was yes. It was just a mission to him. He had no real feelings for me. He would if he had the opportunity. When I turned to Murphy, he briefly met my gaze. He was younger than me but I knew not to underestimate him. I wasn't even sure if he was at that age when he started thinking about things like that. I wanted to say he wouldn't though. When I returned my gaze back to Mr. Barnett, I was afraid to think that he would as well. I know that's what we were originally preparing for as

                                          AMY KULP

well. I was going to sacrifice myself to him. Their leader deserved the world.

I didn't want to be the reason that new girls they brought in were being tortured with a new form. What if these new techniques were worse? Would I be able to fake the bad ones and trick them into using new, easy ways? I didn't want to be the reason that some of these girls were tortured horrifically. If I wasn't their test monkey, who would be though?

"Before you make an offer, let me show you exhibit B." He grabbed the remote and a TV from the corner of the room and turned it on. I could barely see it from where I was sitting but I was able to make up what it was about.

Murphy's gasp filled me in.

On the screen was his mom, Analee. She seemed to be anxious and nervous about being followed because as she drove the van, she kept looking behind her. She kept looking over her shoulder. I was so glad to see her alive. However, it left me with so many questions. Why did she leave Murphy? Did she know about Cyrus?

"You would think she would have more common sense," Mr. Barnett claimed. I saw Murphy's jaw clench as he looked at the ground. Did he know she was alive? "She wants to use one of our vans to escape. That's fine. We have trackers on all of our vehicles." He shrugged his shoulders. "If you choose not to join our team, we will go and get her." He looked at Murphy but the gaze was missed. He wasn't paying attention and I saw the tears in the corner of his eyes. "She will be tortured for the mutiny." He shrugged his shoulders and Murphy refused to look anywhere besides the floor.

How was I supposed to choose my life over hers? I wanted my life. I wanted to live. I don't know how Analee had started in this crew but I had to assume that it was of her own will. I was forced to be here. How could I choose her life over mine? Was Murphy saying that her life was worth more than mine? Maybe that's why he wasn't looking at me. He understood that it was unfair for me to choose. I saw the tears in his eyes and I sighed. I just couldn't agree to it.

"Before you make a decision," Mr. Barnett started. He pressed a button on the remote and it switched screens. I stared at it as it became static and then the picture slowly cleared up. My eyebrows creased down my forehead and it was my turn to stare at the floor. "Chad." Chad made an appearance and walked around the camera. "We have an insight on the safe house that Chad and his mom are at. His mom has done nothing to you. Do you want someone innocent to get hurt?" I opened my mouth but as I watched Chad pass an unknown camera, he smiled.

He looked happy. I have not seen him look that way in a very long time. When he smiled or laughed, the corner of his eyes crinkled. He looked like he aged. From the way the camera was pointed, I could see that he and his mom were having lunch. While I'm sure that his mom was revolted by his actions in getting mixed up here, she was probably relieved that he ended up making the right choice. Would he know that there were cameras watching him? Did he know that he would always have to look over his back? He was considered a traitor. He had to know. Right?

"And before you make your final decision," Mr. Barnett interrupted. I continued to stare at the screen and refused to make eye contact with him. I wanted to continue to watch Chad. That could have been me with my family. I could have been the one smiling and laughing. Mr. Barnett clicked the TV to go to another video and I saw an older woman and an older man sitting down. Unfortunately, there were no sounds in these videos but I could see that they were worried. "I would like to introduce you to your mom and dad."

These people were different from the ones they showed me on the tapes. These people weren't the people who said that they didn't want me. I felt tears collecting in my eyes as I watched them. They sat near the phone and waited patiently. I wasn't sure what for but they both looked like they might cry. Were they waiting for me to call? I gave into Mr. Barnett. They should know that I'm not coming back. Why are they still waiting?

"How do I know you will leave them alone?" I asked. I blinked away any tears that may have formed and stared at him. He smiled sadistically at me and I felt anger boil up in me.

"They don't have anything we want," he clarified. He shrugged his shoulders and pointed at me. "All we wanted was you." Tears started collecting in my eyes as I watched the video. They continued just waiting.

"Can I talk to them?" I asked. "I want them to know that I love them." Next to me, Emmanuel squeezed my inner thigh and I felt myself getting angry. I slapped his hand away but he just gripped tighter.

"No." Mr. Barnett shook his head and got closer to me. "What's your decision, Y?"

I bit my lip as I looked around the room at Murphy. He still wouldn't meet my gaze but I could see his face was hardened. I had to choose between my life and five others. It wasn't even my life though. If I didn't accept the offer, I wasn't being released. I was going to be tortured. I shook my head and sighed as I felt the shaky intake of breath.

"I'll accept."

Cheering and clapping came from the majority of the room. For the first time, Murphy looked up at me and he shook his head. He whispered a 'thank you' to me and I couldn't help but smile at him. It was forced but I knew that Murphy was the one person who was forced to be here. He didn't ask for any of this. The least I could do is show him some gratitude by allowing his mom to escape.

"Now, we are going to get into our first mission as a team." Mr. Barnett passed out manilla folders and everyone instantly started going through them. I sat still and stared at mine. I didn't want to look at who I was helping kidnap. "We are staying in the area as we have one more person to collect before we move camps." I looked over at Emmanuel's papers and saw a familiar face on the page. "Her name is Holli.."

****

"Let's go over the plan again," Agent F mentioned. I felt the van shake as he made a sharp right with the turn of the road. I jolted in my seat and felt my skin crawl when Emmanuel's thigh pressed against mine. He wasn't leaving any room for me to breathe and be by myself. He probably felt responsible for me being here but I wasn't sure if he was sorry for it. "Keep in mind that she will recognize Emmanuel and Y. And if-"

"If I raise an eyebrow, I will be tortured and all bets are off for Murphy's mom, Chad and his mom, and my parents," I recited. I rolled my eyes and felt Emmanuel pinch my thigh. I glared at him but he only smiled at me. I couldn't tell what his emotions were. "Skip over the threats, please."

"Don't talk to your superiors like that," Reggie barked from the front. He turned around and glared at me but I wasn't afraid of him. I glared back and he shifted his gaze to meet Emmanuel's. "Hold back your girl or she will get what's coming for her."

"I'm not his girl," I pouted. I rolled my eyes and folded my arms over my chest. I was tired that they thought they could control everything about me. Yes, I was being forced to be here but I was going to put my mark on this place. Wasn't sure how though. Maybe my attitude would be my lasting mark.

"Not yet," Reggie beamed. I stared at the back of his head as he gave directions to Agent F. He turned back at me and his eyes crinkled at my glare. He was getting enjoyment out of this. "You guys will constantly play a couple until you start to fall for each other. Then boom, you'll become a couple and have a little Murphy." He chuckled again and turned back around in his seat. As much as he loved to taunt me, his job as the navigator was much more important.

I suddenly felt uncomfortable around Emmanuel. Someone who used to be so warm was so cold. His skin was icy against mine and he was trying to keep us touching at all points. I was being suffocated. How did I not see this sadistic and stalker behavior before? Maybe I did but I was too naive to listen to it.

I huffed and immediately got up and stretched my body over the backseats. When I rolled over into the back, I landed with a thump and was dazed for a minute before repositioning myself near Murphy. He eyed me from the corner but wouldn't look directly at me. I scooted closer to him and he shook his head as Agent F continued telling us the plan.

The plan they had played out minute-by-minute.

I don't know if all of the crews go in detail as they do but it was driving me insane. If I swayed from the plan at all, we would have to regroup and decide what we needed to do. How would they predict that all of these girls would react the same way though?

"I'm sorry about your mom," I whispered. Murphy's jaw hardened but he didn't say anything. He motioned for me to stay quiet as the plan was going over again. I shook my head. I was going to put these guys through hell. They all volunteered to be here. Except for Murphy. "We only have each other."

Murphy shook his head as if he was ready to argue with me. Though as we sat in silence and we heard what part of the plan we were on, his face softened. Obviously, I had the smallest role in the entire plot until I would earn experience. After all, I didn't blame them for not trusting me. However, I wanted to argue that my role was of great importance. Maybe the worst part about it was that when Holli would run, she was supposed to be comforted in seeing another girl. She was going to trust me and I would take it away.

I stopped thinking about it once I felt my hand being squeezed. I looked down and saw Murphy holding onto it. I squeezed back and he finally made eye contact with me. His eyes were red and the bags were puffy. He tried to fake a smile for me but I saw it disappear.

"I doubt they let my mom live," he whispered. His voice was shaky as he talked and I wasn't sure if he would be able to finish the sentence without crying. He held to it though. "I doubt that Emmanuel will let you by me for too long though." I crinkle my eyebrows in confusion and whip my head back to see him staring at both of us. "You don't know?" I immediately shook my head and he hung his face lower to the ground. "He picked you." His voice grew lower as he spilled the secrets to me. "Emmanuel has had this twisted fantasy about you for some time now. When he finally got to be in the top-trusted ranks with Mr. Barnett, they targeted you." I stared straight ahead and just blinked. "You were originally going to go to auction with Chad but they would never have let you sell."

"That's enough," Emmanuel boomed as he came over to us. He grabbed me by the shoulder and started taking me away from Murphy. From the tightness of his grip, I knew he was caught in something. I stepped over the seats and sat down beside him - squished into the corner. Emmanuel stared straight ahead as he pushed his body next to mine. He was too close for comfort. Forcefully, he planted his hand on my thigh and left it there.

Now that Murphy had told me that, I could see that Emmanuel was like a robot. The thigh grab was Chad's thing. Emmanuel probably has never had a casual relationship with everyone. He knew romance by being told what to do and observing Chad. His emotions didn't match his body language.

"Is it true?" I asked. Emmanuel's eyes looked at me from the corners and I knew he heard me. He shifted his head for a second and I felt my face twist in disgust.

"It's fine," he whispered. He faced me and leaned toward my body. He pressed his forehead against mine and I felt claustrophobic. "We are going to be just like Cyrus and Analee. Once Cyrus chose her, they fell in love and had Murphy. I can't wait to raise a prodigy son."

                                          AMY KULP

I stared at him in wonder. Did he think that was romantic? I had no idea Analee was a girl who was just chosen. Did Murphy know this? I turned to look at him and he was now openly staring at me. Emmanuel was whispering to me but I felt like Murphy could hear him. I was stuck in this relationship.

I was stuck in this job.

I was stuck.

"Phase A is in action," Agent F called out in front. As soon as the van slowed down, I let my thoughts on my new relationship go and grabbed Emmanuel by the arms.

Time to put on a show.

✳✳

I listened to the screams coming from the end of the streets and felt myself shudder. It was quiet otherwise so every time a new scream rippled through the air, you were able to tell where it was coming from. Any minute now and I would make my appearance. I was one of the most important pieces to this puzzle. I shoved my hands into my pockets and closed my eyes for a second. I could do this. For Chad. For Analee. For my parents.

When I started hearing footsteps coming my way, I stepped underneath the lights. I had to make myself be seen. When I heard the footsteps increase and the scream for help coming my way, I turned. She furiously pushed me away from where she was running. I jolted with her and felt myself gasp out of astonishment. They didn't plan for this.

"We have to run!" she yelled. The blood dripped from her forehead and I watched as it bled into my cloth sleeves. She did a double-take at my face and instantly recognized me. She didn't stop to chat though. She pushed me with all of her might and eventually I started moving with her.

As we ran together, she clutched onto my arms so hard that I felt the marks starting to form. I looked behind us and saw the boys beginning to slow down so I took her down another alley. It was going to be a dead end. As we reached it, she looked around and started panicking. Banging on a different door and trying to climb the wall. When she realized that I wasn't trying to escape like she was, she froze. She did a double-take and looked back at the boys.

"What the hell did you get caught up in Emily?"

"I may not know who this Emily girl is but I do know who I am." As the boys were only steps away she looked at me again and I smiled evilly at her. If I had to come to terms with my situation, I was going to make it fun. I saw the tears forming in her eyes as they grabbed her. One hit, two hits - right to the face. I winced a bit and as they dragged her to the van, I finished my sentence.

"I'm Y. If I have to live in this nightmare, so do you."

National Human Trafficking Hotline

1 (888) 373 - 7888

Read the first chapter of the sequel

Wanted

-**Chapter 1**

The van ride back is always quiet. It has been that way ever since I could remember. However, as soon as our driver parked the van and we unloaded what was in it, we waved goodbye. The proper measures needed to be taken to remove all evidence of blood, hair, and other forensics. After all traces of DNA were out of the van, it was to be shampooed and sanitized again to ensure that it looked brand new. The keys were placed on the ring with the same license plate and as we all made it to the back of the garage, we had to wait patiently for the elevator to come up to the ground floor. While the wait only took about two minutes, it felt like years to me. I made sure there was enough room for everyone, and we all waved again to our driver as he started the preparations to clean out the van. I was just glad it wasn't me who had to do that anymore.

The elevator had four floors in total. The first one was on the ground level and was hidden away from the public eye. Obviously, people would be curious about an elevator that goes underground. The first level underground was to be welcomed back. We were debriefed to ensure that we didn't make any mistakes, scanned to make sure that we didn't have any bugs on us, and medically reviewed to make sure we didn't have too many injuries. Otherwise, we would just be useless. The second floor underground was our home. I, personally, liked to call this my base. The third was where we met with our teams. Only higher-ups got to go to the fourth floor though.

As my team and I split up to go into different lines, I made sure to take everything out of my pockets and place them in the gray bin. I always held up the line when I had to get my gun from my thigh and had to get my pepper spray from my back pocket. The pants I was wearing were too tight today.

"Y'know, with how much you fight, I'm surprised you struggle to get those out of your butt pocket," one of my team members shouted. I looked over at him and saw that he was already getting wanded to see if he had anything medal on him. He smirked at me, and I just rolled my eyes.

This smart-ass was Carlos. He was a little piece of shit who liked to question authority, crack jokes, and demand respect. With how draining this place is on the mental psyche, I never would have thought someone could light up the joint as much as he did. He was good-looking too — his pitch-black hair was cut into a military style, and his muscles were beautifully sculpted underneath his t-shirt, which always hugged him. While I often didn't work with the same people, I worked with Carlos the most. Over the past ten years that we have known each other, we have worked together about nine times. He has watched me grow from a newbie to a leader in no time. However, I knew my husband didn't like him too much. He probably felt threatened.

"I think you should watch where your eyes wander," Santiago warned. I looked behind me and gave a smile of thanks as I watched him start to put his belongings in the gray bin. He looked over at me and smiled.

Santiago was the brains of the group, but he also had a lot of muscle. Although he never talks about his past, I'm pretty sure that Santiago is an ex-soldier. I wasn't there to invade people's backgrounds, so I never brought it up. Should I even ask? We have worked together only twice, but the way he watches out for everyone showed that he cared about the team he was with. That was a rare quality to see in this place. He may care about his team, but he didn't seem to trust anyone. There was always that edge of mystery about him.

"I think you should ice your face," I replied as I spread my legs out for my pat-down. I watched as Carlos's face reacted to my comment. He was already sitting on the bed for his physical examination, and I couldn't help but laugh as the doctor or nurse gave him an ice pack. "I remember that she kicked you pretty hard."

As soon as I was done being patted down, I joined Carlos at the physical examination beds. I sat across from him, and we were instructed to do the same stretches and exercises. Santiago joined us about halfway through, and when we were released we all walked toward our last examination.

This one took the most mental strength: the debriefing. All three of us were separated as we went into stark white rooms. I always dreaded these because someone always got tortured and beaten for how they reacted during the mission. They took all of what was said and determined who was the weak link of the team and then decided they needed to be retrained. By now, I learned not to be emotional during a mission, but I knew for the newer recruits it was hard to listen to someone screaming for their life.

I was desensitized to it though.

After about ten years of doing this job, you get used to the demands and orders. Some things that our new recruits find insulting and surprising, I think of as just another day on the job. Do I get paid to do this? Partially, but I am provided with food, entertainment, and a safe place to live. Our pay depends on how much each girl goes up for auction. Obviously, it depends on their looks and worth. So, a girl in high school with a future ahead of her is worth a lot more than a homeless person. However, you must work yourself up to those good assignments—they're never just given to a newbie.

I liked to think I was one of the best here. Not only have I been here for a long time, but I had adjusted rather quickly to the major changes of this place. Our organization started off with everyone being split into their own groups. This stayed that way for two years. However, things started changing, and the groups were constantly moving when members were being killed and some were moving up the ranks—the only two ways out of here. Originally, I had hoped that my husband would be in the same group as me. It became clear that wasn't the case. He was destined for great things, and he began moving up the ranks faster than anybody else had. He became the leader of the organization and the major reason everything changed.

Instead of always being in the same group, we were now like an underground academy. Every single person in this organization was under the same roof. There were assignments given to different team members. It was made this way so there couldn't be any leaks or undercover agents. If you were constantly switching roles and teams, who could you learn to trust? Nobody.

That's why, as I sat in this debriefing room, I felt myself growing anxious. What if I was the one who everyone thought screwed up today? What if I was too emotional while getting the subject transported to her safe house? That didn't mean I had to be emotional at all, but if I was the weak link of the team I would get tortured and shown how to do everything again. However, out of the four hundred successful kidnappings I have done, I only had to be tortured once.

That was when I was new.

"Welcome back, Y," Dr. Dowell said as he sat down in the chair across the table from me. I nodded to pay my respects but didn't show any emotion. "We're going to get you hooked up to the lie detector test before we begin our usual line of questioning."

I nodded again. I knew the drill by now. Dr. Dowell got the equipment out and quickly attached the wires to various parts of my body. I already felt my nervousness multiply but tried to calm down my breathing. The key was not to get caught lying.

"Are you ready to start?" Dr. Dowell asked. I nodded yes and waited for the first question. It was always the same questions in the same order. "Who was the weakest link of your team excluding you?"

"Howie," I answered.

Howie was our driver. He remained silent and distant from the entire group. He stayed in his seat the entire time and didn't help when our subject was getting a bit too rowdy. Right now, he was responsible for cleaning our van.

"Who was the weakest link including you?"
"Howie."
"Who was the leader of the group excluding you?"
"Santiago."
"Who was the leader of the group including you?"
"Santiago."

I winced when I felt something heavy bang against my knuckles. I watched as Dr. Dowell picked up his metal stapler and placed it back on his desk. Immediately on my skin a blue and purple bruise began to form. I stretched out my fingers to make sure they weren't broken and scrunched them so he would have less to hit.

"You're lying," he stated. "Who was the leader of the group including you?"

"Me," I replied dryly.

"Did your mission go exactly as planned?"

"No."

"What went wrong?"

"Our subject was more interested in Santiago than Carlos," I answered. I watched as Dr. Dowell kept reading my graph as I talked. I had to pause to make sure I wouldn't be slapped with the stapler again. At least he didn't try to staple my fingers. "So, when Carlos suggested that they go back to his place, she rejected him."

"And how did Carlos react?"

"Carlos left like he was supposed to. However, it was Santiago's turn to try to get her to go outside. I don't believe it would have taken much because she was so willing. I think she liked the nerdy type, or maybe Santiago seemed less threatening to her." I shrugged and watched as Dr. Dowell played with the stapler for a second. In an instant flash, he slammed it against my fingers again. I resisted groaning out in pain and clenched my fingers harder. I wanted to slam my head on the table and cry out but knew that could have too many consequences.

"Now tell the truth."

"Okay," I whispered. I cleared my throat before speaking. It would, at least, buy me a bit of time. "She didn't seem interested in either of them. However, she seemed more comfortable around Santiago."

"Why?"

"He wasn't flirting with her."

"Then what happened?"

"Santiago brought her out, and she was dazed. I think he managed to slip a roofie in her drink. However, she didn't drink all of it because she was coherent. She willingly got into the van, but when she saw Carlos she started freaking out and kicked him in the face. She fled the van, and Santiago chased her. That's where I came out from watching them and acted like a random bystander. She trusted me—they always do. You learn from a young age that if you're in trouble, find another female. Carlos and I dragged her back, and Santiago prepared the drug. She fell asleep on Santiago after that." I paused. "Everything else was smooth sailing from there."

"So why do you think Howie was the weak link?" Dr. Dowell asked.

"Because Carlos and I had to drag her back. He could've made it easier and driven after us." I shrugged. "I've worked with Carlos plenty of times. He had to face the dejection or could risk getting the cops called on him."

"Are you sure that you are not projecting feelings onto Carlos? You have worked together multiple times."

"What are you suggesting, Dr. Dowell? I am happily married to the love of my life. Carlos and I are just coworkers." I gritted my teeth and moved my knuckles down to my pants. There, I squeezed the fabric as I let a bit of uneasiness and anger slip through. I hated that he suggested that I would be unfaithful to my husband. He shook his head and wrote something in his notes. "Am I done, or do you have any other questions for me? I'd like to leave."

"You may collect your things and wait for your team to finish with their debriefings."

"Thank you."

I hurriedly snapped all the wires off of me and waited for the buzz for the door to be let open. When it did, I made sure to slam the door behind me. I was met in a little oval hallway space where all the other doors came together. There was only one way to go from here and that was forward. When I met up in the waiting room, I saw Santiago, Carlos, and Howie all waiting for me. My debriefing usually never took the longest, so I was shocked to see that I was the last one.

"Welcome back, Chief," Carlos said. He smiled brightly at me, and I found myself scowling at him. He had lost the icepack somewhere in the debriefing room but as I glanced at his hands I didn't see any additional marks. I glanced over at Santiago and saw a little red bruise forming on his wrist. I wonder what he lied about. The last person I looked at was Howie, who was also looking at me. I annoyingly showed him my fingers without humiliation, and he stared wide-eyed at me. His reaction was how I felt for him being down here. He cleaned the car, came to his debriefing, and finished before me. The debriefings didn't even take that long. "Alright, get ready to stand on the line," he instructed everyone.

I nodded my head and stood in between Carlos and Howie. We waited patiently until the screen that was mounted on the wall was lit up blue. It caught all of our attention at the same time, and we all stood a little quieter with our backs a little straighter. When I looked to the sides of me, I could see everyone else's gaze was trained on the screen. Exactly where mine should be too.

"Congratulations on another job well done," the voice on the screen said. The voice sounded familiar, but I couldn't pinpoint who it used to belong to. Did I work with them? "Listed in order are your most valuable teammates to your least valuable teammates. Once all names are called, everybody but your least valuable teammate will grab your gear and head to the elevators to rest until your next assignment. You can take that time to improve your strategies, physical strength, brainpower, and training techniques. Your most valuable teammate is..."

The screen flickered to a slide with Santiago's name on it. I could see his body relax in line as he read his name. A chorus of claps followed, and I could see a small smile form on his face. Although, he had to of known not to show too much emotion. He might get hurt if he did.

When the screen flickered to another slide, it showed my name. I instantly slouched over and listened to the claps from everyone else. I was safe now. I didn't need to worry about being beaten, tortured, and having my brain picked through for why I did things. I didn't need to worry about having to survive another day or wonder when they would feed me. I didn't have to worry about whether the man coming into the room had intentions of killing me or just using me for my body. I didn't have to worry about anything except getting a good night's sleep.

When the screen flickered again, my eyes immediately read the name on the board. I felt myself sigh and felt the person next to me forget about his posture. Carlos was safe. I knew he was going to be, but I don't remember there being a time when his name was so low on the charts. Granted, we usually had more people on each team. This team was small. Usually, there were five or six of us.

"You may grab your items and step through to the elevators."

I was the one who took the first step. Howie stayed behind as we three grabbed our gear. I made sure to have my gun ready. I watched as the boys took out some money and their wallets as well. After all, we all had fake IDs in case we ever needed them. Nobody was allowed to know our real names except those we worked with. Still, maybe Carlos's name wasn't Carlos. I would only find out if he told me.

But why would he trust me?

When I finally grabbed all my equipment, I stepped inside the elevator. I watched as the doors began to inch close in front of us and watched in horror as Howie was tackled to the ground by the torturers. I could see a bat being thrown at him, and I saw some fists in the air. Without thinking, I closed my eyes and frowned. I wasn't supposed to show emotion though.

How could someone not show emotion for one of their own being beaten like that? They did it on purpose too. Right before the elevator doors closed, they sent the guys who tortured people out. They would beat him up until he was unconscious. They deprived him of food, clothes, water, and safety. They tortured him until he was close to death. Then they rehabilitated him. They talked to him about how to improve. They made sure he got new training and was better before. If he were a girl, he would get so much worse.

"Don't worry, he'll come back better," Carlos reassured. He placed a hand on my shoulder, and I flinched away from him. "You know that it's how we become better."

I nodded because I knew that. He was only going to get better through the torture. He would only come back stronger. It didn't feel right though. It crushed your spirits until you couldn't fight back. It crushed your spirits so much that after a while you just let whatever happen. Sometimes, it just felt like something to prey on the weak. Then again, we were sex traffickers. We shouldn't have any remorse for anybody.

When the elevator doors dinged open, so much relief slipped through my body. We all walked forward into the lobby of where our rooms could be, and I stopped when I saw what station the TV was on. It was always playing the national news coverage because we needed to know if anyone was onto us.

"Damn, Y, is that you?" Santiago asked as they all watched the TV screen too.

"Our girl made national news," Carlos said as he pretended to wipe away a tear.

"Keep a look-out for this girl you see on your screen. She is known to those as Y and is part of a sex trafficking ring. With over four hundred abducted girls in the past ten years, she is known as one of the most ruthless criminals on our list. She is number three on the FBI's Most Wanted. We believe that—"

"Four hundred cases?"

"Technically four-hundred and one," I corrected. I shrugged. "I do about forty a year."

"About three or four a month," Santiago stated. I nodded and his mouth dropped open. "I never would have guessed you have been doing this for so long." He shook his head and excused himself to his room, but I continued to stare at the TV screen, trying to hear what they were saying about me.

"How do you do it?" Carlos asked.

"I don't get to know the girls," I said finally. "Most of the time when I'm on a mission, I'm leading it and am there to give the girl false hope. Girls—"

"Trust other girls," he said over me. I nodded and looked at him. "You are ruthless. You deserve that number three spot but let's hope you don't get too famous."

"You know them, they'll probably have me locked in here for a while, at least until the news coverages stop."

"Yeah, good luck," he said. "I want more money, so I hope I get another job immediately."

"So you can buy hookers?" I asked. I looked over at him and noticed the door he was going into. I didn't realize his bedroom was so close to the lobby area. He smirked at me as he waved goodbye, and I just smiled back.

Guarantee that they won't have Carlos and me together for a very long time. Especially with how Dr. Dowell was questioning me. How could he think that I would cheat on my husband?

Carlos was like too many of the people here. He used to be homeless, and he saw a flyer at his homeless shelter saying he could make quick cash. Once he passed most of the tests, he was trained to be one of us. This job was his opportunity. This job was his saving grace. Like so many other people.

The only other people who came here willingly were ex-soldiers who were dishonorably discharged. They needed an outlet for their anger, so they had a nice fit here. Most of the anger management soldiers were our torturers here. Who else would be a better fit? I'm not sure how they got recruited, but I wasn't sure I wanted to know.

Finally drawing my eyes away from the TV screen, I walked down the silent hallways until I came up to my door. I quickly unlocked the door and jammed the door closed. While our bedrooms were small, I didn't have to sleep here all the time. Whenever my husband comes around, I always sleep in his room. He has the largest room I have ever seen. It could probably fit five king-size beds in it. You would still have room for the dresser and other decorations. However, my room had a twin-size bed, a dresser, and a small bathroom hooked up to the side.

I quickly changed out of my uniform and found myself some comfortable shorts and a t-shirt to lie in. I was planning to skip dinner and just go right to sleep. As soon as my head hit my pillow and I closed my eyes, I was startled awake by a bell going off in my room. With a huge groan, I got out of bed and put my uniform back on. That bell meant that I was being assigned another mission.

I am Y. I'm happily married, have been a part of this operation for ten years with four-hundred and one successful missions, and the FBI's third-most- wanted criminal. I am usually a team lead in missions or a last-minute distraction. I was usually the reason the girls got caught. I was the reason they never escaped. While I can't remember my past, I am proud of the job I do because it is important.

ABOUT THE AUTHOR

Amy Kulp is a middle school math teacher with a passion for writing. She started writing Missing at the age of 14 but quickly scrapped the idea when she wasn't sure where it was leading to. After 6 years of not looking at it, she came back to the idea after watching her favorite binge show, Criminal Minds. After multiple therapeutic sessions with her two dogs, Scooter and Maisey, she had developed a storyline that had turned into the book it is today.

www.ingramcontent.com/pod-product-compliance
Lightning Source LLC
Chambersburg PA
CBHW031200310726
48969CB00001B/162